OF GODS & MONSTERS

SHE WAS DESTINED FOR CHAOS

ELYSIAN GODS BOOK ONE

ZAVI JAMES

This is a work of fiction. Names, characters, places and incidents either are a product of the author's imagination or are used fictitiously. Any resemblance to actual persons, living or dead, events or locales is entirely coincidental.

Cover design by Books and Moods
Interior formatting by AJ Wolf Graphics
Editing by Heart Full of Reads Editing Services

ISBN 978-1-9169030-1-2 (paperback)

Published by Zavi James
www.zavijames.com

TRIGGER WARNING

This series contains topics that some may find triggering. These include but are not limited to sexually explicit scenes, graphic violence, infidelity, death, discussion of suicide and sexual assault.

If you are uncomfortable with reading these situations, then the Elysian Gods series may not be for you.

Reader discretion is advised

To the chaotic ones. The ones who harbour a restless soul, the ones who built their dreams when others told them it couldn't be done and the ones who were made to believe they didn't deserve love – this is for you.

A List of Notable Gods Featured in Of Gods & Monsters

Elite Gods

Hunter – God of protection and forgiveness
Larkin – Goddess of strength
Grayson – God of chaos and destruction
Erik – God of love and desire
Sloan – Goddess of fertility
Ignacio – God of luck and opportunity
Elva – Goddess of death

Minor Gods

Archer – God of secrets and deception

ONE

QUENTIN

"They'll be arriving soon," Gareth announced, bulldozing his way to the front of the room and trying to get everyone's attention.

The conference room in the *Institute of Life Science*, a branch of the British government's Defence Science & Technology laboratories, was filled with scientists, psychologists and security personnel recruited for the project. The *Elysian Liaison Initiative*, E.L.I., would officially begin after two long years of discussions and laying down the groundwork.

During our initial orientation, Gareth had kindly shared with us just how the project had come into existence. He was on the wrong side of fifty and the whispers had made him worry that his mind — the brilliant brain that was once sharp and had elevated him to his position in the government — had finally succumbed to the pressure and snapped. He'd been a hair's breadth away from calling the doctor when the whisper developed into a roar that saw him on his knees in prayer. Concertinaed on the floor of the temple, he'd received all the instructions. The Gods needed work to be done, and Gareth would be their vessel until they saw fit to descend from Elysia and walk among the mortals they watched over.

"You'll be given your assignments," Gareth continued, voice rising above the din as he reached the front of the room.

The chatter died away as attention fell on the bulky manila folders he cradled in his arms.

He'd held off until the morning of the arrival to allocate teams to minimise the time he'd need to soothe bruised egos. Entitlement always reared its ugly head when decisions were taken out of people's hands. We'd already bore witness to a few terse email exchanges.

Gareth had, instead, observed us all for months, making notes as he compiled teams of people who would work together cohesively with the given test subject.

Test subject. It was easier to think of them that way. It allowed me to maintain that this was a serious job rather than an elaborate hoax.

"Please familiarise yourself with your allotted God or Goddess and we can begin work," he told us.

I knew little about Gareth, aside from the fact that he was deeply religious and a man of few words. He didn't invite people to turn to him if they had a problem with the assignments.

Gareth had specifically headhunted every single person in the room. He'd travelled to all corners of the globe to recruit some of the best minds, which was the first reason I'd been hesitant to agree when he set his offer on my table.

As a fresh PhD graduate, I'd been his last pick. It was his riskiest appointment, but my research as a developmental biologist had been published in international journals and spoken about in high regard. Gareth believed that, teamed with other young blood he'd brought on board, we'd help to drive the project in ways he might not have thought of.

Outside in the corridor, visible through the floor-to-ceiling glass panels that made up the walls of the conference room, a parade of people marched past. Security personnel in their dark suits made their way along the hallway, but they weren't what caught my eye.

Breathtakingly beautiful men and women stood between mortals, their wrists cuffed in copper. Gods with ethereal beauty that caused a deep and undeniable ache in the chest of anyone who laid eyes on them, including myself, walked by, with poise and class. Strands of glossy hair perfectly in place with every long stride, crisp suits, and flowing dresses painted on like a second skin. Sharp jawlines and cheekbones that made each face worthy of catwalks and front covers of magazines. Every hair on my arms raised at the power they all emanated. Each of the twelve otherworldly beings looked no older than thirty years of age, but they carried centuries.

A t the back of the pack fell an anomaly. A God, with jet black hair and dark stubble lining his jaw, fought against the restraints as he bellowed, "Hunter! I never agreed to this! I will pull this place apart! Wait until I am out of these cuffs!"

The glass walls of the room trembled with the force of his temper. He swung his head towards the conference room and piercing blue eyes landed on me as I caught full sight of the fury they held. My blood turned to ice in my veins and a crushing pressure constricted my lungs until I lost the ability to breathe. The eye contact lasted for a split second before they pulled the God past the room, colourfully violent threats still being issued.

The vacuum that surrounded me popped as noise erupted in the space and I took in a deep breath, grounding myself again. Eleven of the twelve appeared cooperative. Statistically, it was natural to have an outlier. One that threw off a clean set of results. An anomaly never made things worthless in my eyes but made it more interesting.

"Scott," Gareth called, interrupting my mental workflow on probability.

Walking towards me, he held out a manila folder. It was crisp and clean and contained very little, judging by the thickness of it. That would change soon. Gareth held it out to me, and I took it from his hands.

"I've assigned you to Grayson," he informed me.

I flipped open the folder to see a fact sheet staring back at me. The most striking piece of information provided was names.

They had names like mortals. I wasn't sure what I expected, but the mundanity of it caught me off guard.

"I need my best people on him," Gareth said, clapping a heavy hand on my shoulder.

I narrowed my eyes at him. At twenty-seven, I was the youngest person in the room. My doctorate was awarded two years ago, and I'd originally taken up a postdoctoral role at St Andrews when the government correspondence began. My time in academia had taught me to be wary of sugared words. There was no guarantee that good intentions hid behind them.

"Thanks, Gareth," I said, despite my reservations about his compliments. My parents had taught me to always be polite, even if I had no desire to be. "Any tips?"

The older man let out a sigh and ran a hand through his salt-and-pepper hair. "He's less inclined than the rest of them as you could see by his display."

Gareth rolled his eyes as he spoke, safely knowing that his disrespect went unwitnessed by the deities he worshipped.

Adrenaline flushed through my system at the confirmation that I'd be working with the walking terror, and my mouth grew numb. I pressed my tongue against the roof to regain some feeling. No wonder they'd never disclosed their names. It was easier to keep people in awe if they prayed to the God of chaos rather than trying to call in a favour from Grayson.

"Doesn't understand the need for integration even for a short period," Gareth continued, blissfully unaware of my anxiety. "It's a shame, considering this whole venture was Hunter's idea."

"That was one hell of a tantrum," I muttered, eyes cast down on the page.

"Be careful around him, Scott," Gareth advised me. "Around all of them."

I bit back on a reply about stating the obvious and said, "I won't let you down."

"I know you won't," he told me with a smile. "I suggest you join the rest of your team," he added before walking off.

The room had split off into groups as people joined their colleagues for the project. Glancing down at the folder again, I flipped through the pages, scanning through the information until I saw two familiar names: Charlotte Brown and Matthew Holden. When I looked up again, Charlie waved me over.

"I'm glad we're working together," she said once I'd squeezed my way through the room and joined her.

She opened her arms and I stepped into them, receiving the hug. The silk of her blouse was cool to touch and slipped beneath my fingertips. Charlie was one of the only people I knew who was warm from the first meeting.

"Same," I agreed after she released me from the hug. "Better head to the lab."

We left the conference room, the silence of the corridors wrapping around us as we made our way to the eleventh floor where our lab was based. The institute had thirteen floors; a towering building that had the strictest level of security around it. The ground floor was designated for conference rooms, offices, the canteen, and breakrooms. Every other floor in the main building held lab space and offices, one for every God and Goddess that comprised the Elysian elite.

Stepping into the lift with some others, I reached across and jabbed at the button marked '11' to take us up to our floor.

Charlie's blonde bob swayed around her chin when she turned to look at me. "Trust us to be stuck with the drama queen," she muttered quietly.

"I'm not sure we should call him that," I replied, but the corner of my mouth tugged tellingly.

"What else do you call someone who puts on a spectacular display like that?"

I couldn't argue.

Dr Charlotte Brown, affectionately known as Charlie Brown to her friends, was a behavioural psychologist and the more qualified out of the both of us to refer to the God as a drama queen.

We'd met last January at the initial orientation and quickly formed a friendship. With just under a decade more experience than me, Charlie treated me with the same level of respect as any of the other seasoned colleagues. A gesture that I deeply appreciated.

The crowd thinned as people exited the lift at their desired floors, and I felt a nervous knot forming in the pit of my stomach. It was the same knot that appeared every single time I sat down for an exam or called into an office. The type of knot that soured my tastebuds until I was struggling to keep my breakfast down.

Eventually, we reached the eleventh floor, stepped out of the lift, and took a right. The laboratory had a glass front so that the inside was visible from the corridor. Privacy within the building was a luxury they did not afford us. They arranged workbenches along the room, with an aisle splitting the space through the middle, and a fresh set of white lab coats hung on hooks on the wall.

"Dr Brown. Dr Scott." Matthew Holden greeted us both as we walked into the room.

His strong build, attributed to his military service, and dark attire, placed him as a member of the strict security recruited for the job. But it was the red access card, E.L.I.'s logo boldly emblazoned upon it, that he played with, that singled him out as the head of the project on this floor. That little piece of plastic would grant Matt access to every room on this floor without permission from anyone else.

"Hey, Holden." I returned his greeting in a more casual manner.

Years of protocol dictated that I wore a lab coat inside the lab. Holding the folder between my knees, I shrugged one on over my shirt and straightened up again. The starched white fabric made me feel at home. More in control.

"Did you read through the file yet?" he asked us as I pulled it from between my legs.

"Not really," Charlie replied. "We were just given them, Matthew."

His cheeks coloured a little, and I pushed down on the small spark of jealousy that rose from the depths of my chest. As head of the entire floor, Matt would have been privy to information before the rest of us.

I took a seat at one of the benches, joining Charlie and opening the folder again. My eyes scanned along the information, drinking it in as I pulled my hair up into a messy bun.

"*He's* not happy," Matt informed us.

Charlie glanced up at him. "We already know that. I'd bet the entire institute already knows that."

I only partially paid attention to them as I read over the notes Gareth had provided.

Hunter ruled the Gods of Elysia, and Grayson was one of his younger brothers. Under the section highlighting responsibilities, there were three attributes listed: chaos, vengeance, and destruction.

Thanks a lot, Gareth, I thought to myself. *Rile up the psycho and then give him to us.*

Charlie had read over the same words and quirked a blonde eyebrow. "Oh, I can't wait to observe him."

"Make sure you write that first observation," I reminded her with a snort. Pulling a pen out of the pocket of my jeans, I uncapped it and reached across to scribble on Charlie's page. "Drama queen."

The sound of the lab door unlocking via electronic access card halted our conversation as more of the team settled into their home, away from home. With the lab being the largest space on the floor, Matt would brief us all here before he set us free to work. I itched to implement the months of reading and planning that we'd put in place.

The only thing I was missing was the test subject.

TWO

GRAYSON

Furious didn't cover how I felt about the decision.

There wasn't a single word in any language that could describe the white-hot rage that pulsed through me.

Hunter had been in discussions with the mortals for years and hadn't bothered to inform us all. Not until he'd brought the plans forward to the council. And I had been the only one to object to the ludicrous idea. I thought we'd have more time. I believed I could talk them around. Erik, Ig, Sloan — they were always willing to listen to me, but the days had run together and all the lip service materialised into reality.

Outnumbered, I had no choice. My anger had flourished, and Hunter needed to rebuild the council chambers when I was done.

When they'd wrestled me into cuffs, it had tipped me over the edge. They dulled the powers that coursed through my veins, and I cursed my brother in every tongue I could for agreeing to work with those who were beneath us. To give them power over us so Hunter could have a pet project. I didn't care about his reasoning. It was pure lunacy.

I walked sullenly with the mortals left in charge of me and was ushered into a lab, silent now that they had separated me from my kin.

Even without my clear rage, the team gave me a wide berth, and that was how I preferred it. Slowly surveying the room, I took in the members of my team. All of them lesser beings who needed to be reminded of their place.

"Matthew Holden." A man introduced himself, taking a step forward and stopping in front of me. "I'm the head of the team that'll be in charge of your integration."

I looked at him, already bored by mortal pleasantries.

"You'll also be spending time with Dr Charlotte Brown," Holden pressed on. "She's a behavioural psychologist and heading that branch of the team."

Charlotte stepped forward and offered a bashful smile. It was a smile she had probably perfected for her clients. One that made them feel at ease with her. She dressed demurely, and she'd chewed the lid of her pen until it lost its shape — a tell-tale sign she was nervous to start this job.

"You want to know if I have Daddy issues?" I sneered at her, not taken in by her timid manner. This woman wanted to understand what made me tick, but she had no right to pry inside my head. Nothing would be handed to her easily.

"Well," she responded, not rising to the bait, "it's more than that."

Holden placed a hand on her arm to stop the potential verbal essay she had prepared and was about to unleash from her lips.

"You'll also work with Dr Quentin Scott," Holden told me. "Our resident developmental biologist on this floor."

I was surprised when another woman stepped forward. With a name like Quentin Scott, I'd expected to see a man. Instead, I was faced with a woman, who for a moment, had caught my eye as I was dragged past the meeting earlier. Her eyes were so dark they looked black, but the fear from earlier had been wiped clean.

Standing in front of me now, I sensed the chaos that laid beneath the surface. It didn't run as freely as it did in the others that occupied the room. She buried it deep, kept it under lock and key, but I wanted to crack her open and feed from it. You only restrained something so aggressively when you knew it was a beast that couldn't be controlled.

Holden opened his mouth to continue the introduction, but Quentin Scott cut him off.

"I'm interested in your biological composition and what makes you so different from us."

She walked up to me, with Holden hovering a few steps behind her. This woman was no different from the rest of them. The beat of her heart was prominent in her chest, picking up the pace as she neared me. She'd witnessed the spectacle I'd made of myself, and she feared what I was truly capable of. My reputation wasn't completely shattered yet.

"As if I'm able to show you what makes me superior," I spat bitterly. My fingers flexed, but nothing happened, and the anger stirred in my chest, heating every inch of my skin.

A ghost of a smile tugged at her lips. "The cuffs," she said, realising what had upset me.

They were currently wrapped around my wrists, locking my hands together in front of me, giving me the appearance of a common criminal.

I narrowed my eyes at her and asked, "What do you know about them?"

"Quentin helped create them," Holden answered from behind her. "Along with some of the —"

I looked back down at the woman before me and launched myself at her without a second thought, unable to contain the rage again. She stumbled backwards out of the way, narrowly missing my attack, while Holden pushed past her and joined the other two security guards in grappling with me to regain some control over the situation.

"Let him go," Scott told them, straightening out her lab coat. I'd caught her off guard and rattled the calm composure she'd held. "Let him go. I'm fine."

"Scott," Holden said, looking back at her. "He just tried to attack you."

"I know, but I think we need to defuse the situation, not keep it hostile."

Holden held her gaze for a moment before turning away and instructing his colleagues to release me.

Rather than rushing towards her again, I spat at her feet, just missing the black boots she wore. I should have aimed for her face. It was no more than she deserved for doing this to me. This mortal thought it was fit to bring me down to her level.

Powerless.

Weak.

What had Hunter been thinking when he cooked up this idea?

There was no way they'd devised this alone. There was a single plant in existence that could taint our divinity. A single plant that could weaken the power we'd been gifted with. The next time I saw Hunter, I'd knock some sense into his thick skull.

Scott looked disgustedly at the glob of saliva on the floor, brought her dark eyes up to my face and then without another word, turned away from me.

"Come back here," I demanded as she cut through the centre of the room.

The disrespect made my lip curl into a snarl. I hadn't dismissed her. I hadn't allowed for the conversation to end. Scott threw a look over her shoulder, contemplating my order before thinking better of it and walking to the end of the lab.

The sheer fury of being ignored ricocheted through my system and made the veins at my temple throb.

How fucking dare she?

How dare this mortal walk away from me as if I meant nothing to her? As if my words, my demands, were suggestions she could brush aside.

I wouldn't forget this slight. She'd pay for her ignorance towards me. Hunter may have had his own ideas about what needed to be done down here, but I quickly compiled my agenda that involved reminding every single mortal in this room of who they were working with. Starting with Scott.

Throughout the entire morning, I refused to cooperate with the team as they tried to begin the project. If they expected me to work, they would have to give me something in return. I met anyone who approached me with vicious hostility, reminiscent of a caged animal. That was what the cuffs had reduced me to. My dignity had been stripped away, to help these pathetic beings feel safe.

If they wanted safety, they should have thought twice about agreeing to this imbecilic plan.

Scott kept her distance from me, but I couldn't take my eyes off her. More than anyone in the room, it was this woman who made my blood boil. Even as she left the lab, strolling down the corridor, checking her phone, I couldn't stop thinking about how desperately I wanted to destroy her.

I'd ruin this woman, and in the wreckage, I'd find a sense of peace.

THREE

QUENTIN

Down on the ground floor, I grabbed a much-needed cup of coffee in the breakroom. My ears pricked at the surrounding conversations. Some of my colleagues had already collected samples, while others contemplated removing the cuffs from their subject. I gritted my teeth together so forcefully an ache ran along my jawline. The success of others only highlighted how dramatically I'd failed this morning.

If I hadn't been wary before, the brief interaction with Grayson had proven how they couldn't be trusted. Gods cared for themselves above all else.

There'd been something so vulgar about his actions. An attempt to headbutt me, and when that failed, spitting in my direction. Grayson had been furious when I walked away, but I didn't plan to give him any more of my time than was necessary.

I hadn't agreed to E.L.I. to be the subject of abuse. I'd signed the contract because of the prestige it would bring my name.

That dream was quickly fading, if no one on my team could get the prick to calm down long enough so we could take samples from him.

"Holden said you aren't having much luck."

Gareth joined me at the coffee machine. He popped a pod into the top and set it to start. Mechanical whirring sounded between us before a thin stream of coffee ejected into his cup.

"He hates being here," I explained, unimpressed that Matt had reported back to Gareth. "He hates us. How are we meant to work with that?" I asked, frustration lacing my words.

"Find a way, Scott," Gareth told me unhelpfully.

Visions of me grabbing his coffee mug and tipping it over his head swam through my mind. Shirt stained and hair sticky and wet from caffeine, I wondered if Gareth would be so blasé about my struggle or if I would have hammered home the point that he had given me a nearly impossible task.

"I'm sure Holden has some ideas," he added, picking up the mug before I could act on my impulse.

I liked Matthew. He was polite, made an effort, and was very easy on the eye, but he also liked to think that men could do it all. If he cracked Gray before any of us, we'd never hear the end. Yet another victory that would be added to the stories he regaled us all with over a drink at the pub.

Irritated by the possibility of that reality, I muttered, "I'll speak to you later."

I took my cup, drained it in the lift, and walked back into the lab. The room was empty with everyone taking their break, apart from Grayson, who was sitting on a stool with the same bored expression he'd entered with, written across his features.

In the lab's silence, I studied him. The fluorescent lighting highlighted high cheekbones and a chiselled jaw. His posture didn't falter, causing him to appear like a marble statue. The conclusion was that Grayson had been carved from perfection with fault lines deep beneath it all — far away from the naked eye, so you'd still buy into the pretty facade.

His attention lazily shifted to me as I approached him, and I averted my gaze instantly.

"I would rather you bow when you see me," Grayson

informed me.

His voice was deep, and his tone held such authority that I nearly dropped to my knees before him.

"We don't always get what we want," I shot back. My irritation was still close to the surface, and I was struggling to push it away.

Grayson made an unimpressed sound, and I sucked in a breath.

"We need you to cooperate with us before you can begin integration," I explained, cutting to the chase.

"I never agreed to integrate," he returned coldly. "I didn't even agree to descend into this abysmal —"

"It doesn't sound like you have a choice."

He scowled, transforming his stunning face into something packed with anger.

I placed my empty mug on a nearby bench, folding my arms across my chest, and observed the God in front of me once more.

Grayson was an intimidating figure, with little warmth to him. At first glance, it was easy to be taken in by his ethereal appearance. On closer inspection, beautiful bone structure morphed into a mixture of hard, cutting lines of a body that housed a vicious temper. I couldn't help but think that his looks and temperament fit well with his responsibilities.

"Take these cuffs off me," he ordered.

"I can't do that."

"Take. These. Cuffs. Off. Me," Grayson repeated the words slowly and clearly, as if a different delivery would cause a different outcome.

"I. Can't. Do. That," I mimicked his tone and pace. "Holden has the key, and he won't undo them as long as he thinks you're a threat."

A smile came to Grayson's face, twisting the corners of his mouth upward with a wicked glint in his eye. It was the look that came over a predator as they stalked their prey, smug and self-satisfied with the impending kill. Goosebumps prickled the flesh of my arms, suddenly worried that we'd overestimated the power of the cuffs. We'd never tested them on a subject, only on samples of glittering gold blood with electric blue particles dispersed through it. Even their blood made me feel inferior, shining under the light.

"You need to cooperate," I told him, taking a cautious half-step away from him. "You give us what we want, and we'll give you some freedom."

Grayson scoffed. "I'm not bartering with some mortal."

"If you want to use your hands again and see the outside of this lab, that's exactly what you'll do," I said, turning on my heel.

I was wasting my break talking to him. He didn't have the upper hand and the sooner he realised that, the better. This was my lab. He needed to play by my rules.

"What is it you pray for?" Grayson called after me as I retreated.

The question caused me to stop in my tracks. When I faced him again, the curiosity softened his expression.

"I don't pray," I admitted brazenly.

It'd been years since I folded myself before the Gods and asked anything from them. They'd forsaken me on so many occasions, and I no longer needed to beg them for scraps. I was nothing but an afterthought, an inconsequential speck in their existence, and I refused to reciprocate their apathy with undying devotion.

"I struggle to believe in any of your abilities."

He let out a bark of laughter. "You have Gods throughout this building. You have a God in front of you, and you struggle to believe in what we offer?"

"I'm a scientist," I said, as if that explained everything.

I'd prayed to the Gods once, folded carefully on the floor of the temple beside my parents. As I'd grown older, I'd struggled to connect with the words and gestures, because how could anyone have faith in deities who rarely seemed to hear the prayers of those who needed them most? What right did they have to witness my struggles and decide that I wasn't worth their time?

The entire reason behind the project and integration was to try to renew and restore faith on earth. I had agreed to the job primarily because of ego and pride. An initiative such as this one would write me straight into the history books. I'd be a name known across the globe. But a small part of me, a sliver that I did my best to ignore, wondered if I could find answers to more personal questions. If anyone needed their faith restored, it was me.

"What more proof do you need?" Grayson asked.

"Let me do my job and then I'll have my proof," I replied before leaving the lab.

Following lunch, the space buzzed with activity again. Charlie sat near Grayson and observed him as she typed notes on her laptop. At multiple points during the afternoon, I wished I could have her job. Being able to observe others from a distance had to be nice when the subject was highly volatile.

Instead, I perused through old journal articles, combing over experiments to add to the list. In the months before they'd arrived, we'd carefully mapped out plans and bought the required reagents. I'd been giddy as each request for state-of-the-art equipment was signed off and delivered without resistance.

Although the standard list was devised and distributed among the floors, ambition was rife. We had our own ideas that deviated away from the workflow.

"You," Grayson's voice called out. "Come here."

I tore my gaze away from the screen to see that he was addressing me.

Holden eyed us warily as I got up from my seat and took a tentative step towards the God.

"Keep your distance, Scott," Matthew warned me. I gave him a curt nod and stopped a few feet away from Grayson.

"I'll let you do your work," he told me. "So, you can have your proof."

"Oh?" His sudden willingness to cooperate surprised me. "Okay."

It felt too easy. Grayson had kicked and screamed and shown nothing but contempt for this initiative. I wasn't so doe-eyed to believe that a few terse words exchanged between us would convince him to comply.

Matt joined my side, eyes narrowed, still untrusting of the God.

"Where am I to reside throughout the duration of this

project?" Grayson asked us both.

"You'll stay with Holden," I answered. As head of the project for this floor, Matt would take the lead on Grayson's integration and would also take up the mantle as his host.

"No."

"No?" I echoed.

"No," Gray repeated calmly.

It was so out of character from the way he'd been behaving that the anxiety unfurled in my stomach. This was the calm before the storm.

The room had grown uncomfortably still and silent as colleagues paused their work and shifted their attention to the conversation. Like a car crash — it was impolite to look, but curiosity still made you turn your head towards the wreckage. Disaster was a beautiful theatre when you weren't directly involved.

"I'd rather not deal with this idiot." His eyes flicked over to Matt, mouth curling in disgust, before looking back to me. "I'll cooperate if I reside with you," he finished.

Matthew took a step in front of me, his broad frame shielding me from view. "That isn't what's been agreed to," he informed Grayson.

"Fine," Grayson replied nonchalantly. "Then don't expect me to work with you."

I glanced back over at Charlie, who looked just as baffled at what was unfolding. Her fingers flew over her keyboard as she made notes, and I wondered what her professional opinion was on the display.

"You don't get to call the shots with this," Matt said firmly.

"Do not forget who you're speaking to!" Grayson roared, the force of the words causing a slight tremor in the lab. Glassware clinked together on the shelves until it passed.

"Holden," I said, my fingertips touching his back. His muscles tensed at the contact. "I'll speak to Gareth. We need him to work with us."

Matt turned around; expression unreadable. "Do you think that's a bright idea?"

For a fleeting moment, I believed I had bested a God, which was a foolish notion. Grayson had skilfully wound the argument back in his favour. He dangled the only thing I wanted in front of me and all I had to do was comply with what appeared to be a reasonable demand.

I wanted so badly to complete the job I'd been hired for. Not just complete it. Completion of the project would be a mediocre box-ticking exercise. I'd always strived to be at the top of my field and if that meant having the twisted God live with me, then so be it. Gareth would no doubt have the proper precautions put in place.

"Let Gareth decide," I said as a close on the matter, before Matt could argue.

The rest of the afternoon saw me removed from the lab and settled opposite Gareth in his office. After having the predicament laid out to him, Gareth had spoken to Grayson and Hunter, Matt and me, before finally deciding to allow me to become Grayson's official host. Matt would also temporarily move in as a safety measure, regardless of my objections.

By the time Gareth handed the verdict to us, the sun had disappeared, and the rest of the floor had clocked out for the day, leaving me and Matt to deliver the news to Grayson, who waited patiently in the lab.

"So, shall we remove these now?" Grayson asked, lifting his hands to highlight the copper cuffs.

Matt grudgingly took the key from his pocket and moved towards Grayson. The metallic click sounded loudly in the space as he unlocked the cuffs that bound Grayson's hands and weakened his blood. The moment they came off, Grayson flexed his long fingers and rolled his wrists before smoky black tendrils drifted from his hands.

"Holden!" I cried out when I saw what was happening.

The warning came too late as Grayson used his powers to slam Matthew against the wall, the pressure against his throat restricting the airflow and pinning him in position.

Grayson picked himself fluidly from the stool he'd occupied and rolled his neck, sauntering towards Matt casually.

"As your superior," Grayson told him, "I expect a lot more

respect from you."

"Put him down!" I yelled.

Matt struggled against the black tendrils that held him, his face slowly turning red from lack of oxygen. I moved towards the pair, but another arm of black emitted from Grayson and snaked around my arms, legs, and waist, holding me securely in place. Despite their smoke-like appearance, their grip was solid and powerful.

"I know more about you than you care to admit," Grayson said to Matt, not bothering to spare me a glance. "I know what you pray for. I can see what runs through your head. You better start showing me some respect, or you'll see just what I am capable of."

Grayson let go of him and he slid to the floor, gasping for breath. Done with Matthew, he rounded on me, and panic flooded my system.

"Don't think I'm above hurting a woman," Grayson told me, a wicked glint in his eyes.

Without the cuffs, the full effect of his divinity surrounded us, and he showed no signs of easing up. The grip around my waist tightened like a painful corset, squeezing the last breath out of my lungs.

"I demand respect," Grayson continued. "And I'll take it by force if needs be."

When he finally released his hold, I dropped to my hands and knees, feeling the pain course through my ribs. Grayson leaned down as I heaved in deep breaths, aching with the effort, and tilted my head up towards him, terrified of the situation we'd ended up in.

"That's exactly how I like to see people worship me," he whispered gleefully.

FOUR

GRAYSON

I should have killed him when I had the chance, I thought to myself. It would have been simple and saved me a lot of hassle. But Scott had distracted me, and the delay was costly.

A blinding blue light illuminated the room, causing the long fluorescent bulbs overhead to flicker wildly from the sudden surge of power.

Well, that happened quicker than I'd expected.

When the blue cleared away, Hunter was visible, uncuffed, at the far end of the lab. I would have wagered that they'd released my older brother from the restraints as soon as he had entered his designated lab space. Hunter was the favourite child. A shining beacon for the rest of us to look towards and emulate.

"What are you doing?" Hunter asked me furiously.

His blue eyes, the only common feature among us three brothers, narrowed and focused on me. Where I thrived on chaos, Hunter strived for order. Even now, in his rush to get to the room and get a handle on this situation, Hunter's sandy blonde hair remained perfectly in place. The perpetual poster boy for the elite Gods.

My aura coiled back towards me slowly, receding so that the room appeared less dark. "Just reminding them of their place," I answered, completely unfazed by my brother's anger.

"This is not why we are here," Hunter hissed.

His eyes flicked over to Scott, picking herself up from the floor. As she straightened up, her hands went to her ribs, and she winced in pain. Pride trickled through me, warming my chest. I'd got her on her knees, and considering how pretty she looked there, I'd have been interested in how well she could worship me before the rude interruption.

Pulling my attention away from her, I enunciated every word as I responded to my brother. "May I remind you yet again that I had no desire to be part of this idiotic plan you concocted. You're going soft. Bartering with mortals and wanting us to pretend like we're one of them."

The disgust seeped into every single word, cocooning them in hatred. I couldn't reconcile with the fact he expected us to walk among mortals and behave like them. Integrate and blend in as if we weren't destined to control every aspect of their menial lives. I was a divine being, and to ask me to lower myself was a great, if not the greatest, disrespect I'd suffered in centuries.

The door to the lab behind Hunter opened. Gareth marched in, letting it swing close behind him before making a beeline for Scott. She braced herself against a lab bench, trying to catch her breath that the pain had stolen. Holden had called for reinforcements, and I smirked, knowing that for all his talk, Matthew Holden couldn't handle me on his own.

"We need a better understanding, Grayson," Hunter said, parroting the point he'd made multiple times. "You need to stop this."

Black curls of my aura drifted languidly across the ground, like a sinister fog, towards my brother's feet. I longed for it to consume him, to pull him towards me so I could press a foot against his throat and silence the sanctimonious preaching.

"And if I refuse?" I asked innocently, cocking my head to the side.

One of my favourite pastimes was seeing how far I could push my luck with people. It gave me a thrill to watch the moment they snapped. The moment they lost control, they ventured into my territory.

Apparently, Hunter's patience was already thin. The electric blue of his aura appeared less like the smokiness of my own and more like a solid barrier that slammed into me and pinned me against the wall at the opposite end of the lab.

"See." I laughed maniacally, eyes lighting up at the fight. "Even you can't help but use your powers down here! We aren't meant to mix with them!"

"If you refuse," Hunter said, ignoring my words and walking towards me with purpose, "I'll ensure the council knows about your blatant disregard for their King."

"I am a King in my own right!" I thundered. My voice caused the room to shake for the second time that day.

Sometimes, I wondered if Hunter forgot we belonged to the same bloodline. There were certainly times where I would rather deny the fact that I was related to a pompous, self-righteous airbag like Hunter.

Hunter gritted his teeth, tired of my antics. "And yet it is I who lead the Gods."

I had enough of people trying to force my hand. Unleashing the full strength of my aura, the black of it darkening the room, I let it strike Hunter, knocking him clean off his feet and halfway across the lab.

"You're leading them blindly," I roared, advancing on him.

It was an age-old argument between us that the rest of the Gods no longer batted an eyelid at, but the mortals in the room looked concerned at where this was heading.

Hunter rose to his feet, no sign in his demeanour that he'd just been thrown across the room. He ran a hand through his hair calmly, but I caught the flash of anger in his eyes. Before I had the chance to do anything, Hunter's aura snaked around my throat. We were different in so many ways, and yet we both favoured the same body part for the first line of attack. I was sorely disappointed that the similarity had revealed itself. I'd need to become more creative.

Suspended in the air, feet clean off the ground, Hunter brought me down with such force that the floor cracked beneath me. The room shook from the impact and a few pieces of lab equipment teetered precariously on the edge of the shelves before a symphony of shattering glassware filled the space. My bones rattled beneath my skin as the aftershock ran through my body, and there was a faint ringing in my ears.

"I mean it, Grayson," Hunter warned me, refusing to ease his aura from around my neck. "You need to listen and cooperate, or I will have you stand before the council and let them decide your fate. I will ensure you cease to exist if you ruin this for me."

I looked up, thriving off the chaotic energy around me. It made my blood tingle, like static electricity running through my veins. The ringing had stopped, and I had already recovered from the blow.

A wicked smile came to my face as I pontificated. "Pride is a sin, dear brother."

My gaze flicked over to the three mortals who had congregated by a bench, huddled together, and enraptured by the undignified manner by which those they worshipped behaved. Whereas the men in the room assessed the damage and the strategy between myself and Hunter, Scott was concerned about the state of her lab and Hunter's wellbeing. I could hear their thoughts loud and clear, but it was Scott's that piqued my interest.

Directing my words to her, I said, "This is child's play."

"I'll take my brother back to your residence," Hunter said before Scott could respond. "Please, join us when you can."

He enveloped us both with his aura before we were transported from the lab and reappeared inside what I assumed was Scott's home. We stood in the living room of the house, a bright and open space where bookshelves lined the walls, and a large grey sofa took centre stage.

"I don't intend to warn you again, Grayson," Hunter continued his lecture while I rolled my eyes. "It is not an empty promise this time. It is a guarantee. You may see yourself as invincible, but I wouldn't have set this up unless there was no other option."

"You should have discussed it with me first," I growled at him.

But there had been little chance of that happening. We had never been the type of siblings who shared their ideas and struggles, victories, and defeats. We were brothers who'd been at war for years. Hunter, with his overbearing need to control every aspect of Elysia and the residents, and I with my overwhelming impulse to undermine him in everything he did.

"You aren't exactly the most receptive to new ideas." Hunter scoffed.

It had always been difficult to sway me when I was comfortable and set in my ways. Things were running smoothly. Or, more accurately, things were running smoothly for me. I saw no need to muddy our pristine natures by slumming it with mortals.

"I looked like an idiot when Larkin brought it up before the council meeting," I told him, still livid over my sister-in-law casually dropping the information. "She enjoyed her moment making me squirm."

"She did not," Hunter defended his wife. "She merely thought it would be better to let you know before we were with everyone else. Larkin thought it might soften your reaction."

The harsh laugh left my lips and echoed in the space, loud and empty of joy. It came as no surprise that Hunter would choose to side with Larkin. He tolerated his wife only marginally better than he tolerated me. Their mutual irritation at my existence served as a strong bond between the pair.

"Yes," I said. "I'm sure that's what my dear sister-in-law was doing. Looking out for my wellbeing has always been at the top of her priority list."

Everything to do with Larkin was a power play. I maintained that was the primary reason behind her union with Hunter; power first and love second. She enjoyed being partial to knowledge before others and delivering it in the cruellest ways.

Hunter opened his mouth to respond, but the sound of

footsteps made my ears prick and he seemed to have picked up on them as well.

"Make yourself scarce while I do some damage control," Hunter told me.

I refused to move from my spot. I stood there, looking at my brother with a defiant tilt of my chin.

"That is an order, Grayson!" Hunter barked. "You've already pushed your luck today."

With one last glare and the nagging reminder of what I had to lose, I took myself out of the room and upstairs to find the cell that would be mine for the duration of the sentence Hunter had condemned us all to.

FIVE

QUENTIN

It took some convincing before Gareth allowed me and Matt to leave the facility so that we could return home. The incident had left us all shaken. Two Gods scrapping with each other and damaging the lab had not been on the list for day one of E.L.I.

Matt took a pair of copper cuffs with him in order to restrain Grayson again, although I wasn't sure how he planned to undertake that task. The sharp ache in my ribs that shot through me with every step was a vivid reminder of the fact that we were powerless when he was uncuffed.

The black smoky protrusions that came from Grayson had been fascinating, almost beautiful — like the rest of him. The violent nature of them had been well disguised, but I'd never be caught off guard by them again.

As we pulled up outside the house, a different train of thought took over. I prayed Holden wouldn't make a comment about my living arrangements, but that'd been a dream.

He let out a low whistle as we stepped out of the car. "You can afford this place with what Gareth pays us?"

Charlie was the only person who'd been welcomed to my home. Even Gareth had met me in my tiny flat in Oxford before I returned to London, and then I visited his office.

My cheeks burned, and I stared at the ground. "My family," I mumbled. "I inherited it."

I was grateful when he didn't press the matter any further. The mention of inheritance, the subtle slip of death, usually halted conversations. No one wanted to dig up the memories. Not that I'd have to dig far. My parents were always at the forefront of my mind.

Matt followed me silently as I walked up to the door of my parents' three-bed, detached house that was legally mine, even if I didn't see it that way. I knew I was lucky to have this home. I just wished it were under happier circumstances.

Stepping into the hallway, I wasn't sure what to expect, but the quiet that met me was foreboding. Two Gods had returned here after a vicious fight, and I was meant to believe that they hadn't continued when they arrived here?

"Hello?" I called out, slipping off my boots and leaving them in the hall. I pointed to Matt's feet, and he followed suit.

"Through here," a deep voice replied.

Matt and I walked into the living room, where the voice had come from. I could feel him brushing against my heels and pushed back on the rising irritation at his disregard for my personal space. When I entered the room, Hunter was sitting on my sofa, ankle crossed over his leg, calm and alone.

"Where is he?" I asked, eyes scanning the room, but there was no sign of Grayson.

"Cooling off," Hunter answered me, uncrossing his legs and leaning forward. "He shouldn't cause you any more issues."

Matt scoffed, standing beside me. I couldn't help but agree with the sentiment.

"I thought that was the promise you gave before you joined us down here," he said to Hunter.

I placed a hand on his arm, feeling the muscle tense under

my touch. Antagonising the Gods wouldn't win us any favours. We'd experienced first-hand what happened when Grayson was unhappy with us, and I didn't particularly have any desire to see what Hunter was capable of if we pushed him.

"Why don't you settle in?" I suggested.

"I'd need to get some of my things," Matt told me. We'd come straight to mine from the institute with nothing more than what he'd brought to work that day. "I don't want to leave you."

"She'll be fine," Hunter assured him.

The doubt and distrust were evident in Matt's eyes, and even I wasn't sure I believed Hunter. How could we trust him when his brother had just viciously attacked us? The skin around Matt's neck was brutally red from where Grayson had wrapped his powers.

"I designed this initiative," Hunter reminded the both of us. "I won't jeopardise its progress by being as reckless as my brother."

"How are we meant to trust anything you say?" Matt voiced his concerns.

"Gareth wouldn't have let him come here alone if he thought Hunter was a threat," I pointed out, brain kicking into gear.

Gareth hadn't argued with Hunter when he said he was leaving for my house. He was hosting the head of the Gods and they'd been in contact intermittently for years. If Gareth believed Hunter could be trusted, then I was cautiously inclined to agree.

I watched carefully as Hunter picked himself up from the sofa and straightened the cuffs on his white shirt. He had a distinct energy about him compared to Grayson. Calmer. More mature. Regal. Hunter was the God of forgiveness and protection — the God who led them all. He would not harm us unless he had a reason to.

"I'll be okay," I told Matt firmly. "Just don't be long."

He looked at me for a moment and I could almost see the fight he was having with himself. Matthew liked to be the saviour. He loved telling a tale that cast him as the hero.

Eventually, he gave me a curt nod. "You get in touch with me or Gareth, if anything happens. Understand?"

I resisted the urge to roll my eyes. We had just suffered through the same experience at the hands of Grayson, and yet he had dubbed me the more fragile of the pair. If Grayson or Hunter expressed their anger again, I wasn't sure I'd have the chance to reach for the phone and call for help.

"Scott," Matt said, looking down at me. "I'm being serious."

"I know," I placated him as softly as I could. "I'll call you if anything happens. Spare keys are on the rack in the hall."

He held my gaze for a moment before reluctantly leaving the room.

Slowly, I turned my attention back to Hunter. His pale blue eyes watched my movements, and my mouth ran dry with nerves as the sound of the front door clicking shut sounded through the house.

"I can't apologise enough for my brother's behaviour," Hunter said before the silence could swallow us.

I felt awkward standing there with a God; the God apologising to me. His gift was forgiveness, and yet he was seeking it from me. And how was I meant to deny it? Even if Hunter's motives were driven by his ambition for the initiative to be successful and nothing to do with my wellbeing, I appreciated the gesture.

"You don't need to apologise," I said, my mouth still dry.

Absent-mindedly, my feet led me past him and into the kitchen. The tiles were cool through my socks. Hunter's footsteps sounded behind me, solid and loud. I gestured towards the wooden kitchen table that had once hosted Scott family dinners.

"You did nothing," I said.

"I may not have been directly involved, but Grayson is my responsibility," Hunter explained, ignoring my offer of a seat and standing with his arms folded across his broad chest. "I know he isn't happy about the arrangement, but I was hoping he may at least cooperate." He ran a hand over his clean-shaven jaw. "Our positions are reliant upon mortals and their prayers. If fewer people pray to us, we lose power. The first step is to become a minor God and then we cease to exist."

The information he shared wasn't news. It'd all been laid out with the offer of the job. People prayed less, content with the worldly possessions they could gain themselves. What use were Gods when you could resolve issues in mortal ways? Retail therapy never ghosted you. I understood the apathy that came with being just another number in the long line of sinners to the deities.

Hunter was eager to nip the issue in the bud and believed that a better understanding of the Gods would draw people to them again. I wasn't sure I agreed. Biology might prove they were divine, physics might explain the mechanisms behind the powers they possessed, but how did you install faith in people when you'd let them down time after time?

"Grayson." Hunter sighed. "Well, I guess mortals will always be vengeful."

Hunter led the Gods, both elite tier and minor, because humans relied on him and asked for forgiveness and protection. They didn't just ask those things for themselves but also on behalf of loved ones, and that gave him strength that rivalled the others. He would have been the natural choice for a leader, but that didn't mean the others weren't relied upon.

"He doesn't believe in the need for integration or understanding," Hunter continued. "He thinks he's above it all." The frustration seeped into his words.

"Yeah," I muttered. "I got that vibe from him."

A sad smile crossed Hunter's face. "I hope you won't judge us all based on my brother's actions."

"I really can't judge you," I said, leaning back against the granite countertop gently, trying not to irritate my ribs where the pain was still prominent.

"Ah, yes. My wife sensed that about you. You don't pray. Haven't relied on us. Not quite a believer."

My cheeks flushed with embarrassment. The brazen undecidedness I held towards them dimmed when faced with a God so reasonable. But Hunter didn't appear to be angry with my lack of belief. He looked tired.

Unsure what to tell him, I turned away and grabbed a bottle of wine from the counter, uncorking it with a pop. I opened the cabinet and reached up for a glass, but the motion made me gasp as the pain shot through my ribs.

"Fuck," I breathed and braced myself against the worktop. "Sorry." I wasn't sure if cursing in front of a God counted as a sin.

"Don't worry." Hunter dismissed my apology with a wave

of his hand. He crossed the space in a few steps and stood in front of me. "Would you allow me?" He nodded towards my ribs, and I felt the panic flood my chest and my muscles tensed.

My grip on the neck of the bottle grew tighter as I stared ahead at Hunter's chest. When Grayson had unleashed his powers, it had been unanticipated violence. I wasn't entirely sure if I could trust Hunter, but he didn't come across as threatening. Grayson challenged us all off the bat, but Hunter had exercised reason and understanding. He was softer and more welcoming.

"Okay," I agreed quietly.

Hunter moved a step closer and placed his hands on either side of my waist. The blood rushed to my cheeks again at how intimate the touch felt. It was difficult to ignore the beauty they held. So effortless. So flawless. It clouded my rational thought until I forced myself to think about the experimental set-ups I had to prepare for the week.

A bright, electric blue glow enveloped his hands, and I tried to break away from his touch.

"It's my aura," he explained, holding me in place. "I will not hurt you."

Before long, I felt warmth run through me. It felt like a spring day when the sun kissed my skin and I wished it wouldn't disappear into the horizon. It reminded me of summers that belonged to my childhood, spent on white sand beaches with my brother and parents — luscious and lazy.

After a few moments, Hunter let go of me and I released the breath I'd been holding, along with the nostalgia.

Tentatively twisting my torso, the pain no longer existed. "Thank you," I said in disbelief, patting along my ribs, trying to find a fault in his healing hands.

"It's the least I could do," he replied. "How would you phrase it?" he mused. "This needs to be a symbiotic relationship."

"It needs to be mutually beneficial," I defined.

"Precisely."

I lamented the fact I hadn't been placed with Hunter and envied all of those who had. He was compliant, and that would lead to success. Grayson didn't want symbiosis. He wanted to make us suffer because this was all beneath him.

"I'll take my leave," Hunter said, stepping away from me. "I'm sure my wife is waiting for a full report on what happened today."

"Thank you again for everything you've done," I said to him, feeling like the words weren't enough but having nothing more to give.

He smiled in return and left in the blaze of blue that belonged to him.

Later in the evening, when Matt returned to the house, I was curled up on the end of the sofa with my laptop, scrolling through journals.

He asked, "Is everything okay? You're alone."

"Not alone," I corrected him.

Somewhere in the house, I assumed upstairs, lived our test subject. The residual fear remained and stopped me from climbing the stairs and seeking solace in my room. There was a thin line between bravery and foolishness. I wasn't about to cross it for a second time in twenty-four hours.

"Hunter left?" Matt asked.

"Yes."

"And you haven't seen —"

"Quiet as a mouse."

"How long do you think that'll last?"

The million-dollar question. Grayson didn't strike me as the type of person who took things lying down.

Chaos.

Destruction.

Vengeance.

The words tumbled over each other until they blended into one. Grayson wasn't a docile and domesticated breed. He thrived in a dark wilderness that most people would run from. Sitting in a room and reflecting on his actions wasn't even a remote possibility. Something was brewing. I'd have bet money on that fact.

"Your guess is as good as mine," I muttered, regretting not taking full advantage of my chat with Hunter.

It was going to be a restless night.

SIX

GRAYSON

On a bed, in a dismal room filled with boxes, I seethed throughout the evening. The rage had not simmered down but still blazed uncontrollably in every cell.

It'd been hours since I'd arrived at Scott's house, and silence fell in the early hours of the morning. Breaths became shallow, and streams of conscious thoughts slowed and then stopped. Sleep had taken them both.

I needed to tread carefully. Or Hunter would demote me from my position on the council, and Larkin would love that. There was a mutual understanding between myself and my sister-in-law; we tried not to be in the same room together if we could help it.

Centuries on the council, years serving as an elite God told me that my fellow kin would happily banish me from their ranks. My responsibilities branded me as too much for them to handle, but

I wouldn't be restrained and make myself easier to digest. There was no appeal in becoming palatable. They could all fucking choke as I'd watch on with mirthfulness.

Fed up of the four walls that surrounded me and the incessant train of thoughts that looped in on themselves, I walked out of the room and through the house. My steps were soundless as I trekked down the stairs, noting the surrounding items.

The walls were lined with photographs of Scott's family. A mismatch of people. Scott with golden brown skin and long black hair stuck out. Parents who were Caucasian and blonde. And a boy, a little older than Scott, also Caucasian with darker hair.

None of these people were related by blood, but they appeared together in multiple photos. School plays. Christmas dinners. Holidays. And then the parents disappeared, and a new blonde woman appeared in the photos. Graduations and game nights as a new trio.

In the hallway, by the front door, there was a table stacked with unopened letters, and multiple pairs of shoes haphazardly lining the floor.

My bare feet hit the cool tiles of the kitchen, and I looked around the space. "Let's see what she has," I muttered to myself.

Lazily, I ran a finger across the bottles that were tucked away in the worktop's corner. A collection of different drinks that had been cracked open and enjoyed. Plucking a bottle of gin from the range, I found a glass before pouring myself a measure and dropping at the kitchen table. Just as I let the liquid warm me, my ears pricked to the sound of movement.

Scott padded into the kitchen a few moments later and I used my aura to conceal myself in darkness, wearing it like a cloak. I observed her silently as she grabbed a glass from the cabinet, filling it with water before leaning back against the counter and taking a drink.

Her legs were exposed in the oversized shirt she wore for pyjamas. Smooth, thick thighs rubbing together before the shirt gave her some modesty. The mass of black hair tumbled over her shoulders and down her back in voluminous waves, ending at her waist. That was when I noticed the faint blue glow that surrounded her. Mortal eyes wouldn't have caught it. It wasn't for them. It was a warning for Gods. Hunter delivered a mark of protection.

"I see he's still trying to clean up my mess. He placed a ward on you. So much for him trusting me to do the right thing," I spat, clutching the glass so tight that a crack ran through it.

The shock of my voice emanating from the darkness made her jump. I released my aura from around me as I stood from the chair, leaving the glass on the table. Every muscle in her body tensed when she laid eyes on me. The confidence Scott had possessed yesterday afternoon when she'd told me she didn't believe in our abilities was gone. Now that she had witnessed it first-hand, she'd retreated into her shell.

But it wasn't enough to make her realise my true potential. I wanted some fun. That cocky, bratty personality had got under my skin, and infiltrating her home was the first step. Living together presented the perfect opportunity to destroy her fiery spirit.

"What did it feel like to have the hands of a God on you?" I asked her curiously.

She carefully placed the glass on the counter and shook her head. "Goodnight, Grayson," she said curtly.

Scott took a few steps towards the door, but a dark wisp of my aura pushed it shut with a gentle click. I didn't want to wake Holden. This was a private chat. One on one.

"You don't dismiss the conversation," I told her calmly, feeling anything but. "You don't dismiss me."

The vision of her walking away from me in the lab rushed to the forefront of my mind. In all my existence, I'd never had someone ignore my call, and yet this mortal believed she was above my actions.

As I walked towards her, she panicked and pulled at the handle of the door in a vain attempt to open it. A low rumble of laughter reverberated deep in my chest. At least she had a morsel of common sense knocking around her skull.

"You're scared," I said simply, amused at how easily she thought she could escape me.

Scott didn't want to be alone with me. Her thoughts raced with what to do now that I trapped her in the room. If she was stupid enough to call for Holden, I'd make sure I silenced him permanently this time around. I'd taken him out with ease at the lab and would do so again with no remorse.

Instead of calling for him, she turned around slowly, so that we faced each other. This woman apparently didn't know when to quit.

There was a change in her thoughts that made me raise an eyebrow and look at her with even more interest. Oh, I could definitely have some fun with her.

"You aren't just scared," I noted, continuing towards her.

She took a step back and bumped into the door that sealed her escape route. Standing in front of her, I lifted a hand and trailed my index finger along her jaw. Her breath hitched, and she stiffened under my touch. I used my finger to lift her chin so that she looked me directly in the eye. Something that she would have been told not to do.

To stare a God in the eyes was to challenge us, and there would be no winning this fight. Blue met with brown so deep they could be mistaken for black. When I felt like Scott couldn't support her weight, knees buckling under the intensity of my gaze, I broke eye contact, and my hands grabbed her upper arms and pinned her forcefully against the door. There was nothing gentle about my touch, fingers digging into the soft flesh as I held her upright.

"You're curious," I whispered as a small smile graced my lips.

"I —" Scott floundered to find the words.

I leaned in, my face close to hers, and Scott pulled her focus to my mouth instead of my eyes. Her thoughts were loud and clear. She wanted to pull me in closer and bridge the gap.

"You want to know more about me," I said, matter-of-factly.

"It's my job," she shot back sharply.

What would it take to smother the fire permanently?

There was another rumble of laughter in my chest. "I can read you like a book, Scott."

I had her pinned against the door, and when I leaned in closer, I heard her breath hitch. There was barely enough space to slide a sheet of paper between us. Her mind and her heart raced at the close proximity. My nose ran along her cheekbone and faint notes of honey and orange wrapped around my senses.

"I don't think getting to know me that *intimately* is part of the job description," I whispered in her ear, amused by the salacious thoughts. Who'd have guessed the stiff in the lab coat would have such a dirty mind?

The heat coloured her cheeks, turning them pink and warm. I could read every single one of her thoughts, including those fleeting ones of how it would feel to be pressed against my body.

"Let me make this clear to you," I whispered, sending a shiver down her spine. "I would never touch a filthy mortal like you in such a way."

Quickly, I pulled away, letting her go and giving her some space as I let out a cruel laugh.

The embarrassment overtook her features as I reached past her and pushed the door open, causing her to stumble backwards out of the kitchen. She caught herself before she hit the floor, much to my dismay.

"Goodnight, Scott," I dismissed her, proud of how deeply I'd got under her skin in a short amount of time.

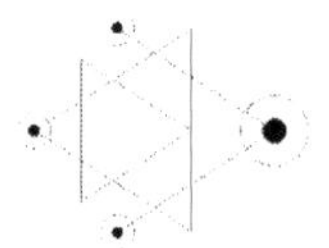

The morning brought with it new possibilities to torture Scott, but disappointingly, she didn't appear at breakfast.

Holden couldn't find her and concluded she must have left for work early. I felt smug, knowing that last night had rattled her so much that she couldn't sit at the same table as me over breakfast. That satisfaction lasted the entire way to the institute and up to the lab. Scott could try to avoid me all she wanted, but I'd find her and continue to play with her.

"Morning," Charlotte greeted us as we walked into the lab. "Where's Quen?"

"She's not here?" Holden asked.

A bruise had formed around his neck and bloomed darkly

across his skin, forcing him to constantly adjust the collar of his shirt. Another one of my achievements proudly on display.

"No, Matthew," Charlotte said dully, with a roll of her eyes. "Or else I wouldn't be asking about her. What the hell happened to your neck?"

I hung back by the door of the lab and watched the mortals chatter and go about their day. Completely mundane and trivial tasks. None of them of any interest to me. They continued to give me space, casting cautious glances my way, but nothing more. I looked forward to the day I wouldn't be required to visit the clinical facility. The plan was to talk my way out of integration. I hoped that Hunter would rather send me back to Elysia than keep me here after they'd taken what they could from me. There were eleven others who could behave like pets if they so desired.

"Things got a little heated last night," Holden replied to Charlotte.

He had the decency to look embarrassed, and the sense of contentment swelled in my chest again. The idiotic mortal had needed to be put in his place, and judging by the tense breakfast and silent journey to the institute, I'd done the job.

"I thought she was coming to work early," Holden said, looking puzzled.

"I'm going to see Gareth." Charlotte brushed past us both before looking back. "Oh, any idea what happened to the lab?" She gestured to the cracks in the floor and empty shelves.

"As I said," Holden repeated, going red, "things got a little heated."

Charlotte shot us both a look but didn't utter another word as she left.

For the rest of the morning, I sat at a lab bench, content as I combed through the thoughts of the team that had been assembled to study me. It was the usual mixture of thoughts, although there were a few mortals that had aimed their prayers in my direction on more than one occasion. People hated when they were wronged and that was when they turned to me.

I was happy to leave Scott to her thoughts wherever she was. Most likely licking her wounds after our run-in last night. Breaking her would be easier than I imagined, and it filled me with a dark and twisted glee to think of her as dispirited. Without the front that she put on for her colleagues, without the confidence that she so falsely possessed, Quentin Scott was another pathetically ordinary mortal with a less than ordinary life.

The clock ticked close to midday when Charlotte walked back into the lab, her thoughts thunderously loud and cutting through the rest of them. I shot up from the bench as I latched on to the main one. The stool tipped backwards, clattering to the floor and drawing attention. Holden instantly moved to place himself between us.

"Are you serious?" I demanded, left eye twitching as I spoke. The sentence came out as a growl, and Charlotte looked a little taken aback.

"What did Gareth say?" Holden asked her.

"Gareth reassigned her," Charlotte broke the news with a shrug.

"To whom?" I asked shortly, but I could make an educated guess.

"Hunter."

The anger swept through me like a tsunami, clearing away any other emotion. Dark shadows of my aura curled around my hands as I struggled to control my temper. My brother had the upper hand in everything since we'd been born, but I'd grown increasingly tired of it. Complacency spread like an untreated disease as Hunter dictated to all of us what needed to be done, and everyone agreed blindly. But I had my own thoughts, and I'd long stopped looking at my big brother through rose-tinted glasses.

"Why would he reassign her?" Holden asked, frowning.

"She asked for it," Charlotte explained.

Holden spun around to face me and eyed my hands, where the pools of black had grown larger. "What did you do to her?"

I thought back to the conversation we had last night. Scott thought she could still dismiss me. She was yet again attempting to walk away.

"Watch your tone with me, Holden," I warned, calculating my next play. "Don't make me regret not snapping your neck last night."

Holden backed down immediately, not wanting to be in the same position as the day before with a bigger audience.

"You have my cooperation if I work with her, otherwise, I refuse to comply," I told them. The tone of my voice dared any of them to question the decision I just made. "I want to speak to her."

Charlotte looked at me curiously, quickly averting her gaze when I caught her eye.

"It can't hurt," she said, glancing at Holden.

He seemed less eager about my demand. There was a protective streak in him that revealed itself when matters regarding Scott came into light. Holden wanted to see her alone and get a handle on the situation, proving he was in control.

"I don't know," he muttered, rubbing his jaw.

"Matt," Charlotte said. "We're going to be the only team who hasn't started. He just wants to talk to her."

I bit the insides of my cheeks, ready to erupt if he refused my request.

"We'll take him up to Hunter's lab," Holden said eventually, agreeing with her.

Holden, Charlotte, and two other security personnel escorted me through the halls, up to the floor above us. Eventually, we stopped outside the lab, and through the glass, I could see Hunter, arm exposed as Scott drew blood from him. She spoke animatedly to those around her, looking completely at ease as she worked, and a fresh flood of fury cascaded over me.

It shouldn't have come as a surprise. She was a mortal. Of course, she'd pick the easiest path she could.

"Let me go in and speak to her first," Charlotte said as she knocked on the glass door and someone allowed her in.

It took all my restraint not to follow her and cause a scene.

Scott would have liked that, for me to seek her out.

No.

She could come to me.

SEVEN

QUENTIN

After a restless night's sleep, I left for work early, without a word. Holden could deal with Grayson. I'd done more than my fair share of babysitting last night. Plus, Holden was probably itching for the chance to show him he hadn't left a lasting impression after the incident in the lab yesterday.

The same couldn't be said for me.

The embarrassment burned through my veins at the thought of last night. I hadn't even realised that Grayson was in the kitchen until he spoke, and it had escalated so quickly. He'd combed through every thought I had, including the ones about how alluring he looked in the darkness.

Why should I be embarrassed? He was a God, and I wasn't the only one who would have noticed how stunning the entire cohort was. Being so close to him had sparked a longing that had me pressing my thighs together. And then the way he'd informed me he'd never touch a 'filthy mortal' such as myself, had left me feeling dirty and worthless.

I refused to be made to feel that way under my roof. Rather than stew and let the anxiety grow into an unmanageable monstrosity, I spent the first thirty minutes of my day locked in my office, straightening out my thoughts. A scientist, a problem solver — that was what I was. Critical thinking was a vital skill.

Gareth could always be found in his office during the early hours before the official start of the workday. This project was his pride and joy, and I assumed his wife was the most understanding woman on the planet with the number of hours he put in.

Knocking on the door, I didn't wait for an answer before pushing it open. My parents would be mortified if they saw the way I breezed into the room, but they'd be disappointed if I didn't stand up for myself. One of those scenarios was easier to live with.

Gareth looked between his two desktop monitors as I walked towards him.

"Scott?" he asked, surprised. "You're a little early today." He glanced at the watch on his wrist.

An invitation wasn't needed, as I took a seat in front of his desk. I crossed one leg over the other and took a deep breath before I said, "I need to talk to you."

"Is everything alright with Grayson?" Gareth asked, sensing the issue.

I took a moment to answer. The last thing I needed was for Gareth to think that I was incapable or weak or worse, that I was blowing everything out of proportion. The thought that he might dismiss me as a hysterical woman made my skin tingle uncomfortably. This went above my pay grade, and I was more than a little concerned, backed by plenty of evidence, over how volatile Grayson had proven to be.

"Everything is —" I thought about how to end the sentence. "Fine." The lie sounded feeble even in my ears, and I cringed internally. "Gareth, I'm requesting a transfer from Grayson," I cut down to the bones of the issue, not willing to trip over myself any more than necessary.

"Scott," Gareth said firmly, leaning forward with his elbows on the table, preparing to start his defence.

Gareth, for all his well-mannered emails and jolly banter, was commander-in-chief. His ego surpassed ours, his drive was more dominant, his ambition bested us all. That didn't mean I was about to retreat with my tail between my legs. It would be a battle of wills.

"He's volatile and unpredictable," I told my boss.

"Which is why I placed you with him in the first place," he responded. "I thought you'd appreciate the challenge. Top of your class. The youngest person I know to have completed a PhD. You're not someone to shy away from work."

Gareth was good at stroking people's egos. During the months leading up to the arrival, he'd worked his way through the staff, getting them to do what he required. We had completed much work under his watch because Gareth wasn't above feeding into people's self-importance, but I wasn't buying it this time. I knew what I was capable of, but that didn't mean he could use it as leverage.

"You're not telling me anything that I don't already know, Gareth," I told him coolly.

No one was going to fight my battles for me, so I had to rely on myself to not get swept up in sugared words that didn't have my best intentions at the heart of them. Kindness was often barbed. People couldn't help but carry their own agendas.

He steepled his fingers and I leaned back in my chair. This was my first job, and I'd never negotiated terms, but I refused to back down easily.

"I'm requesting a transfer," I repeated. "I want to be assigned to a different God."

"I can't say it's a request that I wish to grant."

"You headhunted me for this job," I reminded him. "I had strict conditions, Gareth. I wanted to work on this to publish the findings, but that's a little difficult to do when I can't get what I need from my subject because he behaves like a child. "I want my publications and I want my recognition, and at this rate, it'll be one of the others that gets there first. So, I either get reassigned or I walk away from this project," I said with confidence.

The colour drained from Gareth's face, but his expression

remained calm. Not a muscle in his body twitched. He could replace me. But that would mean finding someone who would agree to the position, going through all the non-disclosure agreements, and getting them up to speed. I was here, and I had a proven track record that I could produce results in the lab if they gave me the correct tools to work with.

This could swing either way; I could get my wish or Gareth could show me the door and I'd be back to applying for postdoctoral positions again, with an unexplainable gap in my employment history.

"You don't mean that," Gareth said, trying to call my bluff.

Sitting up a little straighter in the chair, I relaxed my shoulders. "Yes, I do. You and I both know I could walk into half of the labs across the world without an issue. People want me on their team, and I won't hesitate to find an employer that keeps their word."

The offers had come from St Andrews', Auckland, and Houston Methodist before I'd even submitted my thesis. My external examiner for my viva voce was a Professor from Seville who gave me my fourth job offer if I so wanted it, but I'd turned my back on all those institutes because this job had held the promise of landing in the history books, and it was hard to tame my ego for an offer like that.

Cass was the final push I needed to take the job. My big brother was my sounding board and the person I loved the most on this earth. He'd been hesitant when I explained I was thinking of taking a government post rather than staying in academia. I'd been on the receiving end of a twenty-minute lecture on the dangers of corruption before he concluded I should do what made me happy.

"Fine," Gareth eventually said, blowing out a breath. "You're off Grayson's case."

"And reassigned to?" I asked, flashing him a smile and feeling the knot in my chest ease. "I'm not fussy." There was no need to push my luck, and we hadn't heard of the other Gods causing trouble.

Gareth huffed. "You can work with Hunter, considering you don't seem to have an issue with him."

"I think I can work with that."

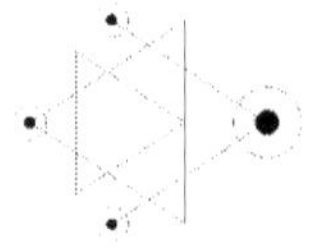

"Quen," Charlie's voice rang across the lab.

I turned around, inverting a tube of blood to mix it with the anticoagulant. Unlike mortal blood, which was a deep red, the Gods housed ichor that was molten gold. Hunter's contained flecks of bright blue, the same shade as his aura. This was the blood we'd been given when creating the cuffs, but I hadn't known who it belonged to.

"Charlie," I said, and felt a blush run to my cheeks. I knew that at some point, I'd need to face my old team but hadn't expected to do so until lunch.

"You asked for reassignment," Charlie cut straight to the point. There was a reason we got on so well.

Moving away from Hunter and the others, I caught Charlie's elbow, aiming for some privacy. When I looked up and outside the glass front of the lab, I saw Holden standing there with two other security agents. However, the most imposing force was Grayson, standing there with a murderous look as his black aura pooled around his hands. It grew, darkening the hallway, when he saw my glance.

"I'm not dealing with the disrespect, Charlie," I said, pulling my eyes back to her. "It's your job to observe his behaviour. My job is to study his biology, not be on the receiving end of his —"

I was at a loss for how to describe it.

"God complex?" Charlie offered.

"Exactly!"

"Quentin." Charlie almost laughed, making my name sound bright and airy. "He's a God. Of course, he has a God complex, but I'm surprised you let him run you out like that."

"He didn't run me out!" I argued loudly, offended by the accusation from my friend. A few members of the lab looked over, and I dropped my voice. "He didn't run me out. I just wanted to work on this project with a little less resistance."

Charlie nodded at the sentiment. She would understand my desire to work hard in a male-dominated field. We were constantly trying to prove our worth.

"He —" Charlie started and bit her lip.

"What?"

She sighed resignedly. "Grayson said he won't comply unless you're working with us again."

"What?" I wasn't sure I'd heard her right.

When I looked past Charlie, I saw Grayson still intensely staring at me from outside the lab, as if trying to burn holes right through me. He probably could, if he wanted to.

"Why?" I asked her.

"I don't know, Quen, but you know Gareth wants a full set of results, and if Gray won't work with anyone else, then we're about to lose a full set."

I glanced around the lab where we were standing. Hunter worked with us without complaint. He allowed samples to be taken and asked questions while answering ours. Grayson looked like he wanted to kill me and then messed with my head. However, Gareth expected twelve sets of results, and the failure would fall squarely on my shoulders in this case.

"Fuck's sake," I hissed, reality sinking in and tears of frustration pricking my eyes. "Let me speak to him." We walked out of the lab where the atmosphere was thick. "I'd like to speak to Grayson," I told them all.

"Be my guest," Holden said.

"On my own, Holden," I snapped, not in the mood to play games.

"No," he responded shortly, folding his arms across his chest.

"Holden!" I barked. "Don't push me today!"

He narrowed his eyes before signalling to the other two colleagues and walked to the end of the corridor, staying in plain sight. Charlie gave me a reassuring smile before joining them.

"Hunter," Grayson sneered his brother's name once we were alone.

"Do you need something, Grayson?" I asked him.

"You chose to work with my brother."

"Actually," I began to correct him, "Gareth placed me with your brother when I requested to be transferred from your team."

"And I bet you jumped at the chance," he said, scathingly. Grayson straightened up and sniffed indignantly before adding, "I won't work with anyone else."

"Why not?"

His anger surfaced quickly. "I don't need to give you a reason!"

From the corner of my eye, I saw Holden move towards us. I looked at him and raised a hand before he stopped in his tracks. This was between me and Grayson.

"This is my job, Grayson. I take it seriously," I told him calmly. "I'm not interested in playing games with you and having you make my life difficult. I asked to be moved so that I could get on with what needed to be done."

"You and I both know that without me, your job is left undone," he retorted.

He took a step closer, but unlike last night, I stood my ground. He was in my domain now. The lab was where I felt most confident. It was clinical and analytical and logical. It was where I'd built myself in the form of late nights and early mornings and missed weekends. I refused to be destroyed in my kingdom.

"It irks you that you can't get me to do what you want," Grayson continued. "It bothers you that I'm an unfinished project."

What irked me was the fact he could read every thought, even when I didn't choose to voice them. There was no running from the truth. I never left projects unfinished, and the fact I couldn't finish his case left me feeling unsettled, even when the transfer was what I'd wanted.

"Come back and I'll give you what you want," Grayson said. "I told you yesterday that I'll work with you to give you your proof."

"How can I trust you?" I asked, narrowing my eyes.

"You can't," he told me honestly. "You just need to decide what matters to you."

A thousand alarm bells blared in my head. I couldn't trust him. I never would, and he'd just told me as such. But all I needed to do was to tolerate him long enough to get the required sample. I wasn't a physicist that would need Grayson to be present for the experiments.

I knew I couldn't trust him, but there was an unfinished project — my project — and the way Charlie had said that Grayson had run me out made my blood boil. Is that what people truly thought had happened? Idle gossip twisting the narrative so that I was the damsel in distress rather than taking charge of my own life.

A black tendril wrapped itself around my wrist and I knew Hunter's ward had worn off and left me at Grayson's mercy. I couldn't let him do this again.

"Gareth is going to be sick of seeing me," I said.

The words were like magic. Grayson's aura dissipated, and I turned back towards the others.

"Get him back to the lab," I ordered, walking down the corridor. "Ask James to prepare some heparin vacutainers and butterfly needles. I'm going to see Gareth."

I didn't wait for a response before taking the stairs down to the offices, giving myself a chance to prepare for my second meeting of the day.

When I walked into Gareth's office unannounced, he looked up with a small frown. This was not the impression I wanted to give my boss.

"What now, Scott?"

He appeared stressed, and I knew it was because of the situation I'd brought to his door this morning. There was no one else willing to take my place on Grayson's team, and even if Gareth could find someone to replace me, it wouldn't matter because Grayson would refuse to work with them.

"If you want me to work with him, then there are a few things that need to happen," I told him.

Gareth sighed and stood up from his desk. "List them and I'll see what I can do."

An hour later, we'd agreed that I would work with Grayson once again, with no option of a transfer, my salary renegotiated, and

I held a single copper cuff in my hand. The last bit was more of an insistence from Gareth, but I didn't argue. It would be nice to have peace of mind that I was safe in my home. Then again, Grayson had got under my skin perfectly fine last night without too much help from his powers.

The corridors flooded with people who were starting their lunch break, and I pushed against the tide to get back to work when I bumped into Charlie.

"Are you coming?" she asked me.

"No. I just want to get things set up so we can start as soon as everyone's back," I explained. "This has already taken longer than it should."

"Do you want me to come with you?"

I shook my head. "Go enjoy your lunch, and I'm sorry I tried to leave without telling you."

"It's fine," Charlie brushed me off. "Don't work too hard."

The silence in the lab suited me just fine as I looked at what James had prepped on my bench. The needles were there, but I could probably do with a larger gauge. Crossing over to the cupboards, I pulled out a box of larger needles before taking a handful.

"You tried to run from me."

I jumped at the silky voice that sounded through the lab. Gods had to be related to cats — quiet, territorial, exalted.

When I glanced over my shoulder, Grayson was leaning against a bench, watching me closely. I turned away and placed the box back into the cupboard.

"If we're going to work together, then I have some conditions," I said.

He cocked his head and raised an eyebrow. "I'm intrigued."

"You do what I ask you in this lab," I said, looking at him. "The progress of this project is important to me."

Grayson shrugged, and I felt the irritation flicker inside me. It meant nothing to him, but it meant a lot to me and others who were recruited.

"Continue," he said.

"You stay away from me when I'm not working with you."

A smirk came to his face, and he pushed himself off from the bench gracefully, stalking towards me. He was definitely part cat.

"I won't be the one that has a problem with that," he breathed. "If I recall correctly, you were the one that wanted to get to know me better."

I refused to be embarrassed by it anymore. After all, I wasn't the only woman or man who had noticed that our twelve new residents were exceptionally attractive.

"A minor lapse in my professional judgement," I told him seriously. "You'll have to forgive me since I am just a mortal."

Grayson had made it perfectly clear what he thought of me.

Filthy mortal.

The words took up more space in my head than I'd like to admit.

"Is that all or anything else?" Grayson took a step back from me.

I pulled out the single copper cuff, fashioned more like a bangle, from my pocket and held it in the space between us. The smirk Grayson wore dropped from his face, and he narrowed his eyes at the offending object.

"You'll wear this when you're in the house with me or going through integrative tasks," I told him.

"Not a chance," he snarled.

"It's non-negotiable."

"You want to strip me of my powers!"

"You said it yourself that I can't trust you."

I caught the twitch of his fingers and the black that crept out from them. Grayson looked as if he was weighing something out in his head. Whatever had transpired between Hunter and himself yesterday when they left the institute had left him hesitant.

"I'll wear it when you sleep," he told me.

"I told you it's non-negotiable," I repeated, ignoring his ridiculous suggestion. "You'll wear it when we're at home and when we need to go out. You don't need to have it on when you're with the others. This isn't just my command. Gareth also agreed."

"Fine!" he spat.

I slipped the cuff back into my pocket. It wouldn't strip him of his powers. One cuff was likely to dampen them. He was an elite God after all, and I had my doubts over just how effective they truly were.

Grayson closed the space between us quickly, his arms on either side of me, hands gripping the bench, so I was trapped in the small space.

"You tried to run from me," he said, looking down at me.

"I did no such thing."

"They put you in my service."

"I'm not in anyone's service. This is my job!" I raised both my hands and slammed my palms into his chest, trying to move him, but Grayson held himself solid beneath my hands without the slightest flinch.

"There it is," he whispered, twisted joy coming over his features. "There's the anger that you worked so hard to keep at bay. That's the anger that would get you to call for me."

"I told you, I don't believe in you. I would never call for you."

"Foolish girl. You've seen plenty of proof that our blood is divine."

Ever since I was a child, I struggled with my temper. The smallest thing set me off in the most explosive ways. The older I got, and with my parents' guidance, I learned to control it, but it never truly left. It'd morphed from physical spats into verbal ones. I became versed in the volley of words and how to use them against my opponent.

"Divine?" I asked, disregarding the way my heart pounded. "You're so insistent that we're so different, but look at you. You're no better than I am. You're selfish and ill-tempered. You sit on a throne and look down at mortals with a river of gold flowing through your veins, but that's it. You walk and talk and are flawed just like the rest of us."

A murderous expression graced his face at my blatant nerve to question his divinity, but I was tired of being pushed. Tired of him thinking that he called the shots when he was on my turf.

A small voice called my name, and I looked past Grayson to see James standing there, surveying the situation.

Only older by three years, James had no issue taking orders from me. The man was so laidback he was practically horizontal.

"James, would you get us some liquid nitrogen buckets, please?" I asked him, trying to keep my voice steady.

He kept his eyes on us and nodded before he left to do as I asked.

Slowly, I turned my attention back to Grayson, careful not to look him directly in the eyes. "I need to work, so move."

Time ticked by at an agonising pace until Grayson eventually removed his arms from either side of me and I picked up the needles from the bench where I'd placed them. Grayson had left little space, so I squeezed past him when he caught my elbow.

"I am nothing like you," he spat with a disgusted look. "Make a comparison again, and I won't think twice about showing you every difference that makes me a divine being, including how easily I could end your pathetic mortal life."

EIGHT

GRAYSON

Scott had batted away the few questions about her disappearance this morning with a tight smile and curt response, refusing to disclose the true reason behind her temporary placement on the floor above us.

It gave me immense pleasure to watch her squirm, especially after her little comment. How dare she compare me to a mortal? Did she truly think we were anything alike? If she made another comment like that again, I'd be sure that she couldn't voice another word. I'd be doing the world a favour.

"Arm," Scott ordered brashly when the lab resumed work. She snapped on a pair of white gloves and picked up a tourniquet.

"I still require respect, Scott," I told her through gritted teeth.

She sighed and tried again. “I need your arm.”

I gave her my most charming smile, perfect pearly whites on display. “Say please.”

“You’re insufferable,” she said, playing with the tourniquet in her hands, and I swallowed a laugh.

Underneath the controlled exterior, something deep inside of Scott belonged to me. Wound a little too tight, like a spring with too much tension, ready to pop at any moment.

“Say please and I’ll do it for you,” I said, making my words sickly sweet.

With a sigh, and probably hoping to avoid another scene today, she gritted out through her teeth, “Please, give me your arm.”

I untucked the bottom of my black shirt out of my trousers but was promptly stopped when Scott wrapped her fingers around my wrists.

“What are you doing?” she asked, eyes wide.

The smirk tugged at my lips again as I answered her, “I can’t roll my sleeves up any higher. If you want blood, I need to take off the shirt.”

She let go of my hands quickly and turned away, busying herself with prepping the materials she needed. Rattled again. With a blush spreading from her cheeks down her neck, the heat emanating from her, those deliciously dirty thoughts had returned. And I enjoyed how well everything fell in my favour.

Slowly, I unbuttoned my shirt, feeling several pairs of eyes on me, but my focus stayed on Scott. Shrugging the clothing from my shoulders, I sat on the stool and folded the shirt across my lap before clearing my throat.

Scott turned back to me. I heard the faint hitch of her breathing and, if possible, she grew a deeper shade of red. The dark pupils dilated, eclipsing the almost black ring of her irises. She took two quiet steps towards me, suddenly lost for words, and avoided looking at my face.

Her gaze travelled along my left forearm, taking in the tanned skin and thick veins that pulsed steadily beneath it. She wrapped the tourniquet tightly around my bicep and pressed her fingers into the crook of my elbow, attempting to find a suitable vessel.

The entire time she worked, she made a point to ignore me, but I was the only thing on her mind; professionally and unprofessionally.

Ripping open an alcohol wipe, she dragged it across my skin and equipped herself with the needle.

"Be gentle now, Scott," I whispered, taunting her quietly.

Her face remained passive as she pressed her fingers along the crease of my arm again. When she was happy, she drove the needle in, giving no warning. I didn't so much as flinch to her disappointment, I imagined, and she attached the tube and watched as gold liquid spilled down the sides, filling the container.

"You have a terrible bedside manner," I informed her haughtily.

"Lucky I'm not a doctor," she quipped back, finally finding her voice.

"I'm not a doctor, but I've been told I have an impeccable bedside manner."

The suggestive tone in my voice made her cheeks heat as she swapped the tube for another one, working quickly. She wanted to escape the embarrassment, but it amused me. Every logical part of her hated me and with good reason. But her basic biology, the subject she'd mastered, betrayed her at every possible chance.

"You can't help but think about it, can you?" I asked her, keeping the conversation between us.

Scott refused to answer me.

When the tube was full, she disconnected it before ripping the needle out of my arm. Unfortunately for her, it didn't do any damage. She handed the tube over to James. The gold blood glinted in the light and contrasted wildly with the black flecks that swam through it. With the tube in hand, James walked off to prepare for the first round of experiments they'd planned.

"I have what I need for now," Scott told me, sharp and business-like. "Charlotte wants to see you for the rest of the afternoon." She snapped the tourniquet off my arm.

"What does she want?" I asked.

My question made her stop and look at me, but I focused on

Charlotte, who was speaking to Holden and gesturing wildly with her hands. There wasn't a moment where those two weren't in some argument.

Scott dropped the tourniquet into the tray with a small clatter and peeled the gloves from her hands, shrugging.

"She'll just ask you some questions, I imagine. Charlie's job is to figure out what goes on inside your head and why you behave the way you do."

I barely allowed her to finish the sentence when I asked, "What will she do with that information?"

"Sorry?"

I focused on Scott again, unfolding the shirt from my lap. The show was for her. To disarm her. I didn't plan to become a circus for unworthy mortal gazes.

Her eyes flicked to my arm, where there wasn't even the smallest scratch where the needle had punctured my skin. Not a single drop of blood was wasted.

"She asks me questions, and she observes me, and then what?" I asked impatiently.

"It adds to our body of evidence."

"It helps with your proof," I said to her.

"Exactly."

The click of Charlotte's heels on the floor caused Scott to turn around.

"Got everything you need, Quen?" she asked her colleague brightly. Charlotte and Scott fell at two ends of the personality spectrum.

"For now," Scott replied. "He's all yours."

I tensed at the way she dismissed me. Palming me off to someone without a second thought. As if it was a chore to deal with me rather than a blessing.

"Fantastic!" Charlotte said, unaware of the tension. "Well, Grayson, if you'd like to follow me, we can get to work." She flashed a smile and then looked at Scott. "Drinks after we finish here?"

"Sure. Why not?"

“A few of us were meeting at Murphy’s,” Charlotte told her the details.

Scott groaned. “Do I have to bring him?”

“Scott,” I hissed her name, unappreciative of the disrespect. How much would it count against me if I ripped out her tongue?

“I think a few of the Gods are joining us,” Charlotte explained. “Baby steps towards integration.”

“You’re doing this for work?” Scott asked, cottoning on to her friend’s plans.

“Oh, please, like you’ve never pulled a few late nights.”

Scott smiled and nodded. “I’ll be there.”

“I won’t,” I announced.

Mortals were ignorant beings, but Scott, reluctant to believe and rely on what was in front of her eyes, always took it a step further. If she was doing her job, then why shouldn’t I be allowed to do mine? Even if it was more of a personal vendetta rather than pride in the job itself.

Grabbing the tray of items that needed to be disposed of, Scott rolled her eyes. As she walked towards the bin, depositing the used item into it, she looked over at me as I rose from my seat.

Charlotte was a talker, and I assumed part of her job was trying to put people at ease. I found the incessant chatter wore on my nerves and made my eye twitch. I walked towards the door of the lab with Charlotte, her heel catching in the crack in the floor, and I caught her elbow roughly and steadied the ditzy woman.

“Careful.” The word came out as a low growl. Considering how accident-prone half the mortals were, I was surprised at the length of their average lifespan.

“Thank you,” Charlotte said, straightening up.

That was when I felt it among the general calm of the room. There was a stab of anger that radiated directly from Scott, and my lips pulled into a smirk.

“You’re very welcome, Charlotte,” I told her, all sweetness.

I removed my hand from her elbow and placed it on the small of her back, guiding her towards the door. The wave of anger pulsed strongly in the room. The lab may well be Scott’s domain, but emotionally, she was in my territory. All the dark, angry thoughts belonged to me and my gift. Whether or not she wanted to admit it, Scott was my disciple.

"How are you settling in?" Charlotte asked.

We exited the lab, and I dropped my hand away from her. The further we went, Scott's anger ebbed away.

"It's an adjustment," I told her.

She nodded and tucked some hair behind her ear. "I can only imagine."

I endured Charlotte's questions for the rest of the afternoon. She had extracted some information from me that included the fact that I was the middle child; I took my job seriously, and I liked to drink. She wanted more, but I was reluctant to tell her much. I'd learned all about her family and boyfriend and what had led her into the job.

"We won't have a lot of one-to-one sessions like this," Charlotte told me, scribbling across a pad of paper in her lap. "I'm more likely to shadow you during integrative tasks."

"Such a shame," I said smoothly. "I've quite enjoyed our time together."

Charlotte flushed pink and smiled as she left the room. "I'll see you later tonight, Grayson."

Back in the lab, I drummed my fingers across the bench as I waited for Scott. The rest of the lab had left an hour ago, but she was sitting in a room with a flow cytometry machine. Her phone vibrated for the millionth time, a few inches away from me. Irritated with the continual buzzing sound, I reached across and saw Holden's face on the screen.

A familiar spark of chaos warmed my soul as I answered, "Quentin Scott's phone. Grayson, Lord of Chaos, speaking. What is it you desire?"

"Where's Scott?" Holden's voice was terse down the line.

"She's with me," I told him.

"What's she doing?"

"I don't think it's appropriate for me to divulge that information," I said with amusement.

There was a flash of fury that transpired down the call. It made me laugh to know how close to the edge Holden was.

"What are you doing?" Scott asked, appearing in the main section of the lab and walking over to me. "Is that my phone? Give it here." She held her hand out, and I dropped the phone into it. "Holden?" Scott put the phone to her ear. "Yeah, we're on our way now. I had to wrap some things up. See you." She put the phone down and eyed me. "Let's get going."

"How are we getting there?" I asked, head cocked to the side, disappointed that she cut my wings before I caused real trouble.

"I'll drive us."

"I have a better way," I told her with a mischievous glint in my eye. Clearly, there was still trouble to be had.

Before she could say anything, my aura wrapped around both of her wrists and pulled her into me. It consumed us both, drowning us in darkness, and when it disappeared, we were standing in the alley at the side of Murphy's.

Scott took in a deep breath, looking slightly shaken. When she recovered, she scolded me. "Grayson! You're not meant to use your powers outside the institute."

"I won't tell if you don't," I said, arching an eyebrow.

Scott told me she wanted proof, and I'd give it to her in all the forms I could, just so I could prove her wrong. Nothing would taste sweeter than getting her to concede.

She shook her head and reached into her pocket, pulling out the copper cuff. "I told you if we're out you need to wear it," she reminded me before I had the chance to object.

"You also said if I'm with the others, I'm not required to wear it."

"You just used your powers," Scott countered. "I think I'm well within my rights to ask you to put this on."

I hesitated because something told me I'd be the only God that was still restrained.

"We could always ask Gareth and Hunter what they think," Scott told me, tipping her chin upward.

My jaw tightened. Scott knew she'd won this round. She unlocked the cuff and placed it around my wrist before fastening it again. The copper sat snug on my arm with no way of pulling it off unless she released me from it.

Scott pushed past me and entered the pub. The noise from the place hit me like a brick wall as soon as the door opened and I lost sight of her among the rest of the punters, but I sensed my kin close by.

"Grayson!"

When I turned my head, I saw Ignacio had called my name. His tie hung loosely around his neck, and a lopsided grin graced his face.

I made my way over and took a seat beside him. Our paths didn't cross often in terms of work, but Ignacio and I had struck up a friendship centuries ago when we were children. Chaos and luck wrapped together in one devious package. I could usually trust Ig to take my side when it came to Hunter and the others.

"Why did you look like you were ready to kill this afternoon?" Ignacio asked. "Other than the usual, of course. Bruna was up in Hunter's lab, and she returned with some salacious gossip, but I'd rather hear it from the horse's mouth."

"Hunter causing yet another inconvenience in my life," I told him bluntly, not wanting to get into it. "Nothing new and it's been resolved now. Let me grab a drink."

I got up from my seat and walked over to the bar, ordering a gin.

"Pace yourself," Charlotte said, appearing next to me.

"Won't even touch the sides," I told her, staring ahead. "I'm sure I'll be able to drink you under the table with ease."

"Not a hard task." She laughed. "I don't drink that much." The man behind the bar returned with my order, and Charlotte smiled. "Tyler, sweetheart, this is Grayson."

"Another one of your new colleagues?" Tyler asked with a thick Irish accent.

"Got that right."

He leaned across the bar and offered his hand. I regarded it for a second before I gripped it and waited for the rush of feeling, but it didn't happen and I remembered the cuff on my wrist, dampening the divinity in my blood.

"Nice to meet you, Grayson," he said. "Don't let this one boss you around."

"I'm sure there are no worries about that happening," I muttered.

Tyler did not know who I was. He did not know who the other eleven were. That was the way it had to be down here.

"Excuse me while I join the other recruits," I said.

Grabbing my drink from the counter, I turned back to see Ignacio in conversation with Elva. There went my company for the night. I'd rather not spend the evening with Elva, Goddess of death. That would be adding fuel to the rumour mill. We'd suffered through almost a millennium of attempted matchmaking, but the truth was we had little in common.

A hand slipped into the crook of my arm, and I looked down to see Sloan had attached herself to me. Her stomach was swollen as she marched towards the end of her pregnancy. This would be her fifth child. No surprise when her gift left her responsible for fertility.

"Gray, come and join us." Sloan steered us towards a table where Hunter, Larkin, and Erik sat together. She tossed long, sandy blonde hair over her shoulder as we walked.

I would have put up a fight, but Sloan was someone I rarely argued with. Her soft-hearted nature and patience had always won me over. I was glad my little brother had found her and welcomed her into our lives and our family.

"I was wondering when we'd be seeing you," Larkin said. This was a woman I had little patience for.

"Come sit with us, Gray," Sloan said as she let go of my arm to join her husband. I sat on the other side of Erik and took a drink from my glass.

"Oh! Look at that!" Larkin said with a smirk, pointing at my wrist. "Hunter mentioned you might still be cuffed, but I didn't expect to see it. Like a dog on a leash. How precious!"

I gritted my teeth. "Shut it, Larkin."

"I never thought I'd see the day that a mortal told you what to do," she said gleefully.

My hand gripped the glass tumbler tighter.

"Larkin," Hunter cut across us. "Enough."

We both looked to Hunter, who wanted to defuse the situation, and Larkin let it go, allowing us to all drift back into conversation.

I promptly zoned out when they started to discuss the project, and my eyes scanned the room until I found Scott. She was talking to a group of others, and Holden stood a hair too close to her than would be polite and professional.

"What are you looking at?" Erik's voice was at my shoulder.

I answered without thinking, "Her."

Erik's bright blue eyes landed on Scott and Holden before a smile came to his face. "He longs to be with her."

I almost choked on my sip of gin. "Excuse me?"

Erik, the youngest of us brothers, was gifted with responsibility for love, desire, and sexual attraction. Between the three of us, we were kept busy with prayers.

"That guy next to her," Erik said with a nod at Holden. "He's harbouring feelings for her. Relatively intense."

I let out an unattractive snort. It didn't surprise me that Holden held feelings for her. I'd witnessed the way the man wanted to mark his territory. The phone call earlier had just about confirmed that he wanted me nowhere near her. An unnecessary challenge in a bid for her attention, and there was no doubt who'd win.

"Who is she?" Erik asked curiously.

"One of the scientists," I told him, shrugging, and then rolled her name off my tongue. "Dr Quentin Scott."

"She placed you in that cuff."

I glared at my younger brother, but Erik only smiled back. We didn't share the same dynamic as I did with Hunter. Although plenty of people would tell you I was wrong for saying it, Erik was my favourite brother. It was a fact that I seldom bothered to hide.

"And her?" I asked him, my curiosity getting the better of me.

We looked back towards the bar. Scott was laughing at something, head tipped back so that her long raven hair cascaded down her back as she clutched a beer bottle by the neck in her hand. Holden looked down at her, and I noticed the hopefulness in his eyes that I had missed before. His hand ghosted over the small of her back and I narrowed my eyes, watching him.

"She's fond of him," Erik said eventually. "Nothing more." He sighed wistfully. "Unrequited love is the worst of all."

I couldn't help but laugh. No. Scott wouldn't be interested in someone like Matthew Holden. Scott strived for perfection. She wanted nothing but the best.

"Gray, you take so much pleasure in people's misery," Erik said, shaking his head and causing platinum blonde strands to fall out of place.

"It's in my blood."

NINE

QUENTIN

As I excused myself from the group at the bar to get another drink, Grayson appeared beside me expectantly.

"What do you want, Grayson?" I asked him, already annoyed by his presence. "I'm off duty."

His voice dropped, and he leaned close so only I could hear him. "Can't a God order a drink without an ulterior motive?"

The words were smooth, wrapped in silk and honey, and sent an involuntary shiver down my spine. It should have been a physical impossibility to be so alluring and infuriating at the same time.

"Any other God and I would say yes. You? No."

"Dr Quentin Scott," a voice said cheerily. "What a pleasure to meet you."

When I turned around to address my name, a beautiful man with shocking platinum blonde hair, struck me, taking my breath away. He was as tall as Grayson, slimmer built, but shared the same blue eyes.

"Hi," I breathed, trying to collect myself. "I'm not sure I know you."

"Erik," he introduced himself with a dazzling smile. "Gray and Hunter's younger brother." He extended a hand out to me.

"Erik," Grayson warned him fiercely.

I reached my hand out towards him, but Grayson's shot out and caught my wrist in a tight and painful hold.

"Let. Go. Of. Me," I hissed, turning my head towards him.

"That's not a wise move," he said, bringing his face close to mine, and I focused on his mouth to avoid his eyes.

"Grayson!" I said, pulling my arm against his grip forcefully. His hold didn't weaken.

"Fine," he huffed, reluctantly letting go and folding his arms across his chest. "But don't say I didn't warn you."

Everything to Grayson was a game, and he was trying to scare me, probably worried that I'd request another transfer. Erik's personality leaned more towards Hunter's, although it was less authoritative and more carefree and open.

I wrapped my hand around Erik's, happy to meet another God who helped prove that Grayson was a complete psychopath and anomaly.

The moment our palms met, there was a surge of emotion that hit me like a runaway freight train. They raced to the surface, making it hard to take a breath. I felt love and affection stronger and purer than I ever had before. Clear in my mind were images of my adoptive parents and brother and an avalanche of memories from my childhood. I saw and felt every crush I had over the years. Ethan broke through them all with the most clarity I'd seen him in so long. Ethan, when we first met, first became a couple, sinking to one knee. Ethan walking away from me and completely shattering my heart as he closed the door.

When Erik released my hand from his hold, my knees buckled, and I gripped the bar to keep myself upright.

"What just happened?" I said, trying to catch my breath as if I'd just run a marathon.

"Sorry," Erik apologised with a kind smile. The expression

lit up his face. "It happens at first touch. We'll pull everything we're responsible for to the surface."

I eventually looked at him. "Love?" I asked.

"And desire," he told me proudly.

Grayson stood close by, looking at me curiously. When he turned to look at his brother, his expression was furious.

"I'm sorry for what happened," Erik said to me gently, sounding like he actually cared. "You shouldn't let it stop you from opening your heart. You have a lot of love to give, Quentin."

Blinking a few times, I let the uncomfortable feeling settle over me. I felt violated. This God had just witnessed many of my personal memories. Memories that I kept under lock and key and buried into the furthest recesses of my mind. Memories I hoped would one day become vague fragments and threads that would stop tripping me up with the smallest trigger.

I went to open my mouth, but Grayson stepped towards Erik, grabbed him by the arm and marched him back to the table where Hunter sat with two women.

"Scott, are you okay?" Matt asked, making his way towards me.

I looked at him for a moment before I said, "You know what, I need to go."

"Why?" He looked over to the table that Grayson and Erik had joined. "What happened? I'll come with you."

"No!" I said and then cleared my throat and regained composure. "No. Stay and enjoy yourself." I forced a smile. "Keep an eye on Grayson. I just want an early night."

With that, I weaved my way out of the bar and took the long walk home.

Saturday morning, I sat up in bed with an uncomfortable knot in the centre of my chest. It'd been there ever since Erik took my hand and I assumed that an early night would ease it, but apparently, I'd been wrong. Considering rest hadn't been the key, I decided that the next option was to knock it out of me at the gym.

When I walked into the kitchen thirty minutes later, Grayson was already at the table, lazily stirring some sugar into his black coffee. He looked at me as I entered the room and raised an eyebrow.

"Where are you going dressed like that?" he asked, eyes roaming down my body and taking in my outfit.

My vividly coloured leggings were a little tight around my thighs and I'd thrown on a black tank top to disguise the little extra weight around my middle. But his gaze made me heat right through to my core.

As I finished braiding my hair, securing it with a hair tie, I plucked an apple from the fruit bowl and shrugged. "Gym. I guess you can come along, if you want."

It was half-hearted at best and more to do with obligation to work rather than a desire to spend time with the arrogant deity.

"Where to?" Matt asked, walking into the kitchen.

I suppressed a sigh. He was undeserving of my short temper.

For two years I'd lived alone and enjoyed the solitary peace. Living with people again felt unnatural, and even more so, when I considered one of those people was Matt.

"Gym," I answered him shortly, unable to curb the irritation entirely.

Matt stretched, t-shirt rising to give a flash of his toned stomach as he nodded. "Give me ten minutes and I'll join you."

"Well," Grayson said, putting his empty mug on the table. "I have nothing better to do so I guess I could grace you with my presence."

I rolled my eyes at the comment. "Hurry up. Both of you."

Waiting outside the house, I leaned against the bonnet of my car and scrolled aimlessly through Instagram until I heard the front door open. When I looked up, I realised that asking Grayson to join me at the gym may have been a mistake.

So far, I'd only encountered Grayson in shirts and trousers and had struggled to keep my thoughts PG rated. Then he'd stripped his shirt off in the lab, and I despised my sleep cycle for bringing his perfectly tanned and toned body into my dreams.

Seeing him in casual clothing stirred something in me that I couldn't bat away so easily. In the vest he'd chosen, I could appreciate his muscular arms that led up to broad shoulders. Shorts showed off strong calves, covered in dark hair that travelled up to powerful thighs. A baseball cap covered his hair, placed backwards on the crown of his head. For someone who hated mortals, he'd done well to blend in. Grayson looked every part the gym goer, with bronzed skin and taut muscles. I had to shake myself to stop staring.

By the time he reached me, the smirk on his face alerted me to the fact he'd read every single one of my thoughts.

"Don't worry, Scott," Grayson said, stopping in front of me. "You can work out all that frustration at the gym."

Grayson wouldn't give me an inch of space as I huffed and pushed myself away from the car. There must have been a foot difference in height, but any time he crowded my space this way, I felt like I'd shrunk.

"As flattered as I am, Scott," he continued smugly. "You need to control yourself."

The front door opened again, and Grayson took a step back as Matthew joined us.

"Let's go," I said briskly, getting into the car.

A short and mostly silent drive later, we arrived at a run-down boxing gym that had been my second home for most of my life when I lived at home. I led the way, pushing open the door and dealing with the receptionist before descending the stairs.

"Scotty!" a deep voice boomed across the room.

"Hey, Sal," I said, spotting the old man.

He made his way over and pulled me into a hug. "Didn't expect to see you today and definitely not this early."

"Are you free?" I asked.

Sal's hair was more salt than pepper these days, but in my heart, there was no one else I'd turn to. Sal would be a permanent fixture in my London life until he was no longer here. He was one of the few people I trusted with my life.

"For you? Of course," Sal told me with a smile.

He looked past my shoulder and clocked Grayson and Matthew before raising an eyebrow. I only ever came to the gym with Cassidy, and he hadn't been here for years. We were too indulgent when he visited to pay a visit to the gym.

"Something I should know?" he asked. "Are you in one of those open relationship things all you young ones seem to be on about these days?"

Pantone could have named a new colour after the shade of red that warmed my skin.

"No, Sal. These are my colleagues, Matthew and Grayson," I mumbled through the embarrassment.

"Pleasure to meet you, lads." Sal shook both of their hands and then said, "Well, what are we standing around for, Scott? Put your gloves on and get in the ring."

As Sal walked off, I spun on my heel and turned to face both men. "Play nice," I warned them.

I pulled my gloves from my bag and stalked off to the ring that took up one side of the gym. Sal trained me and Cassidy since we were teenagers. After our parents passed away, he did his best to keep an eye on us, but with Cass in New York and me in Oxford, contact dropped to the odd phone call. It was only since coming back to London had I stepped back into the ring and reached for the old methods of reigning in my temper and keeping my anxiety at bay.

Sal stood in the ring, adjusting the pads on his hand, and I worked through every drill he gave me. I released all the emotions that Erik had dragged to the surface in each punch thrown. I pounded every ounce of pain the memories brought back into dust. I'd done so well in burying Ethan away that last night had left me dazed.

"Nice to see you haven't lost your touch," Sal said as I kept directing punches his way.

"Taught by the best," I replied between laboured breaths.

Jabs, uppercuts, hooks — I worked through the combos with all my strength while keeping light on my feet. Eventually, the fatigue set in, causing my muscles to burn. I stopped and crouched down on the canvas, taking in a deep lungful of air. The physical pain was a welcome replacement for the emotional damage.

As I sat there, trying to catch my breath and calm my heart rate, the slam of weights on the floor sounded through the room. Across the space, Matthew walked up to Grayson, drawing himself up to full height. The God placed his barbell down on the floor with grace before Matt shoved him.

Without a second thought, I shot to my feet, but Sal had caught the aggressive behaviour and leaned over the ropes of the ring.

"Lads!" he bellowed, voice carrying over to them. "If you want a fight, get in the ring! I don't have fights on the floor of my gym!"

I paled at the suggestion. Refereeing a physical fight between the pair had not been on my agenda today.

"Sounds like a plan to me," Grayson said, looking over his shoulder at Sal.

In moments, both men stood in the ring as Sal laid out the rules. The old man was big on controlled aggression and helped me to deal with my anger until I stopped flipping out over every tiny thing. Under any other circumstance, I might have enjoyed watching a fight, but I had high doubts that this pair could keep it tame.

"Jewellery off," Sal said, pointing to the cuff on Gray's wrist.

"Sal." I took a step towards him, panic not yet giving way to paralysis.

"You know the rules, Scott," he told me.

Swallowing the nervous lump that had grown in my throat, I pulled the key from my leggings and walked up to Grayson. There was a mischievous glint in his eyes that bordered on dangerous.

"You better play fair," I muttered under my breath, loud enough for him to hear.

"Are you telling me what to do?" Grayson asked, looking down at me. "Maybe if you asked nicely."

He held his hand out towards me. I unlocked the cuff and took it from him carefully, not wanting to touch his bare skin. Erik had left a lasting impression, and he was all about love. I didn't want to entertain the thought of what Grayson's power might be capable of. What kind of awful things he could pull to the surface.

"Grayson," I said seriously. "No one else can know."

He was no longer looking at me. Instead, his focus zeroed in on Matthew.

"Grayson," I said, trying to get him to listen to me, but it was pointless.

Sal ushered me out of the ring, and I stood as close as I could, prepared to watch the madness unfold.

TEN

GRAYSON

It was amusing to see just how easy it was to get a rise out of Holden. His anger sat at the surface, bubbling beneath the paper-thin, nice boy exterior, and it took little coaxing to pull it out of him. Holden was a man who took things personally. He thought of himself as the typical alpha male and hated to be questioned or bested, and so, naturally, I'd done both.

What I hadn't expected was for him to be pushed to where he'd agree to a physical fight. The moment Sal mentioned the ring, I was more than happy to oblige and show Holden why he shouldn't have been so stupid. The moment he agreed, he confirmed the lack of functioning neural networks in the lump of grey that sat between his ears.

"You've made a grave mistake," I told him, slipping a fresh mouth guard in.

Scott had taken the cuff from my wrist, and I pulled on some worn boxing gloves with disgust. How strange that mortals fought with their fists. No blazing colours of clashing auras as the Gods had.

"You shouldn't have opened your mouth," Holden hissed.

Wave after wave of nervous energy rolled in from Scott. She hovered directly beside the ring; her face peeking out between the canvas and lowest rope. It was good for her to lose control over situations. A harsh reminder that she wasn't lord and master of her destiny.

Holden and I touched gloves at the centre of the ring, a symbol of respect that neither of us cared for.

I knew as much as the fact that Matthew Holden was an ignorant and arrogant man. He prayed to me regularly, folding his knees in the temple and at home over the pettiest things, and now that I stood before him, he believed he could take me on. For all the prayers answered, he had the audacity to turn against me.

There wasn't a single thought that ran through his head that I couldn't read, and as a result, I knew every move he planned to make.

Ducking and dodging, I fed off Holden's anger and frustration, allowing it to make me sharper and stronger. When I swung for him, I tried to hold back my strength, but it still sent Holden stumbling back towards the ropes.

The mortal pushed himself back towards me and we went blow for blow. It took minimal effort on my part, barely breaking a sweat as I countered each punch that came my way. The longer the fight dragged on, the harder I found it to rein in my powers. There was too much to feed from. Anger, anxiety, chaos; it drove me, and if I wasn't careful, I'd lose control over my aura.

A few more powerful punches, and Holden kissed the canvas. I felt my rage simmering at the surface as I towered over the man, but Sal pushed at my chest to get me away.

"Matt!"

Scott slid into the ring and kneeled beside her colleague. His face was red and already swelling. Holden would sport a beautiful bruise on his cheek to match the one on his neck.

He sat up slowly with her help, dazed from the bout.

"We are done here!" Scott yelled up at me.

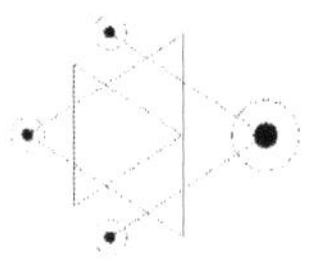

By the time we arrived back at her house, Scott was so furious that she refused to look at or say a word to me. Holden had become her primary concern, as he refused to see a doctor, leaving Scott to play the role of his personal nurse. Her anger stretched to Holden as well, but she seemed to hold it back where the mortal was concerned.

Rather than sitting in silence, being public enemy number one, I changed my plans. Originally, I'd no intention of attending the council meeting today, still livid with the way they had conducted business to create this circus, but it was the more attractive option.

Hunter and Larkin lived at Gareth's home, and they'd been granted the pleasure of using the house as a meeting spot. Wrapping my aura around me, I let it take me to the residence.

"We saved you a spot, Gray," Sloan called over as I arrived in the garden where the rest of the elite were dotted.

I dropped into the seat beside Erik, who rubbed his wife's bump gently. Sloan placed a hand over his and offered a smile. They were sickeningly sweet and if they weren't my favourite people, I would have said something. Even if I had, they wouldn't listen. Erik and Sloan were hard-wired to be openly affectionate.

Elva took the free seat to my left, and I took in a deep breath. She swept the long dark hair that fell like a curtain between us out of the way and wiggled her slender fingers.

"Elva." Her name came out as a pained mumble.

"Hello, Grayson," she greeted me breezily.

"You aren't helping the matters," I told her, my gaze darting along the others. A few caught my eye before hurriedly looking away.

"Let them gossip," Elva said, waving a hand dismissively.

"We're friends, are we not?"

Our work was so intricately entwined that the rest of Elysia assumed it'd be natural for us to fall together in the same way as Erik and Sloan, but I found Elva too calm in her nature. She dealt in death and finality. Instead of taking to it with the same vigour and darkness that pushed me, Elva was comfortable in her routine. Soft-spoken and gentle was her approach.

If I ever considered settling down, I wanted someone that was as chaotic as I was at heart. Balance was not something I craved. I didn't long for someone to calm me down or slow my pace. If it were to ever happen, I'd find a woman to burn beside me, equally bright. But Elysia had yet to create such a being, letting me grow accustomed and comfortable to my solitude.

"We are," I admitted quietly.

No matter how much I tried, I couldn't set the record straight, and it pissed me off how much the others took a vested interest in my love life. A love life they'd created out of nothing more than clucking tongues sharing baseless rumours.

"So? Let them talk."

Hunter stood in front of the eleven of us and called order, hushing the rabble and drawing kin to empty seats.

"I wanted to gather everyone today to remind you why we came to earth."

I couldn't resist the urge to roll my eyes, earning a pointed look from my older sibling.

"As we integrate ourselves with mortals, ensure that anyone outside of the project knows nothing of our powers. We're here to understand —"

I zoned out from the sanctimonious lecture. It wasn't like we hadn't heard it before. There was no doubt in my mind that he had called this meeting for my benefit. A public briefing to remind me that if I set a toe out of line, there were plenty of witnesses to help pin every accusation to me without hesitation.

My brain settled on Scott and the way she'd looked at me from the floor of the ring. It wasn't just anger, but disgust. I was used to it. There were plenty that were sitting around me now, that had the same reaction to me and my responsibilities.

My official title may have been God, but the whispers hissed monster.

"What are you thinking?" Erik had caught me again, and he looked at me curiously.

"Nothing," I said, avoiding his eye.

"Is it her?" he pressed. When I didn't respond, he continued, "Twice in two days, Gray. Why is this mortal taking up so many of your thoughts?"

We kept our voices hushed, but I grew anxious that someone might pick up on the conversation.

"You find her appealing," Erik said, lightbulb going off.

I balled my fists in my lap. "Drop it."

This morning, when she waltzed into the kitchen, dressed in skin-tight gym gear, Scott had piqued another facet of my interest. Beneath the lab coat and baggy jeans that she sported for work, there was a curvaceous body. Thick thighs that demanded to be wrapped around a head, a peachy ass, and wide hips. Her stomach didn't quite lie flat; a lover of the finer things in life and an ample pair of breasts. Beneath the nerd, Scott might have been classified as a temptress.

Then she stepped into the ring and as I lifted the weights, doing my part to blend in, I fixated on the way she moved. All that fury packed into that body sparked something a little more dangerous than vengeance. But it all shattered when I all but knocked out Holden.

Holden.

She ran to Holden's side.

Regardless of how much I despised her, even I could see that Holden fell way below Scott's standards. He was punching above his weight in more ways than one.

Maybe I'd gone about this the wrong way.

Erik cocked his head to the side and stared at me.

"What do you want?" I snapped.

"You've done something," Erik said. "You're worried."

I took it back. Erik wasn't my favourite. I hated my little brother. If anyone could read me, then it was this bastard. He'd never understood personal boundaries, which was why Erik had gone straight for contact when he met Scott.

"It's nothing I can't resolve," I assured him.

A plan formulated in my mind; pieces slotting together quickly, and the familiar warmth spread through my chest and into my fingertips.

"If you need my help —" Erik began, ever the peacemaker.

"It'll be fine," I said, although I wasn't sure about that.

Scott was good at keeping a lid on her rage, but I felt the strength of her anger. I needed to get back into her good graces, or at least inch towards them, if this was going to work.

I was ready to cause complete and utter chaos.

ELEVEN

QUENTIN

"What were you thinking?" I demanded when Matthew finally gathered his wits.

There was a bruise blossoming across his left cheek, staining his skin red as broken vessels allowed the blood to pool. In a day or two, the loss of oxygen would turn it blue-black and make it look worse.

"He gets under my skin," he replied as he stood in the kitchen, watching me extract takeout from the containers and stopping my train of thought running through the blood clotting cascade.

I understood that. It was in Grayson's blood to cause trouble, and I'd be an idiot not to assume that had been his goal when he riled up Matt.

"You shouldn't have reacted to it," I replied. It was my attempt to try and get him to see the bigger picture.

"I know."

Piling heaps of noodles high on the plates, I picked them up before motioning for him to follow me. I walked out the back door and into the garden, taking a seat on the chair and putting the plates on the table.

Out in the afternoon's light, the colouring on his skin looked more vivid. It'd been an uneven and unfair match. Grayson should never have jumped at the chance, and I would struggle to keep my mouth shut the next time I saw him.

"Gareth's going to remove you if you don't pack it in," I reminded him harshly.

"I don't want to talk about work."

"Okay." I stopped twirling the noodles around my fork and looked up at him slowly, trying to fade the red from my vision. "What would you like to talk about?"

"I've never been to your house," he said, turning back to look at it over his shoulder. "It's pretty large, considering it's only you that lives here."

A lump materialised in my throat, knocking the anger out of me, and I suddenly felt exhausted, looking out across the garden. The house had been filled once, before I became the single occupant.

"It's my childhood home," I told him, fighting the wobble that threatened my voice. "My parents left it to me and my brother, Cass, but then Cass left for the States, and now it's only me."

And then Ethan shared this home, staying here as he worked, and I came home to him during the holidays away from my studies. Visions of children and grandchildren used to swim in my mind's eye. The house would grow from quiet to busy and full of love again, and the vast space where I drowned in depression wouldn't consume me.

But it'd all slipped through my fingers until I was alone. I was accustomed to my own company, but there were days where it was difficult to think about what might have been.

"What happened to your parents?" Matthew asked.

It was a punch to the gut every time I had to admit it. Relive it. Almost a decade had passed, and the pain was still as raw as the day it happened.

"Train crash."

The words sounded distant as slender fingers of memories clawed their way out from the back of my mind. The police officers at the door. Identifying bodies. The inquest.

Matthew placed a hand over mine on the table, jolting me back into the present.

"I'm sorry," he said gently, thumb rubbing over the back of my hand.

There was nothing I hated more than people apologising over it. It was a ridiculous notion to apologise over something that had nothing to do with them. An apology didn't right the wrong in my life.

I shrugged. "I was eighteen when it happened. They were on their way to Scotland when the sleeper train derailed."

He squeezed my hand and when I looked at him, an unfamiliar softness laid in the depths of his green eyes.

"I'm sure they're both proud of you, wherever they are," he said.

"I hope so."

The sting of tears caused me to blink rapidly. My grief was private, and I didn't plan to share it with anyone soon.

"Quentin?"

It was strange to hear Matt call me by my given name.

"Yes, Matthew?"

"I was wondering —"

"My, my." Grayson's voice cut across the rest of the sentence. "Doesn't this look cosy?"

I ripped my hand away from Matt's and turned to see the God standing by the back door.

"Cuff, Grayson," I snapped.

"Ask nicely," he replied with just as much heat.

Matthew stood up from his chair. "Do as she says."

"Or what?" The black aura sparked to life around its owner as he walked over to us. "You really are as stupid as you look."

I shot out of my seat and moved towards Grayson, wanting to curb the argument before it started.

"You know the rules, Grayson," I said.

He tore his gaze away from Matthew and looked at me, but I refused to look at his face. He reluctantly held his wrist out to me, and I fastened the cuff around it. At least if they scrapped again, it would be more of an even match.

"I've lost my appetite," I told them, picking up the plate and walking towards the house.

"Quentin," Matt called after me.

"Can I trust you both to keep your egos in check and not ruin my home?" I called back.

"Of course."

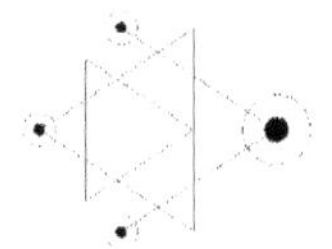

I spent the rest of the night in my bedroom. It had changed little since I was eighteen. The walls were painted sky blue, the desk still had a wobbly leg, and photographs of my parents and my brother and the places I had visited sat on shelves. Clothes were strewn across the floor, and printed copies of scientific and medical papers littered any available surface.

When I glanced at the time on my laptop, I was surprised to see that it was past midnight. Stretching out on the centre of the bed, my back cracked before there was a heavy knock on the door. With a groan, I got up to open it.

"Matth… Grayson?" My brow furrowed in confusion.

He was still dressed in his shirt and trousers while I was in my pyjama shirt yet again. His eyes moved down my body slowly and I wished I had something on hand to cover up a little. Something about his gaze made me feel less modest than I was.

"What do you want?" I asked briskly. "It's late."

"You're still awake," he pointed out.

"I was looking at data."

The reviewers had sent comments on my most recently submitted paper and I hoped to correct what I could as soon as possible so they would accept it for publication.

"Do you need something?"

"Look at me," he said.

So far, I'd been staring and talking at his chest.

"Look at me, Scott," he demanded more forcefully.

Slowly, I raised my head to look him directly in the eye. Unlike the first time, I held my own, probably helped by the cuff, but the colour of his irises rooted me to the spot.

To say Grayson had blue eyes was a disservice. They weren't just pretty baby blues. They were stormy, caging the tornado that was his personality and helped him rip through life. They tumbled from blue to grey and back again in stunning waves that lapped at the shores of his pupils.

"What happened today —" Grayson began.

"You could have hurt him." My senses returned, and the anger flared in my chest, thinking back to the afternoon's mess.

"He started it!"

"I don't care who started it," I said sharply, feeling like a schoolteacher. "You should have never jumped at the chance of that fight."

He shrugged, unbothered by my logic and said, "Sal seemed impressed."

"Sal doesn't know who you are! Stay away from Matthew. He's a friend and I will not see him hurt by you."

Grayson scoffed.

"What?" I asked, narrowing my eyes.

"Holden wants more than a friendship with you."

My stomach coiled uncomfortably at his observation. I wasn't stupid or blind. It was easy to see that Matthew wanted more, but I wasn't sure I saw him in the same way. I wasn't sure I was ready to open myself up to someone and take a chance at something that could end in disaster.

"That's none of your business," I informed him.

"The question is," Grayson said, looking down at me with interest. "Do you want more than a friendship with him?"

I wasn't comfortable discussing the matter with Grayson, let alone when Matthew was asleep down the hallway.

"It's none of your business," I repeated through gritted teeth.

"Because I don't think you see him like that."

"Grayson," I warned.

"You don't think of him the way you've thought of me," he continued, looking smug. "He doesn't spark that same desire in you, does he?"

The smirk that graced his face had me balling my hands into fists. There was no hiding from him when he knew. He'd heard every thought as my body betrayed me and reacted to his.

"You can't help thinking about me in the most primal ways," he said, voice low and dangerous.

"I want nothing to do with you!" I exploded, refusing to give in to his stupid games. "Do you understand? I wouldn't touch you if you were the last being on earth!"

With that, I slammed the door shut with such force that a few sheets of paper fluttered to the floor of my room. Grayson chuckled loudly on the other side of the door, and I let out a frustrated scream.

It would be bliss to have the house to myself again.

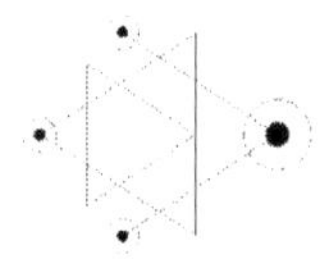

If avoiding Grayson was an Olympic sport, I would have qualified and won every gold medal up for grabs.

It was frustrating just how easily he got under my skin. I hated how well he knew the secrets that I wanted to keep buried and worried about what else he could find out about my life without consent.

My strategy in avoidance had been successful thus far, ensuring I left the house early and returned from work late. The only real interaction I had with him was for research and to deal with the cuff on his wrist. I'd let Matt take the reins on everything else. The men hadn't destroyed the house and Matt sported no new bruises, so I assumed it couldn't be going badly.

We'd managed two whole weeks in our new routine, and I contemplated how much longer we'd be able to maintain it without incident. Things felt too quiet. Too easy.

"Excuse me, are you Dr Scott?"

When I looked up from the PCR plate on the lab bench, I was faced with a beautiful woman. She had a kind face, framed by long, mousy brown hair, and she was heavily pregnant.

"Yes," I said. "That's me."

As far as I knew, none of the deities were due at the facility today, allowing for the staff to plough on with experiments and analysis without distraction. But stranger still was having a Goddess I had no connection with seeking me out.

"I'm Sloan," she smiled. "Gareth said he spoke to you about running some observations."

The door to the lab opened as I processed her words, and Erik strode in with a smile on his face, wide enough to split it in half. He came to a stop just behind the woman.

"Nice to see you again, Quentin," he greeted me as if we were old friends.

I wished I could return the sentiment, but considering our first meeting, I couldn't help but feel wary of him. Erik had pulled up so many memories and feelings that I'd work hard on suppressing. It tainted the airy nature he possessed.

"Hi," I muttered and turned back to Sloan. "Sorry, what observations did he need?"

As I spoke, I pulled out my phone and opened my emails. Something from Gareth had dropped into my inbox earlier, but I'd left it, deciding it could wait until break. But break had come and gone without me leaving the lab and the email remained unopened. Admin had never thrilled me. I longed to be in the lab, practising my craft.

Squinting, I moved my glasses from the top of my head and skimmed through the email.

"He's interested in your pregnancy," I murmured, feeling uncomfortable.

Most things in the project had been pre-defined, but we were slowly realising just how unpredictable this entire situation was.

Pregnancy had not been on the cards. Never outlined in a single document.

"He told me you were the best he has," Sloan said kindly. I forced myself not to roll my eyes. "And that I can trust you with my bump because you had some prior experience."

Sloan placed a protective hand on the swell of her stomach, and Erik wrapped an arm around her shoulder.

"We can trust you to be careful, can't we, Quentin?" he said to me.

"Of course," I replied.

I'd worked with pregnancies throughout the past few years in the lab, so it wasn't uncharted territory. What was uncharted was the pregnancy of a Goddess.

"And I prefer to go by Scott," I added, looking up at the pair and focusing on something I had a little control over. "If you wouldn't mind."

The use of my first name reminded me too much of my parents. Between Erik's powers and Matthew's questions, it'd left me off kilter, and I was trying my hardest to centre myself again.

"Scott," Erik said quietly, looking disappointed that I'd taken the morsel of familiarity away from him. "Okay." Unlike Grayson, he didn't look ready to destroy my lab in return for not getting what he wanted.

"If you follow me through to the patient room," I told them.

Pocketing my phone, I snapped my gloves off and threw them in the bin. The PCR would have to be redone later. A waste of reagents and time, all because I had avoided paperwork.

Each lab contained a patient room — a small space with a bed against the wall to allow for privacy away from the main space. The unspoken reason they existed was so staff could pull late nights without the need to return home. There wasn't a single person on the entire team who planned to drag their feet on this project.

I gestured to the bed as we walked into the room. "If you get yourself comfortable. Erik, there's a seat by there."

Sloan popped herself onto the bed with extreme grace for someone who was so far along in their pregnancy. Erik sat in the chair and watched, who I assumed was his wife, with such adoration that I felt like I was intruding.

Turning away from them, I took a seat at the desk in the room and switched on the desktop, opening a new patient file. I found the email again and split the screen, referencing Gareth's requests as I set things up.

Without proper planning, I was flying solo. There were a few things I could do to get the ball rolling and then I'd need to sit and pull together a more concrete plan that Gareth signed off. Hopefully it would include a midwife or someone who had more experience than I did.

"I need to ask a few questions before I take some samples," I said over my shoulder. "Is that okay?"

"Sure," Sloan replied with a smile, and I was a little more at ease.

Sloan and Erik were proving to have a more calming presence than Grayson. It was a welcomed change in pace.

"Is this your first pregnancy?" I asked, turning back to the screen.

"No." Sloan laughed. "This is my fifth."

My eyes widened. "Wow."

Erik laughed, the deep and wholesome sound filling the room. "We have one girl and three boys," he informed me proudly.

"They didn't come with you?" I asked, swivelling my body in the chair so I could look at the couple. The question flew from my mouth before I could think.

"Unfortunately not," Sloan said. "They're still young. It's hard to handle your powers at such a young age with little experience. It would've caused more trouble than help."

"They're with a… godparent?" I asked.

I wasn't exactly sure of the terminology Gods used. Were godparents a thing for them? The small thrum of the start of a headache appeared behind my brow, and I rubbed the spot.

Erik shook his head, white-blonde hair flying slightly with the motion. "As much as Grayson would have loved to stay behind, that wasn't an option," he explained. "My parents are looking after them."

Deciding it was probably best not to question their choice of guardian for their children, I nodded. After all, if you couldn't say anything nice, you shouldn't say anything at all.

TWELVE

GRAYSON

Two weeks. That was how long Scott had been avoiding me. If she wasn't at work, she was with Sal, leaving me stuck with Holden, who walked me through menial mortal tasks. They were all tedious, and he irritated me to where peeling my skin from my bones felt like a more appealing option.

I needed to talk to Scott. If they required me to do these tasks, I'd prefer to do them with her. There was something more satisfying in getting her to break from her controlled facade.

I'd restrained myself from any more bedroom visits. This only worked if I chipped away at her slowly, and I was happy to play the long game if it meant breaking her into a thousand pieces and reminding her of her place.

In order to shake Holden and allow Scott the space she craved, Murphy's had become a regular haunt for me, and Tyler was someone I had a surprising amount of patience for. He didn't ask many questions, and I helped him behind the bar three times this week to escape Holden and his dull drone.

Unfortunately, it was the middle of the day and Murphy's had yet to open, so I stopped in on Ignacio, who was with Hunter and Larkin.

"A social call?" Hunter said as I appeared in the garden. "To what do we owe the pleasure?"

"I'm not here for you," I told him, distaste running through my words.

Ignacio looked up at me from his seat, looking a little less jovial than he usually was, and I clocked on quickly that I'd walked in on a meeting he'd been aiming to set up for a while. A meeting I'd be desperate for him to conduct so we could both get on with our respective lives.

"Join us. I'm glad to see you listened to my warning, and you've kept yourself out of trouble," Hunter said as Larkin came up beside him.

"Oh, I'm not so sure of that." She laughed. "Is that little scientist of yours still pissed at you?"

"You know nothing, Larkin," I hissed in response.

"That's what I've heard," Larkin continued joyfully. "Julia was telling me she said she had no interest in interacting with you. Strong words even for someone with wavering faith." She let out a laugh. "No surprise. Half of us have no interest in interacting with you."

"Larkin," Ig groaned, running a hand over his face.

Hunter shot his wife a disapproving look.

"What?" she asked, eyes large in feigned innocence. "It's true. Waverly and Aria won't go anywhere near him. Malachi and Flynn aren't fussed either."

The younger elite Gods had always given me a wide berth. They didn't approve of my job, but it wasn't like I had a choice in the matter, and I refused to justify my actions to Waverly, Goddess of rest. Who the fuck was praying for a decent night's sleep?

"Fuck you," I spat. "Enjoy your meeting, Ig."

"Where are you going?" he asked me, looking panicked. He was already losing the courage he needed to submit his request to the pair.

"To Erik's."

"He's not home," Larkin said, looking gleeful.

"Where is he?"

"At the research institute with Sloan," Ignacio answered.

"Why?" I snapped, a lead block settling in the pit of my stomach.

"Gareth asked if Sloan would mind if they looked at her pregnancy," Hunter clarified.

"What?" I asked, trying to process the insanity that had consumed them all.

"Actually, it's your handler that's going to be doing the work if I'm not mistaken," Larkin said with a smirk.

"Are you stupid?!" I yelled.

It was bad enough that they'd consented for Sloan and her unborn child to be treated as an experiment, but to put them into Scott's hands? Scott, who despised me. Scott, who would probably do anything to try and inflict the same misery into my life the way I'd inflicted it into hers.

"Gray, calm down," Hunter said. "They agreed to it."

I didn't listen. Instead, the black of my aura wrapped around me and their cries faded away.

"Gray!" Hunter yelled.

"Let him go, Hunter," Larkin said.

When I released my aura, I appeared in a small room in the lab, causing Scott to startle.

I turned on my brother and sister-in-law. "Are you crazy?!" I asked.

"Hello, Grayson," Sloan said calmly from her place on the bed, swinging her short legs. She looked as if she'd been expecting me.

"What do you think you're doing?" I demanded from her before turning to Erik. "And you! You're allowing this?"

"Most trusted scientist, Gray," Erik said confidently. "What exactly should we be worried about?"

"You believe that drivel Gareth spouted?" My disbelief was clear. "What's there to worry about? Everything!"

"It's not really your decision though, is it, Grayson?" Scott said bluntly, inserting herself into the conversation.

She was flipping through notes in her hands when I rounded on her. She looked up, avoiding my eyes, but I wanted the contact. I wanted to remind her who she was talking to. Bring her to her knees and throw out my carefully plotted plan, because this wasn't a game. This was my family, and I allowed no one to mess with them for the sake of some stupid publications.

"Do you understand what you're working with here?" I asked her.

"Let me think about that," she pondered infuriatingly. "No. I have no idea. I've only studied my entire life to stand here and be utterly clueless."

With most things, I couldn't care less, but I reserved the softest spot in my heart for my niece and three nephews. I'd lose everything I had, relinquish everything I was for them, and the fact that Sloan and Erik thought it was a good idea to let the mortals into this part of their lives struck me as madness.

The black swirled around me, thick and fast. I wasn't about to let Scott use this as an experiment to cement her professional standing.

"Grayson!" Sloan called my name.

A wall of green and red appeared in front of Scott, and she looked confused as she glanced at the couple.

"I suggest you calm down," Erik said.

"Come and sit with me." Sloan patted the space on the bed beside her.

I stared at Scott for a few moments before my aura receded back towards me and I took the seat. It didn't disappear. I was too far gone to control it.

"Gray, I trust her," Sloan said, her tone soft and gentle. "So does Erik."

"That's a stupid move," I muttered.

"You do as well."

Glancing back to Scott, I chewed over Sloan's words. Scott had moved to the other side of the room, allowing us some privacy.

"I just want nothing bad to happen," I admitted, changing the topic of trust and looking between my family.

"You would know if it was," Sloan said, patting my hand.

Erik laughed. "It's your job."

I rubbed my face with a hand and shook my head. "I swear —"

"I think you should apologise to her," Erik suggested.

"What? Why?"

"There's something there," he said with a glint in his eye.

"There's nothing there, Erik. I told you to drop it."

Sloan looked at her husband disapprovingly and said, "Even if there was, he can't act upon it."

"I never said they were in love," Erik countered sulkily. "But I sense an attraction."

"It's a slippery slope, love."

"You're getting as bad as the rest of them now," I cut across them.

"Just apologise to her," Erik said, looking at Scott's back.

"Fine," I relented, if only to get away from Erik trying to make a mountain out of a molehill.

An attraction. There was an attraction. I was a God with eyes. I'd seen her out of the workplace where clothing no longer had to fit workplace regulations to avoid chemical spills on bare skin. No. Outside of her domain, Scott was a little less modest with plunging necklines, fitting clothes, and scandalous hems that left me curious about how to unravel her.

Pushing myself off the bed, I stalked over to Scott, who turned around as she heard me. The look on her face said she was ready for another fight.

"I'm sorry," I gritted out, for Erik's sake. My little brother would one day be my undoing. "For the outburst."

"To be entirely honest, I've grown to expect it from you," she said, pushing past me.

My eye twitched. "You can't just accept the apology, can you?"

She may have been easy to look at. She might have been worth a lingering glance and the uncomfortable tightness in my trousers. But the moment she opened her mouth, every dark desire morphed from sexual to sinister.

"When it comes from you, it's hard to believe it's genuine."

"See, Erik!" I said, throwing my arms out wide. "What a waste of time."

He stared back at me with large eyes, and I hoped that this display popped a bubble in whatever ridiculous notion was forming in his head.

"You had to be told to apologise?" Scott asked, laughing.

I let out a roar of fury before the room darkened and I took my leave.

THIRTEEN

QUENTIN

When Gray disappeared from the patient room, I huffed out a breath and noticed Erik and Sloan both looking at me curiously.

"I'm not sure how you put up with him," I said, wanting to break the awkwardness.

I grabbed a measuring tape from the desk drawer and approached Sloan. The Goddess laid back on the bed without prompting and lifted her shirt to allow for measurements to be taken.

"He's not that bad, really," Erik commented. "My brother is more bark than bite most of the time."

He would say that. He was Grayson's brother. I'd do exactly the same for Cassidy. Regardless of his flaws, no one had a right to pick at them except for me.

Biting back on any comment I had, I placed the tape over his wife's burgeoning belly. My bare fingertips brushed her skin before I realised the mistake and Sloan's gift hit me.

This time, I saw nothing, the way I had with Erik. There were no memories, nothing that was familiar, but a deep pull within me. It was warm and friendly, almost like a glow. It didn't force the breath out of my lungs or knock me off balance. It made me feel strong and protective in a way I'd never felt before.

When I removed my hand from Sloan, my legs gave way and I dropped to the floor, pain pulsing through my kneecaps and up my thighs.

"I'm so sorry," Sloan said, sitting up.

Erik helped me back onto my feet. "Are you okay?" he asked, genuine concern colouring his eyes.

"I'm fine," I said, shrugging him off. "I'm sorry. Sloan, are you alright?"

"Darling?" Erik asked.

Sloan pulled her shirt back down over her bump and looked at me with a gaze that made me shrink.

"Sloan? Honey?" Erik said, moving over to her.

"Erik, I think we need to leave," she said to him.

"Is everything okay?" I asked, feeling panicked at the fact Sloan wanted to leave.

Had she seen something that I couldn't? It was exhausting trying to keep control around beings that knew every inch of you without so much as a word. Could they know things about me I'd yet to discover? Was that how this worked?

"Everything's fine," Sloan told me, but some of the warmth had evaporated. "I just think it's best we go now."

"Sloan, I can't apologise enough. If I did something —"

"It wasn't you, Quentin. It's complicated." Sloan slipped off the bed. "Would it be okay if I stopped by again tomorrow?"

"Yes. That's not a problem."

"Thank you for your time," Erik said with a nod.

His red aura wrapped around them, and within seconds they were gone, leaving me to ponder the sudden departure.

I made the swift decision to finish the rest of the day at home. My phone came off 'do not disturb' for any calls or emails from James. All I could think about was the way the two Gods had rushed out of my care and whether it would count against me if news went back to Gareth.

When I got back to the house, I shut the front door and leaned against it with a sigh. Another God pushed his way to the forefront of my mind.

Maybe I should apologise to Grayson for the way I behaved. I should have just accepted his apology. If we could make it onto civil terms, then maybe I could ask him about what Sloan felt after the contact earlier.

Making my way up the stairs, I crossed the hall to the room Grayson occupied. I wasn't sure if he was home, but it was worth a try. Knocking on the door, I waited and was met by silence. If he was in there, he was probably ignoring me with a smirk on his face. Idiot. I turned the doorknob and pushed it open to see Grayson was in the room, but he wasn't just sitting there.

He was shirtless, on top of a woman that I didn't recognise. She turned her head towards the door, lipstick smudged, looking shocked and embarrassed, and I had to pick my jaw off the floor. Grayson, however, didn't even look at me.

"Busy right now, Scott," he said, burying his face in the crook of the woman's neck.

His voice jolted me from the shock of the scene, and I turned around and slammed the door shut with surprising force.

Racing back down the stairs, I tried to ignore the emotions that welled in my chest. They all fought with each other to rise to the top. Humiliation and anger battled valiantly for centre stage, but stupidity won. How did I think I could ever be on civil terms with that pig?

Automatically, I went into the kitchen and poured myself a glass of wine before walking into the garden. I slammed the back door, watching it bounce off the frame and swing open again.

"Stupid, arrogant prick," I muttered, turning away.

Taking a deep drink from the glass, I leaned against the wall of the house and looked out across the garden. The edges of it still had my mother's rose bushes in full bloom and enjoying the warm, balmy summer weather. Whites and reds, alternating along the border of grass.

"Do you always intend to ruin my fun?" Grayson's voice joined me.

I pushed off the wall, gripping the glass tighter. "My presence didn't seem to have much impact on you."

"Yes, well, Naomi felt a little more embarrassed than I did." Grayson sniffed. "Decided to call it an afternoon."

"Poor you," I hissed.

Grayson appeared at my side, dressed only in jeans that hung low on his hip, glimpsing the sacred V that made my mouth dry and my pulse speed up. Straightening out my thoughts, I walked away from him.

"Why so angry, Scott?" he asked calmly.

"I'm not running a brothel, Grayson," I told him. "This is my home! You don't just bring back whoever you want, whenever you want. I live here! Even when you are gone, I will live here, so I'd rather not have all and sundry know my address!"

It was genuine enough. I couldn't have him bringing whoever he wanted back to my home. I knew nothing about them, and I lived alone. This was a recipe for disaster and if Cass found out, I'd never hear the end of it.

"I don't think it's just that." Gray walked towards me with slow, measured steps.

Putting the glass down on the table, I hurried away from him, walking around the outside of the house until I'd skirted around the side gate and ended up at the front door. He'd followed me with silent footsteps.

"Naomi is a mortal," he informed me, as if I didn't know the fact. "That bothers you, doesn't it?"

"Why the hell would that bother me?" I forced out a laugh.

"Because I told you I'd never touch you. That I'd never want a filthy mortal."

The blood rushed to my cheeks. I hated when this happened. I hated feeling inadequate. Inconsequential. Insignificant. My mind fixated on the words. Foolish. Negligible. Meaningless. They ricocheted against my skull until I wanted to claw them out.

For twenty-seven years, I'd put my all into every aspect of my life to prove to myself and to everyone that I was as good, if not better, than average. The need to be more than the abandoned, angry kid. Grayson was slowly destroying all my hard work with a few simple sentences, and I hated him for it. Hated that I let him have that impact.

"And I told you I wouldn't touch you if you were the last being on earth," I shot back at him, pride punching its way to the surface.

"You have such an independent spirit, Scott," Grayson said with a sinister smile. "But there's a small part of you that wants to obey me. A sliver that would submit to me if I gave you the chance. And I intend to find it."

I opened my mouth to respond but wasn't given the chance. Grayson closed the gap between us. Every time he'd done this, I noticed the way he was careful not to touch me. Grayson had always been wary about being close without contact, but this time, that wasn't his goal.

This time, his hand cupped my face before his lips crashed down on mine.

I'd experienced skin to skin contact with two Gods before him, but the contact with Grayson was stronger than both combined. It was fury and rage in such a deep shade of red that it was basically black.

Multiple memories flashed through my mind. Getting into trouble for things that Cassidy had done. Having boys tell me I couldn't do what they did. Fights with friends. Burying my parents. Watching Ethan walk away from me.

As they flickered in and out of focus, my stomach knotted. So much anger bubbling through my gut and making me nauseous. This was the feeling I'd been accustomed to until my adoption. This was the white-hot pulse that Dad taught me to control. The beast no longer sat caged. It howled, running free for the first time in years.

When all of it faded away, the weakness washed over my limbs and light-headedness rushed through my skull. I gripped onto Grayson as his arms wrapped around me, holding me flush against him and steady. I kissed him back just to bury the pure chaos he'd pulled to the surface.

A deep fire soon replaced it as Grayson's tongue pushed into my mouth, and I didn't resist. Didn't have the energy to refuse him. My body responded in all the ways it had begged to since I'd first laid eyes on him. As if it finally had permission to soak in every inch of the God in the most intimate ways. All of my nerves were on fire from the embrace, and finally I broke away, needing to breathe.

"There it is," Grayson said, still holding me and speaking quietly.

He looked down with a self-satisfied, smug look on his face which brought me back to my senses. Grayson had just been in bed seducing another woman all of five minutes ago, and now he stood there kissing me to prove a point.

And I'd let him.

"Stay the fuck away from me," I said, pushing him away.

"Come on now, Scott. I definitely know that's not what you want." He laughed cruelly. "And my, oh my, do you have a lot running through you? How have you kept all that under control?"

"It's none of your business."

"Even Hunter has lost control of his temper over the years."

I clenched my teeth, feeling completely violated. I didn't trust people. My life was a closed book, and I chose to keep people out of it. Information was given sparingly. Yet, these Gods, these beings who had always forgotten me, assumed it was their right to pick through thoughts and memories that built the different facets of my being.

"And who was the man?" Grayson asked curiously, cocking his head to the side. "The last time you truly lost control. What was he to you?"

"It's none of your business!" I shouted.

"It's okay, Scott. You can submit to me, and I can take away all that anger. Didn't it feel good? Didn't it feel freeing to release it all? Imagine just how good I could make you feel."

The worst thing was that it had felt good. Everything about being wrapped up in Grayson, after the initial fury, felt euphoric. But I couldn't let it happen again. It would allow him to win. He wanted to break me, and I refused to let it happen.

"I'm warning you, Grayson," I told him, lacking conviction.

"What are you going to do, Scott?"

I'd never been so grateful to see Matt's car pull up in front of the house.

I took a few more steps away from Grayson and repeated, "Stay away from me."

"What are you two doing out here?" Matt asked as he got out of the car and walked over to us.

"I wasn't feeling too well," I lied. "Needed some air."

Concern filled his eyes as he looked at me. "Do you need to see a doctor?"

"Probably something to do with the heat," Gray commented slyly.

I shot him a look. How did he continue to be so smug about the situation? How could someone have such little regard for others around them?

"Let's get you inside and grab you a glass of water," Matt said.

He led me towards the door, and I couldn't help but throw one last glance back at Grayson before the door closed, separating us.

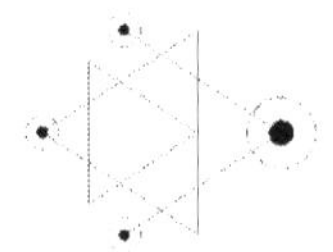

It was a fucking shame that my job didn't offer overtime because the number of early starts I'd pulled would have amounted to a nice bonus. There wasn't an adjective strong enough to describe how I felt with what had transpired between myself and Grayson yesterday, and I didn't want to face him.

Grayson was easily the most frustrating being I knew. He made me lose the control that I had over my aggression and yet I found him alluring. I knew I wasn't the only one who looked at him in that way, evidenced by the woman in his bed, but after that kiss…

In my spare moments, my mind wandered to the embrace.

He'd stolen it, but that didn't mean I hadn't wanted it, and so much more.

Fuck, I cannot be thinking about him like this, I reminded myself.

My thoughts had been filthy enough, but after being that close to him, tasting him, they'd spiralled and become more difficult to tame.

"Quen, are you listening to me?"

"Huh?"

"What's going on up there today?" Charlie asked, tapping my temple gently with a manicured finger.

We were sitting in the breakroom. I held a cold up of coffee in my hands and stared into the dark depths. "I didn't sleep well last night."

It wasn't a lie. I never slept well, but last night had been for reasons other than the usual. Curled up in bed, my heart hammered dangerously as I attempted to pack everything that'd been unleashed back into the box. If Grayson showed up at the door, I didn't know what I'd do, and that was a cause for concern, because it meant I wasn't in control.

"You're spending a lot of time here, Quen," she said, pursing her lips. "Be careful you don't burn yourself out."

I had to bite the insides of my cheeks to stop myself from admitting the truth to Charlie.

"It's fine," I said. "I'm fine. Cass is visiting soon so that'll be a nice break."

"Your brother? Is he bringing his fiancée?"

Cassidy got engaged to Sophie last year. She was a sweet woman who knew how to keep my brother in line. It'd stung a little when he made the announcement, but I quickly pushed it aside. Seeing my brother happy meant the world to me.

"Yeah, Sophie will be here," I confirmed. "Ironing out details for the wedding."

"So, you're taking some leave?"

Nodding, I drained the cold brown liquid from the mug and got up from my seat.

"Quen," Charlie said, looking up at me.

"Mhm?"

"Have you found a plus-one yet?"

I blinked.

No one at this job knew about Ethan. After we'd broken up, I'd methodically removed every photo and post that contained him. A completely clean slate. To everyone here, I didn't date because I didn't have the time, but Charlie bringing up the plus-one reminded me of how single I'd be at Cass's wedding in December.

"Not yet."

"You know, I could always ask my cousin."

FOURTEEN

GRAYSON

Most of my morning had been occupied by helping Tyler stock the pub. It would have been done quicker if I was allowed to use my powers, but I'd already pushed my luck and it was better to tread lightly. Instead, I pulled boxes and placed bottles while Tyler threw in the occasional piece of chatter.

Murphy's was the most interesting place I had stumbled into on earth. It'd given me a chance to speak to and observe mortals at their best and worst. They piled in to celebrate their victories and drown their sorrows. There had been plenty of thoughts to pick through and plenty of decent women to pursue.

And I'd have been successful in my pursuit yesterday afternoon if Scott hadn't barged her way into my room. Apparently, privacy wasn't something to be expected in her household.

"I appreciate you helping out when you can," Tyler said, drawing me from my thoughts.

"It's no trouble."

"I didn't realise you were only part time."

"Agency work," I lied smoothly with the prepared story. "We'll move on once the project is done."

Tyler nodded and continued to wipe down tables. I tolerated him. Never asked too many questions. He had, what I assumed Erik would call, a balanced relationship. Charlie felt the need to fill the silence, but Tyler was comfortable in it.

As the afternoon wore on, I made my way to the institute for an update with Gareth before my scheduled appointment with Scott.

"And you haven't come across any issues?" Gareth asked, eyeing me warily.

I leaned back in the chair opposite him, calm and composed. "None that I can recall."

"Well, Holden has no complaints. Quentin and Charlotte seem pleased with the progress they're making so far. You're due to see Hankle soon —"

It came as no surprise that Holden had said nothing. He wouldn't want a mark on that sterling reputation of his. The mere thought that his superior might see him as incapable forced his mouth to stay shut.

Scott, however, I'd been sure would tell Gareth I'd overstepped the mark again, considering she wasn't at home this morning.

Unless I hadn't actually overstepped the mark.

I knew I could get to her.

Yesterday had been impulsive. A step away from the plans. I'd wanted her to trust me before I made a move. The truth of the matter was that she'd never trust me. Scott was too smart and too guarded, and I was too prone to chaotic situations to prove her wrong.

The insecurity that flowed through Scott when she caught me was not a gentle trickle, but a rushing river that pulled her under.

Frustration, inadequacy, and pure, unadulterated violence rattled through her and drew me in like a magnet. She was mine long before I set my sights on her.

I'd imagined a kiss with her would be lacklustre. After all, how could a mortal ever compare to the centuries of divine indiscretions that made up the notches of my bedpost?

How wrong I was.

Kissing Scott had been drinking darkness that I craved every day. It stirred my soul and woke something I couldn't quite place my finger on. The bitter taste of coffee and the way she clung to me almost made me lose control of my aura, and when she pulled away, it took all my restraint not to push her against the door. The space between us left me unsettled.

I needed more, and I intended to get it.

After finishing up with Gareth, I made my way up to the lab. It was quieter than when we'd first arrived. The team was working on their individual assignments concerning me, so there were only a few technicians in the space.

When I entered, I received a few small nods before I spotted Scott standing by a bench, pen flying over some paper. The office that bore her name was rarely occupied. She brought her laptop and paperwork into the lab, setting up at a bench as if leaving the space would drain her of life.

The same soul-stirring tug occurred now that she was in sight. The same desire to drink from her well until I drowned in it.

Holden turned up yesterday and ruined everything. I could have broken her if he'd stayed away. Could have got what I wanted. That man was truly a thorn in my side, and not a moment passed where I didn't regret my mistake of allowing him to live.

"Scott," I said, walking up to her.

"I'm busy," she told me sharply, not bothering to look up from the papers.

"Don't dismiss me."

She looked up, biting hard on her bottom lip in an attempt to stay calm. Her muscles tensed, and she drew herself up. Always ready for a fight.

"I was asked to come here so that you can add to your

samples," I said. "You being busy directly involves me."

She let out a frustrated breath and went back to her work.

"Come on now, Scott," I said with a wicked smile, taking in her profile. "You aren't scared of me, are you?"

Scott let out a small laugh, and I moved to stand beside her at the bench. There was a pile of paperwork in front of her, and she skimmed over the words.

I leaned down so that my mouth was at her ear. "Or can you not trust yourself around me?"

When she turned her head, our noses almost brushed, but she didn't back away. Scott was a prideful creature, and her fall would be nothing short of spectacular.

"Not even if you were the last being on earth," she told me.

"That's not the message I got yesterday," I said, leaning in so that the tip of my nose touched hers.

Orange blossom and honey and bitter notes of coffee. Scott's scent was purely her; a delectable mixture of sharp and sweet that ensnared and confused.

"James!" she called, pulling back. "Is everything set?!"

She moved away from me as James pushed a trolley of items towards her.

"Patient room, please," she directed him before looking at me. "And you, move it. Sooner I've seen you, sooner you can go, and I can be left in peace."

"You're going to hurt my feelings," I said, following her into the room.

The trolley was laden with pots and tubes for her to store samples. I perched on the edge of the bed, feet planted on the ground, and removed my shirt, knowing by the needles that she needed more blood.

"James, do you want to do the observations?" Scott asked, doing her best to avoid looking at me.

I made a mental note to buy Ignacio a drink because luck was on my side, as James reminded her he needed to leave for a dental appointment. Scott closed her eyes and nodded before James left the room, closing the door behind him, trapping us together in the space.

"I need to take your blood pressure and heart rate," she explained.

She didn't look at me as she attached the cuff to the top of my arm and a clip to my finger, setting the machine to start. Scott pulled out the chart and noted everything down before removing them from me.

"Everything in order?" I asked.

"You know it is," she replied through her teeth.

I was a God. How could anything be less than perfect?

"I need some blood, hair samples, and a cheek swab," Scott listed.

"My body is yours."

Her cheeks coloured, and she turned away quickly, snapping on her gloves vigorously and preparing what she needed to draw blood.

"Your body is for science," Scott corrected my sentence tersely.

But I heard the way her heart rate picked up, and it made my lips twitch into a smirk. I could still break her.

Erik wasn't wrong. An attraction laid between us. Scott had become an itch that I wanted to scratch, and it was becoming harder to ignore. The kiss had tipped the scales. I still wanted to destroy her, but there was no reason I couldn't enjoy the pleasure in all forms.

The more she resisted me, the harder I tried. I was used to getting what I wanted. Women threw themselves at me. So why did she fight so badly against it? How much ego could this mortal maintain? The simple act would satisfy me and ruin her for any other person for the rest of her days. She just needed to give in.

Scott collected the blood into tubes and plucked a few strands of dark hair from my head before storing them away. She pulled out swabs and turned back to me, hesitating. To collect a cheek swab would require a closer proximity.

"I promise I won't bite," I told her, and then raised an eyebrow. "Unless you like that sort of thing."

Goading her always worked. Scott narrowed her eyes, and I opened my legs. She sighed before stepping in between them.

"Open your mouth," she ordered.

"You really need to work on that terrible bedside manner."

"Fuck you."

I wrapped an arm around her waist and pulled her in close, forcing a squeak out of her.

"Tell me where and when," I said, desire darkening my eyes.

"Grayson, I'm trying to work," she said, planting a hand on my chest and trying to keep the swab uncontaminated. Her body had tensed. "Let me go and open your damn mouth so I can get the sample."

She swallowed hard and wriggled out of my grasp, taking a few steps back. Frowning, I pushed myself off the bed and stalked towards her. Why couldn't I hook her in?

"Grayson." Scott took a step back for every step I took towards her.

"Tell me no," I said as she bumped into the worktop, and I trapped her there.

She didn't say the word.

Beneath her golden-brown skin was a faint pink tinge. Her heart pumped rapidly, knocking clumsily against her chest. She'd deny it until she was blue in the face, but I knew Scott felt the rush when we kissed yesterday that had nothing to do with my powers.

"Open your mouth." Her voice was breathy.

I leaned down slowly, bringing my face close to hers, and popped open my mouth so she could get her sample. Scott swabbed the inside of my cheek and avoided all eye contact. With the sample collected, she slipped past me to the trolley and stashed them away.

"So," I said, turning slowly and watching her. "Are you going to tell me where and when?"

Scott took a deep breath. "Keep your hands to yourself from now on or I swear I'm going to cut them off."

She was wholly unaware, and I was becoming more attuned to how much her feisty nature turned me on as much as it irritated me.

Grabbing my shirt, I slipped it on and buttoned it up as she led us out of the room.

"Scott," I said.

She waved a hand at me dismissively, which pissed me off, and disappeared into the room that housed the lab freezers.

Holden walked into the lab. And although I'd been due back at Murphy's, I decided I could stay at the institute a little while longer.

There was nothing more infuriating than the way Scott wouldn't give me the time to speak to her properly but would let Holden hover so close when she clearly didn't desire him in the same way.

She sat at the bench, working, whilst Holden sat opposite her, looking through files. I was certain that they had assigned him an office for this sort of work.

"The other day, I wanted to ask you something," Holden said to her quietly.

"Hmm?" Scott said, half paying attention to him. She was pipetting samples into a plate with precision and kept her focus on her work.

"Quentin."

The use of her given name caught her attention, and I watched from across the room, wondering why she preferred the use of Scott.

Holden hesitated, and I leaned forward in my seat, watching them with curiosity. I was across the lab, but kept an eye on the pair since Holden walked in. It sparked a deep pleasure to see she'd barely paid him any attention when he preened like a peacock for her.

"I'd like to take you out to dinner," Holden said, eyes fixed on her.

"Sure," Scott replied, continuing to work.

I bit back on a laugh. She'd completely disregarded his intention, and her focus was purely on the job in hand. Holden rubbed the back of his neck awkwardly and I pondered how much she'd disregard Holden once I'd shown her what it was like to be with a God. I'd ruin her for life; forever unsatisfied by a mortal because she'd tasted divinity.

"As a date," Holden clarified. "I would like to take you on a date."

Scott completely missed the well that she'd meant to pipette into and finally looked up at him. Holden missed the momentary glance that fell on me before she pulled her attention back to the mortal.

She knew as well as I did where her interest laid in the room. My lips stretched into a half smile to see how much Holden had missed the mark. I leaned back in my seat, ready to enjoy the moment he was shot down. There was no competition.

"Sure," Scott said after a few moments of silence. "A date. I… Yes."

I straightened up in the chair.

What was she doing?

Why was she agreeing to this?

"Tonight?" Holden asked hopefully.

"Why not?" she said, not quite meeting his enthusiasm.

The hesitation caused me to narrow my eyes.

"When will you finish here?" Holden asked.

"Another thirty minutes or so."

"Okay." He nodded. "I'll head back now and when you get home, we can decide on a place."

"Sounds like a plan."

"I'll see you back at the house."

Holden left the lab with an imbecilic grin spread wide across his face, and Scott turned back to her work. As I rose from the chair and crossed the space towards her, my aura bubbled at my fingertips.

"Are you trying to make me jealous, Scott?" I hissed, standing beside her. "That's a very unwise decision."

A tendril of my aura snaked its way up her body and tugged her chin, so she was forced to focus on me.

Scott huffed out a breath, dark eyes focusing on the tip of my nose. "Why on earth would I try to make you jealous?"

I dropped the aura from her, but it stayed around me. There were a few curious glances our way, but no one seemed to possess the courage to come over and question us.

"Because you were jealous last night," I told her.

She let out a harsh laugh before finishing the last well and picking up the plate. Scott moved past me to get to the incubators.

"You want me to believe you have a genuine interest in that sorry excuse of a man?" I asked, echoing her footsteps. "Even by mortal standards, he's pathetic."

"Everyone is pathetic to you, aren't they, Grayson?" There was a bite in her voice, and I sensed the anger building in her. Scott closed the door to the incubator and turned to face me.

"I think your kind are more prone to weaknesses," I told her matter-of-factly.

"Well, we all can't be as perfect as you," she quipped, rolling her eyes and folding her arms across her chest.

When I stepped forward, she moved back — our usual tango of moves. I couldn't deny the pull I felt towards her. The kiss yesterday had pulled at a stray thread that unravelled my plans of wanting to destroy her and had replaced it with a want for her. I needed to get Scott out of my system.

"Personal space, Grayson."

I took yet another step towards her, and she dropped her arms from her chest and held them up in front of her. I took one in my own, twisting and pinning it behind her back, drawing her body against mine. The thumb of my free hand ran across her plump bottom lip and her breath hitched.

"Stop," she whispered.

"I don't believe I'm doing anything," I said in the same hushed tone. I leaned down and she swallowed hard. "Ask," I told her. "All you need to do is ask and I'll give you everything you desire."

Her free hand balled into a fist and slammed into my chest. I let go of her instantly and Scott moved away quickly, striding across the lab to get some space.

"You're desperate for my touch yet you will not beg for it."

I moved to join her as she threw her belongings into her bag.

Apparently, any lab work she had planned was no longer important.

"I'm leaving, Gray," she told me, hitching her bag over her shoulder. "Find your own way home."

Watching her go, I muttered to myself, "You are so proud, Scott. So foolish and stubborn. But I will find a way to break you."

FIFTEEN

QUENTIN

That self-centred, arrogant son of a bitch.

Jealous?

I hadn't been jealous of seeing him with some other woman. And I certainly wasn't playing petty games of trying to make him jealous. Why wasn't I allowed to have a genuine interest in Matthew? Matthew was… nice.

"Home early?" Matt asked as I got in. He was on the sofa, scrolling through his phone.

"Yeah. Work wasn't pressing. It would have been rude to keep you waiting. Let me get changed and then we can go."

"Sure. Of course. Take your time."

I took off up the stairs and into my room to rifle through my wardrobe, pushing all thoughts of a particular God aside.

It had been years since I'd been on a date. It was just dinner. Nothing to be nervous about. Plus, I knew Matthew, so there were things we could discuss without all the awkward silence.

Changing into a pair of skinny jeans and a pink silk blouse that had a deep neckline, I assessed my appearance in the mirror. I pulled my hair from the messy bun and brushed through it carefully before deciding I'd do.

"You scrub up good, Scott," Matthew said, getting to his feet as I entered the living room again.

"You don't look too bad yourself."

Matthew was a man who looked after himself. The blue polo shirt he wore skimmed along his muscular figure, allowing his frame to be appreciated. He was classically handsome; someone you might cast as a prince in a fairy-tale with his blonde hair and baby blues. There were a few colleagues who'd expressed an interest in him. Even I'd let my gaze linger when he left the room.

That was until Grayson arrived and movie star good looks paled in comparison to something darker and wilder.

"Are you ready to go?" Matt asked.

He grabbed his keys from the coffee table, and when I turned around, Grayson was leaning against the door, watching us both. There was a stormy expression on his face, and swirls of black appeared around his hands before the lightbulbs flickered overhead.

"Don't destroy my house while we're out," I told him.

"I give you no promises," he replied shortly through gritted teeth.

His stare burned into the back of us as Matt led us from the house. Grayson could be jealous all he wanted. I couldn't care less.

The restaurant was busy, but we were seated quickly and ordered. A tiny Italian place Matt recommended, and I was happy to let him decide.

"I wasn't sure you'd agree to a date," he admitted as the drinks came to the table.

"Oh?"

"You're always busy and I've never heard you talk much about your dating history."

"There's not much to say."

"I guess you were pretty preoccupied with school and work. You should try to slow down sometimes."

The sentence made me bristle. I was certain that Matt wouldn't be telling James or any of my male counterparts to slow down.

"I can slow down when I'm dead," I muttered.

Picking the napkin off the table, I placed it onto my lap, trying to soothe the ripple in my mood.

"All I'm saying is that you should take some time out for yourself. There's more to life than work," he countered.

Only there wasn't. Not for me. My parents were gone, my brother was across the pond, and the man I thought I'd spend the rest of my life with called it quits. Work got me out of bed each morning. It was a constant, and I knew I was good at it. Success was validation. If I slowed down, if I stopped, I didn't know what would happen.

"Tell me about yours," I said, wanting to shift the conversation away from me.

Over the year I'd known him, it was easy to tell that Matthew's favourite topic was himself. He enjoyed indulging people in tales of his life and needed little prompting to expand on stories or wander off on a tangent.

There was a trickle of guilt as he spoke animatedly about his family, because my mind, as it often did in moments of tedium, returned to Grayson.

I wanted to convince myself that the only reason I thought about Grayson in any capacity was because I was a mortal and we all couldn't help but notice the otherworldly good looks he possessed.

Sharp cheekbones and taut muscles made Grayson catch your eye with no effort on his part. Unlike the other eleven Gods, he was less serene. He was dangerous. Wild. He wasn't inviting in the way his brothers were. Grayson's personality and looks warned you to stay away, and I thought I could… until that kiss.

How could one simple action make me unravel? He'd infected me, and I had no clue how to cure myself. Grayson made me feel like I'd lost control over everything, but at the same time, there was a sense of peace that came along with the kiss. Every other touch I'd shared with someone paled in comparison.

Thinking about it now made me blush, and I crossed my legs under the table, trying to stop the throb that began between my legs. If a kiss had made me feel that way, I wondered what it would feel like if we stumbled further down that forbidden path.

A few hours were simple to waste away in the lab or at Sal's in the ring, but with Matthew, it dragged, and I was glad to finally arrive home and put an end to the evening.

"I really hope you enjoyed the night," he said as we got inside.

"It was… nice."

"You'll let me take you out again?" He sounded so hopeful that I didn't know how to decline.

"Matthew," I started gently.

"We make a good team, Quentin. I just want to show you it doesn't always have to be at work."

What would be the harm in agreeing to another date? He might not have thrilled me, but Matt was polite and had a decent job. He put his foot in his mouth at times, but he treated me well enough.

"Okay," I said eventually. "We can do this again."

"I need to get in early to discuss some things with Gareth, so I'm going to call it a night."

"Thanks for tonight."

"You don't need to thank me."

There was an awkward moment as we stood in the hallway. In a film, you might have expected us to share a goodnight kiss, but in reality, I just nodded and slipped past him to walk into the living room. The night hadn't warranted even a brush of lips. Maybe next time.

I jumped when I saw Grayson lounging casually on the sofa. He closed the book in his hands and sat up slowly.

"For fuck's sake, Grayson." My heart hammered away in my chest.

"Not joining him upstairs?" he asked spitefully.

My jaw twitched as I tried not to rise to the bait.

"Well," he asked expectantly, arching an eyebrow. "Did you enjoy your date?"

I slipped the bag from my shoulder and kicked off my heels, dropping to my actual size. "Yes, actually. I did."

"Liar."

"I'm not lying."

"Of course, you are," he persisted. "How can you enjoy a date, even with that idiot, when you're in love with someone else?"

Of all the arrogant things Grayson said, assuming I was in love with him, had to top the list.

I looked up to give him a piece of my mind, but the words were lost when I saw he had a small velvet box in his hand. As he snapped it open, the colour drained from my face and the ground fell away from beneath my feet. The interior of the box lit up and illuminated a white gold band that hosted a pear-shaped diamond nestled in deep green velvet.

"Quite the ring, Scott," Grayson said, peering down at it. "I wouldn't have thought it was your style, but you're full of surprises."

He adjusted the box, so the light caught the rock.

"You've been in my room," I whispered, eyes never leaving the ring.

The memories all flooded back, pressing down on my lungs and my heart in the most violent way.

The brain was a fascinating organ that worked to protect you. Mine malfunctioned at the worst times. We maintained a love-hate relationship where it usually won and pulled me under the current of misery.

"I wanted to know what kind of person I'm living with, considering we can't seem to have a single civil conversation," Grayson mused.

"You've been in my room!"

This time, it came out angry. The languid way he rolled the words off his tongue flipped the switch inside my chest. I swiped for the box, but Grayson kept it out of my reach.

"Give it here. That's personal," I demanded, eyes stinging with frustration.

"Why have you kept this?"

"Grayson! Give me the damn ring!" I swiped for it again.

"You have a ring and it's not on your finger and I don't see you with anyone else, so, what happened, Scott?"

"IT'S GOT NOTHING TO DO WITH YOU!" I screamed, tears spilling over.

"Temper, temper," he said coolly.

"You've been through my things," I said, wiping roughly at my cheek. "You have one of my belongings in your possession. I swear to you, if you don't hand it over now, I will —"

"What?" Grayson asked as he pushed his aura out around him and let it lazily drift between us. "You might not want to believe in me but that doesn't stop me from being a God."

Matt rushed into the room. "What the fuck is going on?"

I glanced over to him before looking back to Grayson, holding out my hand expectantly. He snapped the box shut but didn't hand it over.

"Does he know?" Grayson asked. "Do any of them? Or is your failure a dirty little secret?"

"Grayson!"

He laughed and held the box out to me. I snatched it away quickly and gripped it tightly in my hand, knuckles turning white as his aura disappeared from between us.

"What is your problem?" Matthew asked, prepared to play the knight in shining armour.

"Just leave it, Holden," I told him sharply.

Grayson picked himself off the sofa. "I can tell you exactly what my problem is." He was toe to toe with Matt. "It seems like you're a glutton for punishment."

I attempted to push Matt away from Grayson, but he'd made the vital mistake of looking the God in the eye. Matthew may have been able to intimidate others, but he'd forgotten who Grayson was. The eye contact alone brought Matt to his knees with a thud on my wooden flooring.

"Grayson, stop!" I said.

He broke eye contact and Matt pushed himself off the ground, ignoring the hand I offered to help him.

"You think —" Matt began.

"Leave it!" I said, frustrated by both men. I shoved Matthew towards the door. "Just leave him."

I didn't look back as I left. Grayson had crossed a line tonight by rifling through my belongings. He continued to drag up painful memories that I wanted to bury and make my job more difficult than it needed to be.

People may have worshipped Grayson as a God, but in my eyes, he was nothing more than a monster.

SIXTEEN

QUENTIN

"I thought you usually ate dinner alone," Matt said the next night, when Grayson joined us in the kitchen.

The God smiled and ignored him before looking at me. I caught his eye, and he lifted his hand and gave it a small shake to indicate the cuff that hung on his wrist. It was a slight comfort.

"I thought I shouldn't deprive myself of fine company," Grayson answered, his eyes still on me. "And I'm curious."

"Curious?" I repeated the word.

The mention of curiosity had pulled me out of my shell. It was a quality I thrived on. I was still furious at him for the stunt he pulled last night, but I was interested in what he was up to.

"Mmm, very much so," he said thoughtfully.

"What are you curious about?" My voice held an air of

suspicion. Nothing with Grayson was straightforward.

"I'm curious how mortal courting compares to that of the Gods."

Matthew placed his glass on the table, harder than was necessary. The liquid inside almost sloshed over the edge.

"Care to find out?" Grayson asked me, his voice low.

Biology won out over sense as a blush stained my cheeks, and Matthew got to his feet.

"What do you say, Scott?" he pushed on, choosing to ignore Matt.

"Pack it in," Matt warned him.

"This conversation doesn't concern you."

"How do you figure that?"

Grayson rolled his neck before turning his attention to Matthew. "You've taken her on one date," he said lazily. "Hardly commitment by any being's standards. Seems to me Scott is free to do as she wishes."

Matt balled his hands into fists, and I put a hand on his arm. "Sit down," I told him.

He ignored me. "I doubt she wishes to spend time with you."

"I would beg to differ," Grayson said with a smug smile. "I'd bet she —"

"Enough!" I yelled. Both men finally looked at me. I was tired and my anger sat closer to the surface than it had done in years. "Matthew. Sit down."

"But —"

"No. This has got to stop. You two can't seem to stop the arguments and I'm sick of it happening under my roof. I come home for peace, and I don't get any of that with the both of you here."

Matthew dropped into his seat again, sulking.

"Matt," I continued, struggling to soften my tone. "I think it's best you moved out."

"What?" he asked, surprised by the request. "Why?"

"You two will never get along, and I can't do it anymore. I don't want to play referee."

"Why me?"

"You have a flat."

"I don't trust him to stay here with you."

I was curious in what context he distrusted Grayson. Did he think he'd cause me harm or try to seduce me? Both were plausible situations.

Maybe this wasn't a good idea. Grayson had proven that he would keep crossing firm boundaries that I set in place. The better plan would be for me to kick them both out, to live with each other so I could live in peace, and the impending inquest into a death wouldn't require me to make an appearance as a witness. Or more likely, prime suspect.

"You know I won't continue to work with you if I don't live here," Grayson reminded me.

He'd given his conditions months ago, and if I changed my mind, then he could do the same. To say I was between a rock and a hard place would have been putting it lightly.

"Matthew." I sighed. "I think it's best you go home."

"You're picking him over me?" he asked incredulously.

"I'm not picking anyone." The throb of a headache hit behind my eyes as I dropped my fork on the plate. "I need this project to work. You have a home, and he doesn't. Just." Cutting myself off, I took in a deep breath. "I think it's best for you to pack up tonight and let everything calm down."

He waited a second before standing up again.

"Where are you going?" I asked.

"No time like the present." He sulked out of the room.

When he cleared it, Grayson looked at me and said, "I'm touched you chose me."

"Fuck off, Grayson."

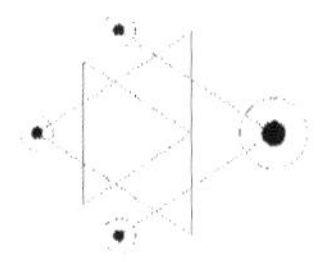

I'd attached a lock to my bedroom door, but the moment I'd finished putting in the last screw, Grayson stood behind me, a smirk in place. A stark reminder that he didn't need to break a lock to enter my domain.

Matt moved out, and there'd been a weird vibe between us ever since. He was mad at me, but I wasn't about to soothe his ego by trying to explain my actions to him. Regardless of the fact he was pissed at me, it had worked. Matthew rarely frequented the lab and testosterone levels at home halved, and that meant the arguments had ceased for the time being.

Despite all the issues we'd encountered, I'd somehow made it through to my annual leave. Finally, I would be spending some time with my brother and future sister-in-law and not think about work.

Rolling over in bed, I shoved my face into the pillow and got comfortable again, begging my body to sleep for a few more hours. We had nothing to be up and alert for.

Somewhere in the distance, a door closed, and I lifted my head up with a groan. Why was the door closing? Pulling myself out of bed, I walked into the hallway and to the top of the stairs before panic flooded me. Grayson stood in the hallway, with Cassidy and Sophie in front of him. Their flight must have got in early.

I'd asked, nearly begged, Gareth if Gray could stay with him while Cass was in town to avoid any awkward questions. The Gods must have truly hated me because this was chaos.

Chaos.

Grayson.

The moment I figured out a way to kill him, I would do it. Fuck every consequence that came my way.

"Duck!" Cass looked past Grayson and beamed at me.

"Cass!"

Seeing and hearing him swept away my previous train of thought. We may not have been blood related, but my brother was my everything. We'd gone from living together to only seeing each other twice a year.

"Come down here and give me a hug."

I raced down the stairs and launched myself at him. It didn't matter that I was nearing thirty — my big brother always felt like home. He was the first person I went to when I felt lost.

Cass hugged me tightly and lifted me off the ground. "It's been too long."

"Way too long," I agreed.

He placed me back on the ground, and I turned to see Sophie smiling at me. I opened my arms to her, and we shared a tamer hug.

"Hi, Quen," she said, southern drawl thick around the words and standing out. "I really appreciate you taking the week off for us."

"It's nothing. I could use the break."

Cass cleared his throat. "Are you going to introduce us?" he asked, nodding in Grayson's direction.

"I… um," I stumbled.

Grayson had taken a step back but remained in the vicinity, watching us all. He put on the most charming smile I'd seen him wear, causing my heart to stutter in my chest. He almost glided towards Cass with an outstretched hand, and my eyes widened as Cass took it. Grayson's free hand covered it, and I saw the cuff on his wrist and let out a sigh of relief.

"Grayson," the God introduced himself.

"Cassidy," Cass said. "Quentin's older brother."

They shook hands for a fraction too long before Sophie stepped in and placed a hand on Cass's shoulder.

"Let the boy go, Cass," she coaxed softly.

"So, Grayson," Cass said, releasing his grip. "How do you know my sister?"

I stepped up next to Grayson. "He's a colleague."

"Come now, Scott," Grayson said. "Don't you think it's better we tell your brother the truth?"

I looked up at him, panicked. I'd lose my job if Gray admitted who he truly was.

"I don't think that's a good idea," I blurted.

"I'd rather not lie to your brother."

"What's going on?" Cass asked. "What do you need to tell me?"

A mischievous grin crossed Grayson's face, and I questioned if I could pass him off as delusional when he broke the news to Cass. I braced myself for what was to come, but Grayson wrapped an arm around my waist, and I tried to keep my expression neutral as I figured out what was going on.

"Your sister and I are seeing each other," Grayson told them confidently.

My jaw dropped as I turned to look at him. What did he just say? I went to step away from him, but Grayson drew me closer to his side with an iron grip.

"You kept that quiet, Quen," Cass said, eyeing us both.

"She doesn't have to tell us everything, Cass," Sophie reminded him.

I stood there, floundering before I said, "You, um… go unpack."

Grayson laughed. "She always gets embarrassed."

I shoved him hard in the side.

"But she has a point," he continued. "It must have been a long trip. Why don't you both unpack and freshen up and then we can all catch up properly?"

"I think that sounds wonderful," Sophie agreed.

She picked her bag from the floor, but Cass took it from her. Shooting us a smile, Sophie walked up the stairs with Cassidy following behind.

He stopped to look back at me. "Good to see you back in the game, duck."

Once I was sure they were both out of earshot, I pushed myself away from Grayson. Gripping his arm, I pulled him through into the living room.

"Hmm," he mused. "I think I like a woman who can take control."

I tried not to let the comment get to me as I pushed the door closed and rounded on him.

"What are you doing?" I asked.

"I needed a plausible excuse why I'm opening the door to your brother at nine-thirty on a Saturday morning," he explained.

If we needed an excuse, it would have been easy to tell them that Grayson was a colleague that rented a room. That was an excuse

I could have lived with.

"You weren't even meant to be here," I told him.

Grayson looked at me knowingly. "How many times do I have to tell you? I hate to be dismissed," he said calmly. "You were going to pack me up and send me off to Gareth."

"That's what we agreed on."

"I never agreed to that arrangement."

I let out a frustrated sigh and ran my hands through my hair. "Why do you insist on being so —"

He took a step towards me. "Yes?"

"Infuriating."

He let out a bark of laughter.

"I'm not seeing you — fake or otherwise," I told him, a tone of finality lacing my words.

"So, what do you intend to do?" Grayson asked, curiously. "Tell them the truth?"

"No. You are going to Gareth's."

"I don't think so."

"Grayson!" Like a child, I stomped my foot, desperate to get out of this situation.

"You see, in the long run, isn't this the type of interaction and integration that Gareth and Hunter are after?" His words rolled around my brain, and he took another step towards me. "You'd be getting me to do what others thought I would rebel against."

I bit on my bottom lip. Grayson was appealing to my desire to succeed. To my ambition.

After a few seconds I whispered, almost pleading with him, "This is my family, Gray. Do you understand that?"

He cocked his head to the side, and I quickly pushed away thoughts of how cute he was whenever he did it. Like a puppy you wanted to take home and keep.

"You need to be on your best behaviour," I laid out for him.

"Aren't I always?" He gave a half-smile, and my heart stuttered again.

"Please," I told him gently, and then even quieter, "Cass and

Sophie are all I have left."

He looked taken aback at how vulnerable and open the sentence was, but I needed him to understand. He couldn't behave around them the same way he had Matthew. I couldn't lose the only people that mattered to me in this life.

"Am I interrupting something?"

I looked over my shoulder to see Cass hovering by the door. I hadn't even heard him open it. With a blush, I shook my head and said, "No. Of course not. I'm going to grab a shower and then we can head out."

"Perfect," he replied. "Let's catch up before Sophie pulls you into all the wedding chaos."

Grayson snorted at the choice of word, and I bit my lip.

"Give me fifteen minutes," I told my brother. "How about breakfast at Gershwin's?"

"That place is still standing?" Cass asked, laughing.

"Yes, it is."

He beamed at me. "Then it would be a crime not to." Cass walked into the living room. His eyes settled on Grayson. "Will you be joining us?"

"No," I answered quickly.

"Yes," Grayson said at the same time.

Cass shot us both a curious look.

"I thought you were busy today," I said to Grayson.

Wasn't it enough that he'd be sharing our home? He didn't need to join us outside of these walls.

Grayson smiled at me. "It's nothing I can't rearrange."

"Good," Cass said with a nod. "It'll give me a chance to get to know you better. Make sure you're treating my sister well."

I could feel the headache creeping in as Cass passed us to move into the kitchen. Turning towards the door, I left, hoping that the shower would ease the pain in my head.

Just as I left the room, I heard Grayson, "You have my word as a God, Scott."

But I wasn't sure how much it counted for.

SEVENTEEN

GRAYSON

My day was spent in the trio's company, observing them carefully. I'd gathered that Cassidy Scott was just as ambitious and hard-headed as the other Scott in my life. An orthopaedic surgeon who had taken up his specialty in America, fallen in love and relocated.

He was protective of his adoptive little sister, warning me to be careful with her heart and I had to bite back on laughter. There was no heart involved in what laid between me and Scott. It was pure need and desire on both parts, but she'd been better at resisting temptation than I'd expected.

"I'll go check if she's ready," I said, getting up from my seat in the living room.

We were heading out for dinner, but our party was missing a guest.

"You'll never get out anywhere on time with Quen," Cass said, rolling his eyes.

Sophie shot him a look. "There's nothing wrong with taking pride in your appearance, Cassidy."

The pair bickered as I left the room.

When I got upstairs, I stopped outside Scott's bedroom door, which was wide open. Her back was to me as she struggled to reach for the zipper. Leaning against the doorframe, I let my eyes run over the smooth skin of her bare back and the curve of her ass.

"Fuck it!" she grumbled as she began to pull the dress off.

I raised an eyebrow. "Careful, Scott. You're awakening a dark desire in me."

She spun on her heel, gripping the front of her dress against her to keep her modesty.

"What are you doing? Go," she hissed at me.

"We're all wondering what's taking so long."

Her cheeks tinged pink, and she huffed. "I can't get the zip up. Can you ask Sophie to come up here?"

Smoothly, I pushed myself off the doorframe and sloped towards her. "Let me help."

"I —"

"We're meant to be seeing each other, Scott. It'll look weird if I go to request someone else to help you."

Scott huffed again before turning around and displaying her back to me. She pulled her mass of dark hair over her shoulder to reveal bare skin, and I reached out, letting my fingers trail down the flesh.

The contact caused her to suck in a breath, and her back arched away from my fingertips.

"Gray." But her voice didn't hold the same fire as it usually did.

"Just trying to help," I said innocently.

"The zip," she instructed, firmer this time.

I smiled, taking hold of the zip at the base of her spine just before the tempting curve. I dragged it, my knuckles brushing against her skin as I went, and her flesh formed goosebumps under my touch. She wouldn't be able to resist me much longer. I'd make sure of it.

Once I reached the top, I whispered in her ear, "All done."

Leaning down, I pressed a kiss to the side of her neck, her pulse strong and fast against my lips. Scott jumped away from me, and I laughed.

"Get out!" she told me, pointing at the door. "Go. I'll be downstairs now."

Eventually, the four of us made it out of the house and sat around the table of a small French bistro. I was surprised at how easily the conversation flowed and even Scott had relaxed from her usual uptight self.

"It's just having to sort out the last few bits," Sophie said.

"You have plenty of time, darling," Cassidy assured her.

"We have five months."

"A winter wedding?" I asked, curious about the choice. The attention of the table turned on me.

Sophie smiled. "It's when we met."

The look Sophie and Cassidy shared was sickening and reminded me of Erik and Sloan. Beside me, Scott suddenly seemed more interested in the food on her plate. Uncomfortable with affection in the way I was.

"I'm sure we'll be seeing you there," Sophie said to me.

"Sophie," Cassidy groaned.

"Oh, I'm not sure about that," Scott said, looking up again.

Beneath the table, I placed a hand on her knee. Her dress choice was relatively short, but it had risen an inch or two since she sat down. Her skin was warm and smooth beneath my palm.

"I think what she means is that we'll wait to see how this plays out," I said.

"Exactly," Cassidy agreed. "And considering that Quen has a lot to do with the ceremony, it's probably not the wisest decision to bring anyone. Don't want him to feel abandoned."

My fingers moved up Scott's leg, and she tensed under my

touch. It was the most contact I'd managed, but I craved more.

"You two are too logical for your own good," Sophie said. "Tell them, Gray. It would be lovely to see Quentin at the wedding with someone. And what about the reception, Quen?"

"Mmm," Quen squeaked.

It sounded a little higher pitched than usual because of my fingers drawing small circles on the inside of her thigh, steadily moving upwards, towards my goal. Scott crossed her legs, trapping my hand between them, and I smiled before removing it slowly.

"Well, we'd love to see you there, Gray." Sophie flashed me a grin, but Cassidy didn't look so certain.

We continued through the main course as Sophie took control, keeping the conversation on wedding arrangements. By the time dessert arrived at the table, Cassidy had steered it in a different direction.

"So, what do you do, Gray? I don't think I caught what your job actually is."

"Biologist," I replied shortly, and Scott choked on her sip of water.

"Oh, so you're in the lab with duck, then?"

"Sometimes. I got contracted to work here on the new project. Once that's done, I'll need to find something else."

"Does that involve moving?"

"More than likely."

He narrowed his eyes at me from across the table.

"Cassidy, drop it," Scott hissed at her brother. She stabbed her fork into the slice of cheesecake in front of her before taking a bite. "Mmmm."

The sound that came from her made my trousers snug, and I dropped my full gaze on the woman beside me. Across the table, Sophie and Cassidy laughed, and when Scott opened her eyes, she turned red.

"Sorry, guys," she mumbled.

"You and food sex." Sophie laughed. "Honestly, I'm surprised you haven't declared cheesecake your true love."

"There's still time." Then she caught my stare. "What?"

The rest of our company had called into conversation again, so I leaned in towards her. "I could give you so much more pleasure than a slice of cake."

Her blush deepened, heat radiating from her, but Scott schooled her face into a nonchalant expression. "I doubt it."

"Is that a challenge?"

She swallowed hard before turning back to her cake.

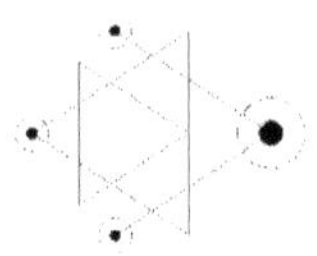

When we arrived home, I left the trio, waiting impatiently for them to finish the evening.

The sound of laughter floated up through the floors and into my room. It was difficult to imagine Scott was capable of such a carefree sound. Happiness wasn't an emotion that rested within her easily from what I'd seen, but with her family, she transformed into a different person. Laughter loud and unencumbered. Talkative and animated. Scott came alive away from work.

Eventually the laughter and chatter died away, and everyone retired to their rooms. I left mine and lingered outside Scott's door as she stood before her mirror.

"Can I help you?" I asked.

She ignored my question and said, "We're not staying together."

"Of course, we are."

"What? No. Why would you think that?" she asked, turning around to face me.

"Won't your guests be curious why we're sleeping separately?"

She closed her eyes before opening them again and setting them on me. All traces of ease had left with my appearance. I unsettled her. Made her raise her defences.

"I'll deal with any questions," she told me. "You sleep in your room and stay away from mine."

Scott crossed over to her desk and grabbed a hair tie before winding her hair up into a bun, revealing the length of her neck. She then reached around to grab her zip, but I stepped into the room and caught it first.

"I can do it," she told me sharply.

"I'm sure you can."

Sighing, she dropped her hand, letting me help her. I pulled the zip down the length of her back, and it took everything in me not to tear the dress from her body. I'd never waited this long for something I wanted.

When I got to the end, I leaned in and spoke in her ear, "Say thank you."

The goosebumps prickled her flesh again and her heartbeat raced.

It took a moment before she whispered the words, "Thank you."

"You must be exhausted."

Scott went to turn, but I didn't allow it. I snaked an arm around her middle and pulled her back into my chest. She took in a deep breath as I pressed my erection against her ass. My free hand grabbed her chin roughly so that she looked at us both in the mirror's reflection. The look of lust was clear between the pair of us.

"Constantly fighting desire and battling against what you really want must be exhausting."

I rolled my hips, pushing my erection further against her. In the reflection, I watched Scott's pupils dilate and her painted lips part. Beneath the thin fabric of her dress, her nipples hardened, only deepening my desire. The way her body responded was beautiful, but I grew impatient, wanting to watch her completely unravel beneath me.

"Give in, Scott," I said by her ear. "Give over to me and I'll help you find a sense of peace."

For a moment, I thought I had her. For a brief second, I could sense her on the precipice, ready and willing to give herself to me. But then Scott ripped herself away from my body.

"I'd like to remind you I'm actually kind of seeing someone," she said. It meant to come across as haughty, but she sounded breathless.

"Holden?" I scoffed. "That's got to be a joke. Have you even spoken since you threw him out?"

She looked at me with a steely glint in her eyes. "I did that because you kept hurting him."

"I think you hurt him worse than I did."

"Excuse me?"

"You hurt his pride, Scott," I informed her.

She bit her lip, and I twitched at the thought of doing the same motion to her. Pulling the plump bottom lip between my teeth and having her flush against me. Kissing her and allowing all her chaos to pull me under.

"Isn't pride a sin?" Scott asked.

I snorted. "You're a fine one to talk."

Scott wore pride like a badge of honour. It buoyed her and protected her. If pride were a sin, then she fashioned it into a second skin to ward us away and live a life that she deemed fulfilling.

"Get out of my room, Grayson." Scott held her dress up with one hand and pushed me out the door with the other.

"Think about it, Scott," I said, unable to let it go.

This woman and my need to see her fall apart at my hands were quickly spiralling into an obsession.

"All you need to do is ask."

EIGHTEEN

QUENTIN

My week with Cass and Sophie ended all too quickly. They boarded a flight back to New York, and I returned to work with a lingering sense of melancholy that I couldn't shake. More frequently, I thought about life after this project was done and moving to the States to be with my family. There was nothing tying me here.

"How's your brother?" Charlie asked, taking a seat at my bench.

I pointed to the wall without looking up and told her, "Lab coat."

Today's experiments included RNA samples and any form of contamination would lead to an anomalous result that I'd have to exclude from analysis.

Charlie huffed before walking off, pulling on a coat, and returning to her seat. "What's wrong with you?" she asked. "I thought you'd be happier after a week off."

That'd been the plan, but I'd returned to work primarily frustrated because of Gray. He hadn't let up all week. A perfect gentleman in front of Cass and Sophie and an utter asshole when we were alone together. Although I hated to admit it, it was becoming more difficult to say no, and I'd resorted to masturbating daily to release some tension and not completely lose my mind.

"Sorry," I mumbled. "I guess I'm more tired than I thought. But yeah, Cass is doing well." When I looked up, Charlie was beaming at me. "Okay, why are you looking at me like that?"

She stuck out her hand in front of my face. It took me a moment to notice a beautiful diamond ring sitting on her ring finger. It glittered under the lights of the lab as she wiggled her fingers.

"Shut up," I whispered. Charlie bit her lip and nodded. "SHUT UP!"

My pipette fell to the bench with a clatter, samples spilling out of the well as I raced around and pulled her into a hug.

Sucker punched. That was the best way to describe how I felt. Her news had hit me, putting another crack in my armour and I worried I wouldn't be able to keep the facade in place much longer.

"Congratulations! Tell me everything," I demanded, ignoring the dull ache in my chest.

Charlie recounted the proposal, and my cheeks ached from smiling. She deserved happiness. Tyler and Charlie were teenage sweethearts, and he was finally making an honest woman out of her.

"I can't believe he asked after all this time," she said wistfully, glancing at her ring.

"He knows he's got a good thing and he doesn't want to lose you. He's ready to make you a Murphy."

Charlie looked up at me with a grin. "Charlotte Murphy."

"You won't be our Charlie Brown anymore."

"Thank Gods for that." She laughed. "My parents are coming into town and throwing us an engagement party Friday night. You'll be there, right?"

"Of course."

"I thought I'd invite everyone here."

"This isn't a small party, is it?"

Charlie offered me a wicked grin. "I don't do small."

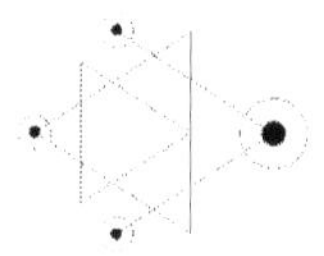

When Friday rolled around, the entire institute buzzed with excitement over the engagement party. Everyone was long gone before I finished and left for home, running straight upstairs to get ready.

Adding the last swipe of lipstick, I looked in the mirror. I tugged at the hem on the pale peach dress and finally satisfied with my look, made my way downstairs.

"Okay, Gray!" I called out, checking the contents of my clutch. "I'll be back later tonight."

He appeared before me, causing me to jump and stumble in my heels. Gray caught me, his arm wrapping around my waist. When I looked up at him, he was dressed in a black suit, black dress shirt, and missing a tie.

"Why are you dressed like that?" I asked.

He'd changed out of the white shirt he'd been in earlier, and I couldn't help but notice how much better the darker shades suited him. Black was Grayson's colour, and he wore it alarmingly well.

"You didn't think I'd attend?" he questioned, arching a brow.

That sobered my thoughts. Of course Gray was coming to the party.

"Do not cause trouble," I warned him through gritted teeth.

"You don't think very highly of me."

"You give me no reason to."

Gray pulled me flush against him, and my mouth ran dry as darkness engulfed us. Once his aura faded, we stood outside the hotel that was hosting the party and I looked at him as he kept a tight grip on me.

"We would have been late if I let you drive," he explained before I had a chance to scold him. "Your time keeping is disgustingly poor."

"Gray!" a voice cut across us before I could lecture him.

A handsome man took long, confident strides towards us, and Gray pushed me away from him. I stumbled on the gravel, finding my balance in time and saving myself from hitting the ground.

"You must be Quentin," he said, smirking. "You're causing quite a stir."

Gray narrowed his eyes. "And you should know better than to listen to gossip."

The man held his hand out to me, and I regarded it warily.

Three.

I had skin to skin contact with three Gods and I wasn't sure I should do it again.

"I'm Ignacio," he introduced himself. "And trust me, you'll like how I make you feel." Ignacio winked, and I laughed at his brazen attempt to flirt.

"Don't," Gray warned sharply, anger warping his features.

That was the push I needed to take Ignacio's hand, and he pressed his lips to the back of mine.

There was a pure rush of elation. Everything I'd achieved ran through my mind. The feeling of victory coursed through my veins and took my breath away. All the recognition I'd got in my life flashed before my eyes. Ignacio's touch was nothing short of euphoric.

When it died away, I realised Gray was standing behind me with his hands placed firmly on my hips, keeping me steady.

Ignacio offered me a devilish smile. "You're a highly successful woman. I told you you'd like my touch."

Suddenly, he was forcefully pushed back a few yards by a black tendril. I turned on the spot, still feeling the heady rush from our interaction.

"Gray! You can't do that," I told him.

He didn't pay attention to me instead, keeping his eyes on Ignacio. Fury blazed in his irises, and I placed a hand on his chest. Gray brought his fiery gaze down on me.

"What's going on?"

Looking over my shoulder, Sloan and Erik had joined us. Erik shot us a curious look, head cocked to the side.

"I need to get inside," I said, dropping my hand from Gray's chest and moving past the Gods to get into the building but not before I heard Sloan.

"You need to stay away from her, Grayson."

A small part of me deflated with the realisation that in their eyes we'd always be mortals who were unworthy to do anything other than worship them. Even Sloan, who appeared so gentle and understanding, had a threshold.

Why did it matter? I wasn't chasing after their approval. They could think little of me because it was reciprocated in every way.

Pushing the thoughts to the back of my mind, I entered the ballroom of the hotel. Charlie's parents had spared no expense, judging by the decorations, and I weaved my way through guests to find the happy couple.

It was easy to forget about the rocky start to the night when I spent most of the evening engaged in conversation with colleagues and celebrating the joyful news.

I slipped from the floor, towards the bar, and watched the room. My finger ran lazily around the lip of the champagne flute as Matthew approached me. I tensed and sat up straight. We hadn't spoken in a while, and we didn't need a stand-off at Charlie's party.

"Hey," he greeted me.

"Hi."

"Can I join you?"

"Sure."

He took the seat next to me and I folded my hands in my lap.

"You look beautiful, Scott," Matthew said.

"Thanks," I replied, looking at the bubbles floating up my glass. "You don't scrub up too badly yourself."

He laughed before it died away. "I missed you at work."

My heart gave a weird little tug. I couldn't be classified as a social butterfly, but we'd always got on well and it'd be strange to be avoided and edged out.

"Look, Quentin," he continued. "I'm sorry for how I behaved. It was childish of me. I know you were just doing your job."

Matt didn't need prompting to apologise. He didn't need someone to remind him to act like a grown man. He'd taken the time to reflect on his actions and approached me with a level head.

"Apology accepted."

"I was wondering if you'd let me take you out on that second date."

I bit on my lip and thought about it for a second before nodding. "You know what, Matthew? I think I'd really like that."

Maybe it was the champagne, or perhaps it was the fact we were at an engagement party, but the ice around my heart thawed. Everyone around me was moving on with their personal lives, so why shouldn't I? I didn't want to be stuck in the past anymore. Maybe if I tried a little harder, I'd find the peace I desperately sought.

Matt flashed me a bright smile before we were interrupted.

"Excuse me," Erik said, running a hand through his white-blonde hair. "Would you mind if I asked Quentin to dance?"

Matthew eyed him for a second before he said, "Sure. I'm going to find Charlie and Tyler."

He hesitated for a split second before leaning over and kissing my cheek.

Erik held his hand out to me as Matt left us. I slipped off the barstool, adjusted my dress, and took it.

Just like with Gray, I was about a foot shorter than him, and my heels barely did anything to make up the difference. He led me out onto the floor full of people and placed a hand respectfully on my waist, holding my other hand.

"Are you sure you're okay to be doing this?" I asked him, unable to keep the ferocity out of my tone.

"What do you mean?"

"I heard Sloan telling Gray to stay away from me. I can look after myself, you know."

Erik chuckled. "We have no doubt about that. I've never seen anyone speak to Gray in the manner that you do. Most wouldn't dare to stand up to him."

I blushed furiously. Our spats had probably seemed rather disrespectful on my half when it was seen from a God's perspective.

"Don't worry, Quentin," Erik assured thoughtfully. "Sloan is just cautious."

Sloan had returned to the lab for observations, but she barely said a word to me as I worked. And then, just like before, she'd disappeared as soon as we were done. It was difficult to figure out what the problem was when courage had failed, and the question never left my lips.

"Have I done something?" I asked, refusing to buckle this time. "Because I don't feel like she likes me very much, but I can't —"

"It's not that," Erik explained. "She's a cautious person. I think she's trying to figure out who you are and how you're fitting in with us."

"I don't really fit with you all. This is my job," I reminded him.

"Hmm." Erik shot me a sceptical look. "Really? I'd be careful lying to a God."

I swallowed hard and chewed nervously on my bottom lip.

"Is there something going on between you and Gray?" Erik asked softly.

"No," I answered quickly.

"It doesn't feel that way. We barely saw him last week."

With all the effort Gray had put in to try and get me into bed, he'd been AWOL from everyone else.

"Word of advice, Quentin," Erik muttered. "What he wants, he shouldn't. Relations between Gods and mortals is strictly prohibited."

I let the words sink in for a moment before Erik continued, "But no one has ever been able to tell him what he can and can't do. Just be careful."

The music ended and Erik let go of me, smiling and walking

away to a table where Sloan was sitting.

When I turned to leave the floor, my eyes landed on Grayson who watched me from the bar, and he subtly motioned me over to him with his head. Sucking in a deep breath, I followed his instruction.

"What did my brother want?" Gray asked as I reached him.

"I think he was warning me off you."

His bright blue eyes narrowed. "They need to mind their own damn business."

"I'm sure they do it because they care," I countered.

"I don't need looking after," Gray snapped, and I rolled my eyes, despite sharing the same attitude. "Tell me, Scott, are you planning to heed my brother's warning?"

He brushed some hair from the side of my face and tucked it behind my ear.

"Apparently, you're not even meant to want this," I replied.

Gray let out a low rumble of laughter as his thumb trailed along my jaw.

"You're going to get us in trouble," I breathed. "Aren't you in enough trouble after what happened outside?"

"Ignacio's fine," Gray said, shrugging. "He'll get me back at some point."

His hand rested against my neck, and I was sure he could feel the unsteady thrum of my pulse underneath his rough palm. Gray guided me gently to a more secluded corner, and my feet obliged.

"You didn't answer me, Scott," Gray pressed. "Are you going to heed my brother's warning?"

He was so close that his lips brushed against mine with every word, and my hands rested on his chest. The sense of peace Gray brought with him muffled several alarm bells that blared in my head. Every time we were close, every time Gray laid his hands on me, he chipped away at my resolve and left me feeling out of my depth.

"Because you don't strike me as the type of person who listens to others," Gray said, smirking.

My nature was curious. I rarely believed what people told me at face value. I hated being told what to do. Between Sloan and Erik tonight, I was hanging on to my will by my fingertips.

Gray's voice was at my ear, causing my hairs to stand on end. "All you have to do is ask, Scott."

He pulled back from me so that I could see the glint in his eye.

What would be so bad about giving in? The world wouldn't end. It might even help to clear my head.

"What do you want, Scott?" he pressed.

I'd never had a problem telling people what I wanted or what I needed, but I'd avoided things with Gray because of the way he was. Insufferable and arrogant. But we were adults. This wasn't a relationship. We were both after sex.

"Gray," I said.

"Scott?"

I let go of the last strand of resolve. "Take me home and fuck me."

I wasn't asking him; I was telling him.

The growl that came from Gray stirred a heat low in my stomach and he glanced up before we were wrapped in black and appeared outside my bedroom door.

Gray's lips crashed down upon mine and my arms wrapped around his neck as I kicked off my heels. My tongue traced across his bottom lip before he let me in, battling for dominance. Gray pinned me up against the doorframe, and my fingers tugged at his hair. As he dipped down and kissed along my bare shoulder and up my neck, I flushed. A soft moan escaped my lips as he hit a sensitive spot of skin.

When we broke apart, Gray's blue eyes were entirely black. The wisps of his aura surrounded us. He was no longer in control. It made my heart thud uncomfortably in my chest to see him as more God than mortal, hammering home just what I was about to do and who I'd be doing it with.

"This is what you want, Scott," he told me.

"I know."

We'd arrived at this point simply because neither of us could resist any longer. Because I couldn't resist him any longer. We'd finally get what each of us desired.

NINETEEN

GRAYSON

Orange blossom. Peach. Honey.

The three distinct scents wrapped around my senses as I leaned in towards Scott. Her eyes fluttered shut, and I wasted no time in closing the gap by kissing her.

The hesitancy rolled off her in waves. As bold as I was, I'd never force myself on a woman. But when the moan escaped her lips, it took all my self-control not to pick her up and fuck her against the door.

"How many times have you thought of me, Scott?" I asked. "How many times have I been in your head while you pleasured yourself?"

The apples of her cheeks turned red, and she remained silent.

"Don't get shy now," I told her with a smirk. "It doesn't suit you."

Quentin Scott wasn't a shy creature. She was ambitious and strong. No matter how many times I'd thought of her as weak. I'd watched the way she took on obstacles in her life, and it'd only strengthened my need for her.

"I've thought about you being in here more than I'd care to admit," she told me.

There she was. Meek and mild and domesticated wasn't her style. She couldn't hide for long behind those walls.

"And tell me exactly what you think of me doing when I'm in here," I coaxed, moving us away from the door.

Perching on the edge of her bed, I took her in as she stood before me. There was something maddening about Scott's body and the way her curves were unapologetically present.

"I think about you touching me."

"How?" I asked, dragging my gaze up her frame and to her face.

She picked the thin strap of her dress off one shoulder and let it fall down her arm before doing the same to the other until her chest was exposed.

I drank her in greedily. The confident nature she possessed was something I admired, but it surprised me that it translated into the bedroom.

Scott wiggled out of the dress, and it dropped to the floor before she stepped out of the pool of material. She was a mass of black hair and bare skin, apart from the black lace that covered my goal.

"You touch me carefully, because you think I might break," she informed me.

Getting up from the end of the bed, I stalked towards her. It was difficult to see her like this and not touch her. My lips found her jaw and Scott tilted her head, letting me move the kisses up to her ear.

"But you refuse to be broken," I whispered in return.

"I won't break, Gray," she replied.

Her fingers started to undo the buttons of my shirt, but I caught her hands.

"You aren't naked," I told her.

"More than you are."

"Do as I say, Scott."

My fingers ghosted over one of her nipples, suddenly pinching it hard. The gasp that came from her slipped into a moan, and my lips twitched into a smirk.

"You're going to show me how you cum when I'm the only thought inside your head," I said.

"And why would I do that?"

"Because if you please me, then I'll do the same for you. Isn't that what you want?"

I looked down at her and knew she was past the point of turning me away now. Instead of answering me, Scott pushed her knickers past her hips and let them drop to the floor. She waltzed past me to make her way to the bed, and I turned slowly on the spot and watched her.

As she laid down on the bed, I unbuttoned the cuffs of my shirt and said, "Show me how you touch yourself."

I moved towards the end of the bed and Scott looked up at me from under her lashes, biting down on her plump bottom lip.

"Show me," I commanded, restless with waiting.

The strength of the order was undeniable, and Scott opened her legs, displaying herself to me. My gaze travelled down her body as my trousers became uncomfortably tight.

"Use your hands and show me. I want to see how you think I should touch you."

Scott licked her lips, moving her hands down her body and along her thighs before touching her wet core and letting out a breathy gasp. Her eyes fluttered shut, and she spoke quietly.

"You start slowly by teasing me with your fingers. But I want more. I want your mouth."

Fuck.

I bit the insides of my cheeks to stop myself from groaning, not wanting to disturb the moment. Pulling off my shirt, I discarded it on the floor as I kept watching her fingers work, circling her clit.

"Do I feel good, Scott?" I asked, voice husky with want.

"So good."

I unbuckled my belt and pulled my trousers and boxers off, allowing my erection to spring free.

"What else are you thinking?" I pressed.

She bit her lip and tipped her head back against the pillows. "I imagine your cock inside me."

Her fingers disappeared inside of her pussy and slid in and out. Scott's other hand played with her clit. I'd never felt so worked up by just watching someone pleasure themselves, but she looked like a piece of art laying on the bed, and it was all thanks to me.

The mattress dipped beneath my weight as I climbed onto the bed. Scott's eyes opened, and she pulled her hands away from herself.

"Don't stop," I told her.

My hands pushed her knees further apart to give me a better view of her glistening pussy. The scent of her arousal made me ache, but I'd given her my terms. I wanted to watch her lose herself before I had my fill.

Scott's hands trailed back down her body, dipping into herself again and making me groan at the sight. She let out a laugh, finding pleasure, knowing the effect she had on me.

Pulling her finger out of herself, Scott said, "I want you to touch me."

I leaned over her, bracing a hand by her shoulder. Her eyes were heavy with lust and desire.

"No," I declined her request.

Her brow furrowed, and I suppressed a laugh.

"You don't get what you want until I get what I want," I explained.

"Fuck you, Gray."

"Which is exactly what you want, so —"

I grabbed her hand and guided it back down to the middle

of her legs. Her fingers once again brushed at her clit and I released her hand to let her work on herself, leaning back so I could take in the view. Her free hand went to her breast while the other dipped lower until it was inside her again.

"I imagine your rough hands all over my body," she told me.

"Do you like it rough?"

Scott writhed against the sheets as she pleasured herself. If I could bring her this much pleasure when she imagined me, I looked forward to seeing what she was like when I finally touched her. But for now, she could work for it. After all, she'd made me do the same.

Reaching out a hand, I stroked her inner thigh, coaxing a moan from her lips.

"Do I tease you, Scott?"

I leaned down and kissed the inside of the opposite thigh.

"I don't think you can help yourself," she whispered.

My fingers inched upwards, stopping short of her core, and Scott bucked her hips in an effort to feel my touch where she ached. Finding no relief, she pushed her head back into the pillows and continued to rub herself.

"Please, Gray," she moaned.

I shook my head, and she continued to push her fingers in and out of herself until her body tensed, shaking as she brought herself to orgasm with a small, high-pitched moan. When she came down from her high, Scott opened her dark eyes and set them on me.

"Happy?" she asked, removing her fingers.

"Ecstatic," I responded, grabbing her wrist and licking her fingers clean. The taste of her added fuel to the fire. "Now you can have what you want."

Leaning down, I kissed her stomach before my thumb moved across her wet pussy. She gasped at the touch and buried her hands in my hair. I let my fingers sink inside of her. My cock ached to replace them, but I wanted to watch her fall off the precipice again. I wanted her to know that she shouldn't have kept me waiting because I was a vengeful God and I'd make her suffer for it.

Her grip tightened as I added a second finger and buried my

head between her legs, finally allowing myself to taste her properly. I groaned against her, causing Scott to arch her back, and her hips rose from the bed as I lapped at her.

"Gray," she breathed.

For centuries, I'd heard people call my name, but the way Scott said it now was all that mattered to me.

My tongue moved between her folds, broad and slow. She squirmed beneath me, and I watched. I was her fantasy. I was all she thought of when she wanted to feel pleasured, and now, I was giving her what she wanted. Scott was kidding herself when she thought I had no power over her.

Her body shook and her grip on my hair became feral, pushing my face into her pussy, and I obliged to her silent demand, moving my tongue quicker. As her back arched, I bit gently on her clit, eliciting a scream from her, legs tightening around my head as she came with a shudder.

I moved, positioning myself above her, braced on both arms. Dipping down, I kissed her, and Scott returned it hungrily. Her hands ran up my arms, the touch setting my skin alight.

My hips angled down slightly so I could rub my cock against her slit, desperate to finally feel her around me.

"Gray, please," she whispered breathlessly.

Scott's hands were on my ribs, fingers digging into my skin. She was insatiable at that moment but tiring. Her stamina couldn't compare to mine.

"You look so pretty when you beg, Scott," I said, drawing back to look at her again.

The fire that she usually came at me with was lost in the hazy clouds of pleasure. She rolled her hips against my hard cock, gaining satisfaction from the simple motion against her sensitive core.

"Are you cumming for me again, Scott?" I whispered into her ear.

I was met with a moan as my lips pressed against her neck. Scott rolled her hip vigorously as I licked at her pulse point, and the friction drove her to the edge again. I felt her heels digging into the back of my thighs as she fell again.

"Fuck," she breathed.

"Are you satisfied?"

Slowly, Scott relaxed her grip on me, sinking back into the bed and nodding. "Gods, yes."

The anger flared in my chest, and my hand wrapped around her throat, commanding her attention. Her eyelids fought back against the lust induced fatigue to stare up at me.

"Only me," I hissed at her. "You only use my name."

The fear was so fleeting that I almost missed it. The logic snaked its way back to her as she asked, "Jealous?"

"I am your focus here."

Her hand reached between us and wrapped around my cock. I groaned at the touch.

"Of course, you are," she assured me.

Letting go of her throat, I grabbed her wrist, so she released my dick from her grasp. Scott believed she was in control of the situation, but she was wrong. Grabbing her other wrist, I pinned them above her head. My cock twitched in anticipation.

"I don't want you to ask," I said, looking down at her. "I don't want you to plead or beg because that won't get you anywhere." I was nose to nose with her and rolled my hips so she could feel me. "If you want me deep inside of you, you'll have to pray."

Gripping both of her hands in one of mine, I let my free hand run down her body, brushing a thumb over her hard nipples. She whimpered in response — the most beautiful sound that almost made me drive straight into her.

"Pray," I commanded.

"Grayson, God of Chaos," Scott whispered after a moment of silence. "I need you. I ask of you to deliver me solace from the chaos I feel. Please. Please, Gray," she muttered, stumbling over the words.

Her hips bucked up, and I pinned them to the bed with my hands. The tip of my cock lined up to her entrance, and she whimpered again.

"I need you to answer this for me," she said, looking

desperate. "I need you in me."

Pushing into her slowly, Scott closed her eyes again, and I kissed her to suppress a moan. She was flushed and covered in a sheen of sweat, completely undone, compared to her usual persona. I deepened the kiss, tongues brushing against each other lazily as I pushed my hips forward, sinking further into her. Scott pulled her legs up, granting me deeper access, and I felt the heat and grip of her pussy tight around me.

We were pressed together, skin sticking to each other. I kissed along her jaw and back to her mouth, setting a rhythm. I'd waited for this and wanted to make it worth it. I picked up the pace before slowing down again.

"Gray, please," Scott begged.

She'd never said please as much as she had in the bedroom tonight.

"Please." It was a moan this time. "Fuck me harder."

I continued to kiss around her neck and shoulder, biting and sucking at the skin. "Since you asked so nicely."

My hips thrust against her, hard and fast, hand slipping between us so I could play with her clit. Scott's nails dug into my shoulders, breaking skin as her body arched up against mine.

"Gray!"

Her walls tightened around me as her body succumbed to the high that I'd given her. Slowly, she opened her eyes, hazy as she tried to focus on me.

"You haven't —" she started.

"Watch," I commanded her.

I wanted her to watch me. Wanted her to see that with every depraved thought she had of me, I had of her.

Pinning her hands above her head again, I bucked into her. There was nothing gentle about my movements. The raw feeling of being inside of her spurred me on. Biting down on her shoulder, I broke the skin with ease, and she gasped at the pain. But I didn't care. I was only focused on myself. On getting my release.

"Let me feel you, Gray."

Looking up at her, with a small trickle of blood on my lips,

I soaked her in. Scott's hair was wild against the pillows, pupils wide, and lips swollen. There were no words in any language, past or present, that could describe the perfection beneath my body. She'd been driven to this point by me. The sight of her made me buck roughly into her, wanting to leave my mark and claim her body. Scott's fingers dug into my flesh and her eyes screwed shut as she took my rage and lust. I fell over the edge as my spine curved and I thrust deep into her one last time, filling her with my cum.

I collapsed on top of Scott, and she buried her head into my hair. Of all the centuries of life, of all the beings I'd pleasured; this night with Scott had topped them all. The sight and feel of her would be burnt into my brain for the rest of my existence.

The thin tendrils of my aura that hung around us dissipated as I regained control.

A silence settled in the room.

We'd crossed the line that both of us believed we were strong enough to resist.

I pulled myself away from her. No words needed to be said. We'd met our understanding. The thing we both wanted, we'd got, and now we could go our separate ways. Continue to live our lives.

Wrapping my aura around me, I left the room without a word.

TWENTY

QUENTIN

The hot beads of water hit my body as I turned on the shower and my muscles ached dully at the soft pressure. Closing my eyes, I let the memories of last night flood my mind, bringing a small smile to my lips and a slickness between my legs.

I don't think I'd ever been so satisfied after sex.

But that was it. I'd fed my curiosity. I had an answer, which meant that I could focus on work and my life again, instead of focusing on Gray.

Stepping out of the shower, I wrapped a towel around my body and scooped my hair into another. When I looked in the mirror, my gaze darted along the bruises that decorated my skin and landed on the harsh bite mark at my shoulder. My fingers brushed against it gingerly. I'd need to wear something that covered it.

On the counter, my phone buzzed with a message from Charlie.

Hey. Didn't see you before you left. Everything okay? x

I typed out a quick response.

All good. Sorry for leaving - headache. Loved the party x

As I placed the phone down on the counter again, it began to ring, and Matt's name appeared on the screen. I swiped to answer and put him on speaker.

"Hey, Matt."

"Scott," he replied. "How are you doing?"

I hesitated. The truth was that I felt at peace; a feeling that had evaded me for years. I'd briefly felt it when Gray kissed me, but after last night, the heavy weight I walked around with had vanished and there was a spring in my step.

"I'm doing good," I told him. "Is this a business call?"

"Completely the opposite, actually. That date we spoke about last night. How are you fixed for today?"

"Today?" My voice didn't hide the surprise.

"Unless you're busy."

"I'm not busy. What did you have in mind?"

"That would be telling," he teased.

I laughed, the uncomfortable knot easing as I dropped the towel and rubbed moisturiser onto my arms.

"Wear something you can move in," Matt instructed.

"Gym gear?"

"Perfect. I'll pick you up at eleven."

"See you then."

I hung up and continued to get ready. By the time I walked down the stairs, kitted out in my gym clothes, the clock read ten-fifty.

"Morning, Scott." A dark voice cut through the silence of the kitchen as I entered the room. "I thought you might sleep in today, and yet here you are, apparently ready to go. Did you not get enough of a workout last night?"

The heat creeped into my cheeks. "Looks like you didn't work me hard enough."

I moved past him to make some coffee, but a black tendril gripped me around the waist and spun me around to face Grayson.

"I heard no complaints from you last night, Scott," he said smoothly.

I bristled at the close proximity. Unless Gray gave me space, this arrangement wouldn't work.

He smirked at my unease. "And here I was thinking I couldn't break you."

Reaching out his hand, Gray brushed the bite mark that'd been revealed as my t-shirt slipped from my shoulder. His palm covered the mark, rough against my smooth skin before a warmth flooded the area. When he removed his arm and aura from around me, I turned my head to see the skin was healed.

"I believe the words you're looking for are thank you," Gray prompted.

"Thanks," I said reluctantly.

"You had much better manners in bed."

"You were worth my manners then," I mumbled.

Popping a pod into the coffee machine, I pushed myself up to sit on the counter and waited for it to finish before taking a long sip. It burned on the way down, but I revelled in the taste of the bitter black brew. As I lowered the mug, I glanced over at Gray.

"What are your plans for today?" I asked.

His expression darkened. "Work matters."

"What do you do, Gray?"

"Excuse me?" He raised an eyebrow.

"What do you do?" I repeated, curiously. "I mean, I have a file that tells me about your responsibilities and I'm working on the biology —"

"I believe we both worked on the biology."

The comment made me roll my eyes. I'd worried things might become awkward, but some tensions had lifted. Gray was still aggravating, and I was still dealing with his mood swings.

"You're ignoring my question," I pointed out.

Grayson stood in front of me and shrugged. "Mostly, I listen to people and decide if I should grant what they desire."

"How do you decide?"

"I just know who's deserving. When someone prays to me,

I can feel it. I understand the depth of the request being put to me," he explained. "If they're worthy, then I give them my time. If their reason resonates enough, then I'll grant it."

I pulled a face. "But you've been doing that while you've been here. That's the bare minimum you do, right?"

Gray advanced, stopping in between my legs and looking down at me. I refused to meet his eye and sipped from my mug to keep myself occupied.

"There's plenty up there that you don't know about," he reminded me. "Plenty of things we do to keep your world nice and safe."

The way he said it made my hairs stand on end. "Like what?"

"I don't think so, Scott," Gray said. "Just because we slept together doesn't make us equals. You don't need to know divine business."

That comment irked me. For a split second, I thought about tossing the contents of my mug at him, but took another sip instead, preparing an argument, when a loud knock broke the silence.

"You need to move," I said, putting the mug on the counter.

"Where are those impeccable manners from last night?"

"Move."

Gray's face came close to mine, the tip of his nose running along my cheek. "Say please."

My brain struggled to run along logical tracks. My mind and body ran carelessly along a tightrope towards what he wanted.

"Please."

With a smirk in place, Gray straightened up and took two steps back as I slipped off the counter.

"If you're going to Sal's, I'll join you," he said casually.

"I'm not going to Sal's," I called as I left the kitchen.

I needed to put as much space as possible between us.

Gray followed me through the house. "Where are you going?"

Opening the front door, Matt stood on the doorstep. He was dressed in a t-shirt and pair of shorts, flashing me a smile so wide that his dimples showed.

"Hey," he said brightly. "Ready for our date?"

"Date?" Gray asked, his tone darker than it had been all morning.

"Yes, and yes," I said, matching Holden's brightness. "Do I need anything else?"

"Perfect as you are," Matt told me.

"Enjoy work, Gray," I said over my shoulder. "See you later."

TWENTY ONE

GRAYSON

A furious rush of anger filled my chest as Scott closed the door.

I struggled to understand what she saw in Matthew Holden. A woman who prided herself on years of education, whose grey matter was consistently in use, chose to date an oaf like Holden. It begged sense and logic.

Originally, I thought she'd said yes to the mortal because she was trying to make me jealous, and I'd stamped that out when

I'd forced her hand to make Holden move out. A spanner in his plan. But somewhere along the way, they'd patched things up and were on another date.

I wasn't interested in her for anything other than sex, but I couldn't wrap my head around why she'd choose someone so unlike me. Holden attempted to behave as an alpha and could convince others, but he picked fights he couldn't win. I'd shown that repeatedly. And while Scott had a lot of bite, our one-to-one session confirmed she wanted someone who could take control.

Last night was meant to drive her out of my head, but she still took up space. The vision of her spread out on the bed like a feast. The taste of her like the sweetest nectar that had been created. The feel of her body, so perfectly against mine. Scott had cemented herself as an obsession, and I didn't plan to share.

As easy as it would be to sit and spiral and plot Holden's downfall, other matters required my attention. Forcefully, I pushed her and the current predicament from my mind and prepared for the council
meeting.

Sitting together in Gareth's living room felt suffocating. Time away from Elysia and from my kin had given me space to breathe. Reminded me how invasive and judgemental they were. Every time we gathered together these days, all twelve of us, my skin itched, and I looked for an excuse to leave.

As usual, I took my position beside Erik. The moment I sat down, his head snapped in my direction.

"Please tell me you didn't," he hissed.

My expression remained neutral. "What?"

"Grayson, as much as I think you're an idiot right now, I know you aren't stupid." Erik lowered his voice. "What were you thinking?"

Erik's responsibilities meant he could vaguely sense what had transpired. He wouldn't be able to tell with who, but as starry-eyed as my little brother was, he remained sharp. There was no use in denying what he knew as a fact.

"I was thinking," I replied coolly. "I needed to get her out of my system. It's done and dusted and no one else needs to know." There was a warning tone lacing my words.

Erik shook his head. "I told her —"

"Yes, she told me about your little conversation. I should thank you. You gave her the push she needed," I told him, grinning.

"If Sloan finds out, she's going to kill you."

"Why?"

"She hasn't told you —"

"What haven't I told him?"

Both of us jumped, too invested in our conversation to have sensed her behind us. She lovingly kissed Erik on the cheek and ran a hand through his hair in a disgusting display of affection before taking the seat on the other side of him.

"Nothing, dear," Erik assured her with a smile.

"What's your issue with Scott?" I asked her, no time for manners.

Erik shot me daggers, but Sloan took in a deep breath and replied.

"I don't have an issue with her. I just don't want you getting in trouble, Gray. First, you're getting too close to her by the looks of it, and if anyone else sees the way you two behave, that'll get you in shit with Hunter. Second, she works hard, so let her work. Hunter might actually kill you if you ruin this for us."

I clenched my teeth and leaned back in the chair. "Fine."

There was more to it than that, and I wouldn't let the topic go with ease. Sloan must have seen something, and I wanted to know what. She dealt with fertility, so it was to do with Scott having children or her own conception.

Ignacio took the seat on my left and bumped his shoulder against mine, asking, "Are you done being an asshole?"

"Am I ever?" I asked in response, and Ig laughed. "Sorry about the other night."

"I didn't realise you'd staked a claim."

I gave a noncommittal shrug. Ig wouldn't have gone any further than harmless flirting. His moral compass pointed less south than my own and he had his hands tied with a certain Goddess.

"What are we doing here?" Ig asked, glancing around the

room.

"Hunter had some words with the minor Gods."

"He went home?"

"Apparently."

As if on cue, Hunter stood and called for our attention.

"Some of you may know that I went to talk to the minor Gods earlier this week," he started. "They've been restless for years. It comes in waves, but I think Archer is trying to stir the pot again. He's insistent that we should also involve them in the project."

"They want to come down here?" A voice lifted from the small crowd.

The minor Gods had been an issue for some time. They believed it was unfair that there were tiers, and that they were beneath us. Archer was the most vocal minor God and had proven a difficulty for us. We'd come to blows on more than one occasion.

"Yes," Hunter said. "And I think it might be a good way to build some bridges."

The room erupted, but it was my voice that was the loudest. "You can't be serious, Hunter. What is wrong with you?"

My brother fixed me with a stare. "We need to try to placate them."

"They cause issues in Elysia, and you want to bring them to earth?"

"They'll be cuffed until they can prove they can be trusted."

I bit the insides of my cheeks as the noise in the room continued to mount.

"Enough!" Hunter stood there with his aura blazing blue around him and multiple others sparked into life, including mine, Erik, and Ig's. The swirl of blue, black, red, and orange lit up the room.

"We need to make a decision on this," Hunter told us all. "In the long run, I think it'll be beneficial for us. So, I put it to our council. All in favour of allowing the minor Gods to join us?"

Hunter, Larkin, Waverly, Malachi, Flynn, Aria, Elva, Bexley. A flurry of hands shot into the air.

"And those against?"

The small group of us that comprised Ig, Sloan, Erik, and me. I was surprised to see Sloan had joined us on this matter.

"Looks like I'll be talking to Gareth to set the wheels in motion," Hunter said. He continued to discuss matters concerning Elysia before he adjourned the meeting. When we rose from our seats, Hunter called out, "Erik. Grayson. A moment, please."

Gritting my teeth, I walked over to join my older brother.

With every decision he made, the less fitting I found him as a leader. Minor Gods on earth had been the primary bone of contention that led to the last war. Was he really pretending like decades of bloodshed in the heavens hadn't happened? Was he prepared to plunge us into that darkness again?

"I don't appreciate you both showing me up," Hunter told us both quietly, looking as irritated as I felt.

"Hunter," Erik began. "You asked for a vote."

"You're going to make me look weak."

"You do a good job of that on your own," I muttered.

"I'll remind you both of who is in charge," he shot back.

"And let us remind you, you can't force us to do shit."

Blue and black swirled out the three of us. Our volatile relationship had grown more explosive over the past few years. I didn't give a fuck about respect or loyalty. Not when it came to Hunter.

"Both of you need to stop," Erik said firmly. "Hunter, you got what you wanted without me and Gray. Now, if you don't mind, we'll take our leave."

Erik looked at me and I dropped my aura first, even if I wanted to take Hunter out in front of everyone. We walked away, back to Sloan.

"Ignore him," Erik pleaded, knowing that my temper was still swirling behind the calm facade. "He has a lot riding on this project and it's not as if it'll be the entire cohort of minor Gods."

"If Archer is coming, then it's going to be chaos," I said, staring ahead.

"Good thing you're here then."

Erik threw me a smile, and I gave my little brother a gentle shove.

If the God of secrets was joining us, then we'd all have to watch our step.

TWENTY TWO

QUENTIN

Matt had arranged a date at a rock-climbing centre. Strapped into a harness, we dangled from the wall, racing to the top and easing ourselves back down. If I was honest, I hadn't laughed so much in a long time. The conversation was light, and once we'd exhausted ourselves, we returned home and agreed to meet at Murphy's for a drink.

"My best paying customer!" Tyler greeted me as I walked into the pub.

I curtsied deeply and walked over to the bar.

"Hey, Quen," Charlie said, appearing next to her partner.

"What did he promise you to get you behind the bar?" I

asked.

"A life sentence."

I laughed hard, and Tyler wore a sheepish grin as he looked at me.

"No," I said, sobering up. "No, Ty."

"Please, Scott. I'm short staffed, and just look at the place," Tyler pleaded.

Glancing around, it was easy to see that the pub was packed to the brim with only Charlie, Tyler, and one other member of staff behind the bar.

I sighed. "You owe me."

"You're a star!"

He threw me an apron that I tied around my waist before pulling my hair into a ponytail and making my way behind the bar.

As I finished serving my first customer, a pair of fingers brushed against the small of my back, and I tensed.

"How was the date?" Gray's voice was at my ear.

I turned on my heel to see his signature smirk and my eyes trailed down his body. He was dressed casually again, and it caught me off guard each time. The plain black t-shirt fitted his form like a second skin, and I flushed, thinking of the sculpted body that laid beneath the fabric.

"Can't have gone that well if you're looking at me like I'm your last meal." He raised a brow, looking pleased with himself, and I shook my head, stepping away from him.

"I had a great time," I corrected him. "We went rock climbing. I can't believe I haven't tried it before. What are you doing behind the bar?"

"Helping," he answered.

"You do bar work?" I asked, surprised.

"You do bar work?" he echoed. "I thought the lab was your domain."

"I did it throughout my undergraduate."

I'd worked at the local bar just to eat up time. The money had been a bonus. My inheritance had seen me want for nothing.

"Hey, sweetheart," I said, turning away from Gray when a

customer caught my eye. "What can I get you?"

"I like to host people back in Elysia," Gray said to me as I grabbed a pint glass.

His voice was close enough so that only I could pick up what he was saying, but that also meant his body was uncomfortably close to mine. The heat rolled off him in waves and my mind strayed towards the gutter and dived right into the memories of last night.

I handed the pint over to the customer and put the cash in the till, trying desperately to ignore the recollection of how his body felt pressed against mine.

"Personal space, Grayson," I reminded him quietly.

Gray's response was to stand behind me and play with the frayed edges of my denim shorts. Rough fingers skimming across my thighs, and I ached with longing for his fingers to be elsewhere. It was worrying how quickly my afternoon with Matthew had slipped from my mind now that Grayson was around.

"Wrong side of the bar, beautiful," Matt said, taking a seat.

"Ty asked me for a favour," I answered him.

"Do you need another pair of hands?"

"I think we have it covered," Gray said. I made to move away from him, but he pinched my shorts and kept me in place. "I've got this. How about you go collect glasses?"

I wanted to argue with him, but he'd let go of my shorts and I left to collect the empty glasses from around the room so we could have some space. Every so often, I looked over to Gray to see if he was behaving with Matt, and thankfully, he'd been served and Gray moved on.

When I'd finished clearing the tables, I walked back to Matt.

"I'm sorry," I apologised. "I know we were meant to sort of continue our date."

"It's fine," Matthew told me. "We can still spend time together, though, that might mean you'll have to carry me home by the end of the night."

I laughed as he snaked an arm around my waist. Charlie stood behind the bar, and I flushed pink at the pointed look she shot us.

"I should probably get behind the bar," I mumbled, trying to untangle myself from him. "Can I get you anything else?"

"I could use a kiss."

He looked up at me earnestly, and my cheeks burnt. We hadn't kissed yet. As well as both of the dates had gone, the physical chemistry felt like it was lacking.

"I'm not sure Tyler serves those," I joked uncomfortably.

I couldn't figure out if requesting a kiss in public was a calculative move on Matt's part. The naïve stance would be to think it was just an innocent request, but I was a cynic and hated being forced into anything.

"Good thing I'm not asking Murphy."

He pulled me in closer, and I noticed Gray was watching us from the other side of the bar, expression unreadable.

I owed it to myself to date properly, and that included a physical relationship. Staying celibate for the rest of my life was not an option, and I didn't want meaningless sex for the rest of my days, no matter how mind blowing it was. Deep inside, I craved the stability and love that you discovered in a relationship.

Cupping Matt's face, I leaned down and pressed my lips against his. His tongue ran across my bottom lip, and I took a moment before deepening the kiss. He tasted of beer and the kiss was… nice.

It was nice, and he was a decent kisser. Even so, I couldn't help but compare it to Gray. I quickly pushed those thoughts out of my head, and when we broke apart, Matt was grinning at me, dimples visible in his cheeks.

"I guess I can let you go back to work now," he said.

He pulled me down again and brushed his lips against mine before letting me go.

Grabbing the glasses quickly, I walked behind the bar.

"Ugh! I've been waiting so long to see that," Charlie said as I squeezed past her.

"Yes. Quite the display, Scott." Gray's expression was still blank, but his voice had an edge to it.

I shrugged. "I'm not opposed to PDA."

That was a lie. Ethan had never been the most openly affectionate, and I'd never batted an eyelid. It meant that displays like Matt had just cornered me into left me red and feeling off balance.

"No. I can see that."

The intensity of Gray's gaze made my knees buckle. Disapproval and vexation coated his features, but I reminded myself that I shouldn't care what he or any of the Gods thought about how I conducted my life.

"Excuse me." I moved past him to put the glasses down and went to serve a customer.

Most of the night passed without event. Gray kept himself away from me and we served the rush of people. Matt left just before closing, telling me he'd see me on Monday at work.

Ty eventually rang the bell, and we finished up the last orders.

"Well, I would say we could head back to mine." Gray's voice was clear. "But my roommate is a little hostile."

From across the bar, I watched as Gray leaned over the counter and chatted up a petite blonde woman.

"So, how about we head back to yours?" he suggested.

The woman let out a giggle and nodded her head.

The ferric tang of blood filled my mouth as I bit on my cheeks.

The woman got off the stool, and Gray turned to leave the bar, catching my eye. "Don't wait up, Scott," he told me spitefully.

Balling up his apron, he threw it at me before joining the blonde, and I tried to dampen the feeling of disappointment and anger that spread through my gut.

This was never more than a one-time thing. Mindless want and satisfied curiosity.

Then why did envy pull me under for the rest of the night?

TWENTY THREE

GRAYSON

Three weeks.

For three weeks, we'd fallen into a pattern.

My presence wasn't needed at the institute, and I'd only seen Scott at home. Most nights she brought work home and took it to her room, barely saying two words to me.

The nights she didn't work, Scott spent them with Holden. Last week, she'd brought him home afterwards, and I almost smashed every glass object in the house. And I would have brought the house down to its foundations when I saw Holden's smug face the next morning, had it not been for Scott's unsatisfied thoughts.

Unsurprisingly, he'd been unable to please her. Mediocre sex wasn't enough to gratify her. Scott required a connection. She demanded an adversary in the bedroom who could make her bend, who could serve her as she relinquished control.

To avoid the pseudo-couple, I busied myself by visiting Erik and Sloan. She was close to her due date, and many of us stopped in on her. When I wasn't with them, I picked up women from Murphy's, taking them home as long as the others weren't around. My solace was always in the depths of chaos.

The problem was that every woman I chose was timid. None of them had the brash confidence and inflated ego that Scott possessed, and it irritated me she'd left a lasting impression and then decided her time and effort was better wasted on Holden.

We wouldn't be able to avoid each other today. Gareth had invited the entire institute to Brighton to celebrate his birthday and that meant a mixture of Gods and mortals littered around the beach.

If we ever made it.

"Hurry up, Scott!" I called through the house. "Otherwise, I'm using my aura to get us there."

"I'm coming," she yelled back. "Stop being so impatient."

If I'd learned anything about this woman, it was that she was rarely on time for anything that wasn't work.

She came down the stairs a few minutes later, and we slipped into the car, heading out of London on a silent trip.

Throughout the drive, I kept my gaze on her with no concern for subtlety. My goal was not to make her feel comfortable. My goal was to understand why this mortal had taken up so much headspace and drove me to the brink of insanity.

Scott had a foul temper, triggered by small things like bad traffic. Her time management was poor. Her house was a mess, books and items stacked haphazardly on any available surface. She was the furthest thing from divinity that I'd encountered, and yet I was drawn to her indescribably.

When we arrived, Scott pulled a cooler and her bag out of the back of the car and slung the bag over her shoulder.

"Hand it here," I told her, holding a hand out.

"I can manage," she brushed me off sharply.

"Hand it here, Scott."

"I don't need you to carry it," she snapped. "Lock the car."

She tossed the keys at me and carried the cooler, using both arms, down to the mass of people on the beach. She melted in among the rest of the mortals, and I clocked the Gods spread between them.

"They make so many poor decisions," Erik said as I joined him, pocketing Scott's keys into my shorts. "But I love seeing when they get it right."

He watched Gareth with his wife and young daughter. The three of them sat in the sand, building sandcastles with smiles plastered across their faces. A perfect, happy family.

"You're a sap," I told him, disgusted.

"And you're a cynic," he replied airily.

"Where's Sloan?"

Erik nodded over to some loungers and a parasol where Sloan was laid out comfortably in the shade, bump proudly on display.

"Not long now," I said.

Erik grinned. "Two more weeks."

"Are you going to bring the rest of the kids down?"

"Gareth's trying to clear it. I think Archer might pay a visit then. We'll have to see. The project is growing, and I think it's unsettling him. He's worried it might be more than he can handle."

"Fantastic," I said through gritted teeth.

"Come on," Erik said. "Let's join the rest of them."

A small group, comprising a few male colleagues, had formed and tossed a rugby ball between them. I pulled off my t-shirt, leaving me in my shorts, and let the sun warm my skin as we joined them.

I could feel the eyes on me and then the thoughts, but there was only one string of thoughts that caught my attention. One stream of consciousness that interested me above all else.

My eyes combed through the faces on the beach until I found Scott standing by a lounger with her sole focus on me. It appeared that we were both having a similar issue.

I smirked and watched as her face flushed, looking away once she knew I had caught her. She'd need to be more subtle than that if she wanted to get away with eye-fucking.

"You playing, Grayson?" Holden tossed a ball between his hands.

When I glanced back to Scott, she'd stripped off her shorts and tank top, and my dick twitched in my shorts. Outside the lab, she didn't do modest when it came down to her clothes but seeing her stripped down to two pieces didn't help my predicament.

"I'm not sure you're going to want to play games with me," I muttered in response, brain already formulating a plan as he turned away to talk to other colleagues.

"Bet you get a similar view all the time at home," Ig said, jogging up next to me and watching Scott as she stretched out on a lounger in the sun.

Golden skin glistened under the sun, begging the rays to kiss it and luring me to do the same.

Internally, I scolded myself for not being more astute. The last thing I wanted was for anyone else's eye to be drawn to what I'd made mine.

"I wish," I replied honestly. "She's too caught up in work most of the time."

"Can't deny it, she looks damn good in my colour."

I bristled at the comment. So far, I hadn't seen her wear all black, and I felt a prick of annoyance as she basked in the sun in an orange bikini.

It meant nothing. She wasn't a Goddess, so none of the traditions applied to her. Ig was merely trying to get me back after I'd landed him on his ass the other night.

I bit back on the comment that Scott actually looked better in nothing. It was bad enough that Erik knew. I wasn't about to air it and risk Hunter pulling me up on conduct and behaviour.

"No one looks good in your colour," I retorted.

Ig snorted. "They wear black at funerals."

"At least it stands for something. Orange? Why does anyone wear orange?"

"Fuck you, Gray."

Letting out a hearty laugh, I watched Ig sulk towards Elva. I went to follow him, but after one more glance at Scott and I instantly changed my course.

"Enjoying the sun?" I asked when I reached her.

Placing myself on the lounger beside Scott, parasol shielding me from the brightness, I let my eyes roam over her figure. The skin at her thighs and hips was decorated with white stretch marks where she'd grown to accommodate the curves that attracted attention.

She turned her head towards me, eyes hidden behind large, dark sunglasses. "Mmm. It feels good," she replied lazily.

"I know what else could make you feel good," I said, leaning towards her.

"Grayson," she warned me.

"What?"

"It's not happening."

"So, you know what I'm talking about then?"

She sat up slowly and turned to look at me.

"You know, you should really get some shade," I advised her, patting the space next to me.

She shook her head. "I'm good."

Moving off the lounger, I took a seat beside her. Scott pushed her glasses up onto her head now that my body cast shadows over her. I took the chance to check her out again, causing her to raise an eyebrow.

"Don't look at me like that, Scott. I caught you looking earlier."

"There's nothing against looking," she told me indignantly.

"In my eyes, there's nothing against touching."

"Gray."

"Come on, Scott," I coaxed gently. "I know you weren't happy the other night."

Her eyes grew wide, and her cheeks coloured. "I have no idea —"

"You're really going to lie to me?"

She huffed at being caught out.

"You hate when you don't get your way," I said, amused by her behaviour.

I'd seen how wilful she was and appreciated the quality until it meant her resisting me. She could possess all the fire in the world as long as it didn't stop me from getting what I wanted.

"You're the same," she shot back.

"I never said it was an undesirable trait."

She softened again. "What do you want, Gray?"

"Exactly the same as you." I leaned in and played with a loose strand of her hair. "Satisfaction." I dropped a light kiss at her jaw.

"Gray," she whispered.

"Mmm?"

"We're going to get in trouble."

She hadn't told me to stop.

"Then we should leave," I told her.

My aura wrapped around us, taking us back to hers. In moments, we were standing inside of the front hallway of her house, and she pushed me away.

"Gray!" Scott yelled, looking furious. "Do you ever listen? We were around loads of people. You can get in serious trouble. And… Matthew —"

I rolled my eyes in response to her outburst. "I'll deal with the consequences if they come."

Cupping her face with one hand, I put the other arm around her bare waist. Scott was still warm from the sun, but goosebumps rose across the surface of her skin. Whether or not she wanted to admit it, she was mine. Her body listened to me, and her mind followed.

"Tell me I'm wrong, Scott."

Her hands were planted on my bare chest, and she bit her lip, fighting with herself.

"You tell me you don't want this, and I'll leave you alone," I explained.

In her eyes, the decision had been made, but I wanted her to tell me. It took a few moments before she finally broke.

"What are you waiting for?"

TWENTY FOUR

QUENTIN

I struggled to focus when Gray was this close and semi-naked. Every part of me wanted to stick to my guns and tell him no, but my body craved to feel him again. The pleasure and the peace that Gray provided were something I desperately searched for in late nights and early mornings. It evaded me at every turn until I'd given into him.

Grayson was my twisted salvation that I never knew I needed.

How fucked up that a God I'd forsaken, a God I would never turn to, ended up being the one who kept my sanity and brought balance to my life?

"What are you waiting for?" I asked him, losing all my resolve.

Gray smirked as he unclasped my top, and it fell from my body. I hooked my thumbs into my bottoms and pulled them down my legs. When I straightened up, I looked at Gray through my lashes.

"Tell me what you're thinking." His voice had a gravelly edge to it.

If Gray wanted, he could find out exactly what I was thinking, but he wanted me to tell him. This was another layer to the game. Asking me for my thoughts instead of taking them was another sign of me giving into him. I preferred it this way. Preferred to offer them before he took them from me.

"I want you inside me," I told him simply.

With that sentence, Gray lost control. His eyes turned black, the veins running up his arm took on the same colour, standing out against his skin, and his aura swirled to life around him. This was the reminder, if one was ever needed, that Gray was a God and not a typical man.

His hand curled into my hair, fingers tangled in the strands, and he tugged, bringing my head up before claiming my mouth as his own. I smiled into the kiss, turned on by his rough behaviour. Gray's free hand ran down my back, cupping my ass before moving to the front and in between my legs, making me groan in delight.

I was already wet for him, and his fingers teased along my folds before he slipped two into me.

"Fuck." He breathed the word into my hair, and I moaned into his chest, my hands gripping onto him.

Gray smelled like bitter coffee, books, and bonfire. It was a heady mix that I associated with him. It was what I sensed before I saw him in the lab or the house. A mixture of all the things I loved.

He pushed another finger into me, and I squirmed against his hand.

"Please. Please," I begged him.

A dark chuckle that came from Gray before he removed his fingers. He picked me up with ease, carrying me until my back hit the wall of the hallway.

“Always so impatient,” he muttered, looking at me.

My fingers sunk into his hair, and he lowered his mouth to suck and lick at my nipple. I nipped at his ear, and he responded in kind, making me gasp at the mix of pleasure and pain.

It was Gray’s aura that held me against the wall as he took off his shorts and discarded them before turning his attention to the other nipple, making my back arch to his touch.

“Gray, please.” I wasn’t capable of stringing together more of a sentence.

The burning desire for him had grown over the past few weeks, and to have him so close and yet not close enough was driving me insane. I dug my fingers into his hair again and pulled his head back so I could look at him, panting.

Gray let me down from against the wall and my shaky feet hit the ground. If I wanted something from him, I was going to have to get it because Gray liked to make me beg and I wasn’t in the mood for those games.

Hooking a leg around his, Gray looked at me in confusion as I pushed his chest and sent him to the ground with a thump. He looked up at me from the floor, and I gave him a sultry smile before sitting on top of him and pinning him with my knees.

“You can’t help but tease, can you?” I asked.

I reached behind me and grabbed his hard cock, thumb rubbing over the head. Slowly, I lifted myself, lining him up to me before sinking onto it. I kept my eyes on him and watched his face go slack with desire as he filled me inch by inch. It felt so good to have him there again. And the moan that came from Gray pushed me further.

“Quentin. Fuck,” he uttered.

Quentin. No longer Scott. He was just as caught up as I was if he’d dropped the formality of using my family name. I usually hated people calling me Quentin, but when Gray said it, it sounded musical, and I wanted to hear it again.

“More?” I asked him.

He looked at me, eyes pitch black and almost demonic, as he nodded his head. I was in control. Instead of seating myself fully onto his dick, I lifted, only leaving the head of him inside me. Gray let out a growl, and I felt the vibrations through his chest.

"Always so impatient, Gray," I repeated the words he told me.

The smirk was wiped clean from my face when Gray flipped us over and my back hit the wooden floorboards. His hard muscles pushed against the curves of my body, pressing me down against the surface.

"You just don't know when to stop, do you?" he hissed.

Gray grabbed my legs, forcing them apart, and buried his dick deep inside me. I squeezed my eyes shut and bit down on my lip to stop from screaming out. He thrust his hips, and I met every movement, finally allowing myself to moan at the pleasure he provided.

"Does he fuck you like this?" Gray asked, pressing his forehead against mine.

I wanted to respond to him, but I couldn't form the words, instead my fingers pulled at his hair. Gray's hand pulled my head up so that our mouths met again, and soon our tongues battled for dominance.

"You feel so good, Gray," I mumbled against his lips.

"Maybe we should stop."

I whimpered at the thought, and Gray smirked.

"Oh, I love when you make that sound," he told me.

Gray didn't stop. He placed an arm around my waist so that my back arched up and angled me so he could drive in deeper.

"Cum for me, Quentin."

He picked up the pace, and my nails dug into his forearms as he pushed me over the edge. My muscles tensed, and I threw my head back in pure ecstasy.

I'd barely come down from the orgasm when Gray's hand stroked my sensitive clit, making me whimper again. He growled in response, pulling out of me as he played with my overstimulated bundle of nerves and then pushed back into me.

"No," I breathed, unable to find a moment of clarity with the way he played with my body. "Oh, Gods."

Gray removed his hands. "What did I tell you? Only me."

I looked at him, lips parted and nodded, desperately needing to feel his hand again.

"Say my name," he demanded.

"Gray." It was a pathetic whimper of a sound.

"Louder."

I bit my lip as his fingers teased over my clit again, and I ached for him to move.

"Gray!"

"Such a good girl," he crooned, and there was a sense of satisfaction at his approval.

He pressed his fingers down on my clit and rubbed, thrusting in and out until I found myself on the edge. Before long, my legs began to shake, and soon, Gray had delivered my second orgasm. My body was spent from a morning in the sun and the ecstasy he had supplied me.

He pulled himself out of me, his dick resting against my thigh, slick and hard and throbbing. My chest heaved as I tried to catch my breath. Gray's hands found my hips, and he flipped me over so that my front was against the floor before pulling me to my knees.

I didn't protest. I didn't want to.

His rough fingers brushed against my ass gently before he brought his palm down against it in a stinging slap and I yelped in pain. Anger filled me, but the fire was doused as he massaged the spot, soothing the sting that he'd brought with his blow.

Suddenly, Gray entered me again, without warning. The side of my face pushed against the floor with the force.

"Fuck me, Quen," Gray groaned. "You feel like heaven." He pushed his hips until he found the spot.

I cried out his name. "Gray! Yes!"

"You cum only for me. Do you understand?"

He continued to thrust into me, setting a pace again. My legs felt weak, knees in pain from the hard wood beneath them. His aura wrapped around me to keep me in the position. Gray wasn't trying to satisfy me anymore. He was using me to find his own high, and I let him.

"No one but you," I agreed.

The words fell out of my mouth with no prompting. I curved my spine, pushing my ass further back so Gray could go deeper. Every inch of him filled me, and it was better than I remembered.

"Fuck," he grunted.

Gray's fingers sank into the soft flesh of my hips. There was no doubt in my mind that he'd leave bruises. He jerked before shuddering and cumming inside of me.

He slipped himself out of me, and I felt the trickle down my inner thighs. Both times we had sex, Gray had left me in a complete mess. His aura placed me gently on the floor, where he joined me.

I rolled onto my back, head turning to face Gray, and I watched as the darkness faded from him. His veins returned to a dull blue, his eyes sharp and bright again, and his aura disappeared from around us as he gained control and composure again.

"See how much better it feels when you give in to me?" he asked.

Groaning, I pushed myself, so I was sitting up. My legs shook and I willed them to keep steady. "I shouldn't be doing this," I replied.

"You aren't his girlfriend."

"I know."

"So?" Gray sat up next to me. "Keep dating him and when needs be…" He placed a kiss on my back, and I shivered and closed my eyes. "We'll keep each other satisfied."

Letting out a shaky breath, I glanced over my shoulder at him. "Aren't you meant to be convincing me to do good?"

"Need I remind you what I'm responsible for?"

Nothing good would come of this. We were breaking too many rules too quickly.

"We can't do this again," I told him firmly.

He narrowed his eyes. "We'll see about that."

"It's not a challenge, Gray."

"Isn't it?"

He pulled me in towards him before kissing me again. I melted into the embrace and Gray pulled me so that I straddled his lap. I couldn't help the groan that escaped my lips.

Gray broke the kiss and laughed. "I guess it can't be called a challenge if you give in so easily."

I slammed both of my palms against his chest and stood up, a little unsteadily, thanks to the lack of strength in my legs.

"This isn't happening again," I repeated.

I started my slow ascent up the stairs, and Gray called after me, "Whatever you say, Scott!"

"And you better bring my car back here!"

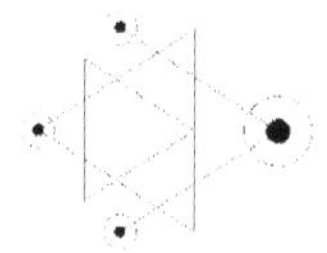

I'd attempted to see Matthew in some way, shape or form, every night this week. If it wasn't a date, then I went to his place, or he came to the house so that my evenings were filled with ways to avoid Gray.

Although my evenings were free of him, my mornings and some of my working days were not. It was in those moments that Gray tried to get under my skin. He was a mixture of subtle and blunt, swapping between gentle brushes of skin and standing an inch too close to pinning me against surfaces and telling me exactly what he wanted to do to me between stolen kisses.

I was proud to say I hadn't given into him again; however, it had led to plenty of dreams of Gray. There was an undeniable attraction between us, but if anyone found out, there would be disciplinary action at work, consequences from the Gods, and worst of all, Gray would have won.

When I returned from Sal's on Saturday morning, having channelled my frustrations in the ring, Gray was lying on the floor of the living room in the most ungodly fashion.

"Everything okay?" I asked, peering down at him.

He sat boldly upright and beamed at me. My heart skittered erratically behind my breastbone. Gray was all pearly whites and shining blue eyes. Waves of pure joy rolled off him, and I tried to ignore the tornado of butterflies that'd been unleashed in my gut.

"Sloan had the baby," he announced.

"She gave birth already?"

He nodded in response, and I grinned.

"That's amazing news! Boy or girl?" I asked.

"A baby boy. I've been waiting for you."

"What for?"

"We're going to visit."

I sat on the arm of the sofa and stared down at him. "Aren't they going to want only family there?"

"The others will be there," Gray informed me. "I'm sure your friend Charlotte will be there."

"Yeah, well, that's kind of their assignment and I'm not working today."

"You'll come as a friend to the family. I'm sure Erik will be thrilled to see you."

The way Gray looked at me told me he wasn't playing a game. It was a simple request and even though there was a nagging voice in the back of my mind, my curiosity had me agreeing.

"Sure," I said. "Why not? But I need to shower and get changed first."

As I left the room he shouted after me, "Wear something red!"

"Why red?" I asked, popping my head back into the room.

"We're honouring Erik and the birth of his child. Red is his colour. Simple tradition, Scott. You don't want to be disrespectful, do you?"

I sighed. "I'll check if I have anything, otherwise I'll have to attend naked."

A spark flickered in Gray's eyes, and they turned black.

"Don't even think about it," I warned him.

"Too late."

Before he had any more ideas, I ran up the stairs to get ready.

Red was not a colour I wore often, and it took some time before I found an old red jumpsuit in the back of the wardrobe. I slipped it on and gave myself a onceover. The plunging neckline might be deemed a little inappropriate, but it was all I had.

I met Gray back in the living room to find him dressed in a red suit with a white shirt.

"What do you think?" he asked.

"I don't like it," I replied, shaking my head. "Red doesn't suit you."

"Scott." Gray laughed. "Only you would be that blatantly honest and oblivious to offending a God."

My cheeks heated at my misstep.

"But I agree," he said. "Red is much more Erik's colour. I prefer black."

His gaze ran over my body, taking me in from head to toe and lingering on my curves.

"It's all I have," I said, wrapping my arms around myself.

"I have no complaints."

"Grayson."

"But I will say that I'd prefer you in black as well."

I wasn't sure how to take the compliment, so I let it slide. "How are we getting there?"

He rolled his eyes before stepping up to me. Gray's knuckles brushed against my cheek as he said, "Best behaviour now, Scott. This is my family."

The world went dark and when it brightened again, we were in Dr Martyn Hankel's living room. He was hosting Sloan and Erik. Martyn was a prominent physicist with a soft nature and the perfect host for the couple.

The house was packed with Gods and Goddesses, and a few people working on the project.

The first thing I noticed was how most of the room was dressed in shades of green and there were five people dressed in red — Erik, Gray, Hunter, Larkin, and myself. I felt several sets of eyes look curiously in my direction.

"Quen!" Charlie greeted me. "What are you doing here?"

I'd never been so happy to see her. As she came my way, I pulled her into a hug, and Gray left my side.

"I didn't realise you were assigned here," Charlie said, letting me go.

"I wasn't," I said, shaking my head. "Gray asked me to come with him."

Charlie's eyebrows practically disappeared into her hairline. "I'm surprised."

"So was I. Maybe he's actually adjusting."

"Hmm," Charlie hummed, fishing a notepad out of her bag and scribbled things down. "Okay, well, I need to follow Gray. Come over Friday and help me choose centrepieces?"

I nodded. "Sure thing. Go work."

Charlie kissed my cheek and left me again, making me feel like I stuck out like a sore thumb.

"Bold choice," Larkin, Hunter's wife, said, giving me a onceover.

"Grayson said red."

Larkin laughed and threw her long blonde hair over her shoulder. "I wouldn't listen to half the things Grayson says. You realise that it's his job to cause trouble, right?"

Hunter came up behind his wife and wrapped his arms around her waist, resting his chin on her shoulder. "Nice to see you again, Quentin. Was the colour Grayson's idea?"

I bit the insides of my cheek, nodding.

"He's never going to play by the rules," Hunter said, rolling his eyes.

"Is it a problem?" I asked.

"Not really. Just breaks protocol. Maybe check with one of us next time." He kissed Larkin on the cheek. "Come on, love."

He pulled his wife away, and I shrank back towards the wall, wondering what the fuck Gray pulled me into.

I spied Erik and Sloan, along with four children and their new baby. They glowed faintly with the aura, nestled among a crowd of family and psychologists. You could feel the swell of love in the room, and it almost threw me off balance as the Gods gathered around the family and their new arrival. Erik must have been in his element.

"Kind of sickening, no?"

When I looked to my right, there was a man standing a few steps away. A quick glance at his wrists in copper locked in front of him confirmed he was a God — as if their stunningly good looks alone weren't enough.

"Archer," he introduced himself.

"You're not one of them," I said.

"Technically, I am."

"You're a minor God," I said, but he seemed unhappy with my assessment.

"I'm a God, nonetheless. Care to introduce yourself to me?"

"Scott."

"I don't think that's quite right."

TWENTY FIVE

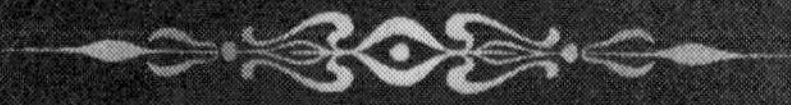

GRAYSON

I would never have guessed that Erik would be the family man out of the three of us. Sure, he was in charge of love, but when he'd first come into the role properly, he was so focused on everyone else that he hadn't left time for himself. Then he met Sloan, and everything changed. They'd started slowly, but now they had baby number five.

Making my way over to the couple, I grinned at my sister-in-law. "Everything went okay then?"

"No problems at all," Sloan replied.

Three young children launched themselves at me and I grappled with them, winning by using my aura to restrain the rascals.

"Gray," Sloan warned, but she was smiling.

These were my little troublemakers, and I'd even let them get away with murder.

Erik joined us, holding their new-born son.

"Congratulations to you both," Larkin said.

"He looks just like you, Erik," Hunter commented.

He was right. Their boy had a shock of platinum blonde hair and bright blue eyes, just like his brothers and sister. None of the children had taken after Sloan. A fact that irritated her to no end.

"Give me my adorable nephew," I demanded. The rest of my godchildren whined as I placed them on the ground, and Erik carefully handed over the baby. I cradled the tiny thing in my arms. "Have you named him yet?"

"Cato," Erik answered.

My eyes fell to Cato, who yawned, and my heart melted.

"You know," Hunter said quietly to Larkin. "Maybe we should think about having our own."

Everyone's attention turned to Hunter, and those who weren't immediate family backed away as Larkin turned on him.

"I don't think so," she said coolly.

"Larkin."

"No!"

She didn't say another word before wrapping herself in her silver aura and leaving us. The crowd dispersed, not wanting to pry on the family matter, leaving the four of us together with the kids.

"Nice job," I muttered, holding Cato in one arm and giving my big brother a thumbs-up with the free one.

Hunter disappeared after his wife, and I handed Cato over to Sloan while the kids ran around us.

Erik had been surveying the room when his head snapped to me. "Again? Really? I thought you said that it was a one off to get her out of your system."

Sloan looked up. "Please tell me you're joking. I told you to stay away from her."

"You won't tell me why," I shot back.

"She's here," Erik said.

"Where?" Sloan asked.

I didn't turn, but Sloan found her without any help.

"She's in red! You put her in red!" Sloan was outraged and Erik took Cato from her arms. The rest of the children scarpered as they sensed the change in mood. "What is wrong with you?"

"What?" I shrugged.

"I'm surprised Hunter didn't rip you apart for this."

"Sloan, what is your problem with her?"

Erik was only vaguely paying attention to the argument. "Archer's with her," he said, cutting across us.

I turned around to see Archer standing next to Scott and talking to her. When he reached his bound hands towards her, I left Sloan and Erik in a swirl of black and appeared between the pair in time to feel Scott's hand hit my back.

"Gray!" she hissed.

"Grayson," Archer greeted me.

"Archer." I nodded in return.

"Gray, move," Scott demanded from behind me.

"You heard the lady, Grayson."

"You couldn't even show some respect," I spat, noticing Archer hadn't dressed in green like protocol dictated.

"Interesting that the mortal's in red, don't you think? Do you have something to tell us? Or is it Hunter that's been so stupid?"

"Why don't you go back to Elysia and cause your trouble there?"

"Oh, I'm not here for long. A flying visit this time."

"Gray," Scott exclaimed. "I mean it."

Turning on my heel, Scott's furious expression met me. I gripped her upper arm and said, "Come with me."

I held a little tighter than I should have, and in return, she punched me in the ribs. It didn't hurt, but it caught me by surprise, and I let go of her while Archer howled with laughter.

"I like her," he said as he recovered.

Scott stormed off towards Erik and Sloan and I trailed after her, furious at how the day had spiralled into chaos and irritated that I'd expected anything else.

"Congratulations," Scott said to the pair.

"Thank you, Scott," Erik replied, hugging her.

"Would you like to hold him?" Sloan asked.

The panic was clear across her features. "Um, no. That's okay."

She stepped back and bumped straight into me. I held her shoulders and said, "What are you scared of, Scott?"

"I'm not scared," she replied tersely.

"Take Cato."

Scott nodded, and Sloan passed him over. Cato laid in Scott's arm as she held him delicately. I stood behind her, looking over her shoulder and down at the little bundle. Cato fussed slightly and Scott rocked him while I reached over her shoulder to stroke his chubby red cheek.

"What's wrong, little man?" I asked.

Cato settled again and when I looked up, I was aware that Sloan and Erik were both giving me very different looks. I wasn't sure which I wanted to address first. Sloan's look dropped quickly, and I felt more eyes on me.

"I think you should give him back to the parents," I suggested quietly.

Scott didn't need to be told twice. She wasn't as comfortable around children as the rest of us.

"I'm sorry I didn't bring a gift," she apologised.

I perked up and my aura materialised a small black bear in my hands. "That reminds me," I said, handing it over.

"Black for a baby? Really?" Scott asked.

"Aura colours are important to us. It's a mark of respect. To gift someone your colour shows a great deal of love," Sloan explained.

"What are you gifting him?" I asked.

"We thought we'd wait a while," Erik told me. "There's going to be enough going on down here. Plus, it gives us a chance to think about it."

"I want to be there."

"I think we'll all be there when it happens."

Scott stood quietly as we spoke, watching the other children play with their pale auras fluttering around them.

Sloan sighed gently. "I think it's best we called it a day. The kids are getting restless."

"Are they staying long?" I asked, curiously.

"They're here until tomorrow evening."

"Am I good to come over and spend time with them?"

"Of course."

I looked back to Scott. "Ready to go home?"

She nodded but her eyes flicked over to Archer, who was leaning against the wall, watching us all.

I pulled her close, gently this time, and wrapped the black around us but not in time to miss Archer raising his hands to wave her goodbye.

Once we were back in the house, Scott pulled away from me quickly, and I could sense the chaotic anger that pulsed through her. She hadn't been this angry in weeks.

"What have I done now?" I almost rolled my eyes.

"Honestly? You have to ask?"

"Well, technically, no. But you get so mad when I rummage through your head so at the risk of pissing you off further, I will repeat the question. What have I done now?"

She let out an exasperated scream. "Why, Grayson, was I the only other person in red, apart from your family? I felt like an utter idiot."

"That's what you're angry about?" I asked, surprised.

"Yes! That's what I'm angry about! Larkin and Hunter and the rest of the godsdamn room looking at me like I've done something wrong." She started to pace. "Everyone else was in green!"

"I know."

"You knew?"

I took a moment before confirming. "Yes, I knew."

"So, you knew everyone would be in green and that only your family would be in red, and you still told me to wear red?"

"Correct."

There was nothing for me to be angry about, so I let her yell and pace while I stood and watched her. It was fascinating; the things that worried, irritated, and angered this woman.

"Gray! I'm not being part of whatever game you're playing to piss off Hunter."

My brow furrowed. "I wasn't playing a game."

"Sure, because Hunter and Larkin sure think it's something you'd do to wind them up. I'm not being humiliated by you so you can get some enjoyment out of it."

Her anger was morphing. There was a quiver in her voice as then anger turned into upset at being embarrassed in front of a room full of people.

I stepped towards her, and she stopped pacing, sticking her hands out, warning me to keep away. She wasn't crying, but her eyes became glassy, and I didn't know how to deal with someone when they cried.

"I wasn't trying to embarrass you," I told her calmly. "On my duties as a God, I swear that wasn't my intention."

"What was your intention then, Gray? Because you knew what you were doing."

"I wanted people to know you were with me. I wanted them to know you belonged to me, especially after Ignacio —"

"Excuse me?" The sadness was replaced by anger again, and I was struggling to keep up with her. "I do not *belong* to anyone. Do you understand me? And I sure as fuck do not belong to you!"

Scott turned on her heel and walked out of the room.

"Scott!" I called after her, following her steps into the hallway. "Quentin, wait! I still don't see the problem."

She didn't look at me as she climbed the stairs. "Oh, fuck off, Gray, and stay away from me!"

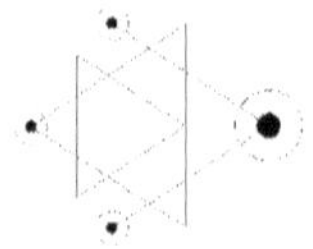

Scott wouldn't even look at me. She moved around the house in silence, aside from the slamming doors. I usually thrived off the anger, but I couldn't understand why she'd be so angry over such a small thing.

It wasn't my concern. I had better things to preoccupy myself with.

"I miss you, monsters!" I said, lounging on the sofa at Erik's place while his children clambered over me. All except for Beckett, who, as a teenager, believed he was too old to join in with the mess his younger siblings made.

"Do you think you'll have more?" I asked Erik.

Sloan beat him to the answer. "Definitely."

"She still refuses to tell me how many," Erik mumbled as Cato fussed in his arms. He rocked the baby gently. "Are you up for more nieces and nephews? More godchildren?"

I laughed at the question. Erik and Sloan's children were my life. Much to Hunter's dismay, Erik had made it clear I was his first choice as godparent, and I wouldn't let them down.

Cato continued to fuss, and Erik kissed the top of his head.

"Let me take him," Sloan said. "I think he needs to feed and sleep." She took their latest addition out of her husband's arms.

"Can you take them all for a little while?" Erik asked. "I want to speak to Grayson."

Sloan shot him a look and nodded. "Come on, little ones."

The brood followed her out of the room, and I straightened up. Without the kids around, the unease and anxiety rose again because Erik would only want to discuss one thing.

Most people assumed I had the most difficult job in the family, but I'd come to expect disaster at every turn, and I revelled in it. Erik's responsibility, on the other hand, was two-fold because love could be wonderful and exhilarating, but it could also be damagingly heart breaking.

I'd seen the early days when the heartbreak made him fall apart. We learned to dampen the sense of feeling so we could continue with our lives. When Erik learned to control it, he was happier, but he was wavering again.

As a general rule of thumb, we didn't interfere in each other's lives. No Gods did unless they were directly asked, but Erik was my little brother and boundaries were always blurry, so I had no doubt he'd let himself into my affairs more than I'd have considered polite.

"What happened between the both of you?" he asked, and I tensed. Erik leaned forward. "You looked very cosy yesterday. When Scott held Cato and you… You'd make such a good husband and father, Gray. Despite what the others think, you have a big heart."

"You're seeing things that aren't there. I don't wish to discuss this."

"Well, we are," Erik said, in a show of strength. "You need to keep your emotions in check, or the others are going to ask questions."

It was rare that he told me what to do, but this was Erik's element. And maybe he could help rid me of the nagging feeling I had.

"I made her angry," I blurted out.

Erik looked as confused as I felt. "Yes," he said. "That's what you do."

"No. I mean, I made her angry when I wasn't trying to."

He blinked a few times and asked, "How?"

Letting out a deep breath, I said, "She thought I asked her to wear red because I wanted to embarrass her in front of everyone."

"It was a stupid move."

"It was not! I didn't try to humiliate her. I was trying to prove a point to Ignacio."

"What point were you trying to prove?" Erik asked, eyes narrowing.

"That she's mine."

He rubbed his hands down his face and looked at me. "You need to stop."

"I know the rules."

"Do you?"

"Yes, Erik. I just don't always follow them."

Erik shook his head. "She's been through enough."

"What do you mean?"

"It's not my place to say, but she's been through enough and she doesn't need you adding to it."

"We're both adults, Erik. We both know what this is."

"Do you? I've never seen you so possessive of a being. Things, sure, but never another being. Please, Gray. Just let the girl be."

"Why are you making it sound like it's all down to me?"

"Isn't it?"

"You tell me. She seems to be as eager as I am."

"But you should know better."

"We grant people's desires. That's all I do for her."

"She doesn't pray to you!"

"She still wants me!"

The conversation had broken down, and as the anger flared, auras sparked into life.

Green wisps moved in front of Erik, and we turned to see Sloan, childless, standing in the room.

"Grayson," she said firmly. "I'd appreciate you not starting a fight today. I think we're both too tired for that."

I dropped my aura, and so did Sloan.

"Do either of you want to tell me what's going on?" I asked them, trying to control my anger.

"Scott," Erik said quietly.

"Ah," Sloan said.

I fixed Sloan with a stare, and she fidgeted. Erik opened an arm to her, and she joined him on the arm of the sofa.

"I just want you to steer clear of her," Sloan told me carefully.

"WHY?"

"Grayson, don't raise your voice at her," Erik warned me. My brother would get into a fight with ease if it boiled down to his wife.

"Why am I meant to stay away from her? Because she might suffer a bit of heartbreak? Because I'll get in trouble with the council?" I asked, dialling back.

Sloan sighed. "It's more than that."

"Sloan?" Erik looked at her.

I leaned forward. "Share with the group, Sloan."

"I don't have a definite answer," she mumbled. "But I don't think Quentin is mortal."

"What?" Erik spluttered. "You didn't mention this."

"At least not fully mortal."

"You're crazy." I laughed.

"Grayson!" Erik warned me again.

"So, she's what then?" I asked. "Part nymph?"

Sloan looked at Erik, and he squeezed her hand gently. "Go on, love," he encouraged.

"I think she might be a demigoddess."

I stood up from the sofa, laughing. "You need more sleep because that's impossible."

"Is it?" she asked.

"Erik, talk to your wife."

"What makes you think that?" Erik asked.

"When we touched, there was something there," Sloan explained. "Her conception didn't feel mortal. It happened all too fast and then —"

"There's more?" I said incredulously.

"She'll have children, but they don't feel mortal either."

"It's not possible!" I began to pace the room. "It's not possible because we destroyed every demigod centuries ago. We haven't been allowed here for hundreds of years to avoid the creation of anymore."

Demigods were dangerous. Not fully mortal and not fully

divine, they had the best of both worlds. They learned how to hide their divinity to live among mortals and then caused trouble of catastrophic proportions. To stop it, all the elite had destroyed them and ensured no more would be made.

"You have no proof," I said, stopping to look at her. "She's completely ordinary."

"Is she, Grayson?" Sloan asked softly. "You don't think it's strange how she's had an alarming amount of success."

"She's worked hard."

Sloan laughed. "I don't deny it, but it still doesn't sit right with me."

"Fine. Let me indulge in your madness. Who?"

"I have my theories."

"Who, Sloan?"

"Mallory."

Mallory was Elva's younger cousin. A minor Goddess who'd been responsible for greed.

Sloan pushed on. "Quentin is how old?"

"Twenty-seven," I answered without hesitation.

"Mallory ceased to exist twenty-six years ago, and we never knew why."

"Elva said she requested it and we can't deny a direct request from another God when it comes to our responsibilities."

"But don't you remember how Mallory was?"

It was difficult to forget Mallory. She'd visit Elva regularly until they'd argued over something, and then she rarely visited upper Elysia, preferring to stay with the minor Gods.

We saw little of her for months and when she returned, Erik had said he felt such a sense of love and heartbreak, but he never asked her what happened. None of us had, and then it was too late.

"I don't believe you," I said.

"You don't have to but if she is… If she is a demigoddess, then that's even more reason to stay away from her, Gray."

"And why is that?"

"Archer," Erik said. We both turned to look at him. "Keep

Archer away from her. If it's true and he finds out, he's going to find a way to use her."

I sank back onto the sofa. "We need proof first. I need proof."

"I plan to look next time we're in Elysia. And Gray, perhaps you could speak to Elva," Sloan suggested.

I nodded.

"I'm sorry," she continued. "I want my family to be safe, and that means staying away from her, Gray. Please."

TWENTY SIX

GRAYSON

It was late when I arrived back at Scott's house, close to midnight. The conversation with Sloan and Erik ricocheted around my head. It was an impossibility. Sloan must have sensed it wrong. Maybe the pregnancy had made her less perceptive.

The shuffling from the kitchen was loud, and I stood quietly in the doorway, under the cover of darkness, and watched Scott.

She pushed herself up onto the counter, hissing in pain as

she bashed her leg on the edge. Getting unsteadily to her feet, she reached up on top of the cabinet, fingers searching for a box just out of her grasp.

One thing that struck me most about Scott was her inability to ask for help. Whereas others sought it at the first sign of trouble, Scott exhausted every possibility before she reluctantly called in reinforcements.

After a few more minutes of searching for the box of coffee capsules, she sighed and dropped her arm. Silently, she stood on the counter, and then her thoughts drifted to me. She contemplated swallowing her pride to get a fix.

Without a word, I wrapped my aura around myself and returned to my room. Perching on the edge of the bed, I dropped my head in my hands.

Of all the people that could have worked on this project, of course, we'd stumble onto the demigoddess.

No.

She wasn't divine.

The creak of the flooring gave her away, and I picked my head out of my hands to look at her.

"If you're here for a fight, Scott, then I hate to disappoint you, but I'm not in the mood," I told her.

"I don't want a fight. I wanted to ask if you could grab something from the top of the cabinet for me?" she said, and then quickly added, "Please."

"What is it?" I played along, although I already knew.

"Coffee," she responded sheepishly.

"It's a filthy habit you need to kick. It's almost midnight."

"I don't sleep much, anyway. I was going to try to do some more work."

She didn't sleep. I often heard her pottering around her room and walking up and down the stairs. When she did sleep, it was restless, and I was curious about what kept her away from peace.

"Is something wrong?" she asked, looking at me properly.

I didn't respond.

"Do you want to talk about it?" she said, stepping into the

room.

“Not really.”

“It might help.”

“I highly doubt it.”

“Okay.”

She sighed and turned away. But I couldn’t let her leave. Scott presented herself as a mystery. A physical manifestation of everything I stood against. If that were true, if she was what Sloan thought her to be, then this obsession had stepped beyond dangerous and become fatal.

My aura swept across the room, dark and strong, wrapping around her waist and pulling her back towards me. Scott stood between my legs, and my hands found her hips. There was something comforting about touching her. Like if I had physical contact with her, it cemented that she was nothing more than a mortal.

The need to touch her was always there. The moment she walked into the same room, there was an urge to lay my hands on her. Our communication skills were poor but when I touched her, I conveyed everything I thought and felt. My displeasures and my desires.

“Stay,” I said.

It wasn’t a demand, but it wasn’t a question. This wasn’t like the other times I’d kept her with me. It wasn’t full of want and lust.

“Just stay,” I repeated.

She nodded, and I stood up from the bed, letting her go and pulling back the duvet.

“I sleep on the left,” she told me.

“So do I.”

“I’m your guest.”

That coaxed a smile from me. “This is your house, Scott.”

She shrugged and climbed into the bed, taking the left side. I growled in irritation, stripping down to underwear before appearing on the right side of the bed and muttering, “You’re a pain in the ass.”

Scott flashed me a grin, cheeks red, and I rolled my eyes, but the melancholy lifted slightly. That smile she possessed was rarely shared. The last time she'd used it was with Cassidy and Sophie. I wasn't someone that was allowed the private slice of Scott that bled pure joy.

"If you don't want to talk about it, then what do you want to do?" she asked.

"Sleep."

She sighed. "Coffee is a better option, but fine."

She sank down into the bed and rolled over, facing away from me. She knew I'd gone to see Erik and Sloan today. It should have put me in a better mood, but all it'd done was tie me in knots and Scott had read the room.

As a God, it was no surprise that I could read her mood, but when she returned the gesture, it always caught me off guard. More than once, she'd dialled back her temper after I'd returned from a council meeting. Like she didn't want to continue to poke the bear. Almost like she cared.

Suddenly, I placed an arm around her waist and pulled her flush against my body so that we spooned, needing her close. I buried my face in her hair and placed a kiss on the back of her head.

"I'm sorry I made you so angry," I whispered.

I still didn't understand it, but the radio silence had driven me insane. If she wanted an apology, then she could have it. In the privacy of her home, in the intimacy of us pressed together, I folded.

Scott relaxed in my arms, and slowly she turned around to face me. I didn't let go of her but loosened my grip to allow her to move. We laid there, face to face, tips of our noses touching. Her long eyelashes brushed against my skin, leaving a faint ticklish sensation.

"Tell me everything next time," she breathed.

"I will," I agreed.

"I'm not a possession."

"I know." I didn't want to fight with her tonight. After a few moments, I asked her, "Do you want to be here, Quentin?"

Her name rolled off my tongue. I enjoyed being able to address her by a moniker she refused everyone else. Despite her refusal at being a possession, I'd marked her as mine and that meant I had privileges others were denied.

She looked at me curiously. "Like, on the planet?"

"No. Nothing so deep. I can't cope with that tonight. Do you want to be here? With me, right now?"

"Yes," she said firmly. "I don't do things unless I want to."

Nodding, I bridged the gap, kissing her. Quentin's hand rested on the side of my face as she returned the gesture. Legs tangled together as we laid there, making out and allowing the physicality to ground us.

"You should get some sleep," I told her, breaking away.

It could have so easily turned into something more. Pinned beneath my body, I could have made Quentin scream my name and left us both satisfied, but the conversation with Erik and Sloan kept me sober.

"So should you," she replied, brushing her lips against mine.

The gentleness stirred something inside my chest. I didn't know how to handle softness when my life was encompassed by poor decisions and viciousness.

"I'm an immortal being who doesn't necessarily need sleep."

"I will if you do," she compromised, her fingers trailing down my cheek.

I closed my eyes and chuckled quietly. "Alright. Goodnight, Quentin."

"Night, Gray."

Leaving my arm around her waist, I waited. Her breathing slowed, and her stream of consciousness stopped.

Opening my eyes again, I took her in. Funnily enough, this was the most peaceful she'd ever looked. Scott was a ball of energy most of the time. She was either working or at Sal's. Even when she afforded herself time to watch Netflix, her mind was still ticking. It was like something inside of her refused to stop and I wished I knew what drove her to constant unease.

Cautiously, I brushed some hair from her face, and she stirred, an arm coming around me as she nestled against my body.

Affectionate wouldn't be a word used to describe her. Not unless you'd caught glimpses of it the way I had. She hugged Sophie tightly, squeezed her brother's hand, cried when Charlotte shared happy news. Behind all the walls and armour, Quentin was a woman filled with love who gave it away sparingly.

The longer I looked at her, the more I was sure that Sloan was going mad.

This woman may have been extraordinary by mortal standards, but there wasn't a single thing I could find that would make her divine.

She was messy and unorganised. She had the worst temper I'd encountered. She was never on time for anything other than work. Divinity equated perfection and Quentin wasn't perfect. She was a fucking mess.

"For your sake, Quentin, I really hope I'm right."

TWENTY SEVEN

QUENTIN

It'd been a few days since the night I'd fallen asleep with Gray, but neither of us had discussed it. It was as if it'd never happened. He was back to his snarky ways and whatever crumb of vulnerability had shone through had well and truly evaporated. And I was grateful. Whatever laid between Gray and I was uncomplicated and that was how it needed to stay.

Not that there was anything between us.

I had split my time between the lab and with Sloan, Erik, and Cato. Babies weren't really my thing, but he was cute as a button and generally well behaved. His development was much quicker than an average human baby, and at a cellular level, it was fascinating to observe. The question was what mechanisms were behind the rapid growth that then stalled entirely to make them immortal. Several papers on telomeres littered the office and the house, but I was struggling to find an answer that related to these deities.

That was the question that fuelled my curiosity so much so that I was starting to lose track of time in the lab. My starts became earlier and my finishes were past five o'clock, but I didn't complain because this was what I loved beyond anything else.

So when Gray turned up at the door of the tissue culture lab, I jumped.

"Can I come in?" he asked.

"If you put a lab coat on."

He abided by the rule and shrugged on a coat, walking into the room. "We have a meeting."

I didn't look at him but returned my focus to my work. The flasks were stacked to the left, all of them with Cato's cells in. Six needed a media change, and another three needed to be emptied and cryopreserved. Well plates were set up earlier in the day for scratch tests tomorrow and I felt on top of everything for the first time in weeks.

"What time is it?" I asked him distractedly.

"Nine."

That got my attention. "It's nine already? Shit."

He took the seat next to me.

"Why have you got a meeting this late?" I asked, trying to pick up the pace.

"Hunter's request, since it concerns us returning to Elysia," Gray explained, and I almost dropped the flask in my hand.

"You're going back?"

There was a small knot of panic in me, and I couldn't figure out why. The past three months, I'd grown accustomed to having Gray around, and I guessed I wasn't entirely sure I was ready to go back to living on my own again.

"For Cato's gifting ceremony," Gray clarified.

The knot eased, and I continued with my work. "Why aren't you at the meeting?"

"Gareth asked me to come and get you."

"Why?"

"How would I know?"

I placed everything down and looked at him. "Because I know you and I would bet money that you had a look at his thoughts."

"This constant character assassination is very damaging to my ego. Now say something nice about me."

"There's nothing nice to say."

A wicked glint came to his eye. "We both know that's not true."

I grabbed the flasks out of the hood and put them back in the incubator. I could finish this after the meeting. Diving back into the hood, I capped the bottle of medium and dropped it in the water bath.

"Are you going to tell me what he wants?" I asked, snapping off the gloves and putting them in the bin. Hanging up the lab coat, I washed my hands, with Gray mimicking my actions.

"He's coming with us," Gray said.

"Wait, what? He's going with you? To Elysia?"

Gray nodded.

"Shit," I mumbled.

"And we'd like you to come too."

I walked straight into the lab door and Gray barked out a laugh. Once I'd recovered, I bit the insides of my cheeks and opened the door before walking through it.

"Why would he want me there?" I asked.

"I might have put in a few words."

"Gray! Why?"

"You want proof so I thought I would give you proof."

He had me there, although we'd already been banking away proof slowly as the results from analysis trickled in.

Gray preyed on the silence between us. “Scared, Scott?”

He knew how to bait me.

“Absolutely not,” I said.

“Prove it.”

We walked into Gareth’s office to find Hunter was already there. The meeting lasted a full two hours as I was briefed on where and when and how and why.

Originally it was just Gareth who would go to witness the tradition, but Hunter worried about the sanity of a mortal in Elysia alone and decided that it would be better for someone else to accompany him. Gray volunteered me, and with Gareth and Hunter’s approval, it was done. Insanity loved company.

In two days’ time, the hosting would be reversed. Gareth would stay with Hunter and Larkin, and I’d live with Gray. All that was left to do was wait for the weekend.

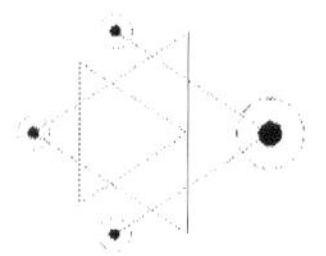

When Saturday arrived, Gray took us to the institute, and I shook as we stood on the ground floor. Whether it was from the nerves or the four cups of coffee, I couldn’t tell.

“Stop fidgeting,” Gray hissed.

“I can’t help it.”

He rolled his eyes in response.

Slowly, we were joined by other Gods and Gareth as they gathered to return home.

The Gods pressed together and I felt Gray’s hands on my hips, pressing up behind me. I subtly reached for one of his hands to pull it away, but he had an iron grip. I glanced around, only to have Ignacio catch my eye and wink, setting my cheeks aflame.

I don’t know who started the process or how long it took, but there was a blinding mix of colours and a heady rush that I’d never experienced before. When the light dimmed and my eyes adjusted, Gray removed his hands from me. The other Gods left in bursts of their aura, glad to be home.

"Come on then, Scott. Don't be shy." Gray patted me on the ass, and I swatted him before taking in the view.

It wasn't all clouds like people depicted paradise as, but it was beautiful enough to take my breath away and make my eyes sting with tears.

We stood in a park filled with the most vibrant colours that I was incapable of describing. Trees full of green leaves and flowers in bloom. Something inside of me tugged, as if there was a distant familiarity to it.

Gray placed a gentle hand on the small of my back. "Welcome to Elysia. As much as I'd love to leave you standing here, I'd very much like to go home and I'd be a terrible host if I didn't take you with me. So, shall we?"

I turned my head and noticed that he seemed more relaxed in this environment.

"Of course." I nodded.

The black surrounded us, and the scent of bonfires and books calmed me. When Gray's aura disappeared, we were outside a large gothic mansion on top of a cliff. The beauty of it was in stark contrast to the park we'd just been in. It was darker, moodier, and fit Gray to a tee.

"You live here?" I stumbled, taking it all in as he walked us through iron gates.

Even the weather was darker in his domain, oppressive and static, as if on the verge of a thunderstorm.

"Mhm," he confirmed. "Do you like it?"

"It looks amazing."

I felt embarrassed at the fact he'd been staying at my house when his usual residence was so opulent.

He placed a hand on my back again and guided me up the stairs and into the house.

"Let me show you to your room."

"Okay," I agreed.

He walked confidently through the house and I drank it in,

surprised at how sleek everything was. Gray was chaotic and well kept — a walking contradiction. I didn't know what I'd expected his home to be like, but I'd never imagined it like this.

Eventually, he stopped at a room.

"You'll stay here," he informed me. "If there's anything you need, let me know. My room is down the hall if you find yourself lonely —"

"Don't even think about it."

He leaned down and placed a kiss on my neck, whispering, "I'm always thinking about it."

Giving him a gentle shove, I got some distance, and Gray laughed heartily.

"Freshen up, and then I can show you around Elysia," he said.

I did as he said, taking my time to scope the bedroom and en-suite. When I finished, I knew I should have found Gray, but I wanted to be nosey. What was his home like? What would the God who was destined to destroy everything want his residence to be?

Walking through the corridors, it came as no surprise that everything was decorated in black. Photo frames, chandeliers, door handles. Delicate filigree design touched corners and fixtures, giving the space an understated classiness. The floors were dark herringbone wood, and my footsteps echoed around me as I explored.

On the ground floor, I peeked into the rooms. A living room that was twice the size of mine, a study, and a library. I stopped at a large room that was completely empty aside from a single chair at the back and placed in the centre. Faint rays of sunlight broke through the clouds and filtered through the windows, bathing the room in a soft, golden glow.

"I should have known you couldn't follow simple instructions." A pair of arms snaked around me, and Gray's chest was against my back. "Impressed?" he asked smugly.

"Wondering how you and your ego fit on that chair," I shot.

"It's a throne."

In less than a second, he was sitting on it, and I was sitting on his lap.

"Stop that," I scolded, but I rested against his body.

"My home, so we play by my rules," he reminded me.

I looked out on the space again from the new vantage point. "Why do you even have a room like this? It's not like you have mortals come up here."

"No, but we all have one for special occasions. Birthdays and the like. We'll use this room tomorrow for Cato's gifting ball."

I shifted in his arms to face him. But whatever words I'd prepared were lost. I'd seen Gray in casual clothing, and I'd seen him in what I'd considered formal clothing, but this was something else.

He was dressed in an ornately decorated doublet. Black on black and on his head, nestled against his tufts of dark hair, was a black crown.

"Do you approve, Quentin?" he asked, his nose running along my throat and making me turn pink.

He screamed royalty, and I couldn't untangle my thoughts.

"Looks like I'm not the only one who can't stop thinking about it," he murmured against my skin. "I suggest I take you on the tour unless you'd rather spend your day here with me."

"Tour. Now," I said, swallowing hard.

Gray let me go and we both stood. He straightened out his clothes and caught me looking at him again.

"You can change your mind," he teased, grinning wolfishly.

"Shut up and get moving."

He spent the entire day taking me around upper Elysia, the highest heaven. Everything took my breath away, and my resolve was wavering. It was hard not to want to give them my devotion when I walked among their homes and all they held dear.

We sat down to dinner at a restaurant. Food was a luxury here, something to do rather than a necessity. The plates were intricate and mouth-watering, and I wasn't sure how I was meant to go back to my limited repertoire in the kitchen.

I watched the way people acknowledged Gray. More than once, we'd been interrupted until he told a server he wanted no more disturbances.

"I'm not sure Holden would approve of me taking you to dinner," Gray commented from across the table.

"It's just work."

"He doesn't like me very much."

"You're a difficult being to like."

"You have no problems."

"I tolerate you."

"For the sex?"

"For the sex."

"I feel used."

I laughed, and Gray joined in. Low and husky, the sound lit a fire deep in my stomach.

I wanted to stay away from him and every cell in my body knew I should, but Gray was like a drug. Everything about him drew me in. He was quick-witted and sharp and charming and undeniably good looking. He fought me at every step, but I enjoyed it and I know he did too. It was as if we were evenly matched, although he'd deny it.

"What happens tomorrow?" I asked, trying to keep us on the straight and narrow.

He leaned back in his chair.

"We meet with Erik and Sloan, and they gift Cato his responsibility?" I guessed.

"Not quite. We gather at the reflecting pool. Erik and Sloan have an idea of what they'd like to gift him, but it's not really in our hands. Most of the time, we're in line with the pool, but now and then, it has ideas of its own."

"What about the aura colour?"

"You'll watch the pool change colour when Cato is given his gift. As he grows older, he'll learn how to summon and control it."

Desserts were placed in front of us.

"Then I'll host the gifting ball," Gray continued when we were left alone. "Actually, we'll need to find you something to wear for that —"

There was a forkful of cake halfway to my mouth, but I

stopped. "I don't trust you with my outfit choice. Plus, I have a dress."

"I told you I'd give you the full story from now on."

I thought back to that night we laid in bed together when he didn't seem like his usual self. He was quieter, less aggressive, and the words held more weight.

"To honour Cato, you'll need to wear whatever colour his aura is. Everyone will be dressed in that colour. I give you my word."

"… Okay."

I lifted the fork back to my mouth and savoured the most delicious slice of fudge cake I'd tasted, letting out a moan of pleasure.

"Scott, am I ever going to be able to take you anywhere?" Gray shifted uncomfortably in his seat, and I grinned.

"Problem, Gray?"

"Nothing you can't fix."

"Dream on."

By the time we finished and returned to Gray's, I was yawning.

"Maybe you should head to bed. It'll be a busy day tomorrow," Gray said, running his fingers through my hair.

"What about you?"

"I need to visit Elva and sort out some arrangements before tomorrow."

"Can I help with anything?"

"I have it all in hand, Scott. Go on up and I'll see you in the morning."

Halfway up the stairs, I turned back to him. "Thank you for everything today, Gray. I really enjoyed myself."

"You're welcome."

Upstairs, I changed into my pyjamas and crawled into bed. Sleep found me easily, but not long after, I woke to the sound of whispers. I tried to ignore them, but it was no use. Getting up from bed, I followed them out into the hallway.

"Gray?"

Nothing. He must still be with Elva.

The whispers were a rush, and a pulling sensation joined them. My feet moved of their own accord. Even though I didn't know where I was heading, it was like my body knew where it needed to be.

It lured me out of Gray's house and barefoot through the streets before I reached the reflecting pool. A beautiful body of water that was crystal clear and mirrored the night sky above.

The desire to step in was overwhelming. The whispers were no longer soft and gentle but roared around me. I had to step in. I needed to obey.

My feet hit the waters, ice cold and making me shiver, but I didn't stop. Instead, there was a desire to wade in deeper.

"QUENTIN!"

I heard my name, but it didn't deter me. I only stopped when I was swept up from the water and into Gray's arms. The noise disappeared as he held me and the waters around us turned a deep black colour.

"I don't know what happened," I said, confused as to why I was in the pool.

He moved out of the water and up onto the shore. Erik and Sloan were standing on the banks with Elva, looking horrified.

"I'm so sorry," I said to him, realising I'd done something wrong.

Gray placed me on the ground, and the tug to return to the waters started again. It was like I was being dragged back towards it. Gray picked me up and it vanished.

"What's happening, Gray?" I asked, looking up at him.

It wasn't often that I got scared, but I wasn't in control of my actions and the panic was setting in.

"You're shielding her," Elva said. "As long as you're with her, it can't sense her."

"I told you this would happen!" Erik yelled, looking furious. "Is this enough proof for you, Gray? On top of everything else, we've seen tonight. Will you let it be now? Will you listen?"

Gray growled, "I'm taking her home. We'll discuss this

tomorrow."

He didn't wait for a response before we were back in his home, in his room. Gray placed me down on the edge of the bed and kneeled before me.

"What happened?" he asked seriously.

"I have no idea. I fell asleep and then I woke up to voices. It was like I had to listen to them. I had to get in the water."

He squeezed his eyes shut for a second and then opened them again. "Did anything happen? Did you see anything?"

"No. I stepped in. I would have gone further if you didn't show up," I whispered. "What's happening?"

Gray looked up at me. "It's a lot for a mortal to take in, Quentin. You'll stay with me or one of the others from now on, understand?"

I nodded, and he rose from the floor. "You're staying with me tonight."

I didn't argue, but I hated the fact that I appeared so weak in front of him. I wanted to tell him I'd be fine, but the loss of control had rattled me. Crawling up the bed, I got under the covers and Gray joined me.

"Gray?"

"What?"

"What did Erik mean when he asked about proof?"

I hadn't realised I was shaking until Gray took me into his arms and rubbed my back. It was a gesture of comfort, and I rested my head on his chest. I hadn't had a panic attack in a year, and I used his heartbeat to steady my nerves.

After a few moments, Gray answered the question, "It's the same argument he's been having with me since we got down there. No mortal and God should have relations."

"But what does that have to do with what happened?"

"He doesn't think mortals should be up here."

There was a hesitation in all his answers, and I wished I knew what he was thinking. If I had to guess, Gray thought I was weaker than he first assumed and that he was correct when he met me. That thought alone made my heart sink as we laid in silence.

TWENTY EIGHT

GRAYSON

I'd heard every single thought that ran through her head, and she couldn't have been more wrong. Quentin wasn't weak.

The Goddess in her had woken the moment the pool realised someone unclaimed was nearby. Her divinity wasn't strong enough to be sensed by the pool when she was near a pure God, so the moment I'd left her alone, it began to call to her. If we hadn't reached her in time, the whole of Elysia would have been in uproar.

"Don't worry about Erik. It isn't your fault," I told her as she laid next to me.

Unsurprisingly, she had a soft spot for my brother. Aside from panicking over her loss of control, Quentin worried that she'd upset Erik.

"Will it happen again?" she asked.

"Not if you stay with us."

"But what if you need to be somewhere?"

Quentin was nestled against me in bed and thin wisps of black grew from me as a heat ran from my body to hers.

"You have my mark," I told her. "A ward to keep you safe."

"Do you think Gareth felt it?"

"I doubt it. Hunter and Larkin would've been with him all day." I sighed. "Scott, try to get some rest. I promise things are fine. You got overwhelmed."

I couldn't tell her. Not yet. We still hadn't decided what to do with the information.

I'd spent the evening in talks with Elva, Erik, and Sloan, explaining what I believed to be a preposterous theory. But Elva filled in the blanks and when she brought out Mallory's old robes, a simple touch allowed Sloan and Erik to see everything unfold.

Mallory visited mortals with only a single God knowing her whereabouts. Archer, God of secrets. She had felt out of place in Elysia and sought solace on earth. She'd fallen in love and became pregnant, but the mortal died before she could tell him. Finding herself in a bind, she stayed hidden on earth and gave birth before giving up the child, knowing what its fate would be if she brought it back to Elysia.

In her grief and heartache, she visited Elva and requested death, having lost the man she loved and unable to watch her child from a distance. Elva had no option but to grant her cousin's direct request.

Quentin had spent twenty-seven years on earth and passed through the care system until Alexander and Vanessa Scott, two surgeons who struggled to conceive, adopted her into their family as a younger sister for their adopted son.

Her time on earth, coupled with her lack of faith, had led to the suppression of her divinity, but bringing her back to Elysia had caused it to stir.

"I'm sorry," she whispered into my chest.

It wasn't often I waded into Quentin's thoughts because I enjoyed her telling me things. It felt like a victory when she offered what ran through her mind, but all bets were off. She believed she'd inconvenienced me. That people were angry with her. That there was something wrong with her and that she was weak.

"Stop," I demanded. "You'll drive yourself and me completely mad."

I stroked her hair, and she curled up closer to my body, limbs tangling together as she got comfortable. After a while, she fell asleep, and I spent the rest of the night watching the demigoddess in my arms.

Early into the morning, Quentin stirred, burying herself into my side, and I laughed softly. Her eyes fluttered open.

"What now?" she muttered groggily.

"I didn't take you as someone who liked to cuddle."

"You never stick around long enough to find out."

"You never stick around long enough to let me find out."

Neither of us hung around after we got what we wanted, but the warmth of her body through the night made me wonder if I should stop by longer.

Not that Erik would let me stop by at all after last night's fiasco.

At the same time it hit me, the penny dropped for Quentin too because she quickly untangled herself, sitting up and running her hands through her hair.

"Don't worry," I said, noting she looked more fragile than usual. "I won't let anything happen."

I surprised myself with how much force was behind the words, but it was true. I wouldn't let anything happen to her while we were up here.

She smiled weakly and got out of bed, and immediately, I missed her presence by my side. The small pockets of vulnerability selfishly made me want more. I longed to keep her at my side and unravel her until she inducted me into the inner circle that was so elusive to reach. I wanted to matter to her.

"I should get ready," she said, pulling her hair up.

"Yes. You brought a black dress with you?"

"Yeah. And Gareth's going to be in blue, right?"

"He'll be wearing his host's colours," I confirmed and watched as Quentin left my room, leaning over to get a magnificent view as she went.

As per usual, I was the first to get ready. Her time-keeping was truly appalling and showed no signs of improvement, no matter how many comments I made.

When she finally made it down the stairs, I struggled to keep my thoughts in check. Her punctuality was the last thing on my mind. The black dress skimmed over her curves, clinging to her like a second skin and had a generous, plunging neckline.

She didn't notice the effect she had on me today. Instead, she looked nervous and watched her feet as she came down the stairs cautiously.

"Get out of your head, Scott," I told her, using my aura to tip her chin upwards as she came off the last step. "You're in control."

At least, she would be if she stayed around the Gods. And I had no plans to let her out of my sight. Especially when she looked like a temptress.

We left the house for the reflecting pool. My teeth clenched as I silently cursed the lack of time to appreciate her. Along with the others, we stood on the banks with the water crystal clear, reflecting the skies above. Unlike last night, Quentin stood next to me without a problem.

"Maybe we should tell Hunter what happened," Quentin suggested when she waved hello to Gareth.

"No! No. We don't want him thinking this entire project is a bad idea."

She mulled the comment over before Gareth came towards her.

"How are you finding it?" he asked her.

"Intense," she replied.

"That's one way to describe it. You look beautiful, Scott."

"Thank you. You don't look too bad yourself."

Something pulled inside of me when he complimented her. I should have told her how she looked when she came down the stairs. Should have let her know she would take up many of my thoughts for the day and beyond.

"Are you okay?" Quentin asked. Her hand was on my arm, pulling my mind from the gutter.

"I'm fine."

It came out short and sharp, and she instantly dropped her hand from me. I wanted to grab it, but Erik and Sloan appeared, and I needed to focus.

My mood lifted considerably as my godchildren stumbled over in our direction. As I played with the children, I heard Quentin's voice.

"Oh, hello," she mumbled.

When I looked up, Tenley, Erik's only daughter and youngest until Cato, stared up at Quentin. She lifted her arms, and I watched the woman panic.

"She won't break," I said, amused at her reaction. "She just wants to be held. I can —"

"It's okay."

Quentin leaned down and scooped her up, placing the little girl on her hip, and Tenley laughed, wrapping her arms around Quentin's neck. Carefully, Quen moved towards me, and I felt Erik's eyes on us. There was a flash of warning in his blues. But who would pay attention to us when we were gathered here for Cato?

Tenley rested her head on Quen's shoulder, and I smirked. She wasn't a natural with children, and Ten had thrown her in at the deep end.

"What?" she asked, looking at me.

"Nothing."

Hunter moved forward to begin the gifting ceremony. The crowd comprised the elite, and minor Gods that had ascended from lower Elysia.

"It is our divine right, when we are born, to be bestowed a gift that mortals will call upon," Hunter's voice rang out clearly.

Erik cradled Cato in one arm while the other wrapped around Sloan. They were dressed in their colours, beaming proudly.

"Erik. Sloan. You have welcomed a new God among us. As head of the council, I ask on behalf of us all here today that you step into the pool and allow us to bear witness to the gift he shall carry for his eternal life."

The couple waded into the water, up to their waists. The calm pool pulsed. It swirled itself almost like a vortex around the trio, and I heard Quen gasp.

"They're fine," I whispered. "Keep watching."

My aura kept her steady as a rush of knowledge passed over us and left as quickly as it came. The water around the family spiralled quicker and changed from crystal clear to an electric blue, and the crowd around us burst into cheers and applause.

Quentin popped her fingers into her mouth and leaned away from Tenley to give a shrill whistle. I grinned and let my aura slink away from her waist.

The water calmed down to reveal my brother and his family, looking as happy as the rest of us.

"They chose knowledge?" Quen asked me.

"Intelligence."

"And his aura will be blue?"

"Precisely."

Hunter stood on the banks again and opened his arms wide. "May I be the first to present to you all, Cato, God of intelligence."

Another eruption of noise and Tenley wriggled out of Quen's arms as all the children rushed towards their parents who'd stepped onto dry land.

They made their way around the familiar faces before reaching us.

"Congratulations!" Quen greeted them.

I picked Cato out of Erik's arms. "You'll have enough brains for all of us. That might mean some extra work on your uncle Hunter's behalf."

"Grayson, stop corrupting my child before he can even speak," Erik scolded.

Sloan pulled Quen into a hug and asked, “How did you find it?”

“Fascinating,” she replied.

I bounced the baby gently and softly tried to persuade him I was his favourite uncle.

“Hand my son back over, Gray,” Erik said. “You’re stopping him from seeing everyone else.”

Placing a kiss on Cato’s head, I handed him back over carefully.

“We’ll see you later tonight,” Sloan said before they left to mingle with others.

“What happens now?” Quentin asked.

“We are going to get away and find you a dress for tonight.”

I took her hand and pulled her away from the crowd of people.

Being in Elysia, being at Cato’s gifting ceremony, made the blood in my veins sing with joy. When we were clear of the pool, clear of people, and in the silence of the streets, I pulled Quen into me and kissed her roughly. It took a split second for her to respond, moaning into my mouth before pulling away.

“Gray…”

Her cheeks were flushed pink as she looked around the empty streets.

“There’s no one here,” I assured her.

“It’s still a risk.”

Usually, I wouldn’t let her words stop me, but after last night, I needed to be cautious. Things between us were a relatively simple arrangement, but the knowledge of her divinity added an extra layer of complication into the mix.

Of course, if I could stop anyone else from finding out her true identity, there was no reason our arrangement couldn’t stay in place until I was back in Elysia permanently.

Her reservations were different from mine. She wanted to prove I had no sway over her, but we both knew that was a lie.

“You said we were going to find a dress,” she reminded me.

I sighed. “Are you saying you’d rather find a dress than have sex with me?"

"That's exactly what I'm saying."

She broke free of my arms and continued to walk down the path. I watched her for a few moments, dressed in black with wisps of my ward around her, hips swaying as she walked away. Quen looked like she belonged in Elysia as much as I did. I wondered if in another life…

I quickly shook the thoughts from my head, surprised that they'd flourished in the first place. That was a dangerous line of thought that didn't need entertaining. Quentin belonged back on earth with the rest of the ordinary mortals.

Jogging, I caught up with her and guided her towards a small boutique I knew Larkin and Sloan frequented. When we entered, a minor God appeared, bowing, and Quentin rolled her eyes. She'd done it every time she'd seen someone bow to me, and I enjoyed the fact it irritated her.

"Lord Grayson." The minor God looked at Quentin, tipping her head to the side. "Mortal?"

"No concern of yours," I told her briskly. "I'm looking for a dress for my nephew's gifting ball."

"Of course. Did you have anything in mind? Colour? Cut?"

"Blue. Something that hugs her figure."

"Gray," Quen started.

"Trust me."

Modesty wasn't really an option among the Gods. Not when you could have pride and ego on display. Plus, what she was wearing now wasn't exactly covering her curves, so why worry?

Ah.

Quentin's thoughts were loud and clear as she watched the minor God walk away.

It was one thing to have a dozen divinely attractive beings around you. It was another entirely when you were one of two people in Elysia who were so obviously flawed.

"Gray," she said. "Do I have to attend tonight?"

It wasn't often I'd seen her doubt herself, but I disliked it. She had no reason to, and I had no idea how to stop it.

"It'd be a shame if you didn't."

The minor God returned to us and led us through to a large changing room. On the rail sat a variety of blue dresses for Quentin to try on. Dropping into a chair in the room, I gestured to them.

"Knock yourself out," I told her before turning to the minor God. "You can leave us now."

"Are you sure there won't be anything else, sir?"

I looked at her, and she faltered under my gaze before bowing her head and leaving us alone.

"Well, we don't have all day," I said, turning back to Quen.

"Get out."

"Oh, please. I've seen you naked plenty of times."

She flushed again, and the doubt filled her mind, lifting me to my feet and causing me to stride over to her.

"Would you like to explain to me why you're so shy all of a sudden?" Placing my hands on her hips, I turned her to look at me, but she dropped her gaze. "Scott."

I kissed her neck gently, and she brought her hands up to my chest.

"Stop," she whispered.

"Is that what you want?" My teeth grazed along the soft flesh, and her pulse picked up. "You've never been shy around me."

One of my hands moved to her back and found the zipper of her dress, dragging it open.

"I'm still not shy around you," she told me quietly, and I smiled against her skin.

I peeled the dress from Quen's body, and she didn't resist. Instead, it slipped past her curves and dropped on the floor before she stepped out of it. I held her at arm's length and took her in, gaze travelling down her body, clad only in lace underwear and heels.

The inside of her forearms was decorated in marker — calculations and journal titles for when she didn't have scrap paper to hand. Stretch marks like forks of lightning creeped along her thighs and hips. Scars from old scrapes and a fresh bruise from where she hit her leg the other night stood out against her golden skin.

When I looked back up, I glanced past her to the full-length mirror and saw the blues of my eyes replaced by black and my aura uncoiling around me.

"See what you do to me?" I asked, bringing my focus back to her. "See how easily you can make me lose control?"

Quentin was so concerned about everything she'd seen here, and how she could compare. An old habit that was ingrained into her and she couldn't help herself from trying to figure out how she could be better.

But for me, there was no one like her. I couldn't recall any other being that made me lose control the way she had. It was why I kept returning to her when I told Erik that it'd only be once to get her out of my system. In a life where I'd grown accustomed to perfection, her every flaw became my kryptonite.

"Whatever is going on in your head." I pressed my lips against her forehead. "It needn't be. When I run my hands along your curves."

My hands slid along her sides, savouring the smooth skin, and she shivered.

"When I taste your lips."

I leaned down and kissed her, flicking my tongue along her plump bottom lip and earning a whimper.

"When I have you all to myself, I have pure perfection. Now, may I suggest you get dressed or I really won't be able to control myself."

A smile played on her lips, and I could sense her thoughts had calmed down.

"I'm glad you're at least trying to behave," she said.

I let go of her and as she walked towards the rail of dresses, she brushed her palm against my dick. It was already semi-hard from looking at her, but it throbbed in anticipation of her touch, wanting more.

I caught her wrist and dragged her back towards me roughly. "Don't start something you aren't prepared to finish."

"I'm not starting anything."

She looked up at me through her lashes, and I was glad to see her restored to former glory. So confident that she thought she could take me on, and I relished the challenge. But she should have known by now that she'd never win.

Bending down, I whispered in her ear, "Don't play coy, Scott. I could have you screaming my name in seconds."

She took in a sharp breath, and I knew she was thinking of what I could do to her. What I'd done to her before.

A knock on the door made us both stop.

"Would you like any help?" the minor God called.

"I don't believe so," I called back, then looked to Quentin. "I'm too selfish to share."

She laughed quietly, turning pink.

"I hate to hurry you, sir, but I have customers waiting," she said.

I let out a frustrated sigh. "The next time I have you, I plan to take my time." Straightening up, I called out, "We'll be out now."

Letting go of Quen, she stepped back into her dress, covering every delicious slope that I'd grown familiar with. I helped her zip it up, and she turned back around to face me.

"Gray, you can't go out there like that," she told me.

"Why not?"

"Look at you."

She stepped aside so I could look at myself in the mirror to see I hadn't regained control. It was difficult when my mind was running over everything I'd like to do to her.

Cupping her face with my hand, I said, "You do this to me."

I could feel it from her, the sense of pride she had in knowing how she could make me lose it entirely without doing much.

"You need to calm down," Quentin told me, straightening the tie at my neck.

She placed a hand on my chest, and I took a deep breath, trying to clear my head but struggling to do so.

"Promise me," I muttered.

"What?"

"Promise me, I can have you later."

This was stepping slightly out of our spoken agreement. Sex just happened between us. There were never plans or promises. One of us craved it and sought the other. This time, I was asking for her specifically. No spur of the moment but asking her to let me come to her after the festivities were over.

"Okay," she said eventually. "Okay. I promise."

The knowledge that she'd be mine later calmed me down enough that I regained control. Looking in the mirror, I ran a hand through my hair, smoothing it down again.

"Yeah, yeah. You're presentable enough," Quentin said, grabbing my arm. "Let's get out of here."

She led us out of the room, and the boutique was filled with beings that inhabited Elysia. She made a beeline for the door, and I caught the owner's eye on the way out.

"Third dress on the left," I instructed before leaving.

TWENTY NINE

QUENTIN

Gray's home was a flurry of people when we arrived, and he excused himself to help with the preparations for the evening.

I made my way to my room and took a cold shower, which was much needed after the stop at the boutique. The dress had been forgotten, so maybe I wouldn't need to attend tonight.

Drying my hair, I changed into pyjamas for comfort. I laid down on the bed and closed my eyes for a moment and when I opened them again, I realised I must have fallen asleep. I was snug under the covers, and on the pillow next to me, laid a box. Sitting up, I rubbed my eyes before looking at it again. There was a note pinned to it with Gray's swirling font.

If you need a hand, you know I'm always happy to help.

He must have come in when he'd finished setting up.

I pulled the box onto my lap and lifted the lid, sucking in a breath.

"Can't say he doesn't have good taste," I mumbled.

Pulling the dress out of the box, tissue paper fell around me on the bed. I didn't even notice this dress on the rail, but Gray must have and had it delivered. An electric blue strapless mermaid dress with gold detailing along the bodice. Like everything else here, it was painstakingly beautiful.

Getting out of bed, I got ready. By the time I was done, I could hear the voices of people downstairs and music carried itself up to the room.

My heels clicked down the hallway as I made my way to the stairs and onto the ground floor. The entire house seemed to be packed with people and I made my way through them without a worry, thanks to Gray's ward.

I'd no idea where he was as I wandered through the rooms slowly, searching for him. There were definitely more guests than I'd expected, but Gray's family was royalty, so people were eager to celebrate.

When I opened the door to a room, I was surprised to see Hunter in there with a woman on his lap that clearly wasn't Larkin. They paid me no attention as they continued to run their hands over each other.

I left the room quickly and ended up outside on the grounds. I wasn't sure if I was meant to have seen that, and I needed some space to breathe.

"What's spooked you, Quentin Scott?"

When I turned around, Archer walked steadily towards me.

"I… Nothing. I just needed some air. It's busy in there."

Archer shot me a look before holding a champagne flute out. I took it from him as he looked me up and down and I sipped from the glass.

"Walk with me? Our last meeting was cut short," he said smoothly.

Gray had blocked us from talking to each other last time, but considering I didn't know where Gray was and the fact I didn't know many people here, taking a stroll with Archer didn't seem like a bad idea.

"Sure," I replied.

He offered me his arm, and I slipped a hand through it. Archer was dressed in blue like the rest of us, apparently not wanting to break protocol and tradition tonight.

"I'm surprised Grayson isn't with you," he commented.

Even though I'd been looking for him, I didn't like the fact that Archer thought I needed Gray around.

"He's not my keeper," I told him.

Archer laughed and waved a free hand up and down my body. "That ward around you would suggest otherwise. He wanted nothing to get to you, but I'm surprised he's not here himself. He seems rather protective of you."

"We work closely together. I'm his host. A part of his team."

He nodded. "I just want to make sure you aren't falling for his charm."

The comment caught me off guard.

"Relations between Gods and mortals are prohibited," I parroted the line.

It seemed safe to feed him it. If anyone thought something was going on between me and Gray, we'd get into all kinds of trouble.

"True enough, but then again, if we were to think someone was worth the trouble… Gods are used to getting what they want."

"You have nothing to worry about with me," I assured him.

"Perhaps he'll take the plunge tonight."

"The plunge?"

We were walking along the paths that cut through the grounds. The evening was warm and there was a soft breeze. Just as with everything in Elysia, it was perfect.

Archer took a sip from his glass before answering, "Mmm. Every time he throws one of these parties, we assume he'll do it, but we're always left disappointed."

"I don't understand."

I hated riddles and wished he'd just tell me what Gray was meant to be doing.

"A proposal," Archer said.

"For what?"

"Marriage, of course."

My brow furrowed, and Archer continued.

"We're all waiting for him to ask Elva to be his wife. It's inevitable that it'll happen. The entire council would be only too happy to grant the union."

My heart stopped in my chest. "Elva?"

"Goddess of death."

"I know who she is."

There was an ugly, raw feeling of jealousy in my chest that I tried to push down on. There was nothing to be jealous over. We had sex occasionally. We weren't dating. We sure as hell weren't in a relationship. He was free to do whatever he wanted.

"Though everyone really wants to know if he'll take after Hunter or Erik," Archer mused.

"What do you mean?"

"Erik is a real family man. I find it quite sickening, but Hunter — well, monogamy isn't really his cup of tea."

That explained what I'd witnessed inside.

"Scott!"

Archer and I walked back around towards the house. Up by the doors, Gray looked furious with Elva beside him.

I took them both in, standing together, adorned in blue, and my stomach dropped. Why hadn't I seen it before? They looked like a couple that belonged on the front of a magazine and gracing red carpets. They looked perfect, with Gray in his tailored suit emanating power, and Elva beside him, dainty and ethereal in a ballgown.

Archer leaned down and spoke to me, "You might want to make it clear to him he's not your keeper."

"Scott! Get here now," Gray demanded.

Elva placed a hand on his arm, and the jealousy reared its head again.

"Better get back to him before he destroys the place," Archer muttered, straightening up.

He unlinked his arm from mine and took the glass before it disappeared.

Gray approached us, with Elva trailing behind him. He looked livid.

"Grayson," Archer greeted him with a smile.

"Archer," Gray said shortly. "Scott, get inside."

"Excuse me?" I asked.

"Get. Inside."

"You don't tell me what to do."

"I do when it's my house."

"Grayson, calm down," Elva implored.

"You might want to listen to her," Archer quipped. "Wouldn't want to cause a scene."

"You need to stay away from her," Gray warned him.

"And why's that, Grayson?"

Gray's aura sprung to life, and it was joined by another in deep forest green. Archer didn't look remotely worried about taking on an elite God.

"GET INSIDE!" Grayson roared. He looked at me with pure fury in his eyes, and it sparked up my irrational anger at the whole situation.

"Fine!" I yelled back. "Archer." The minor God looked at me, not dropping his aura. "Come and dance with me. I don't know many people here."

"Scott," Gray warned, but I didn't want to listen.

Archer dropped his aura, and the air cleared of green before he offered his arm again. "What kind of gentleman would I be if I declined such a request?"

I took his arm and looked at the pure disbelief that took over Gray's face as we walked past him. He raised an arm, but Elva grabbed it before he could do any damage. Good. She could deal with his moody, irrational ass for the night. I just wanted to enjoy myself, considering this was a celebration.

Archer led me through into Gray's throne room, where the music flowed. I scanned the room and saw a few familiar faces before I was pulled against Archer's body, his hands on my waist.

"Are you okay, angel?" he asked.

"My name's Scott."

"I know. You're a brave one to take on Gods," he commented.

I probably shouldn't have risen to the bait and yelled back. I could sense Gray when he entered the room again. The anger was palpable, and it was probably, thanks to the wards around me, that it felt so strong. It was an extension of him and his powers.

"I don't like being told what to do," I said to Archer.

"I can see that."

"Excuse me, Archer," Ig said, reaching us. "Would you mind if I took Scott from you?"

"You're a popular woman. There's no question as to why," Archer complimented me.

"Scott," Ig prompted.

"Thank you, Archer," I said.

He flashed me a smile and leaned in to place a kiss on my cheek. "Anytime, angel. I look forward to seeing more of you when I'm down there."

Archer left, and Ig took his spot.

"You know how to pick them, Scott," he muttered.

"What?"

"First, Gray, and now Archer."

"I have no idea —"

"I know," he said.

My stomach dropped. "How?"

"Scott, I've known him long enough. He's drunk with me less and less, and the way he's currently fuming over there says that there's something between you."

"Is it that obvious?"

Ig shook his head. "Most people don't know Gray well

enough. That's his general attitude. Pissed at the world. It's his job."

I nodded.

"I wouldn't trust Archer," Ig advised me.

"I don't think I should trust any of you."

"Woah! What have we done?"

"Nothing."

We swayed on the floor among the pairs.

"Why doesn't he propose to her?" I asked eventually. "And how is she okay with him sleeping with me if it's that serious?"

"Who? Who's proposing to who?" Ignacio asked, perplexed.

"Gray and Elva."

When Ig laughed, it was a beautiful, full sound that attracted a few stares.

"He's not proposing to her," Ig informed me.

"Everyone's waiting for it."

"They'll be waiting a long time. If he even thought about it, I'd rip his head off."

"Wait. You —"

"And Elva. Yes."

The irrational anger I felt dissipated from my chest.

"Although, we've kept it quiet. Not entirely sure the council would approve since they'd very much like for Elva and Gray to settle together."

"So, they aren't?"

"They're good friends. Work close together but they've never been anything more."

I chewed on my bottom lip.

"You got jealous very easily, Scott. You want to be careful with that," he warned me with a smug smile.

"I wasn't jealous."

"Do mortals call it something else?"

THIRTY

GRAYSON

When I'd seen Archer with Quentin, I'd lost it. If my ward hadn't been placed around her, Archer would have known exactly what she was, and I couldn't risk that happening.

As she stormed past me to go back inside, hanging off his arm, I destroyed two of the stone benches on the grounds before going to find them.

Standing by the wall of my throne room, I watched them and allowed the anger to course through my veins, making my blood white-hot.

She was angry at me and I'd no idea what I'd done to piss her off, when a single word hadn't been exchanged between us since we arrived home. My hands balled into fists when Archer pulled her closer and rested his hands on her hips.

"Are you planning on destroying your entire house?" Ig asked, joining me. His tie was loose around his neck, and he wore a grin. I didn't reply, and he followed my eye line before sighing. "I thought she was just sex."

"She is, but that doesn't mean I want anyone else around her," I muttered sullenly.

"What about that mortal she's dating?"

I snorted. Holden wasn't a threat. Quen kept coming back to me, no matter how much she told herself she shouldn't.

"Try reining it in, Gray, or you're going to have a lot more questions coming your way," Ig said.

I had enough of seeing them together. I pushed myself from the wall, but Ig caught my shoulder.

"Let me," he said.

He strode off towards them, and I watched. The moment Archer kissed her cheek, the row of crystal glasses and the punch bowl on the table near me shattered. I repaired them instantly and got a few curious stares.

"Calm. Down."

Erik appeared next to me and when I looked back to the floor, Archer had disappeared, and Ignacio was with her.

"Grayson, I honestly think you should stop whatever you have with her. This." He gestured vaguely. "It's becoming too much. There's more at risk now," Erik explained.

"I shouldn't have brought her here," I admitted quietly.

If I'd kept Quentin down on earth, I could have convinced the others to not look into her birth. We'd have been blissfully unaware. We could have continued like nothing happened and that could have still been the case if we didn't have to worry about Archer sniffing around.

"I need to talk to her," I said.

"Gray."

"Erik, I just…" I couldn't describe it, and Erik looked worried.

"Let me read you," he said quietly.

"No! No. That's not happening."

I jerked away from my brother as he put his hands out towards me. Turning my back on him, I walked straight over to Ig and Quen.

"I'll take it from here," I said, reaching the pair.

"No," Quen said simply.

"Scott."

"You're going to cause a scene," Ig warned us both.

They broke apart, and I looked at Scott.

"I think it's in everyone's interest, Scott," Ig said. "You're not the only one who gets jealous." Ig kissed her cheek, and my aura sparked. "Get over yourself." He laughed, knocking his shoulder into mine as he left.

I controlled my aura and offered Quen my hand. After a few moments, she took it and I led her out of the throne room. The entire ground floor was filled with people, so I took the steps down to the basement and pulled her into a room.

"What are you playing at?" I demanded once the door was closed.

We were facing each other, and my words echoed in the space.

"I'm not playing at anything," she said.

"That display with Archer?"

"I went looking for you and I couldn't find you and then…" She trailed off.

"What?"

"I walked in on Hunter with… I don't know who, but it wasn't Larkin. Does she know that he's with other people?"

I groaned, rubbing my temples. I wished my older brother would try to be discreet about it.

"Yes. Larkin knows," I confirmed.

"And she lets him?!"

"She got the ring and the position so she couldn't care less."

"That's awful!"

"They make it work," I said, trying to get us back on track. "You stay away from Archer from now on."

"You can't tell me what to do."

"You don't know him! He tries to stir up trouble."

"A lot of people say the same thing about you."

"We're different!" It echoed loudly as we stared at each other.

I half expected her to storm out of the room and find him just to prove a point. The incessant need to be right would be her undoing. But if she so much as thought of seeking him out, I'd lock her in a room and throw away the key.

"He said you were going to marry Elva," Quen said so quietly that I almost missed it.

I laughed. "You're as bad as the rest of them if you believe that."

A whole century I'd been dealing with people asking about Elva, trying to set us up and push us together. It aggravated me and it washed over her. And then a decade ago, Elva and Ig started to date, and I waited for the day they'd tell the heavens, so I'd be set free.

"Well, you don't exactly talk to me about your life," she pointed out. "And I don't want to be the other woman."

I looked at her for a second before closing the gap between us. "We started this because neither of us were exclusively with others."

Truth be told, I hadn't slept with anyone aside from Quen since we'd started. It wasn't worth it. No one would satisfy me the way she did. I knew she went on dates with Holden, but I also knew their sex life was lacking, and she often made an excuse to keep their physical relationship to a minimum, so it didn't bother me.

I wrapped an arm around her waist and pulled her flush against my body. Where she usually resisted, this time she moved with ease, resting her hands on my chest.

"Were you jealous, Scott?"

"No." Her answer was too sharp and too quick.

The smirk pulled at my lips. "I was jealous," I admitted.

She looked up at me with surprise.

"When I saw you with Archer," I continued.

"Gray."

"I don't want him near you, Quen."

The reason was two-fold. I didn't want Archer to find out, and I hated him touching her. I'd always dealt with anger and chaos, but what I felt in the throne room when Archer kissed her cheek was beyond anything I'd experienced before.

"Promise me you'll stay away from him. I don't trust him."

She hesitated.

"Ask any of the others and I swear they'll give you the same sort of answer."

It took a few moments before she spoke, "I'll stay away from Archer."

"Good."

I knew it wouldn't be that simple. I knew that when Archer joined the project, he'd try to get to her. He appreciated her physical appearance. But there was so much more to Quen that Archer didn't see, and I wasn't willing to let him see.

When I looked at her again, I smiled. "You wore the dress."

"You have decent taste."

"I have impeccable taste."

She rolled her eyes at me, and I held her close. Her arms wrapped around my neck, and she reached up to kiss me, fingers sliding into my hair. Her touch set my blood on fire, and I needed her close. Always.

I needed to make sure Erik didn't find out that I had no intention of keeping away from her.

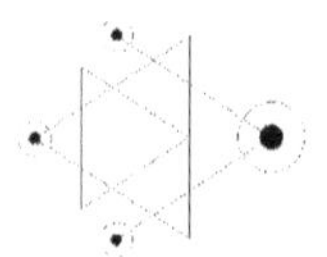

"Hello, Gray," Sloan greeted me when I walked into their home.

"What do we do with Quentin now that we know?" Erik asked, cutting straight to the chase.

"Hello to you too," I muttered, sitting on the sofa. I sensed Erik's anger instantly. "Woah now, little brother."

"Gray! Please stop this!"

"Erik, why does anything need to change?"

He looked at me blankly, and I continued to explain.

"We don't need to tell her. Her life doesn't need to change. We'll be the only ones who know and when we get back to Elysia, we'll forget about her."

Last night, when the guests had finally returned home and after I'd watched the beautiful woman fall apart under my touch, a plan had formed. A plan that meant life could continue with no disruption.

"You're simplifying it too much," Erik told me. "What about when she has children, Grayson? What then?"

"She won't have children. Have you seen her around yours?" I laughed.

Sloan shot me a withering stare. "Please, remind me again what my job is and what you are in charge of."

I flushed slightly and grumbled. Something about Quentin having children made me uncomfortable. Children implied family, implied trusting someone to take that step with.

"This isn't as simple as papering over the cracks, Gray," Erik stressed.

"Why can't it be? We don't have to worry about any of that until the future."

"You're being selfish. You want to continue to toy with her for your benefit without worrying about the risk."

"I'm sure that's not true," Sloan commented.

But Erik had tripped my temper. "And why shouldn't I be selfish?" I asked. "I need something to preoccupy my time while we're down there."

"Why couldn't you just try to date Elva instead?" Erik asked.

My aura blazed into life, and Erik's followed, shielding his wife. The innate need to protect her would always win out over self-preservation. It was the stupidest reaction anyone could have. To let someone infiltrate their most basic needs until they would risk their life for them.

"Grayson, we're just asking you to think. If they find out about her, they will kill her," Sloan said.

A flicker of doubt came to my chest before I disappeared from the house, unable to carry out the discussion with two irrational participants.

They were blowing this out of proportion.

THIRTY ONE

QUENTIN

Since coming back down from Elysia, I'd committed myself to the lab again. As beautiful as the place was, it was good to be back in familiar territory. Fields, parks, pools, and cliffs were all glorious, but being around perfection was exhausting. Glassware, cells, and cursing colleagues were my comfort zone.

It had been another long day, and the last thing on my list was to gather fresh samples from Cato. Rather than come by the institute, I stopped by the house to see Sloan, Erik, and the baby.

"He's grown so much," I said.

Despite being a few weeks old, Cato looked months older.

"They don't stay babies for long," Sloan told me.

"Mortals have the same saying but this is a whole different level."

I carefully took some cheek swabs from him and sealed them, ready to take back to the lab.

"I guess I'll see you both soon," I said, packing things away.

"Actually, Quentin, would you mind staying for a chat?"

"Sure. I don't have to rush off. Is everything okay?"

"Take a seat."

I sat back down, and Sloan and Erik took the seat opposite me.

"It's about Gray," Erik started.

The nerves twisted in my stomach, making me feel sick. "What about Gray?"

"Quentin, we know you've both been seeing each other."

My face heated. I didn't want to discuss my sex life with anyone, let alone with Gray's brother and sister-in-law.

"You know that it's against the rules," Sloan reminded me.

"No one knows, if that's what you're worried about."

I didn't count Ignacio and probably Elva, both who seemed too close to Gray to betray him.

"That's what we're worried about," Sloan said.

"Scott, under any other circumstance, I wouldn't interfere, but I need to ask you to stop seeing my brother," Erik told me.

There was a small spark of anger. I wasn't doing any harm. We weren't hurting anyone. We were two consenting adults enjoying each other's intimate company.

"Erik, no offence, but this really has nothing to do with you. Either of you. Gray and I know what we're doing," I sniffed.

I got up from my seat, no longer wanting to be lectured by these Gods.

"If Hunter finds out, he won't hesitate to kill Gray," Erik said quietly.

That stopped me in my tracks.

"What?" I asked.

Whenever I thought of the repercussions of our arrangement, I imagined Gareth calling me into the office and firing me. My employment record would have a red mark on it, and I'd have to come up with a plausible excuse for future interviews that didn't involve me admitting that I'd fucked the test subject on numerous occasions. Not once had I thought Gray would suffer any consequences.

"Hunter's wanted to make an example of Grayson for some time. I wouldn't put it past him to do what he has to, making sure the rest of us remember to abide by the rules."

My blood felt like ice in my veins. I'd seen Hunter and Gray go toe-to-toe when they first arrived. There was no love lost between the pair.

"Surely, you know what it's like to want to protect family, Scott," Erik continued.

I thought of Cassidy. I thought of my parents. I'd do anything to protect them. I'd have done anything to stop them from taking that trip and boarding the train.

"That's all we want — to protect our family. Gray means a lot to us and to our children. We would have spoken to him, but I think you know that would've been a lost cause," Sloan explained.

Gray would have kicked off the moment they started talking to him. He didn't deal well with people telling him what to do. Neither did I, but I was more inclined to let someone finish making their point.

"We just want to protect our family," Sloan reiterated.

"I need to go," I replied.

Erik called after me, "Think about it, Quentin. You would have had to break your arrangement, eventually."

I left the house and got into my car.

Everything that Erik and Sloan said banged around my skull the entire way to the institute and back home. I knew what it was like to want to protect the people you love. How was I meant to argue with that? Especially if it meant that Gray wouldn't exist anymore.

I knew that we'd get in trouble if anyone found out, and maybe it'd been reckless. Nearly half the elite Gods appeared to know, and it wouldn't take long for the rest to find out. Not only that, but if Gareth got wind of this, my job would be on the line.

Feeling deflated, I headed over to Murphy's, wanting to drown my sorrows before they consumed me and left me wallowing on the sofa.

Entering the pub, a burst of noise hit my eardrums and a crowd of familiar faces was scattered in booths and along the bar. Sometimes I wondered if our work force alone would be the ones paying for Charlie and Tyler's wedding.

"Hey, gorgeous." Holden appeared next to me, and I kissed him half-heartedly.

"Hey."

We had seen little of each other, thanks to work, but he served as a pleasant distraction for now. Maybe it would do me some good to spend some time with my kind again.

"We're up at the bar," he told me.

Matthew guided me through the crowd until we both sat at the bar with some others. Tyler was serving one end and Gray appeared in front of me, a charming grin on his face.

"Pick your poison, Scott," he told me.

"Bombay sapphire."

"Gin? Rough day?"

He'd picked up on my habits as we lived together. Gin after a rough day, wine when I attempted to cook, and coffee at any given hour I could get my hands on it. Gray was trying to break the last habit, keeping things out of reach and hiding the coffee machine, but I always won.

You're like a truffle pig, he'd said, aura catching me as I slipped from the kitchen counter. *Only for something a lot less valuable.*

"Something like that," I muttered in response, bringing myself back to the present.

Gray shot me a quizzical look, pouring me a measure of blue gin. He didn't press the conversation. I'd tell him later, like I usually did nowadays. I came home late, banged around the kitchen and recounted my day over dinner. Exhausted from the day, I retired to bed and tried to read before I made my way to Gray's room, or he came to mine. Sex was a good stress relief and Gray appreciated how stressful my job could get.

He placed the drink down in front of me and moved away to serve another customer.

"I've missed having you around, Scott," Holden said to me.

"Sorry. Things have been busy. We should try to schedule something in."

"Quentin —"

"You can pick."

"Actually —"

"Yes?"

"I was thinking maybe we should stop dating."

"Oh! Um…" I said, surprised at his request. He'd always seemed more interested in our dates than I did.

"I'm not interested in seeing anyone else, Quen."

From the corner of my eye, I saw Gray stop cleaning a glass, and I knew he was listening to the conversation.

"I guess, I'm asking if you'd be my girlfriend?"

The air had been sucked out of me. When my eyes flicked up to Gray, he looked highly amused. He'd always maintained Holden wasn't good enough, and I had no genuine interest in him. He wasn't wrong, but Erik and Sloan came to mind. I didn't want anything to happen to Gray. And all it took was for one person to slip and Hunter would have the excuse he needed.

"Quentin?" Matthew said, looking hopeful.

"… Yes."

He beamed at me, leaning in, and kissing me deeply.

This was it now. No more Gray. I was officially off the market.

THIRTY TWO

GRAYSON

I'd heard it all.

Holden wanted commitment from Quentin. Exclusivity. I could have laughed. When she looked my way, I failed to hide my amusement. How could I?

Foremost, it was hilarious that he thought he was worthy of her. Quentin was a demigoddess, and she deserved someone that could hold her in that esteem. An equal to tread through life beside her. Holden was a bumbling idiot who didn't appreciate her full potential and wanted to keep her three steps behind him.

Second, Quentin would not commit to Holden when she had me in her life.

"… Yes," she answered.

I stopped cleaning the glass in my hands, and the smile dropped off my face. It took every ounce of self-restraint not to spark up my aura and destroy the entire building.

Yes? Yes. She'd said yes with brief hesitation. What the fuck had happened that Scott suddenly wanted a serious relationship with Holden? I could only assume that she was having a breakdown of some sort, because she was smarter than this.

When Holden kissed her, I turned away, and the glass shattered in my hand before I dropped the pieces to the floor.

"Everything okay, Gray?" Tyler asked.

"Glass slipped."

I cleaned the mess and turned around to see Quentin was no longer in her seat. It took a moment to sense where she was before I left the bar to find her.

She was leaving the bathroom when she walked straight into me.

"Sorry," she apologised instantly, before looking up. "Gray?"

Roughly, I pushed her back into the room and locked the door behind me.

"What do you think you're doing?" I hissed.

"What?" she bit back. "What are you doing?"

I'd backed her up against the wall and she put her hands up on my chest in a feeble attempt to keep some space between us. Space that I wasn't willing to give her after the stunt she'd pulled.

"Holden! Really?" I raged, unable to keep this civil and calm.

Any trace of fear, any speck of confusion, was wiped away from her dark eyes. The shutters came down and Quen drew herself up, ready to fight.

"It's not any of your business, Grayson," she told me sharply.

None of my business. As if I wasn't the one she came home

to every night. As if I didn't satisfy her every need. As if I wasn't enough.

"You don't even like him," I spat.

"That's not true!" She tipped her chin up indignantly.

Okay. She liked Holden as a friend, but I couldn't fathom why she'd want anything more from him.

"You don't like him enough to stay away from me," I corrected myself, falling back on the truth.

I pressed against her, placing my forehead against hers, and took in the honey and orange scent. This woman belonged to me in every sense. She'd infiltrated my life until I couldn't stop my thoughts from straying to her. I'd brought her home and into my bed. How did she choose him when I'd given her so much?

"I'm not doing this." Her voice was quiet, and she refused to look me in the eye.

"Aren't you?" I asked, voice low.

My lips found hers, and she didn't hesitate to respond. It was instinctive. Reactive. Her body bent to my whim without fail each and every time. We were a chaotic mess that created comfort for each other. But the moment my hands ran down her sides, she broke the kiss and pushed me away forcefully.

"I'm not doing this, Gray," Quen said firmly.

"Why not?"

"I'm not being a cheat. I'm with Matthew now, so all this needs to stop. Okay?"

There were so many words on the tip of my tongue. A myriad of questions. What made him so special that he was granted the duty of being her boyfriend? Why did he deserve her loyalty? How had he cracked into the circle of people she cared for so deeply?

None of them left my brain. Pride forced the words to lodge in my throat and get stuck to the roof of my mouth. If she wanted to lower her standards, then why should I try to convince her otherwise?

"Whatever you say," I spat vitriolically.

She pushed past me, and I heard the door unlock before she

left the room.

A strange pain pulsed through my chest, making me wince, but I ignored it, resuming my position back behind the bar.

Quentin sat with Holden again. He had an arm around her waist while they talked. She didn't look relaxed or interested in what he said. Her eyes flicked up to me, but I looked away, disgusted.

What did I care? Our arrangement was only ever temporary.

Mortals, demi or otherwise, were pathetic.

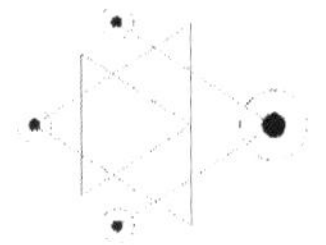

When I arrived at Erik's late on Friday night, I didn't say much, just that I needed a place to stay. It wasn't until the following morning, when Erik found me sitting in the garden in the early hours, slowly destroying my surroundings, that he watched me knowingly. Worry creased his brow, and the concern aggravated me.

As Erik sat down on the grass beside me, I said, "What do you want, Erik?"

"I'm wondering why you are currently taking up residence here?"

"Can't I come visit my favourite brother and sister-in-law?"

"I'd be more inclined to believe that if you'd bothered to say more than two words to us since you got here." Erik turned his head to look at me properly. "You can't keep going like this."

He gestured out to the garden. I'd destroyed nearly everything in it. It wouldn't take us a second to repair, but Erik had never been fond of my destructive phases.

"What happened?" he asked.

I refused to answer him.

"I assume it has something to do with Scott," Erik continued.

I obliterated the small birdhouse at the end of the garden into pieces, shards of wood flying across the space. There was a sick sense of joy that rose inside as I imagined Holden being impaled on one.

"Grayson."

"She's in a relationship with that oaf."

"Holden?"

I didn't respond. Instead, I pulled up every plant from the roots while I sat next to him in silence.

"Why is that a problem?" Erik asked curiously.

"She refuses to sleep with me anymore," I said, the words harsh as they tumbled from my lips. "She says she won't be a cheat."

"Your agreement was only temporary."

"I know that, Erik, but —"

"But?"

I let out a frustrated sigh. "Holden? Matthew Holden doesn't deserve her." There was a ferocity behind the words.

"And why not?"

"Look at him! He's a pathetic, blundering mortal and she… well, she's a demigoddess."

Silence settled between us, heavy with words that neither of us wanted to voice.

"So, who deserves her then, Gray?" Erik eventually asked as the sun started to rise over the horizon.

A single answer, one word, sprung to mind, but I swallowed it. Turning to him, I said, "You tell me, Erik. This is your department, no? You know whether she's meant to be with Holden."

"Even if they aren't meant to be together, many people make mistakes before finding their life partner. Even immortals get it wrong sometimes," he reasoned.

"Hunter doesn't count."

Hunter's affairs were illustrious and well known. Erik should count himself lucky to have found Sloan.

"They might bond," Erik said hopefully.

Wrong thing to say, because I went ahead and uprooted an entire tree at the end of the garden at the thought.

The thought of them bonding stirred jealousy in me to the same degree as when Archer kissed her cheek. Visions of Holden sitting at dinner with her brother and Sophie drifted into my mind. Scott resting against him as she laughed, openly and freely, in her element surrounded by her family. By people she loved and allowed to have her heart.

How the fuck had Holden cemented himself by her side?

"Grayson, this needs to stop," Erik said firmly. "She needs to find happiness."

"Let her then," I spat the words into the early morning as pain shot through my chest. "I couldn't care less what she does."

THIRTY THREE

QUENTIN

I was sitting in a beautiful park, the delicate scent of flowers drifting in the gentle breeze. Glancing around, I was alone, and getting to my feet, I realised I was back in Elysia. They led me along the paths, the surrounding heavens eerily silent.

Why was I here?

"Hello, angel."

I spun around, heart thudding nervously, to find Archer standing there, smirking.

"Archer, what are you doing here?"

"This is my home."

He stretched a hand out towards me, and I walked in his

direction and took it. It felt solid and warm in my own.

"And I wanted to see you," he said, green eyes fixed on mine.

"You wanted to see me?" I repeated, confused by the statement.

"You intrigue me, Quentin. There's something about you I can't quite put my finger on. I don't just think it's me that sees it. They all seem protective of you."

Archer reached up and tucked a lock of my hair behind my ear, and his knuckles brushed against my cheek gently.

"What is it about you, Quentin?" he asked, looking at me curiously.

"I work with them," I answered.

"There's more than that."

He leaned towards me and looked me in the eye. I wanted to snap them shut, worried he'd read every single thought that ran through my mind.

"They're my friends."

It wasn't quite a lie, but it wasn't the truth, either. Erik and Sloan fostered a rocky relationship with me. Ig seemed to offer some advice that might have strayed us into the territory of friendship. And Gray — it was just as complicated as when I first laid eyes on him.

That earned me a laugh from Archer that unsettled my insides.

"So naïve, angel. They aren't your friends. We're Gods. We're always after something."

I processed the words and blinked. I'd spent most of my time with Grayson and it'd been pretty clear what both of us had wanted, but there were times when he'd slipped into my bed and held me while we talked, and I felt like we'd crossed into a weird friendship.

"You can't trust them," Archer said. "They destroy anything that they feel threatens them."

"I don't threaten them."

Arched cupped my face in his hand. "Something about

you…"

I shook my head and pulled his hand from my face, but he laced our fingers together.

"It's nice to have you alone," he said.

In the back of my mind, I could hear Gray's voice warning me to stay away.

"I should go," I told him.

"Is that what you want?"

I nodded, and Archer mimicked the movement.

"Remember what I said. I'll see you soon." He kissed my forehead gently before letting me go.

When I opened my eyes, I was nestled in my bed. Had I just dreamed about Archer? Everything had felt so real. His touch felt solid. Why would I dream about him when we'd barely spoken?

Burying my face in the pillow, I decided I needed to spend time away from the Gods. This was getting ridiculous. I'd transitioned from never calling their name to being tangled with the elites in more ways than one.

Gray hadn't come home from Tyler's after his shift Friday night, and he hadn't come home for dinner last night either. But he was free to do what he wanted, even if the house was eerily quiet without him.

It'd been completely foolish of me to assume that things would be plain sailing after agreeing to date Matt. I wanted Gray and I had to maintain the strange relationship we had without the physical aspect and the fact he avoided me to the point he hadn't come home hurt. A fresh wave of tears stung my eyes, and I swallowed the thick lump that formed in my throat.

Life had to progress. Gray would leave eventually and when he was back in Elysia, he wouldn't remember the mortal who hosted him. Not when he was surrounded by beauty and grace. I'd become nothing more than a vague memory or the butt of the joke.

A knock on the front door made me finish the bite of cereal before I answered it. A man stood there with two round boxes, and I signed off for them before taking them through to the living room.

When I took the lid off them, I found the brightest yellow tulips I'd ever seen. There must have been a hundred blooms in total, and I blushed at the gesture. I hadn't received flowers since Ethan.

Pulling my phone off the table, I instantly called Matthew.

"Hey, Quentin," he answered. "Everything okay?"

"Hey. Yeah, everything's great. I just wanted to call and say thank you."

"For what?"

"For the flowers."

"What flowers?"

"The tulips you sent me."

"I haven't sent you any flowers."

I narrowed my eyes and looked around the box. There was no card. No inclination who the sender was. I'd assumed they were from him.

"Who sent you flowers?" Matt asked, sounding wary.

"Oh, they're from my brother. I didn't see the note."

Holden laughed down the phone. "You're such a scatterbrain sometimes, Scott."

"I know." I laughed nervously. "I know. Anyway, I have to go."

"I'll pick you up tomorrow for work?"

"Um, sure."

"See you then, babe."

I put the phone down and felt my blood boil. If those flowers hadn't come from Matt, then there was only one other person they'd come from. I raced upstairs and got dressed before getting into the car.

If Gray wasn't at home, Erik might know where he was.

When I reached Martyn's house, I knocked on the door, and Erik answered.

"Scott? I didn't think we had —"

"Is he here?" I asked.

"Who?"

"Who? Gray. That's who."

"He's… Yes. Gray!"

I didn't wait to be let in, instead pushing past Erik into the house.

"Grayson!"

Moving into the living room, I spotted Gray lounging in a chair and looking as sinful as he always did.

"To what do I owe the pleasure, Scott?" he asked darkly.

"Quentin!" Sloan came into the room with a smile that disappeared almost instantly when she saw the tension between me and Gray.

"What are you playing at?" I asked him, ignoring her.

"Excuse me?" he replied, sitting up straight. "Shall I remind you who you're talking to?"

"I know exactly who I'm talking to. As if I give a shit."

Gray stood, with his aura flaring to life around him. Erik stood behind me and Sloan behind Gray in a weird stand-off.

"Gray, back down," Erik told him.

"No," he replied, smoky aura reaching out towards me. "I'd like to know what I'm being accused of doing."

"I don't know what you're trying to do, but you can keep your flowers," I spat.

"Flowers?" Gray asked.

"The tulips you sent. I don't want them."

He barked out a laugh. "Don't flatter yourself, Scott. I'd never send anyone flowers. Especially not you."

The comment stung. I brushed it off and narrowed my eyes. "Hilarious, Gray. I don't appreciate you trying to cause trouble."

"I didn't send you anything! They must have come from your boyfriend."

He spat out the last words, and the lightbulbs above us shattered. I threw up a hand to shield myself from the shards, but Erik had cast his aura around us, so everything was tinted red and no glass hit me.

"Calm yourself!" Erik yelled, sounding angrier than I'd ever heard him before.

"They didn't come from Matthew," I told them.

Gray suddenly stalked towards me. "What flowers did you

say they were?"

Erik let his aura sink away from me slowly.

"Tulips," I said. "Yellow tulips."

"GRAY!" Erik yelled.

But it was too late. Gray wrapped his aura around us both and took us back to the house.

"Where are they?" he demanded.

I wasn't even phased by the fact that we'd arrived back home and pointed to the two boxes sitting on the coffee table.

Gray walked over to them and picked up a box. His aura engulfed it and turned the entire piece to dust. He picked up the second box to do the same.

"Grayson!"

He turned on me and strode across the space with such purpose than my first instinct was to run. Gray was furious, and I was in the firing line.

"Have you seen him?" he asked, stopping when the toes of his shoes hit mine.

"Who?" I squeaked.

"Archer! Have you seen him?"

"Archer?"

He let out a frustrated growl.

"Gray, just explain."

Tentatively, I put a hand out and placed it on his arm. Since the night in the pub, Gray had kept clear of me, but it'd been difficult. I missed him being around, and the small contact soothed my soul.

"Sit," he commanded.

"I'm not a dog."

"Sit your ass down," he told me again, words clipped and through gritted teeth.

I dropped my hand and perched on the edge of the couch.

"Yellow tulips are Archer's flowers. We all have a colour. We all have a flower," he explained.

"I know that."

"Have you seen him?" Gray asked. I maintained the quiet. "SIMPLE QUESTION!"

"No!" I barked. "No. I haven't seen him."

He took a deep breath. "Scott, I don't know what he's doing, but I don't trust him, and neither should you. Do you understand?"

"We've been through this before. I know."

"Then why is he sending you flowers?"

"I don't know, Grayson. I didn't even know they were from him."

"If he comes near you, call for me."

"Why?"

"Do you have to question everything?"

"I just don't understand. He seems alright."

"You don't know him."

I shrugged.

Gray snarled, "You need to listen to me on this. Stay away from him."

"You can't tell me what to do," I said.

The light fixtures shattered, and I jumped, raising my arms to protect myself.

"Gray! Stop!"

"Then do this one thing!"

"Fine!"

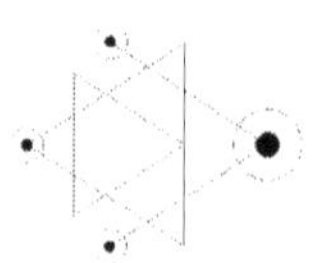

It would be fair to say that I'd slipped back into avoiding Gray again. These days, we couldn't seem to stop ourselves from getting into fights, but I didn't have the energy to keep doing it. The lab work was piling up, and I'd decided to try with Matt. We went on dates, and I stayed with him a few times in the past few weeks. When I crawled into bed at home, I'd call him, but the fact remained… We lacked a spark.

The problem only got worse when we went to Murphy's and

Gray lived behind the bar. On those nights, I struggled to keep my eyes off him. Jeans hanging low off his hips and t-shirts stretched tight across his chest, he made casual look like something you'd devour in private.

It was meant to be a one-time thing, but I couldn't stay away from him and with the threat of others finding out, it felt safer to end things.

A Saturday night in September, I pulled Matt early from Murphy's and took him home. Gray was working, and the house was empty, so I led him into my room. I pushed the window open and let in a gentle breeze before approaching Matt again.

Sex with Matthew was different. He focused on himself more than on me. Selfish was the adjective that often came to mind. Gray wouldn't allow himself an orgasm until I had at least one, most of the time more. I was his priority. But that wasn't the case anymore.

Matt also handled me with great care. He treated me as if I'd break, and even when I tried to show him what I liked by biting and letting my nails sink into his skin, he reminded me to be careful, further dousing the already precarious flame.

So, with Matt above me now thrusting into me, I lied. I faked the pleasure because a relationship didn't need to have great sex. A relationship was more than physical.

"You're amazing, babe." He rolled off and laid beside me on the bed.

I wished I could say the same about him.

"I'm going to grab a glass of water. Do you want anything?" I asked.

"I'm good."

I leaned over and kissed him chastely before getting out of bed. I picked his hoodie up from the floor, pulled it over my head, and left the room.

In the kitchen, I grabbed myself a glass of cold water and drank deeply. When I turned around, the glass fell from my hand when I saw Gray standing in the shadows. His aura caught the glass, keeping it from shattering and causing a scene.

"Are you trying to give me a heart attack?! I thought you

were working tonight." I placed a hand on my chest and felt the organ hammering beneath my touch.

"I got off early. I'd kindly ask you to stop bringing people back to the house."

I scoffed. "It's my home, and Matthew is hardly a stranger. He's my boyfriend."

Gray stalked towards me, and I backed myself away into the kitchen counter. He looked as livid as he had on the first night in the lab. The first time he'd cornered me in the kitchen.

"You smell of him," he said, crowding my space. "It's disgusting."

I blushed, feeling ashamed and embarrassed. "Well, move and then you can go back to creeping around in the shadows."

As I went to move, he caged me in, placing his hands on either side of me and gripping the counter until his knuckles turned white.

"I heard you," he whispered furiously. "I heard every fake moan."

I looked up into his eyes. Something about the God of chaos and vengeance and destruction standing in front of me, completely pissed off, should have made me fold in on myself. But I'd grown so used to him and his temper.

Gray leaned into me, and I swallowed, not because I was worried but because I hadn't been this close to his body in weeks, and I desperately craved for him to be closer.

He picked up on the thoughts, smirk gracing his face.

"He doesn't satisfy your needs, does he, Scott?" Gray looked amused. I shoved him, but he didn't move an inch. Instead, he came closer, leaning down and whispering, "He can't make you scream the way I can."

His lips brushed against my neck, and I took in a sharp breath.

"Quentin?" Matt's voice rang out before he came into the kitchen.

Gray took a calm step away from me.

"What's taking so long?" Matt asked, glancing between us

both. “I was beginning to miss you.”

“She’s a human being, not a vital organ,” Gray informed him bluntly. “Unfortunately, you survived her absence.”

“This is a private conversation.”

“You’re in my house.”

“It’s Scott’s house.”

“I live here.”

“Here we go again,” I mumbled. “Matt, maybe you should head home.”

He gave me a look. “Are you going to be okay?”

“I always am.”

He let out a sigh and nodded. “You have my hoodie, babe.”

I grabbed the bottom of it, ready to pull it over my head, when Matt grabbed my hands and pulled me tight against him.

“Woah!” he said. “What do you think you’re doing?”

I hadn’t realised I was about to strip off with Gray there. I was used to him seeing me naked.

“Sorry,” I blushed. “I wasn’t thinking.”

“Oh, don’t apologise on my behalf. I think I’d rather enjoy the view,” Gray said smugly.

Matt let go of me, puffing out his chest, but I pushed him back.

“He’s not worth it. Come on. Let’s go.” I turned back to Gray as we left the kitchen. “Stay away from me.”

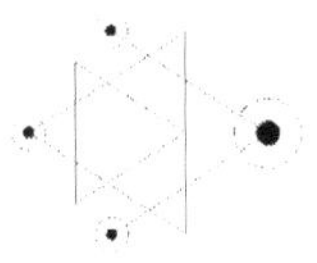

When I fell asleep, I found myself in Elysia again.

“Archer?” I called out.

He appeared in front of me. “Right here.”

Even though I didn’t know why I kept dreaming of him, he calmed me when I found myself here. Maybe it was because of my experience with the pool, and the fact he was a God, kept me safe from the waters and whispers.

"Are we walking tonight?" he asked. I nodded and slipped a hand through his arm before we walked down the path. "You seem upset."

I bit the insides of my cheeks and shrugged.

He stopped us and used a hand to tip my chin up, so I looked at him. "Tell me what's wrong."

"Gray." His name spilled from my mouth before I could stop myself.

"What's he done?"

"He's being an ass."

Archer laughed. "What did I tell you? Not to trust him."

"He says the same about you."

"He would. Listen to me. You have no idea what he and the other elites are capable of."

"So tell me."

"Sweetheart, I keep secrets. I don't spill them. Not unless I get something in return."

"What do you want?"

"There's an interesting question," he said, looking at me curiously, and I felt like I'd made a mistake.

Bartering with a God felt like it was asking for trouble. But at the same time, I was tired of them being so cryptic. I wanted answers, and I needed to get them somehow.

"If you tell me what you want, I'm willing to make a trade," I pressed.

"You're playing dangerous games but that's a very tempting offer you bring to the table."

I swallowed, watching him. Archer ran a hand through his dark hair, and I noticed a small scar he sported down the side of his face. It was faint and pale, almost unnoticeable, until the light caught it perfectly.

"How did you get that?" I asked, confused that a God would bear such imperfection.

My fingers slowly reached out to touch it.

"I should go," he said suddenly, moving his face out of reach.

"You're leaving?"

"Don't worry. I'll see you soon." He brushed his lips against my forehead and disappeared.

Elysia crumbled away, and I woke up from the dream.

Groaning, I buried my face into the pillow before I felt something else against my cheek. When I opened my eyes, I saw a yellow tulip. Sitting up in bed, I realised I was surrounded by them.

"GRAY!" I yelled.

He appeared at the door of the bedroom in just a pair of boxers, and for two seconds, I forgot why I called him. And then his aura filled the room.

"Why are there yellow tulips in here?" he demanded. The darkness of his aura was almost suffocating, but when it disappeared, it took the flowers with it. "Scott?!"

"I don't know!" I lied.

Gray stormed away from the room, muttering about seeing Hunter, and I sank back down into bed, too afraid to go back to sleep.

THIRTY FOUR

GRAYSON

Yellow tulips would be the fucking death of me.

I made my way to visit Hunter, hoping to discuss the problem that had arisen. For once, I needed my big brother for his status and title.

"And you wonder why I refused to have children with you," Larkin yelled.

"You can't complain if I have them by someone else then," Hunter shot back.

"Trouble in paradise?" I cut in with a smirk, unable to hold back.

They both turned to me, and I was grateful that Larkin

wasn't responsible for death because I would have ceased to exist, time and time again. Much to my dismay, she disappeared in silver, and I turned back to my big brother, packing my fight away for another day.

"What do you want, Grayson?" Hunter asked.

"A discussion."

"About?"

"Archer."

"What now?"

"He's," I started. How was I meant to phrase this? "He's causing issues."

"How exactly? He doesn't arrive until tomorrow."

"Yellow tulips everywhere at Scott's place."

Hunter raised an eyebrow. "Why would he leave a mark with her? Has something happened between them?"

It better not have, I thought, the jealousy uncoiling deep in the pit of my stomach.

I'd make sure Archer didn't exist anymore if he so much as tried. But considering Quentin wouldn't let me near her, I doubted she'd let Archer close.

"Not as far as I know," I answered coolly.

"Hmm, he's not that stupid," Hunter agreed. "He knows it'd be punishable by death."

If you're stupid enough to get caught.

"It's irritating her," I said.

"So?" he barked. "Let it irritate her, Grayson. She's a mortal. Surely, you can put up with her whining. I have bigger things to deal with than this."

And there it was in a nutshell — my older brother and ruler of all of us was forever a selfish prick under the layers of fake niceties.

He left me with no choice. I'd have to figure out a way to deal with Archer myself.

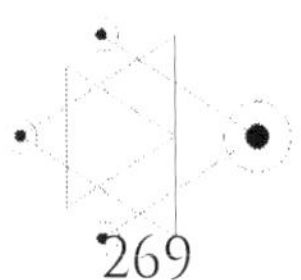

It was a grim Monday when I entered the institute. My presence wasn't required in the lab with Quentin. Instead, I was seeing Charlotte. As if I didn't see enough of her. She shadowed most of my moves and was generally exhausting to be around. Tyler deserved a medal for even considering tying his life to hers.

"Gray, is something wrong?" she asked.

Charlotte wasn't a bad mortal as far as they went. She attended temple weekly and prayed. Those prayers had never been directed at me but aimed at my brothers and Sloan. Protection, love, children — everything Charlotte wished for her life to be filled with.

"No. Why do you ask?" I answered curtly.

"You've seemed volatile the last few weeks."

Volatile was one way of putting it. I was constantly livid or in pain, and I couldn't decipher why.

When people prayed to me, I granted it with a little more tenacity than usual and I was waiting for Hunter to call me out on it, but it looked like his marital problems were taking centre stage at the moment, allowing me to get away with my misdemeanours.

I shrugged in response.

"You know." Charlotte sighed. "You can talk to me if you need anything."

I looked at her for a few moments and wondered what she might say or what advice she might offer if I told her, I'd fucked her friend multiple times and that she was actually a demigoddess, and if any of that came to light, we'd both be dead.

"I'll pass if it's all the same."

"I don't know how Quentin puts up with you sometimes."

I huffed.

"And Tyler. You can be impossible, Grayson."

I'd much rather talk to Quentin. That was the strange thing about it. I didn't just crave her physically. I missed finding out about her day. I wanted to lie in bed with her and listen to her complain about an experiment that didn't work until she finally gave into sleep. There was a growing chasm between us, and it felt too much.

And it was partially my fault. Avoiding her had seemed like

the only logical option, but without her, I felt empty. No one challenged me the way she did. No one amused me with their antics the way Quentin could.

When I left Charlotte's office, the institute was quiet. It was just gone five and if I knew Quen, which I'd like to say I did, then she wouldn't have finished with the rest. She'd still be in the lab.

Quentin had told me to stay away from her, but I couldn't. No one had successfully told me what to do in centuries. The desire to be around her was too strong and so I'd attempt to be around her and stay in control.

Tonight, I'd make us both dinner and she could tell me about work and whatever else she wanted just so I could spend time with her.

Why wait until tonight? I could find her in the lab and wait for her to finish.

When I walked into the room, the benches were empty, but something felt off. I picked up the pace, walking down the aisle.

"Scott," I called out. "I wanted to… ARCHER!"

He was standing in front of Scott and before I could stop him, his bare fingers brushed against the skin of her cheek.

I didn't think before unleashing my aura, pushing him away and leaving a wall of it in front of her for protection.

"Leave her alone," I growled, striding up beside her.

"I just wanted to know what's so interesting about her, but I'm starting to see it now. I couldn't get a read."

I faltered slightly. "No read?"

"Not a single thing. I mean, I know she's an angel, but you're telling me she's got no secrets? It makes no sense."

I shook my head. "She's spent a lot of time with Gods. She's been up to Elysia. Who knows how her body is coping with those changes?"

"We should! Perhaps I'll talk to Gareth and Hunter about extending this little project." He turned to Quentin. "You need control samples, right? Maybe you can add yourself to the mix because something isn't right here."

Archer dropped his aura and stalked out of the lab. Turning

at the door, he said, "I'll be in touch, Scott."

Once he'd gone, I dropped my aura. "I need to go."

"Gray." Quentin caught my arm, looking pale. "Why couldn't he read me?"

"I don't know, Scott. I have to see Erik."

"Why? What's wrong?"

"Nothing!" I snapped. "Nothing's wrong. Like I said, it's probably a case of overexposure to all of us."

I told her no more as I disappeared in black, straight to my brother.

"Erik!" I called out, appearing at his host's house.

"Gray?" Sloan asked, rocking Cato in her arms. Elva was there and looked alarmed at my sudden appearance.

"Where is he?" I asked.

"I'll get him now. Is everything okay?"

All I could do was shake my head. In less than a second, Sloan disappeared and reappeared with Erik by her side.

"What's wrong?" Erik asked me.

"Archer is hanging around her," I told him. "He wants to know why we're all so interested in her."

"I'm sorry. Could you repeat that?" Erik asked.

"Archer thinks we're protective of her. Thinks there must be something special about her we aren't disclosing. He couldn't read her today and he's going to be like a dog with a bone."

Elva spoke quietly, "Why do we need permission to read each other?"

"Because we're divine," Sloan answered.

"Her powers," Erik muttered.

"No! No! She doesn't have powers. This needs to stop!" I hissed, grabbing at my hair.

"She's a demigoddess. She's my blood. Of course, she has powers," Elva told me seriously.

The stress continued to build, and there was a sharp pain in my chest that I tried to ignore.

"They might not be dormant anymore," Sloan mused.

"She came to Elysia. It's her home. It might have done something. We may not need to worry about him ever reading her," Elva added.

"She didn't make it into the pool," I argued.

"She did. She just didn't get very far."

"What am I meant to do?" I couldn't keep the desperation from my voice.

"Stay away from her," Erik answered shortly.

"I'm not the problem here. Archer is."

"Keep a ward on her," Elva suggested.

"That won't work. Archer's interested in her because of how much Gray's involved with her. He doesn't know the full extent, but Gray's interest has piqued his," Sloan said.

I sighed, the pain growing stronger in my chest until it felt like it might split me in two.

"I don't know," Erik whispered. "I wish we'd never come down here."

A single stray tear fell down his porcelain cheek. And I was beginning to think maybe we wouldn't find a way out of this.

THIRTY FIVE

QUENTIN

I sat at the bar at *Murphy's*, next to Charlotte, as she flicked through a large binder of wedding details. This woman was efficient, to say the least, and I was impressed by the way she'd organised things.

"I need to get the dress sorted," Charlie muttered.

"Isn't it a little soon?"

With just under a year left, I was amazed at how much she'd managed to arrange already. I guess that was what happened when you truly intended to get married.

"Not really," Charlie said. "You'll come with me, right?"

"Of course."

There was a vague memory in my head that tried to push itself forward from when I went searching for a dress. No bridal party, just me brushing my fingers across rails of white dresses, trying to decide what I wanted to look like on my big day. Lace and satin and organza. The whites were too blinding and the choices too overwhelming. I'd left without trying on a single thing.

"You're a star." Charlie leaned over and kissed my cheek, no doubt leaving behind a lipstick stain.

"Ready to go, babe?" Tyler asked her.

"You're not working close?" I asked in return.

"Nope," Charlie answered. "He's promised me a date night and Gray said he'd close up, which is sweet of him."

I glanced across the bar to see Gray serving. He was more at ease around mortals than when he first arrived. I could almost imagine him doing this for a living if he wasn't divine. Looking at him now, it would be easy to see how you could frequent the bar because of the sexy bartender with bright blue eyes and a brighter smile.

The way things had deteriorated between us hurt me deeply. Most nights, I struggled to sleep, missing his body beside mine. The house was quiet as we avoided each other. More than once, I wanted to find him and have the colossal argument I felt was simmering under the surface. But more than that, I wanted to tell him I missed him.

"Did you hear me?" Charlie asked, drawing me out of my thoughts.

"Huh?"

"I said, have you noticed anything weird about Gray? He seems a little more closed off again, but I can't put my finger on it, and he won't tell me anything."

"I don't think so," I lied, ignoring the guilt. "I mean, it's Gray. He's always closed off."

"No. No, he isn't. For the last month or so, he seemed happy to talk. He came back from the gifting ceremony, and he was like a different person than the past few weeks." She shrugged. "I don't know. I feel like something's upset him."

My heart clenched as I wondered if it had anything to do

with the way we'd been. Did he feel it too? The emptiness that devoured every moment we were apart. That would be giving myself too much credit.

"Anyway, if you find anything out, let me know. See you soon, Scotty!" Charlie said. She hopped off the chair and left with Tyler, binder securely under her arm.

I sighed and turned to look back at Gray, but my view was obscured by Archer.

"What are you doing all alone at the bar?" he asked.

"I was with Charlie."

Between Gray and Archer, I didn't know who to believe. I wished I could talk to someone on neutral ground to understand things better. It was making me uncomfortable not knowing who to trust. Life had been a lot simpler when I lived on my own, worked with cells that couldn't talk back, and refused to acknowledge the Gods.

"I'm sorry for the outburst in your lab," Archer apologised softly.

I was surprised at the apology. "Can you not make it a habit? Actually, I'd prefer it remains a one-time thing."

"Understood."

I ran my fingers along the rim of my wine glass.

"I would like to get to know you better if you'd allow me to do so," Archer said, watching me.

To anyone else, it'd seem like a harmless request, but Archer was a God. He'd invaded my dreams and my space, and the attention was suffocating. Anyone could see that he was after something, but so was I.

"I want something in return," I said, fixing him with a look. "I want answers to questions."

"Of course. What would you like to know?"

"What's the deal between you and Gray? It's like you can't stand to be in the same room with each other."

His features darkened, and I watched as his body language changed. Archer was usually confident and open, but he'd closed himself off.

"He took something from me," he said darkly. "I think Grayson should tell you, lest I be called biased and accused of manipulating facts."

I furrowed my brow and Archer raised a hand to brush his fingers across my forehead, trying to smooth the creases. Just like in the lab, there was a rush of feeling, but nothing came of it. Unlike with every other God, it felt like Archer couldn't quite pull anything to the surface.

"Still nothing," he whispered. "I need to get going," he said, dropping his hand. "Perhaps we can meet again soon."

"Maybe."

"All you need to do is think of me and I'll be there in a heartbeat."

Archer left, and the night wore on. Gray didn't visit my side of the bar, keeping as far away as possible.

I watched him as he worked and paid attention to a petite woman with an ample amount of cleavage on display. He eventually rang the bell for last order and the pub emptied, but the woman pulled him over the bar, and I witnessed them kiss.

Something deep inside me twisted uncomfortably and made me nauseous. There was a sharp pain in my chest that made me gasp for air. Whatever had unfolded in front of me, I no longer wanted a front row seat.

I needed to get away.

THIRTY SIX

GRAYSON

I sensed her all night, and I chose to stay as far away as possible. Whatever the pain in my chest was, it radiated more when Quentin was nearby. This woman was destined to kill me in one way or another.

Staying away from her proved more difficult when Archer appeared. But it wasn't my problem. Archer couldn't read her. There was no need to worry. And even if Archer could and he found out the truth, what did it matter? I owed her nothing.

A woman displaying her ample assets frequented the bar area, catching my eye so I laid on all the charm to distract myself. By the end of the night, she'd pulled me over the bar for a kiss. It was a confident move, but it was calculated. Contrived. A move she'd used on men before. It wasn't like Quentin who did as she felt based on instinct.

The kiss was wet and tasted of stale smoke, and then I heard it. A small gasp. When I pulled away, I saw Quentin pushing her way out of the pub with traces of anger running through her.

"Not tonight," I said. "I think it's best you go home."

She wasn't happy with my refusal, but I wasn't focused on her anymore. I was focused on Quentin and her reaction.

The pub emptied out, and I locked up before taking myself home. Quen still hadn't arrived and so I stood outside the door, waiting for her.

"Where have you been?" I asked when she finally walked up the street.

"Walking home. Took the scenic route."

Controlled aggression was what Scott was best at. If something pissed her off, she dealt with it privately before facing it. I was amazed by the restraint, though I'd watched the way it slipped around me at times.

She came up to the door, stopping to fish her keys from her bag.

"Why'd you rush off?" I asked.

She sighed, and the keys fell from her hand, clattering on the ground. Quen reached down to grab them, but my aura snatched them before she had a chance.

"Gray," she said, straightening up. "I'm not in the mood to play games tonight."

"I'm not playing games, Scott. I want an answer."

"I didn't feel well."

The keys hung from my index finger, and she reached out. I pulled them back quickly, and she stumbled.

"I thought you said you weren't playing games," Quen muttered.

"I think you're lying to me."

"Give me my keys."

"Tell me the truth."

"What do you want me to say, Gray?"

There it was. There was the flash of anger I fed off.

"You want me to say that I hated seeing you all over someone else at the bar?" she asked.

I smirked. She was jealous. Just like she'd been jealous over Elva. The same way I found myself jealous of Holden and Archer.

I pushed the key into the lock and opened the door, letting us into the house. I closed and locked it once we were both inside, and Quen kicked off her heels, sinking down to size.

"I'm going to bed," she announced.

She took off up the stairs two at a time, and I followed suit. The door to her bedroom slammed shut, and I growled before letting my aura carry me through to the other side.

"Privacy, Grayson," Quentin told me, but she didn't sound surprised at my lack of boundaries.

"She kissed me, you know," I clarified coolly.

"You encouraged it!"

How was she standing there having this conversation when she had a boyfriend to concern herself with now?

I advanced on her, like a hunter closing in on prey, until she hit the wall of her room.

"What do you want from me, Quentin?" My arms caged her in, and I stared down at her.

Her answer surprised me. "A friendship."

She was looking up at me in such earnest that I almost laughed.

"I'm sorry?"

Quentin looked away from me. "I'm in a relationship," she stated, "but I miss you."

The words were so quiet, but they came crystal clear to my ears.

I could see it all over her face. This was only ever temporary. Quentin Scott was the type of woman who wanted commitment and a relationship. She wouldn't get that from me and we both knew it, so she'd made a choice.

But she still wanted me here.

"You're the one who stopped talking to me," I pointed out.

She looked up at me again. “I know. I’m sorry.”

What was I meant to do with this woman?

I missed her. The way we avoided each other now was uncalled for, but I wasn’t sure I could trust myself around her. The obsession had morphed and spiralled until I no longer had control over it.

We stood there for a few minutes, and I fought with myself, unsure I could give her what she wanted, but being around her again, talking to her, eased all the pain in my chest.

“Okay. We’re friends,” I told her, pushing away from the wall so she could get some space. “I’ll leave you to sleep.”

I left the room and headed into my own.

Friends.

She wanted to be friends.

If she wanted to be friends, then why get so jealous of a random woman who threw herself at me?

No. She wanted more than a friendship, but she wouldn’t allow herself. Quentin was too practical. She was thinking beyond the project.

I shook my head, stripping off my clothes before getting into bed. I put my hands behind my head and stared at the ceiling.

It wasn’t even like I wanted that woman at the pub. She’d thrown herself at me, and I still couldn’t help but compare her to Quentin. It was maddening how she’d taken over my life without me realising.

The quicker this project was over, the better. Maybe then we’d actually get things back to normal. Being on earth was throwing things out of sync. At home in Elysia, I’d be free of Quen and whatever hold she had over me.

But even I knew I was lying to myself.

A knock on the door made me turn my head. Quen stood in her pyjamas, looking at me.

“Is something wrong?” I asked.

“No. I… It doesn’t matter.”

She turned around, but I let a tendril of aura snake towards her, coiling around her waist.

"What is it?" I asked again.

Quen let out a heavy sigh. "I just… Can I stay with you?"

This woman was going to kill me. I clenched my jaw for a moment and then let my aura drag her towards the bed.

"Of course," I said tightly.

Before Holden waded in with his size nines, we'd spent nights together. She would sit in bed, working on presentations and spreadsheets, and with a book in my hand, I'd watch her silently.

Something about waking up to her in the morning, before she had a chance to caffeinate and spark up on ambition, was like a drug to me. I saw her first thing before anyone else did. I saw her when she was most vulnerable.

"I like the left side," she pointed out.

"Tough shit. Get in or get out."

She rolled her eyes before crawling into bed and settling down beside me. I turned over to face her.

"Is this what friends do?" I asked, unable to help myself.

Quen shrugged in response. "I used to share a bed with friends when I went to sleepovers."

She'd come prepared with a justification.

"Would you also like to paint my nails and braid my hair?" I quizzed her.

She lifted a hand and ran it through my hair. There was a tenderness in the gesture that revealed itself in the privacy of our bubble. It'd be so easy to kiss her, but I pushed down on those thoughts. She'd done well to justify lying in bed with me, and I wasn't about to do anything to scare her off.

"Friends also talk," she continued.

"We are talking."

"I mean honestly."

"What do you think I'm dishonest about?"

"Archer."

I tensed and commented, "I saw you speak to him at the bar."

"He keeps finding me. He said you took something from

him and that if I wanted to know more, I should ask you."

Archer would plant little seeds of doubt everywhere. God of secrets. The pool should have gifted him powers for shit stirring since he had a penchant for the art.

I couldn't tell her. I wouldn't have wanted to tell her before we found out her status, but now that I knew what she was, I'd never be able to speak to her about that part of my past. Not if I wanted her to keep thinking of me the way she did.

"You obviously don't like each other," she pressed.

"I've got years on you, Scott. I've done a lot of things in my lifetime. He's taken some of those decisions more personally than he should have."

"Such as?"

"It's divine business, Scott. And it's the past. I don't really want to bring it all up again."

She bit her bottom lip.

"He's trying to stir up trouble," I told her firmly. "Don't let him. He's bitter he hasn't made it to the elites."

Quen considered this quietly, and I tried to pull her mind from it.

"Any other questions?" I asked her.

Her lips quirked into a smile. "Millions."

"Fire away."

"What's your flower?"

"Millions of questions and you start that?"

"My brain is a little fried right now. It's been a long week."

I lifted a hand, closing my fist tight and opening it again. In my palm was a single Odessa calla lily. Slender and black, it stood out against my skin.

"That's beautiful," she breathed. "I don't think I've seen them before."

Archer could fuck off with his yellow tulips. Quentin was drawn to my colour, just like she was drawn to me. I let the flower disappear and settled an arm over her waist.

"Gray," she said.

"I'm getting comfortable. Will you let me ask you a question?"

"Sure."

I knew what I wanted to ask her, but I wasn't sure she'd answer. Intensely private, Quen kept her cards close to her chest.

"That ring," I started, and she tensed under my touch, body rigid as I touched on the uncomfortable topic. "What's the story?"

There were a few moments of silence, but she didn't run.

"What happened?" I prompted, curiously.

I'd been curious ever since Erik touched her and spoke to her at the bar. The curiosity grew ever since I'd found the ring. I could find out with ease, but I wanted her to tell me.

Maybe Erik was right and I enjoyed people's misery, or perhaps it was because she decided to open up about things to me, it felt like a win.

"He left," she said abruptly. Quentin was all about facts.

"And?"

"What, Gray?" she snapped. "What do you want to know?"

"Why does it make you so angry?"

"Can't you just find out?"

"You wouldn't appreciate that."

She looked at me and then closed her eyes. "I fell in love with a guy called Ethan when I was an undergraduate student."

"How old were you?"

"Nineteen."

"You weren't in love."

"Fuck off."

She twitched under my arm as if to leave, so I pulled her closer to my body. Quentin wasn't going anywhere. This was the most content I felt in weeks. This was where she belonged.

"Sorry," I said. "I reserve my judgements until the end."

Sighing heavily, she continued, "He looked after me. My parents died the year before and Cass was in New York. Ethan made sure I was alright. Kept my head screwed on."

She looked at my chest, fingers tracing patterns carefully as she recalled the memories. Not angry or protective or business-like. This was Quen when she was vulnerable.

"When we graduated, he went into industry, and I started my PhD. It was fine. Things were good. They were better than good. He proposed."

"The ring —"

"Yes. That was the ring he gave me." She looked up slowly with a wry smile. "You were right. It's not really to my taste."

"What happened?"

Quen shrugged. "He got bothered by things. We set the date for after I graduated and then his colleagues would joke it'd be Mr and Dr. I worked hard for my title, so I mean, I'd use it when I had to."

"As you should."

She raised an eyebrow at me. But I was a prideful being, so I understood.

"He got more and more hostile about everything. Suggested I quit and take up a job with him instead. He was already working his way up the ranks, but I'm not interested in big Pharma."

"He wanted you to leave without finishing?"

"Mhm. And then —"

Quentin buried her face in the pillow, and I wondered if she was crying. Then she lifted it again, and I saw she was completely calm.

"And then," she continued, "he told me one morning that he wasn't in love with me anymore. That I loved my work more than him. So Ethan packed his things and left me. I had to face cancelling the wedding and telling everyone. I blocked him on everything and buried my head in work and now I'm here."

Quen was on a roll, and I felt like maybe she needed to get this off her chest. How many people knew the truth of what unfolded in her life?

"I gave five years of my life to someone and thought it was just the start, only for him to turn around and say he didn't even love me anymore. People find it easy to leave me. I don't know what it is, but I'm not worth sticking around for. I learned the hard way that I'm the only person I can rely on."

She looked me in the eye as if telling me to challenge her and then thought I knew I could bend her easily. I didn't. I kept my powers under control and nodded.

"Fair enough," I said. "Scott belongs to Scott and no one else."

She was quiet and then said, "No teasing? No telling me how I'm a pathetic mortal?"

"No."

"I'm surprised."

I shrugged, rolling around the information in my head.

It made sense why she would behave the way she did. She worked hard and gave selected people her time. It was a knock-on effect from that sorry excuse of a man.

Who would leave her like that? Quentin could be difficult. There was no doubt about that, but she didn't deserve to be left so heartlessly.

The anger bubbled just beneath the surface. Why hadn't she sought me out sooner? If she'd prayed to me, I'd have helped her get revenge. But she hadn't. Quen had dealt with it the way she dealt with everything. Alone and in her own time.

"I don't think you were in love," I told her honestly.

She opened her mouth to protest, but I continued.

"You weren't soulbound."

"Soulbound? Like soulmates?"

I hummed. "Is that what mortals call it? You're all fickle beings. Anyone you marry is deemed a soulmate. Erik knows more about it than I do, but if you're soulbound to a person, then it means they were created for you. He and Sloan are soulbound."

"I don't believe in soulmates. Or soul binding."

"You don't believe in much, do you, Scott?"

She smiled and nestled herself against me. "I'm a realist, Gray. Love is a series of chemical reactions. It's not some grand, sweeping gesture that people make it out to be. No soulmates or love at first sight. It's two people having to work out if they should settle together and hoping it won't completely implode and destroy them."

"Is that what you truly believe?" I asked, shocked by her

cold and calculated summary.

"It's what I know."

THIRTY SEVEN

GRAYSON

All the Gods had gathered at Gareth's house for the weekly briefing, and the small selection of minor Gods joined our ranks.

"How's Quentin doing?" Archer asked, gliding towards us.

My eye twitched. "Stop trying to stir up shit, Archer."

"She asked you about it then?" He laughed. "She'll find out what you're like, Grayson. You'll lose that shine."

Erik clapped a hand on my shoulder and pulled me away before we could start a fight.

Hunter had become more irritable lately, as he always did when Sloan and Erik had children. He wanted an heir and Larkin outright refused him. Their relationship was a complicated one, and he had the tendency to take it out on the rest of us. We didn't need to give him any more ammunition to reprimand us over nothing.

"You seem in a better mood," Erik commented as we took a seat and Hunter started.

I shrugged.

"What's going on?" Erik asked suspiciously. "You haven't slept with her. I can tell you haven't."

"Nothing."

"Do you two ever listen to these things?" Sloan asked.

"Why bother when you can fill us in later?" I replied.

"Gray," Erik said. "What's going on between you and Scott?"

"Honestly? Nothing. We're friends."

His blonde eyebrows disappeared into his hairline. He was probably surprised that I'd managed a friendship with anyone other than Ignacio and Elva.

"And you're happy?" Erik asked incredulously.

"For now."

There were always stipulations. I might not be able to keep it up, but for now, I was content.

I didn't know why it made me happy, but it did. Talking to Quen, knowing things about her daily life, and coaxing her to share things with me was something I enjoyed. I couldn't deny there were times I wanted more, but I was learning to control the appetite I had for her.

Hunter wrapped up and I rolled my eyes. He was a prick in general, but worse when Larkin fought with him. He made a beeline towards Erik and me, with Elva and Sloan making themselves scarce.

Cowards.

"I was thinking about a family dinner together, soon. I feel like we're seeing less of each other at the moment," Hunter said.

"What's the matter, Hunter?" I asked. "Can't control Larkin

on your own?"

There was a flash of blue, and I laughed. On the scale of hot heads, Hunter fell closer to Erik than me. Seeing him lose it so easily told me I'd hit a nerve.

"You can invite Elva," Hunter told me sharply. "It's about time you thought of settling down."

Ig was nearby, and I caught him duck his head. Outside of family, Ig was who I was close to, and he was usually happy-go-lucky. Lately, it bothered him how much people pushed for Elva and I to get together, regardless of the fact neither of us had an intention to fulfil the council's wishes.

"Why?" I asked.

"You know things aren't exactly settled in Elysia. The minor Gods are getting restless. The more of a united front we show, the better it'll be."

Erik looked at him wide-eyed. "No. No. No. No more marriages of convenience. Look at where it's got you."

When Hunter proposed to Larkin, Erik was against the idea. He went through the entire wedding looking ready to kill someone. It was in Erik's nature to believe in true love, and he'd be the first to tell you that wasn't what laid between Hunter and his wife.

"Sometimes our duty has to come before feelings, Erik," Hunter reminded him.

"How is that working for you, exactly?" Erik asked.

I folded my arms across my chest and watched them. It was rare that Erik would take on Hunter, but this was something he'd die on a hill for.

"Erik," Sloan said gently, making her way back towards us.

"I understand the importance of keeping Elysia at peace. Not all of us can hang around for centuries until we find the one," Hunter barked.

"No," Erik said. "But you should have learned how to rule on your own without Larkin pulling the strings in the background."

The blue flared into life, and it was joined by red.

"Stop trying to force decisions on people, Hunter," Erik said fiercely. "Love and marriage aren't a game or bargaining chips."

"You're so jaded by your responsibilities you don't see the bigger picture."

"Maybe you should take yours a little more seriously, big brother, because you're not doing well to protect your family."

The blue struck out at Erik, but he blocked it while I pushed my aura out around me. Erik didn't need my help. A wall of red rushed at Hunter quicker than he could recover from the block and our big brother was flung to the other end of the room, all eyes landing on him.

Erik looked furious, and Sloan appeared next to him as Hunter got back up to his feet.

There wasn't a single wisp of blue that reached Erik as it was blocked by red, green, and then black.

"Hunter. Give it a rest," I warned him.

The Gods around us all watched, whispering at the display. Fights between us were conducted privately, where Hunter could keep his spotless image intact.

"GET OUT!" Hunter roared. "ALL OF YOU!"

I opened my mouth, wanting to poke at the bear but green wrapped around me and I appeared at Martyn Hankel's home with Erik and Sloan.

"Are you okay?" Sloan asked her husband.

"Fine."

Erik shook himself, aura still drifting around him as he wasn't fully in control.

"You shouldn't have done that," I told him, trying to be a responsible older brother.

"He's using people like chess pieces. It's fine if he wants to mess up his own life but he shouldn't play with others."

"Brother, I appreciate the support." I held him by the shoulders and made him look at me. "But you have a wife and children to think of. I can fight my own battles."

Erik sighed, and I watched the red fade away from around him.

"Thanks though. Also, you're welcome to knock Hunter on his ass for any other reason. Just don't want Sloan to kill me because

I'm the cause of your death."

Erik laughed and rubbed the back of his neck. "It got a little heated."

"Just a little, love," Sloan said.

"I'm heading back to Scott's. If you need anything, if he comes here trying to pick a fight, Sloan, come and get me," I told them.

Sloan nodded, and I made my way back to Quentin's place.

The house was quiet, and I found myself laughing. Hunter was losing the plot and so what if I revelled in people's misery? Someone had to, right? It was about time Hunter was put in his place.

Looking around the living room, I saw a stack of dusty vinyl records tucked away and I thumbed through them before pulling one out and placing it in the player. Smooth music made its way through the house, filling the silence, and I was surprised she'd listen to such old music.

The voice crooned through the house, and my mood lifted to the rafters.

No one was going to find out about her.

They were too busy with their own shit.

THIRTY EIGHT

QUENTIN

Sitting in a small cafe, Matthew and I ordered brunch and chatted away. We were tucked away in a cosy booth with the scent of sugary syrup surrounding us.

"Cass isn't having any of it," I told him. "But you can't blame Sophie for trying."

Matt smiled and bit into a slice of toast. "I'm looking forward to meeting them both at the wedding."

I choked on my coffee, spluttering in the most unladylike fashion.

"I'm sorry?" I said once I'd recovered.

"You get a plus one to the wedding, right? I assume you

aren't taking anyone else."

I'd completely forgotten about that. Cass thought I was dating Gray, and I'd be attending the wedding with him. Matthew wanted to be the guest because we were actually dating.

"I didn't think we were at a point to introduce each other to family," I said.

"Well, the wedding is in December. That's still three months away. You don't think we'll be ready by then?"

I couldn't breathe. At every turn, Matt took the lead, guiding our relationship and the pace of it. This time, I tried to learn from my past mistakes. With Ethan, I'd dug my heels in and picked small fights and it'd landed me alone. So, with Matt, I bit my tongue, but even I had my limits.

"Maybe… I'll have to see. You'd probably get bored. I'll be running around after the pair of them all week and on the day."

"I don't mind, Quentin."

"We'll see, Matt."

It came out as a bite, and he looked taken aback and then shrugged.

"Whatever you say."

My phone pinged on the table, and I picked it up to see a new email.

"I thought I told you no phones on dates," he said firmly.

I had a horrible habit of being tied to my phone for emails and work. Typing out emails or receiving them, and Matt became so irritated that he placed a ban. My first instinct was to say 'fuck you' but I swallowed that unsavoury response and agreed that I should focus on us when we were together.

My eyes scanned over the email. "I know, but I've been waiting… YES!"

I jumped in my seat, thighs bashing against the table and causing the plates and mugs to wobble noisily.

"Quentin!"

I'd learned some things about Matthew since being in a relationship with him. He liked a trophy. When I dressed down, he complained. When I drew attention for what he thought were the wrong reasons, he complained. Most of the time I rolled my eyes and ignored him, not willing to start a fight. Like now. I didn't care if people stared, but it bothered him.

"Look!" I said, shoving my phone in his face. He took it from me and read the email. "The presentation I submitted. It got accepted for the conference!"

I waited for his congratulations, but it never came.

"Are you sure you're ready for it?" he asked, handing the phone back over.

"Sorry?"

The pride and joy that had swelled in my chest deflated.

"You're good, Scott, but it's a world congress and you're going to present in front of a lot of people."

My brow furrowed. "And?"

"And I'm just making sure you're ready for it. You're twenty-seven, you've got to be one of the youngest —"

"So?" I felt myself getting defensive about it.

"Are you going to be able to stand up to experts in the field?"

I blinked at him a few times; the happiness completely wiped out by his lack of enthusiasm.

My PhD project had been my baby. The number of hours I'd sunk into research, learning new skills so that I could fully understand my work, was unfathomable to most. I was more than capable of presenting my findings and discussing them with my colleagues who were more advanced in the field. Even if I couldn't answer, it'd be a great learning curve, and I'd get my name out there.

"I need to go," I said to him, letting the anger win out.

"Oh, come on, Quentin. You're not hurt, are you? I'm just looking out for you, babe."

"I'm fine, but I need to get some things together for this conference. I'm going to need some things to wear and —"

His eyes lit up. "I'll come with you."

Matt would love nothing more than to keep a check on me and help me pick out my clothes, but he could go fuck himself. I wasn't playing Barbie to his airhead Ken.

"That's alright," I said curtly. "I'll call Charlie."

I pulled out my purse, and Matt put a hand on my wrist.

"I'll get it," he said. "You know, I am proud of you."

Empty words. He knew he should say it, and that's why he had. Too little, too late.

"Thanks." I leaned over and kissed his cheek, lips barely touching the skin. "I'll see you later."

I got up and left with no intention of calling Charlie. I wanted to be alone.

When I finally arrived home, I dropped the bags in the hallway and kicked off my boots. I'd picked up a few pieces and everything else could be found in my wardrobe.

The sound of music drifted from the living room. A familiar song that I hadn't heard in years. Gray had stuck on one of Dad's old vinyl records.

I wanted to be mad at him for touching things that belonged to my dad, for going through my belongings again. But Nat King Cole's smooth voice flared through the room and when Gray saw me, he reached out a hand. It brought back a flood of memories that warmed my insides.

"Come and dance with me," he said.

"Gray, I just got in," I argued nervously. "It's been a long day."

"So?" he said, not seeing the issue. "Come dance with me, Scott. I didn't get the chance at the gifting ball." After a moment he added, "Please."

The please was what broke me. He didn't say it unless he really wanted something.

After the day I had, what would be the harm?

Walking over to Gray, he placed a hand on my waist, and I put one on his shoulder as the free ones clasped together.

I hadn't played the records in years. My father loved Nat King Cole and Cass and I had fallen hard for his voice.

Gray moved us around the furniture in the living room, swaying us around the place until I laughed.

"Mum and Dad used to dance to this. It was the first dance at their wedding."

"They had good taste."

The music built and Gray moved gracefully, moving me around the space, and I followed his lead with ease, humming along to the song.

All the anger and sadness I'd felt when I was with Matt drained away, and I enjoyed the moment. And then I let it take over me — the urge to share the news with Gray.

"You know that presentation I've been working on?"

"The one that kept me up at night because you wouldn't put it away in bed?"

Gray would mock that he couldn't sleep, thanks to the bright light of my laptop, but he didn't need the sleep, and even if he did, he could have pulled his aura around him. Instead, he'd lay next to me, reading a book from the glow of my screen and only finish when I got too tired to work anymore.

"Yes, that's the one."

"What about it?"

We didn't stop moving as we carried out the conversation.

"I got my acceptance today. I fly to Malaysia in two weeks for the conference. Gray!!"

He'd stopped us dancing and wrapped both his arms around my waist, picking me up from the floor and spinning me around until I laughed at the ridiculousness of the situation.

"That's my girl!"

I blushed at his words but didn't correct him. He held me up off the floor, and I rested my hands on his broad shoulders.

"All that hard work paid off? How long are you there?" he asked, genuinely interested.

He slowly let me down so my feet touched the floor and my hands slid down to his chest.

"Conference is for four days, but I'm asking for a week. I've never been to Malaysia."

"You're going to take them by storm. I'm so fucking proud of you."

Gray leaned down and kissed me, and I forgot.

I forgot I had a boyfriend.

I forgot Gray was a God.

I forgot that this was trouble.

Instead, I wound my arms around his neck and kissed him back. Every kiss I shared with Gray turned my insides molten and sparked something dangerous in my chest. It was only when we broke apart, breathing heavily, with his forehead against mine, did I think.

Gray opened his eyes, and they were entirely black.

"Quentin." His voice was deep and husky, and I knew I'd made a mistake.

I pushed away from him gently and shook my head.

"I'm sorry," he said, looking pained.

"It's fine. It just can't happen again," I stumbled, trying to straighten my thoughts. "I need to go and get things ready."

Hurrying out of the room, I felt my heart sink at the silence that followed me out.

Why couldn't I stay away from him? It wasn't for lack of trying, but when I tried, it hurt so badly. When we didn't talk, it was as if something was missing.

He irritated me. His general attitude towards life was annoying and yet he listened, and he was brutally honest, and I appreciated that.

But even though we were friends, and it dulled the ache, inside I craved more.

I had no right to be jealous when he kissed another woman, but it'd be easier if I didn't have to see it happen. I wanted it to be me, but that wasn't a good idea. It was too dangerous, and I didn't want Gray to be punished, to be killed, because we couldn't keep it in our trousers.

But the most worrying thing about the whole situation was that it was beginning to feel like more than sex.

It was starting to feel like something a lot more complicated.

THIRTY NINE

GRAYSON

"Do you need any help?"

She jumped, still not used to how quietly I moved. Too caught up in her own tangle of thoughts.

I leaned against her bedroom door, having just finished a shift at Murphy's. It was late and Quentin stood by her bed, suitcase on top, open and partially filled.

"I'm good, thanks. Nearly done," she replied, moving to her drawers and pulling out some pyjamas.

"Quentin, about the other week —"

"Mhm?" She kept her back to me.

Walking into the room, I grabbed her by the hips and turned her around to face me. Beneath my hands, she trembled nervously.

"I'm sorry," I said without prompt. "I overstepped the mark, and I shouldn't have."

Ever since our impromptu kiss, things had changed between us. Another round of avoiding each other without underlying anger. Quen wouldn't look at me. She'd disappear the moment I walked into a room, locking herself away upstairs. It drove me mad that she'd slipped through my fingers again.

She shook her head, her focus on the floor.

"Please, Scott," I said, lifting her chin, so she'd look at me. The pain in my chest eased as we locked eyes. "It won't happen again." There was a pause. "Not unless you want it to."

The smile pulled at her lips, and she smacked me in the chest. I laughed and pulled her into a hug. Her body moulded against mine and I took in a deep breath, revelling in honey and orange. She wrapped her arms tight around me and I basked in the peace the simple gesture brought.

When we came apart, I regretted letting her go. The cold space that was left felt too prominent. Demanded too much attention to be rectified, but I couldn't keep her with me no matter how much I wanted to.

"I can drop you off at the airport, if you want," I offered. "I could take you straight to the hotel."

"Matthew's taking me."

"Of course." I ran a hand through my hair, messing the neat style. "I should let you finish packing and get some rest." I moved towards the door and looked over my shoulder. "I'll miss you, Scott."

When she didn't say anything, I left the room. Halfway down the hall, I heard a soft whisper.

"I'll miss you too, Gray."

"What are you doing here?" Erik asked, walking into the kitchen of his host's house.

I sat in the dark, nursing a glass of whiskey in the early hours of the morning. The dim light of the moon shone through the window and left a patch of light on the tiles.

"I couldn't be in the house on my own any longer," I explained.

"What?"

"Scott. She left for her conference two days ago. The house is too quiet. I can't stay there."

Erik nodded, and I poured another glass, pushing it towards him.

"Gray, are you hurt?" he asked me suddenly.

I drained my glass and shook my head. "No."

"I can feel —"

"I have this weird pain here."

I gestured around my chest. Erik paled. I might not have wanted to admit it, but we both knew this wasn't a medical issue. If it was, Aria would have been here in a flash. This was a pain only Erik could pick up on.

This was heartache.

"Gray, please let me read you," he pleaded in the darkness.

I'd been fighting against this for weeks, but I was tired. For the first time in my existence, I was exhausted, and I needed him to tell me what I already knew; that I'd fucked up and caught feelings for a woman that I shouldn't have.

It would pass. Hearts healed, given time. We'd forget about each other and move on with our lives once the project was completed.

The thought made the ache turn to a searing pain, and I grimaced.

Erik looked surprised as I nodded my head, finally giving into his request.

To read another God was no small ask. We knew everything when it came to our responsibilities, except when it came to one another. We could sense things, but it was never the full picture.

I put out both my hands towards Erik, and he took in a deep breath before holding them. The red of his aura spiralled its way up my arms rapidly, and I was hit with an overwhelming surge of emotion.

It appeared crystal clear before my eyes, the myriad of memories I had with Quentin over the past few months and Erik was partial to all of them.

I saw her when I was first dragged through the facility. She had large brown eyes that held no fear, and I was instantly interested in this woman who didn't shy away from watching me in full fury.

We interacted through our annoyances at one another, and the first time we touched, skin to skin, I basked in all the chaos that came from her. And something happened that I didn't realise. Deep black, like my aura, seeped into her the moment we touched.

The months passed, and I couldn't keep away from her. Sex became something more. My desire for her ran deeper, no longer just content with the physical. I craved the gentlest touch. I shared in her victories and comforted her in her losses. I laid next to her in bed and had long conversations.

Quen calmed me when I was upset with a hand on my arm or a simple look. She frustrated me most days, but it pained me to have her away from me.

Archer and Matthew came into view, and the black from my body pulled to be with her. It wrapped around her, and it caused the physical pain I was feeling. Every time we avoided each other, I watched the black seep away towards her, but I'd never sent my aura to her. It wasn't a ward, so what had been happening?

The last image that played out before us was the hug we'd shared before she left. Quen gripped me tightly and I bit my tongue from asking her to stay. Our days were numbered, and I didn't want to waste any more away from her. When she peeled herself away from me, something golden shimmered between us.

Erik's aura receded from my arms, spiralling back towards him before it disappeared. He let go of my hands, and a golden glow illuminated mine.

"Erik?" I panicked. "What is this?"

Gold was not my colour. It didn't belong to Erik. This wasn't natural.

When I looked at my brother, tears fell down his cheeks.

I rose from the chair quickly and noticed the golden glow came from my chest, lighting up the kitchen and silhouetting my ribs.

"What the fuck is this?!" I touched my chest and looked at him.

The panic was rising at the unknown substance that'd lit me up like a beacon.

"I'm so sorry," he whispered.

"What? Why? What have you done to me?"

"I haven't done anything."

"What is this?!" I demanded.

"Her soul."

I froze.

Looking at my hands, I shook my head.

"No. No. It can't. I can't —"

"Grayson. You were specifically made for each other."

"No. No, we weren't!"

"You were." Erik nodded to my hands and chest. "It's why you physically ache without her. It's why you're so drawn to each other without reason."

"It's so bright," I said, staring at my hands.

Erik nodded and choked out, "I'm so sorry."

"Why?"

"I didn't know you were bound until now," he admitted. "I pushed her to leave you. I pushed her towards Holden. I told her what would happen if Hunter found out."

"What?" My eyes darkened.

"I didn't know she was made for you. She's a demigoddess. It explains why I couldn't see everything. I'd have needed her permission."

The black of my aura hit Erik so quickly that he slammed against the wall.

"She's MINE," I roared. "She's meant to be with me and now she's with him!"

Sloan appeared in the kitchen. "Grayson!"

The glasses around us shattered as the rage pulsed through me, stronger than I'd ever felt.

"Gray! Stop!" Sloan yelled.

"Think. Of. Scott," Erik choked out.

He knew Quentin had a soft spot for him, and she wouldn't forgive me if I hurt him. Struggling, I regained control, and Erik slid down the wall and dropped to the floor.

"What do you think you're doing?" Sloan yelled, looking at me. She stopped as she took me in. "Oh…"

The glow still hadn't disappeared from me. I turned towards Erik.

"How do I stop it?" I asked him desperately.

Erik shook his head violently, getting up off the floor. "Don't do it, Gray."

"I can't be with her! How did this happen?"

"You can break a soul bond, but you'd be in so much pain. Please, don't do it. I've seen it once. I don't want you to go through that."

I leaned against the wall and slumped to the floor. "What am I meant to do, Erik?"

"Tell her."

"What would be the point? I can't be with her."

"We'll find a way," Sloan said. She walked over to me and kneeled down on the floor.

"If they think she's mortal, then I die. If they find out she's a demigoddess, then she dies."

There was no winning. Whatever way we painted it, this was forbidden.

"If they find out she's a demigoddess, then we can convince the council somehow. There's one of her, Gray. Not an army like before," Sloan told me.

Erik joined his wife. "Tell her. She'll leave Holden for you."

I looked up at him slowly and shook my head. "I want her to leave him because she chose me. Not because she feels obliged to. I can't give her what she wants. Commitment. A life. A family. You know that. I know that. Fuck, even she knows that."

We were Gods, and we took what we wanted. But it wasn't the case here. Quentin needed to make this decision. And even if she did, what could I offer her?

"Okay, don't tell her, but be with her, Gray. You both need to be near each other if you want to ease the pain," Erik said.

"She's working," I told him.

"You don't think she'd want to see you?"

"Will she?"

"Gray, everything you feel, she'll be feeling too."

I nodded. "Don't tell anyone. I mean it, Erik. I need to figure out what to do."

"Of course."

We were soulbound.

That infuriating and brilliant woman was designed for me, and yet she wasn't mine. The glow of her soul had faded as Erik's powers left my system. It had been so bright, but I wasn't surprised. Mine was dark in comparison. We balanced each other.

"I need to see her," I said.

I had no plans to tell her. I knew Quen well enough. If I told her, then she'd think and rationalise, and I didn't want that. I wanted her to fall in love with me, and then and only then would I tell her about the binding. Or maybe I wouldn't. What use would it be to put her mind in the same turmoil as mine? I didn't understand it completely either. Only Erik truly knew the extent, and he'd confirmed it.

I let my aura drop me where she was. I found myself in a quiet corner of a hotel with boards signposting what was going on in each room, but I didn't need directions. I could sense her in the building and followed my instincts.

The room was packed with chairs, and I took a seat at the back. The stage at the front boasted a large projection screen, and the opening slide for Quen's presentation was displayed. She was announced and walked out onto the stage, and I swallowed hard.

I had behaved around her. I did what she'd asked, and I'd tried to be a good friend minus the single slip up, but knowing she was mine, that part of my soul sat in her, made this so much harder. I took a deep breath and watched her carefully, hands gripping my seat and turning my knuckles white.

"Good afternoon, everyone. I'm Dr Quentin Scott and I'll be talking to you today about developmental programming in regard to fetal growth and the effects of hormonal imbalance during pregnancy."

She didn't falter. Instead, for thirty minutes, Quentin moved back and forth across the stage, flipping through her slides and explaining her research. She handled it all as if she'd been doing this her entire life.

Part of her soul resided in me, and I felt lucky. I felt lucky that such a confident and amazing woman was made for me.

"Thank you for taking the time to listen to my talk. I'll be happy to answer any questions."

There was a flurry of hands, and for the next fifteen minutes, she answered questions from the audience. Once or twice, she flushed red when she didn't know the answer, but kept her cool. The chair called time on the session and Quentin was allowed off the stage.

The room buzzed as people got up and left to mingle. I made my way through the crowded space and found Quentin surrounded by a small group of people. I kept my distance. As badly as I wanted to see her, she was working. This might not mean anything to me, but it meant everything to her, and she wouldn't forgive me if I intruded.

I heard her laugh, and a smile broke out on my face. That sound, hearty and uninhibited, had become one of my favourites. Music that only she knew the notes to.

The crowd slowly thinned, but an older man stayed close by. He had a hand on the small of her back and she was grinning up at him. I walked over and cleared my throat, wanting to break up the cosy setting.

"Gray? What are you doing here?" she asked.

Her tone wasn't accusatory, but she sounded surprised and

happy to see me. Quentin moved away from the man, old enough to be her father, and hugged me.

"Gray," she said. "This is my old supervisor, Professor Dylan Watts. Dylan, this is a friend and colleague of mine, Grayson."

Dylan Watts extended his hand towards me, and I took it, gripping it with more force than necessary.

"Pleased to meet you," he said.

I let go of his hand, and Dylan told Quen he'd see her at dinner and placed a kiss on her cheek. It took all my control not to bring down the entire room.

Any anger seeped away when she turned her smile towards me.

"What are you doing here?"

She was still on a high after her presentation. Ig would have loved to read her now and feel how grateful she was for the opportunity.

"You didn't think I'd miss it, right?" I asked coolly.

"You saw?"

"Very impressive, Scott."

"I didn't look stupid?"

"Not in the slightest."

She let out a big breath.

"I should probably leave you to work," I said.

I had seen her. That was all I wanted. All I needed for my soul to calm down. I wondered if she really felt everything the way I did.

"Oh," Quen said, biting her bottom lip. "Well, today's sessions are done. And —"

"Yes?"

"There's a conference dinner tonight —"

"So you're busy."

"There are… families. People are bringing their… It's not just conference delegates."

She was getting flustered. The eloquent woman on the stage

was starting to ramble, and I tried not to grin. Nervous. I made Quentin nervous.

"I see," I said, refusing to give her an inch.

"You could stay if you want."

"You won't be networking?"

Her face fell, and I realised how it came across. I must have sounded like her ex, who had issues with her success.

"I mean, you won't mind me being there whilst you network?" I clarified.

Quen looked at me for a moment before she smiled again. "Absolutely not."

"Then I guess I could grace you with my presence and be your plus one."

She rolled her eyes. "I am blessed."

"Yes, you are."

FORTY

GRAYSON

I attended the conference dinner with Quentin, and she spent the next day in sessions. When I suggested I leave her to enjoy the rest of her holiday, she asked if I had anything pressing to do.

Nothing.

Not a single thing.

I was almost certain that nothing would ever appear urgent again, as long as she was in the vicinity.

So, for the past few days, I'd trekked around the area with her, exploring the country.

Culture and history fascinated Quen. The guidebook she brought with her was a mess by the time we reached the last day —

pages folded and battered from use. I was rendered useless when she refused to take any shortcuts I offered.

"I can't believe we're going home tomorrow." She sighed and perched on the edge of the bed.

A week in the sun had turned her golden skin into a richer tone, but she didn't try to find shade. Quen was a sun seeker, and it loved her in return.

"You've enjoyed the break?" I asked.

"It's been amazing."

"I have something planned for tonight."

"Oh?" she asked, surprised.

"Get changed and we can go."

"You aren't going to tell me what you have planned?"

"No, it's a surprise."

Quentin hated surprises. She hated not being in control, but sometimes, it was healthy for her to relinquish the tight hold she had on everything, even if I forced her hand.

"Fine," she huffed.

She grabbed some clothes from her case and disappeared into the bathroom.

I knew this wasn't helping my case. I'd hid with Scott, away from facing the reality of what was happening between us. Away from the truth of the binding. There would be no point when I'd have to break it because I'd be back in Elysia with the rest. And maybe it'd be smarter to stay away, but it was easier said than done.

When I returned from the trip, I needed to talk to Erik. We needed to figure out the best way of resolving this. For now, I intended to enjoy my time with her. It was rare to have her undivided attention.

"You seem deep in thought."

I turned around and clenched my jaw. Quentin was dressed in a little black dress that skimmed the top of her thighs and made my mouth run dry.

"Presentable enough for whatever you have planned?" she asked.

I loved it when she wore black. I loved seeing her draped in my colour and I noticed more and more how she opted for black when she was with me. An unconscious decision that stirred something primal and feral deep inside.

"Perfect." I walked towards her, keeping my resolve by a fraying thread. "You have everything?"

She nodded, picking up her purse from the bed before I offered her my arm and we left.

I took Quentin out to dinner. In keeping with having her let go of her control, it was a restaurant that served in complete darkness. We sat in pitch black, which was my comfort zone, and ate together. She was tense at first, but by dessert, she let go, relaxing and enjoying the experience.

"I didn't know they even had restaurants like that," she commented as we left.

"Something a little different. I thought you might appreciate it."

"Thank you, Gray. I've had a wonderful evening."

"Actually, I have one more surprise."

She narrowed her eyes but took my arm. I let my aura transport us both to the edge of a body of water where a small boat stood on the shore.

"You got me dressed up for a boat trip?"

"I promise you'll love it."

"Bold statement, Grayson."

I rolled my eyes behind her. I had one-hundred per cent confidence that she'd enjoy the evening. Carefully, I helped her into the boat, my hands brushing against the bare skin on her back where the dress was cut away to reveal her skin. Once she sat herself down, I got in and set us off down the water.

"You know that this is perfect for murder? Successful woman gets into a boat with a strange man and that's the end of her," Quen mused.

I fixed her with a look. "Why am I the murderer in this instance?"

"You have a temper."

"So do you."

"I have better control of mine."

I rowed us quietly as the sun set, letting her valid point drift away without response.

"Thank you for staying with me the past few days," she said, breaking the silence.

"You don't have to thank me."

"I've got used to doing a lot on my own. I forgot how nice it was to have company."

The sentiment was something I was familiar with. I kept few close to me, mainly because there weren't many that chose to be close. When you had responsibilities like I did, people made their judgements quickly. They failed to remember that I didn't ask for my gifts. They were bestowed upon me, and I was living up to them.

Quentin's independence was different. Stemming from abandonment, she chose loneliness. She protected herself by beating them to the punch.

"I'm surprised you didn't ask Holden to come here with you," I said.

She looked at her feet and shrugged. "He wouldn't have enjoyed it."

"He's not into travel?"

"No, not that bit. I..."

I knew exactly what she meant, but wanted her to say it aloud. Wanted to hear her admit what I'd known all along.

"What is it?" I pressed.

"He's not a bad guy."

She was trying to protect him from me.

"But?" I pressed.

"I don't think it's going to work."

It felt like a heavy weight had lifted from my chest. I knew it. I knew she had no genuine desire for Holden. The entire relationship was a farce.

"I think he just wants a pretty face," Quen explained quietly.

"And you're so much more than that."

Her cheeks flushed pink. "Sometimes I wonder…" She

trailed off and bit her lip. "Sometimes I wonder if I should ease up with work. Give my time to someone again."

It angered me that she thought she had to bend just to get approval from some male.

"And then I think of my parents," she continued. "And I think if someone loves me that much, they'll meet me halfway."

I wondered if she realised that we'd met each other halfway. I'd never interrupt her work, and she didn't judge me for mine.

Quen looked at me and laughed. "Sorry. You must think I'm such an idiot."

"Completely the opposite, Scott. I think you're an ambitious woman and you deserve someone who appreciates that."

She smiled. "Who would have known you could be so sweet?"

"Don't go telling people. I have a reputation to uphold."

"Do you find it difficult?"

I raised an eyebrow.

"Your job," she clarified. "You and Elva seem like you got the shit end of the deal."

It was my turn to shrug. "It's my gift."

"But it's..." She was trying to find the words. "It's a little darker than the rest. It's not exactly joyous."

My defences rose. Maybe I was wrong. Maybe she did judge me.

"I find joy in it." The words were short and clipped.

Her brow furrowed, and she leaned in towards me, putting a hand on my knee. "I wasn't trying to dig at you, Gray. I get you take pride in your work. I just thought it must be difficult when others expect you to justify it."

Her thumb was rubbing against my knee, and I took a deep breath.

"I gave up trying to explain myself to anyone."

She nodded, and I stopped rowing, letting us float on the water as the sun sank away.

"Why have we stopped?" she asked.

"You'll see. Come sit with me."

Quen moved cautiously, taking the spot at my side.

"I'm sorry if you thought I was judging you," she said.

I let out a breath and looked at her. I didn't usually care, but I didn't want her to judge me. I was well aware that what I did caused more issues than fixed them, but it was in my blood and people called to me. Denying my gift would have made me deeply unhappy.

"I know you wouldn't," I told her.

That earned me a smile.

When the sun had set and the space around us turned dark, Quentin inched herself towards me and I felt the nervous energy.

"What's wrong?" I asked. She didn't answer, and I laughed. "Scott, are you scared? Are you afraid of the dark?"

"No! Not the dark."

"What is it then?"

She heaved a sigh. "I don't like deep, dark water. It freaks me out. We know more about the moon than we do about our oceans."

"You can't be serious."

"I don't want to know what's down there."

I laughed heartily, and she thumped me on the arm before I pulled her into my side. Quen rested herself against my body, tension melting away.

"I'll do my best to protect you from any unknown water creature," I muttered against her hair.

"Rephrase that from 'do your best' to 'you will'."

"You don't ask for much, do you, Scott?"

"Not at all."

The urge to kiss her was overwhelming, and it took a lot of self-control not to. I was used to getting what I wanted, and this was fast becoming torture. She admitted it herself that things wouldn't last with Holden, but I knew that didn't mean she wanted me to step into the spot.

I heard the gasp as she looked past me. Pulling away to give her space, she saw why I'd brought her here.

"Are these fireflies?" she breathed.

"Yes, they are," I answered.

"This is beautiful."

Her eyes were large as she looked around us at the bugs lighting up the space.

"It's luciferase and luciferin that makes them glow like this," she explained.

Quen reached out a hand and waited until one bug landed on her palm.

"They use the same complex in the lab. You can test promoter strength of genes if you… Sorry. Sorry."

She looked embarrassed at having drifted back into work, but I shook my head. I knew all the facts, but she could tell me. Watching her get lost in the world she was comfortable in made my heart thud in double time. It was access into a life that she worked hard for and protected fiercely.

"Don't apologise, Quentin."

The bug flew off her hand and joined the others around us. She rested her head against my shoulder, and I put an arm around her, keeping her as close as I could.

She sighed and said, "I think this is possibly the sweetest thing anyone has done for me."

There was a swell of pride in my chest to know I'd presented her with something that had beaten the rest. Something I hoped would stay with her even when I couldn't. A lasting memory as a gift when we were eventually separated.

"Gray?"

"Yes?"

"Aren't the others going to wonder where you've been most of this week?"

"Erik knows."

"You trust him with a lot, don't you?"

I thought of Erik. He was the most harmless out of the three of us brothers. He tried to do what was right, even if it didn't always work out. He separated me from Quentin, but that was before he knew about the binding, and I knew Erik would never forgive himself for that, so what would be the use in being angry at him?

"Just like you trust Cassidy with everything, no?"

There was a beat of silence.

"It must be nice to have blood. I wonder sometimes what it would be like to have blood relatives," she said.

I wanted to tell her it was overrated. That for every Erik, there was a Hunter. I wanted to tell her that her biological mother was also a force to be reckoned with, but her heartbreak was too much. That she couldn't live without Quentin, so she refused to live at all. I wanted to take her to Elva so that they could bond.

I didn't say or do any of those things, because to do so would be to put her life in danger.

"Your adopted family was good to you, though?" I probed.

"I wouldn't have swapped Mum and Dad for the world. Couldn't cope without Cass even though he's a giant pain in the ass most of the time."

"If I were a mortal, I might actually fear your brother."

She laughed as I hugged her close.

"He likes you," she assured me.

"It's hard not to."

We sat out on the water, watching quietly and making the occasional comment, until she yawned, and her weight felt heavier against my body.

"How about we go back?" I suggested.

Scott nodded against me, and I wrapped my aura around the both of us, boat be damned, and took us back to the hotel. She was tired beyond sense and kept yawning.

"You need to get some sleep," I told her.

"You'll stay with me?" The words were muffled with yet another yawn.

"Haven't I every night?"

She hummed and started undressing herself, and I clenched my jaw again. Clad only in her underwear, she crawled into the bed — left side, of course.

I took off my shirt and tossed it to her. "Put that on if you aren't getting into pyjamas."

She sleepily tugged on my shirt as I took off my shoes and trousers and got into bed beside her. Putting her in my shirt was a mistake. Quentin looked so small in it, completely nestled up, and my heart felt funny. She took in a deep breath and smiled to herself, eyes closed, rolling over so she faced away from me.

I moulded my body against hers, spooning.

"What are you smiling about?" I asked, kissing the back of her neck.

"You smell so good."

She was definitely tired. Quen's tongue loosened when she was on the brink of sleep. The filter grew less effective.

"So do you, Quen."

"Thank you, Gray."

She yawned and pushed herself back into me, and I wrapped an arm around her, pulling her in as close as I could.

"It's my pleasure. Now get some sleep." I dotted a kiss on the back of her head.

Everything fell quiet, and after some time, I heard her voice; quiet and thick with sleep.

"Love you, Gray."

FORTY ONE

GRAYSON

I hadn't slept all night thinking about what she'd said. I had no proof she meant it. I wasn't even sure that she'd remember saying it, considering that when she woke up, she didn't mention it. If I brought it up with her, no doubt it would turn into a fight. Or maybe I didn't raise the issue because I didn't want to hear her tell me I was wrong. That those words had been a mistake.

I watched her like a hawk as she finished the last bits of packing.

Did she love me?

Did I love her?

Quentin was attractive. There was no denying that. I'd worshipped her body every time she'd allowed it. The Gods had carved her for me and me alone. Our attraction was purely primal at the beginning.

But I enjoyed spending time with her during more mundane moments. She challenged and intrigued me, but did that mean I loved her? How was something that was meant to be a fuck and chuck turn out so complicated?

Quentin took a flight back home as Holden was due to pick her up. After moping around, getting tied with my thoughts for hours, I used my aura to take me back to Erik's place. My brother wasn't there, but I found Sloan, Elva, and Ignacio.

"The wanderer returns," Sloan greeted me.

"Glad to see you back, Grayson," Elva said.

"Never thought I'd live to see you chase a mortal around the globe." Ignacio laughed.

There was an awkwardness in the air.

"Am I missing something here?" Ig asked, picking up on it.

I looked to Sloan and Elva.

"It's up to you, Gray," Sloan said. "Maybe another opinion, another set of thoughts, wouldn't hurt."

"What is it?" Ig asked, getting antsy.

I took a seat and looked at my friend, deciding to bring him into the circle of trust.

"She's not mortal."

"Yeah, and I'm a demigod." He scoffed.

"No. But she is."

Ignacio laughed heartily, and when none of us joined in, he looked at me.

"It's not possible," he said, sobering up.

Elva took his hand. "Mallory," she said simply.

"Of course, it'd be fucking Mallory." He was out of his seat and Elva looked unhappy.

"Don't speak ill of the dead, Ig," she told him sharply.

"Especially when it's my family."

Elva's cool tone made him rethink just how much fire he had lit inside, and he sat back down.

"How?" he asked. "How long have you known?"

And so, we filled him in on everything.

Almost everything.

The soulbound knowledge stayed between Sloan and me, and by the time we finished, Ignacio looked like he had the worst headache.

"Why can you never keep things simple?" he muttered.

"Not in my nature," I responded.

"Even this is a bit much for you. Hand her in and be done with it."

I had to stop myself from striking out at Ig. He didn't know everything. I couldn't do what he asked of me. Sending Quentin to her death was a reality I couldn’t bear to think of.

"Ignacio." There was a warning tone in Elva's voice.

"What? You were both at the forefront of it, millennia ago. We didn't have to touch a single one of them when both of you were happy to help bear the brunt of killing them all."

I felt ashamed now, knowing that Quen was one of them. That I’d so easily helped to round up her kin and help them meet their demise.

Elva's face read the same as mine and I wondered if she regretted it as much as I did. I wondered if she regretted not investing more time in Mallory.

"She's harmless," Sloan said.

"She's family," Elva pointed out.

"She's harmless until she finds out what happened to the rest of her kin. And if she has children, Sloan?" Ig asked.

Sloan looked away quickly.

"She's going to have children!” Ig exclaimed.

There was a small spark of thought in the back of my mind that wondered if those children were mine. If in some impossible future, we created a family together. I squashed it quickly because it was highly unlikely and focused on Ignacio.

"I'm not sitting around waiting to be slaughtered by her and the minor Gods. I say we tell Hunter and spare ourselves," Ig told us all.

Any other comment he may have had was cut off when Elva finally gave in to her aura. A rich purple knocked Ignacio out of his seat next to her and had him pinned against the floor. He wouldn't fight her. Not when he loved her the way he did.

"Enough!" Elva demanded. "May I remind you she is our kin as well? Divinity runs through her as it does through me and as it did through Mallory. If you're willing to see her put to death for something she cannot help, for who she is, then you aren't the man I thought you were."

Elva eased her aura from him, and Ig recovered quickly.

"He'll have us all if he finds out we haven't told him," he mumbled.

Sloan sighed. "We're trying to find a way around that."

"Keep her hidden until we get back to Elysia?"

"That's the plan," I confirmed.

But even as I said it, I wondered how it'd be possible. I ached for her when she was miles away. How was I meant to go home and be without her? There had to be a way to break this. I needed my brother to present a solution.

"Sloan, where's Erik?" I asked.

"Hunter requested to see him."

"That's not good."

"Why?" Ig asked.

Sloan shook her head, and I shot out of my seat.

"Ignacio," I said. "You tell no one about this."

It took a moment, but he glanced at Elva and said, "You have my word as a God."

That was all I needed before I left to join my brothers.

Gareth was going to lose the plot when he saw this. Hunter and Erik hadn't been able to keep their calm and the entire living room had been transformed into a war zone. Furniture was tipped onto its side and books pulled from the shelves. Shattered glass scattered across the floor, and my brothers stood at opposite ends of the room.

"Hunter! Stop!" I called out.

The force at which Hunter hit Erik sent him flying into the wall, leaving a dent as he slumped down it. I pulled out my aura and waded in front of Erik.

"Move, Grayson!" Hunter demanded.

"No! What are you doing?"

"I'm sick and tired of the disrespect that's shown from both of you!"

There was a ripple of blue before I was knocked off my feet, and I caught myself before I hit the ground.

"Disrespect is what you've earned from us both!" I told him.

Erik was still on the ground, bleeding from his injuries. I looked over my shoulder and said, "Go back home."

Erik didn't argue, but disappeared in wisps of red.

"You're going soft, Grayson," Hunter said.

"No, I'm just trying not to be a prick like you."

A bolt of blue came at me, but I deflected it.

"The both of you have always teamed up against me. What is it that you want?" he asked, looking feral.

What I would have given for Elysia to witness the madness that consumed him. The mask was slipping, and it struck the tinderbox of glee in my heart. We were more alike than Hunter would ever want to admit.

He was advancing quickly, with his aura flexed around him. Hunter had been fired up for a while, but I only realised how much. Erik's little outburst at the last meeting must have hit a nerve, and I hadn't been around to see if they'd managed to work through it. Evidently not. Erik wouldn't have been able to let it go, knowing that I was soulbound.

"I'll get my way," Hunter told me. "You will marry Elva and we are going to strengthen our hold on Elysia."

"You're delusional."

His aura hit me square in the chest, and I went flying into a bookcase. Hunter's attack was relentless, and I could barely call on my aura to protect myself. He was too quick. Too powerful.

"Then the council will decide it! Now, get out!" he yelled.

I didn't need to be told twice. Against all my instincts to stay and make matters worse, to take on my brother with all my rage, I left.

I needed to pick my battles with Hunter wisely, especially when I was beginning to think I couldn't be without a certain demigoddess.

FORTY TWO

QUENTIN

When Matt picked me up at the airport, he grinned and scooped me into his arms. I hugged him back, but was riddled with guilt. It slammed through my veins and made my skin prickle.

"I've missed you," he said.

"It's only been a week," I quipped weakly in return as he let go of me.

"You didn't miss me?"

"I never said that."

He leaned down to kiss me, and I pulled away before it could get any deeper. Matt took my case and put it in the back of the car.

"How was it?" he asked.

"Amazing. The talk went really well. There were loads of

people who wanted to discuss it with me. And Dylan was there, which was unexpected. I have a few new emails from people who are interested in setting up some collaborative work."

Matt looked over at me. "You're not seriously thinking about taking on more work, are you?"

"What do you mean?"

"I barely see you, Quentin." He sounded annoyed. "And when I see you, I have to compete with emails and spreadsheets. You didn't have time for me preparing for this stupid presentation."

"Stupid presentation?"

"That's not what I meant."

"Well, what did you mean, Matthew?"

He let out a frustrated sigh. "You're impossible sometimes, Quentin. You take everything as a personal attack. I just want to spend time with my girlfriend. Why is that such a bad thing?"

"I enjoy my work."

"You make it your entire life."

No, I didn't.

There was more to life than my work. I was just cautious who I gave my time to. I spent it on Cass, Charlie, Sal.

And Gray.

I gave a lot of my time to Gray these days.

Matt had rarely been a priority. Even when I was with him, I was focusing on other things.

"I've worked hard. I want to keep working hard," I argued, banishing thoughts of Gray.

"Sometimes people don't want to sit on the side-lines and cheer you on all the time."

The words stung and robbed me of the power of speech. He reminded me too much of Ethan. Ethan had the tendency to make it about himself. He couldn't be happy for me. Not truly.

When Matt pulled up outside the house, I went to open the car door, but he caught my wrist, a little harder than I was used to.

"Let go," I told him.

"Scott, listen. I don't want to fight with you. I haven't seen you all week."

I turned to face him, biting my cheeks to stop the tears that burnt in my eyes.

"It's a stupid argument," he told me, softening. "I'm sorry I brought it up, but like I said, I just want to spend time with my beautiful girlfriend."

That was all I ever was to him. Beautiful. I wondered if I gave Matt five words to describe me, what they would be? I'd bet the house that they would all have something to do with my physical appearance.

He cupped my face and leaned in to kiss me, but I pulled away, opening the door.

"I said I was sorry, Quentin." The frustration laced his words again, making him sound like a child. "What more do you want?"

I opened the back door of the car and pulled my case out. "If you have to ask, then what's the point? Thanks for the lift."

Slamming the door closed, I stormed up to the house. Unlocking the door, I threw it shut behind me and let my case drop. When I looked around, my anger blossomed from vague irritation into something more tangible.

The floor of the hallway was completely covered in a carpet of yellow tulips.

"For fuck's sake," I hissed.

My words echoed in a deeper tone. "For fuck's sake!"

"Gray?"

"Scott?"

Moving out of the hallway, I found Grayson on the couch, also surrounded by tulips. When I looked at him, I saw he was bleeding.

"What the hell happened to you?" I asked, panic flooding my chest and making my heart skitter uncomfortably. "Let me go grab the first aid kit."

Gray laughed, and I remembered he wasn't mortal.

"Felt the brunt of Hunter's wrath," he answered. "I got off lightly. Erik not so much. It'll heal. It just takes a little longer since it was inflicted by another God."

I nodded and moved over to him. Hunter got him good. Worse than when they'd first arrived.

"I'm surprised that he did that to you and Erik. He seemed so —"

"Saintly?" Gray looked up at me with a raised eyebrow.

"He's meant to be a protector."

"He's also a God and unequivocally selfish. He'll protect himself before anyone else."

"Even his brothers?" I asked. "Larkin?"

There was a bark of laughter. It was a laugh that was harsh, and he used it when he found something stupid, causing me to blush.

"Hunter will look out for himself before anyone else," he said.

"Why is he being like that?"

I couldn't help myself. As I watched Gray, my fingers reached out towards his lip where it was split. The cut was already starting to heal, but there was a thin trail of gold smeared across it. When they brushed his lips, he caught my wrist and kissed the inside.

My heart fluttered wildly. Gray had woken it from the frosty cage I'd locked it inside, and it thrived under his touch. Worryingly, it answered his call and nothing I tried could restrain it again.

When he spoke, his voice was gentle. "I assure you I'm fine. Stop worrying."

He pulled me gently, so I sat on his lap and any of the residual anger I felt disappeared.

"Hunter is losing favour with the council. He's not entirely popular with the minor Gods either, so I think he's worried about being replaced. And with no heir…" He trailed off.

"Wait," I said as the penny dropped. "You?"

He laughed. "You seem surprised."

I shrugged. "A little. You like to break the rules. Not enforce them."

Tucking a lock of his dark hair back in place, I saw his lip had fully healed.

"I only break the rules under special circumstances," Gray whispered.

His gaze was intense and if I were to read between the lines, I'd say Gray was trying to tell me something. But I didn't want to read between the lines. Everything was meant to be uncomplicated between us.

But they had complicated a long time ago, and Gray made it worse when he came to Malaysia. Spending time alone with him, fully clothed and away from everyone else, I realised just how supportive he could be and how sweet he was. And whatever part of me shut down when Ethan left had woken up again. And that was disastrous.

"Quentin." His voice was a whisper, and his eyes scanned over my face before settling on my mouth. "I think you need to unpack before I do something we both regret."

He ran a thumb gently across my bottom lip, and I let out a shaky breath. I prided myself on my determination, but the willpower that carried me through life dwindled the moment I was faced with Gray.

Quietly, I unfolded myself up from his lap, instantly missing the heat of his body.

"Stay away from Hunter," I said.

"Stay away from Archer." He gestured around the room, and I bit my lip. Gray cleared the mess in an instant.

"Thank you."

"Don't encourage him," Gray cautioned.

"I won't." Then I corrected myself. "I don't."

Gray smirked. "You think you don't."

I blushed and left the room, picking up the suitcase and dragging it upstairs. I unpacked and put my clothes in the laundry.

When Gray said we'd both regret it, would he regret it because I was mortal? Did he regret every time we'd tumbled into bed together? Was he regretting spending time with me over the last week? My thoughts looped in on themselves and tied me in knots.

It was only after I came out of the shower that I noticed there was a vase on my desk with a single Odessa calla lily.

All my worries disappeared, and my heart skipped a beat.

FORTY THREE

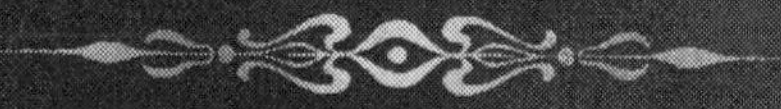

QUENTIN

It was Ember's Day. Gray's day. His birthday, to be exact. Affectionately referred to as Ember's Day because people symbolically burned things as an homage to the destruction he was in charge of.

He'd invited me to dinner with a few of the others and I'd eagerly agreed but was already running late.

"I'm sorry!" I called, bursting through the front door of my home with a large box in hand.

I went straight through to the kitchen and put it on the table.

"I swear I lost track of time. Give me ten minutes."

When I rushed back into the living room, Gray stood by the

sofa, and I stopped in my tracks. He was dressed head-to-toe in black. The sleeves of his shirt were rolled up to his elbows, top two buttons undone, and trousers hugging the curve of his ass and making my brain short-circuit.

Fuck. This man never had a bad day.

"You scrub up well," I managed, hoping it came out casually.

"As if you didn't know that already," Gray said, straightening up.

The shine dropped instantly. "Cocky piece of shit."

I moved past him to get ready. It took me twenty minutes. Not the ten I'd promised.

The pink dress I'd planned to wear had a mysterious stain I couldn't remove and had been replaced by a black satin number instead. The fabric skimmed along my curves and thin straps criss-crossed along my bare back. I grabbed a leather jacket before leaving the room.

"Okay, I swear I'm ready now!" I said, tottering back into the living room in my heels.

Gray was lounging on the sofa as I stepped in front of him, rummaging through my small black clutch.

"Gray," I said, looking up and blushing deeply.

"What is it, Scott?" He rose from the sofa swiftly and moved towards me.

The blue of his eyes had switched to black, and I could see the way the fabric of his trousers was strained around his dick.

"You need to gain a little control."

The wisps of his aura flexed towards me, and he took a deep breath.

"I can change," I said, rooted to the spot.

"No," he gritted out from between his teeth. "No, that won't be necessary."

He did his best to regain control, but the smirk was plastered on his face.

"Come on," he said. "We're already running late."

Pulling me against his body, he used his aura to take us to a secluded area, a street away from the restaurant.

"Are you sure the others won't mind me being there?" I asked.

"You're my guest. Plus, you get on with Erik, Sloan, and Ig. I'm sure you'll like Elva now that you know I'm not marrying her."

I pushed Gray, and he slipped an arm around my waist as we walked into the building. I didn't stop or correct him.

When we got to the table, Elva stood up to greet us. Gray let go of me to hug her, and she kissed both of his cheeks. She reached out for me, but Gray stood like a wall between us.

"You don't have a cuff. I don't think we need that right now," Gray told her, slightly viciously.

"I'm sorry." Elva sounded disappointed.

"It's nice to meet you," I said, peering around Gray and offering a smile.

Ig grabbed me by the waist and pulled me into a hug, and I jumped and let out a squeak of surprise. Laughing, I squeezed him back. The moment he let me go, Gray pulled me back towards him before Ig grabbed him and they rough-housed.

"Happy birthday," Ignacio said. "And I'll remind you again to get over yourself."

We took our seats at the table, ordering drinks before Erik and Sloan arrived. Gray got up and hugged them both. When he sat back down, I laughed and wiped Sloan's lipstick from his cheek with my thumb.

"How come you guys were so late?" I asked once Gray's cheek was clean.

"There's a reason they have five children," Ig replied with a smirk.

I choked on my sip of wine and Elva slapped Ignacio's arm.

"We're here now," Erik said, completely unfazed. "Shall we order food?"

It was a strange feeling for me to be sitting with Gods, having dinner as if there wasn't the vast expanse of divinity between us all.

I never cared about the specific dates in the calendar and in particular Ember's Day. Revenge just seemed like a waste of energy, but I didn't voice that out loud. I wasn't willing to watch the smile slip from Gray's face.

During the evening, I was highly aware of Gray's presence next to mine. When our hands rested on the table, my fingers gravitated towards his hand. Gray didn't move, he just glanced in my direction, and I knew he was leaving the decision to me.

I couldn't figure out why my need for him was so great. Maybe it was because we were sitting with two other couples who seemed to be so desperately in love. Or maybe I'd just given up on following the rules.

There was something between Gray and I. Something more than sex. Neither of us could keep away from each other, but neither was addressing the mammoth in the room.

My fingertips grazed his skin before I laced our fingers together. His fingers locked around mine, and there was a sense of peace that flooded me.

My gaze shifted to Erik, and he looked at our hands before his blue eyes found mine and I was ready for him to hit the roof. Instead, the corner of his mouth curled into a smile, and he gave me a subtle nod.

Perhaps he'd given up trying to keep us apart.

I was giving up on trying to keep us apart.

For the rest of the night, I relaxed, nudging against Gray gently. I traced the numbers one, four, three on his palm over and over until the skin on the pad of my index finger felt numb. They were the numbers tattooed on my inner wrist of my left hand.

I.IV.III

The first time I did it, he looked curious, but when I offered no explanation, he continued his conversation.

"Can you try to behave?" Gray whispered into my ear as dessert was brought to the table.

I turned to face him and whispered back, "I wasn't the one struggling to control myself before we left."

"Touché."

Gray opted for a decadent dark chocolate cake. It was rich and almost black, so it came as no surprise that he'd chosen it. I went for a lemon and blueberry creation. As I took a bite, I made sure to keep myself in check.

"Do you want to try some of this?" Gray asked.

"Sure."

I went to reach towards his plate, but he stuck a fork into the cake and held it out towards me. I took a bite and closed my eyes, letting the rich taste spread over my tongue and it happened before I realised. I let out a moan.

When I opened my eyes, it was only Gray that had noticed. The blue of his irises flickered black.

"You just can't help yourself," he said.

Gray tucked some hair behind my ear and stared down at me.

I wanted to close the gap. I needed to close the gap.

"You two need to get a room," Ig said from across the table.

I pulled away from Gray quickly to see Ig smirking at us. Gray threw a napkin at him, and we lapsed into conversation again.

By the time we got back home, I was grateful to step out of my heels. My feet ached with each step I took into the kitchen.

"Thank you for inviting me tonight. I really enjoyed it," I said to Gray.

The box I'd brought in with me earlier today sat on the kitchen table.

"Shit," I muttered. "I forgot to take this with me. I got it for you."

I stood by the table and Gray stood behind me, leaving barely any space.

"What is it?" he asked.

"A present. Kind of. It's difficult to shop for a God."

He reached around me, arms encircling my waist, and pulled the lid off the box. His aura pulled out a cake and set it on the table. It was decorated in black and gold marbling to honour him.

"I thought we could all have some, but I forgot to take it," I said, turning around to face him.

"Thank you," he replied.

It was too much. The pulling sensation in my chest and the need to feel him against me again was just too much.

My hands went to his face, and Gray looked at me curiously before I stepped up on my toes and kissed him. It took a moment before Gray responded, nipping at my lip before I opened my mouth for him. Our tongues met in a heated dance. It'd been too long since I'd felt this hot, heavy desire.

Gray grabbed my hips, pulling me flush against him, and I felt his erection pressed against my lower stomach. Clumsily, I pushed his jacket off his shoulders and let it drop to the floor.

He moved the kisses away from my lips and along the edge of my jaw slowly while my fingers worked on the buttons of his shirt. Gray reached my neck and sucked at the skin, making me tip my head for him.

"I've waited long enough," Gray said.

"But you were so well-behaved," I teased breathlessly.

Gray growled at me, "Do you know how fucking hard it is to have you in bed every night and keep my hands to myself?"

My hands slid down his chest until I found the waistband of his trousers, untucking his shirt. Gray ripped the flimsy strands of my dress as he nipped at the crook of my neck. I gasped quietly before the silky fabric pooled around my feet.

"You're going to leave a mark, Gray," I warned.

"I fully intend to."

His hands ran along my bare sides, and I trembled under his touch. I needed him badly.

Gray's hands moved up to my breasts, thumbing my nipples so that my back arched. My own kept undoing the buttons of his shirt before pushing it off his body. The pile of clothes at our feet was growing.

My mouth found his shoulder, and I kissed and sucked at the skin, but Gray claimed it with his own again.

There was nothing soft or tender or gentle here. It was a raw, primal need for each other that we'd denied for too long.

One of his hands fisted into my hair as he deepened the kiss and the heat pooled between my legs.

I made quick work of the button and zipper on his trousers. Gray rid himself of his shoes and socks as I pushed the trousers past his hips and let them fall. He hooked his thumbs into the waistband of my knickers, and I brushed a hand over his cock, earning a satisfied groan from him.

The kitchen grew dark with his aura as his control wavered, shedding his boxers until we were entirely naked in my kitchen.

I took his hand, the one that wasn't tangled in my hair, and guided it between my legs.

"Always so impatient, Scott," he told me.

"I just know what I —"

I couldn't finish the sentence as Gray thumbed at my clit, making me moan. His other arm moved around my waist to hold me close, and the smile on his face was devilish. I hooked a leg around his hip to give him better access, and he slid a finger into me.

"Fuck," I breathed, closing my eyes as he worked his fingers.

I caught his wrist to stop him. When I looked up at Gray, his eyes were completely black, and I realised how much I missed seeing him like this.

Unhooking my leg from him, I pulled his fingers from me, lifting his hand and sucking them clean. I sank to my knees in front of him, not breaking eye contact. My tongue flicked out against his rock-hard cock, and he hissed in pleasure. Both of his hands tangled in my hair, and I swirled my tongue around the head.

"Scott," he said darkly. "Don't tease."

I took him into my mouth, laughter sending vibrations along the length of him.

Gray grunted and pushed my head, testing my gag reflex. My eyes watered as I bobbed my head, taking as much of him as I could and letting my tongue run along him. Sounds of his breath hitching and the groans filled the room around us.

When his body tensed, when his movements became more erratic, I let him out of my mouth with a wet pop. I didn't want to feel his release in my mouth. I wanted to feel it inside of me.

Gray looked down at me desperately as I got up off my knees.

He pushed me roughly against the wall, pinning me in place with his hand around my throat.

"Why the fuck did you stop?" he demanded.

"I need you inside of me," I answered, struggling for breath.

Gray licked his lips and leaned in, keeping his hand on my throat. "Tell me this isn't a one-time thing."

I wrapped my leg around his hip again and ground against him. "You better leave me wanting more."

Releasing my throat, Gray gripped my ass in his hands and lifted me up. My back slammed against the icy wall, causing me to arch into him. He guided himself into me without question or hesitation, stretching my pussy to him, and I bit on his shoulder to silence myself.

"You feel so good," Gray told me.

He pulled out almost the whole way before slamming into me again, and I yelped at how rough he was.

Gray's mouth found mine again and my fingers buried into his hair as he held me up and set a rhythm. My nails dug into the flesh of his back.

"Fuck," he growled. "I've missed you."

I knew what he meant.

There was no one that could make me feel the way he did. No sex had ever felt so achingly satisfying than when it was with Gray. Nothing made me feel as complete as when I submitted to him.

Curses and moans echoed around the kitchen as he thrust into me and his hand slipped between my legs, dancing along my folds and tactfully avoiding my clit until I whimpered.

"There's the sound I love to hear," he said smugly.

"Stop," I panted. "Stop being so mean."

There was a rumble of laughter before he ran his finger along the bundle of nerves.

"Gray!" I called out his name in pure pleasure.

His aura held me up, freeing both of his hands. While one worked on my clit, the other rolled my nipple and I felt light-headed from the ecstasy. Gray leaned down and bit my other nipple before letting his tongue run across it.

"Don't stop," I pleaded. "Please. *Please.*"

My back arched from the wall and he didn't ease or slow the pace. He nipped at my chest, and I whimpered again. Tomorrow morning, my body would bear the marks of tonight, but I loved the thought of reminders of where he'd been and what he'd claimed.

A few more thrusts, teamed with him rubbing against me, caused me to spasm around his cock, legs locking around Gray's waist, so he was deep inside me. I curled against him, biting on his shoulder as my orgasm crashed around me.

Gray continued to grind against me when I opened my eyes weakly. He groaned and bit at my neck before his body tensed and trembled and he released into me.

We stayed like that for a few moments, wrapped around each other; sweat slicked bodies and our breathing heavy.

Slowly, Gray nudged my face, so I'd look at him. His eyes were fading back to blue now. My legs were tired and started to slip from his waist, and he slid himself out of me before my feet touched the ground. Gray kept me upright as my legs struggled to do their job, and evidence of his pleasure dripped down my thighs.

When he spoke, it was a whisper. "What do you want, Quentin?"

"I want you." The answer came without a thought.

"I can't give you everything you desire."

He meant he couldn't give me a relationship. He meant he couldn't let anyone know about us.

I knew this. I knew all of this, and it should have been red flags because the way he made my heart thud and the way I couldn't stop thinking about him… If he couldn't give me those things, I should walk away from him because I deserved them.

But I couldn't. I'd take whatever scrap he could give me because Gray was my damnation.

"I know," I told him.

"Does it change your answer?"

"No. I know what I want."

He leaned his forehead against mine. His voice was low and

deep and authoritative. “I won’t share you.”

My hand reached up to cup his face. “You won’t have to. The same rule applies to you.”

I’d leave Matt. I’d see him tomorrow and end things. I knew I should feel bad that this happened while I had a boyfriend, but I didn’t. He’d never know, and I’d end things before anything happened again.

Gray nodded at me and kissed me again. “I’ve missed you.”

It seemed such a strange thing to say when we lived together, talked every day and spent each night together in bed, but I’d missed being able to have him like this.

“My kitchen is a mess because of you,” I stated quietly.

“You started this.”

There was a blush of colour on my cheeks. “Happy birthday, Gray.”

“Happy fucking birthday to me.”

FORTY FOUR

QUENTIN

When I woke up the next morning, the space next to me was empty, but the bed wasn't cold. Gray couldn't have woken up much earlier than I had.

Rolling over, I groaned. My body ached. My chest, my hips, in between my legs. Gray had ensured he'd left his mark on me over and over again, and I did nothing to stop him. Something about being tangled with him again felt right.

Eventually, I pulled myself out of bed and found his shirt folded over the back of a chair, slipping it over my head. I took in a deep breath and let his scent fill my nose before padding downstairs.

Gray was in the kitchen. The mess we'd made last night was

gone, and I watched from the doorway as he poured a mug of coffee.

"You should have woken me up. I'm going to be late for work," I said, pulling my hair into a messy bun.

"Morning to you too."

"Morning, Gray."

When he turned back to look at me, his irises flickered black and set off butterflies in my stomach, adrenaline rushing through my veins and making me dizzy.

In moments, he was across the kitchen, mouth on mine, and I gave in easily.

"No," I said, pulling away grudgingly. "No, I can't."

"Why not?"

"I will definitely be late for work, and we spent most of last night…" I trailed off. "How are you still going?"

"Gods have a lot more stamina."

He picked me up, and I wrapped my legs around him. Gray kissed me again, placing me on the counter. Somewhere in the room, my phone buzzed from where it'd been left last night, and for the first time in years, I didn't rush to answer it or see who it was. I was content in the moment.

Gray handed me a mug of black coffee, and I chugged from it.

"I can get you to work faster than the car," he argued.

"Are you trying to coerce me?"

"Coerce suggests that you're unwilling. You, Scott, are anything but."

I flicked out my leg to kick him, but he moved away.

"Are you trying to attack me?" he asked.

He stood just out of reach, arms folded across his chest, eyebrow raised and looking amused. I could kick his ass, I was certain. I was going to get him in the ring at Sal's, cuff on, and see how smug he looked then.

"You're scared, and that's why you moved," I told him simply.

His face dropped, and I grinned.

"You think I'm scared of you?" he asked, arching an eyebrow.

"I think you're terrified of me."

He dropped his arms and stalked back towards me. "You remember who I am, right?"

"Some God or other."

I waved a hand through the air vaguely and took another sip from my coffee mug, but Gray took it from my hand and placed it away.

"Hey!" I argued.

He stood between my legs, and I looked up at him.

"You're a pain in the ass," he told me.

He was taking up all my personal space. His eyes pulled me in, large and blue, and his scent wrapped around me, familiar and welcoming.

I could be a little late. I'd worked enough late nights to give me some time. Still sitting on the counter, I wrapped my legs around his waist, and he leaned down to kiss me. It was desperate and lustful. We couldn't get our fill of each other after spending so long apart.

When we broke the kiss, we were both breathing heavily, and he pressed his forehead against mine.

"You'll leave him today," Gray said. It wasn't a question.

I nodded my head. I had no intention of staying with Matthew. Even if it weren't for Gray, it was never a long-term relationship. He wanted things I couldn't provide for him, and I wanted things he wasn't happy to even contemplate.

Gray gripped my thighs in his hands and levered me back so that I was lying on the worktop. He kissed up my legs, and I felt myself grow wet.

"I'm an extremely selfish being, Scott," Gray reminded me.

"Mhm."

He kissed along my thighs. I was completely naked under his shirt, and he smiled as he realised that fact. He spoke so close that I felt his mouth ghost against my pussy, and I shifted my hips, but he moved out of reach.

"I want you to myself," Gray said firmly. "Do you understand me?"

I nodded again, and he cocked his head to the side.

"Use your words, Scott. You usually have plenty of them."

"Yes. Yes, I understand. Please, Gray."

I fucking hated the fact he knew how to get me to do anything he wanted.

Gray laughed, and I had the urge to get up and leave, but just as I pushed myself to sit up, his tongue flicked out at me, and I gasped.

"Where are you going?" he asked.

Short, sharp flicks of his tongue against my pussy, and my hands grasped his hair, pulling him closer.

"Nowhere," I managed to rasp out.

I laid back on the counter, feet planted on the surface, and Gray's head between my legs. He alternated between short bursts and long, broad strokes, and I couldn't stay quiet, writhing in pleasure.

I felt him smile against me and wondered how I could ever have feelings for such a smug prick.

When Gray slid a finger into me, I let out a low groan and ground my hips.

"Gray." It was a breathy whisper.

"Mmmm?" He hummed his response against my clit, pushing in another finger.

"Keep going," I urged. My back arched off the counter, and I closed my eyes at the pleasure.

"You're my favourite meal, Scott."

Gray curved his fingers and hit the spot, forcing my toes to curl.

"Yes. Gray, yes!"

His fingers and tongue picked up speed, and I gripped his hair as my body tensed. Before long, I tightened around his fingers and my thighs closed around his head as my body trembled through the climax. I screamed his name, blood thundering through my ears as my body hit its high from my drug.

"WHAT THE FUCK?"

Everything happened so fast.

Gray pulled his fingers from me as I sat upright on the counter. Gray moved his body in front of mine, but I saw Matt standing in the kitchen, looking furious, and my stomach dropped, nausea hitting me.

"WHAT THE FUCK IS GOING ON HERE?"

Matthew's voice shook from the anger, and I tried to move Gray from in front of me, but he didn't give an inch.

I'd given Matt back his keys for the mornings when he came to pick me up for work. He must have been the one messaging me this morning.

"Calm down, Holden," Grayson told him.

"Calm down? Calm down?! Are you fucking kidding me? I've just caught you fucking my girlfriend in her kitchen!"

My face heated. There was no way to get around this now. Matthew just walked in on us.

Oh, Gods.

Matthew just walked in on us.

What was I meant to say to him?

"Matthew." My voice was quiet as I peered out from behind Gray.

When Matt clapped his eyes on me, his fury only seemed to increase. "Gods, Quentin! Are you serious right now? You've been fucking him while you were seeing me?"

"No! No. It's not like that!"

I swung my leg over and pushed myself off the counter, taking a few steps towards him.

"You're in his shirt!" Matt yelled. "This isn't the first time!"

I closed my eyes for a second. Why didn't I get showered and dressed this morning?

"Matt, just listen to me," I pleaded.

"I don't want to listen to anything you have to say, Scott! Fuck, I thought you were an absolute gem, but you're nothing more than a common whore!"

The words barely left his mouth when Gray's aura sent Matt clean across the room.

"Gray! Stop!" I cried.

"Don't you dare insult her in front of me," Gray said, voice shaking with authority.

He started to advance on Matt, and I caught hold of his arm.

"Stop it! Just stop!" I told him.

Gray looked down at me, his own anger clear in his eyes. This was going to make things ten times worse. Matt picked himself up off the floor and I turned to face him.

"I'm so sorry," I said. "I'm so so sorry."

"Save your pathetic apology," Matt spat. "We'll see what Gareth has to say about this. We're forbidden from any relations with them. You're not immune to the rules."

Gray's aura moved around me, and I turned on him. "I said stop it!"

Matt stalked out of the house, and I ran after him. I might not have felt for him in a romantic sense, but that didn't mean I wanted to hurt him.

"Matthew, let's talk about this."

He opened the door and stormed towards his car. I went to follow, but Gray's arms grabbed me around the waist.

"Let me go!" I screamed.

"You're half naked, Quentin," he reminded me calmly, slamming the door closed on my escape.

"I need to go after him. I can't… He can't tell Gareth. Hunter's going to find out."

The panic clawed its way through my body. Gray pulled me into the living room, and I was struggling to breathe.

I planned things. I planned through everything, so when something unexpected happened, I lost my shit.

Gray set me down and grabbed my face in his hands. "Listen to me. Look at me and listen to me."

I focused on him, and he got me to mirror his breathing. In for three counts and out for five and before long, it was regulated.

"I'm going to Gareth now," Gray told me. "Get yourself

dressed and come straight to the institute and find us. I'll sort this. I promise."

I nodded at him, and he pressed a kiss to my forehead.

"I'll sort this, Quentin."

Gray stepped away from me and disappeared in wisps of black, and I prayed that there was a way out of this.

FORTY FIVE

GRAYSON

Holden was a liability on a regular day, but with this information, he graduated to dangerous.

I'd never seen Quen look or feel so panicked. This level of chaos was something she didn't deal well with, but it was where I thrived. I needed to smooth this over before it got out of hand. Before she'd be put in the firing line by more than just her boss.

Gareth looked up as I appeared in his office. "Grayson!" he said, surprised. "I wasn't expecting you today. None of you are due here —"

"I need to speak to you," I cut across him.

"Take a seat," he said.

I sat down opposite him.

"How can I help you?" Gareth asked, well-meaning as always.

"I need to discuss Quentin with you."

Gareth stopped clicking through the files on his desktop and gave me his full attention. He narrowed his eyes momentarily and then said, "What about Scott?"

"Scott and I," I started and cleared my throat.

I had to tell him so that we could squash this. I had to tell Gareth to make sure Hunter didn't find out. Because if that happened, then I risked another skeleton falling out of the closet and I couldn't entertain the thoughts of the consequences if that happened.

"What about you and Scott?" His words were slow and measured, like he didn't really want to know what came next.

"Scott and I are —"

The sentence was lost as Gareth's office door flew open and Holden strode into the room.

"What are you doing here?" Holden said, eyes landing on me. "Trying to cover up?"

"Holden?" Gareth asked, eyebrows knitting together. "Do you want to tell me why you're storming into my office?"

I stood from my seat, but Holden was dead set on his mission.

"He's fucking Scott!" Holden announced.

My aura slammed the door shut. We didn't need the entire institute to see or hear this as they arrived for work.

Gareth rose from his chair, looking between us both. "I thought she was dating you," he said, settling his gaze on Holden.

"Yeah. Apparently, that didn't stop them."

There was a lot of anger swirling in the room, and I tried my hardest not to feed from it. But between Holden and Gareth, it was a difficult task.

"Explain. Now," Gareth demanded.

I looked to Gareth, ready to try to calm him down.

"What do you need, Gareth?" Holden yelled. "A drawing? I walked in on them all over each other!"

I had enough of Holden and his childish behaviour. The wounded act might have broken Quen, but it only served to irritate me. My aura wrapped tightly around his throat to silence him.

"You talk way too much," I hissed, watching him turn red.

"Grayson!" Gareth called out.

He was trying to keep a handle on the situation, but unlike Holden, he also knew what was at stake and who he was talking to.

"Let him go," Gareth said firmly.

I loosened my grip, so Holden could breathe properly, but refused to release him. This wouldn't have been an issue if I'd just killed him on the first night. The one time I chose to show some mercy, the one time my head turned for a bigger target, I'd miscalculated.

"Please tell me what he said isn't true," Gareth continued through gritted teeth.

"Scott and I are seeing each other," I confirmed.

Gareth let out a breath and closed his eyes. "You both know the rules," he said, looking at me again. "You know that's not allowed."

"And do you intend to enforce that?" I asked, challenging him.

"I'll have to inform your brother and he can enforce it."

My aura blazed around me, darkening the room. "You'll do nothing of the sort!"

Gareth shrank back from his desk in a feeble attempt to put some distance between us.

"Hunter is going through enough at the moment. He doesn't need anything else on his plate," I told him.

As if I gave a shit what my brother was going through. He couldn't find out because that would lead to all sorts of problems.

There was a weak knock on the door before it opened and Quentin walked in, surveying the scene.

"Put him down, Gray," she told me.

At her request, I took my aura away from Holden and he rubbed his throat, taking in air.

Quentin closed the door and looked at Gareth. For the first time since I'd met her, I was struck by how young she was. She shook with each movement, shoulders hunched as if trying to protect herself from whatever would be thrown her way.

"Gareth," Quen started.

"What they're saying is true?" he asked, cutting to the point.

She swallowed before nodding, and he shook his head.

"I didn't expect this from you, Scott." He sighed.

Her cheeks flamed red. And I wanted to go to her, but that wouldn't help our case.

"Gareth. I... It just happened," she spluttered, eyes turning glassy.

"Fucking slut," Holden hissed.

I whirled around on him and pinned him to the ground with my aura. He needed to stop insulting her. She was my soulbound and I wouldn't have anyone disrespect her. Holden writhed against the floor, trying to get free of my hold.

"STOP! GRAY!" Quentin yelled.

She came over and grabbed my arm, and I fought against the urge to destroy Holden because she didn't want me to. I let him go and looked at her.

"You're making it worse," she said.

"I've stopped," I replied.

My fingers brushed against her cheek gently, wiping at a stray tear. How was I meant to keep a lid on this now?

"Look at them!" Holden said, sitting up.

"Give it a rest!" Gareth told him. He pinched the bridge of his nose and said, "Holden, I'm enforcing two weeks of leave."

"What?!"

"You heard me."

"I didn't do anything!"

"You need to calm down."

Holden was up on his feet, looking furious. "Why am I being

punished for something they did?"

"It's not a punishment! You need to calm down. This information doesn't leave this office or there will be disciplinary action taken."

Holden looked ready to argue, but he wrenched the door open and left the office, slamming it shut behind him. Quentin flinched, and I moved towards her.

"Both of you," Gareth said. "Sit."

Quentin dropped into a seat obediently, and I sat beside her.

"I don't want to know how or why," Gareth told us. "You both know this isn't allowed."

Quen wrung her hands in her lap.

"Grayson, I'd like to speak to Quentin alone," Gareth said to me.

"No." I wasn't about to leave her on her own.

"Gray," she whispered, without looking up. "Let me speak to him."

I didn't feel comfortable leaving her. It was my job to protect her, and although most of the time I knew she didn't need it, she wasn't herself. She needed someone to take the reins. But how was I meant to argue without making it worse?

"I'm okay," she assured me poorly.

I got up from the seat. "I'll be in the lab."

FORTY SIX

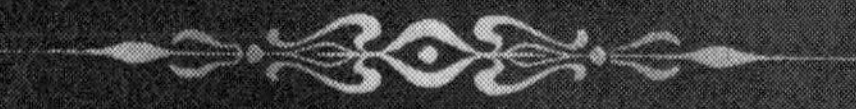

QUENTIN

I listened to the click of the door as Gray left the room, and a sense of dread filled my stomach worse than it had in years. I couldn't bring myself to look Gareth in the eye.

"Scott." He heaved a laboured sigh. "What is going on?"

"I don't know."

"Really?"

I didn't know. I had no idea what was going on. I knew I needed Gray. I knew I couldn't stay away from him, but I couldn't tell Gareth that. My gaze drifted to the ceiling, searching for an answer in between the tiles.

"Whatever it is, it's more than what Holden saw, isn't it?"

Gareth asked. My head snapped back to argue, but he held up a hand. "Don't. The way he was looking at you. The way you calmed him down."

My heart thudded violently in my chest, and I felt light-headed. We'd spent so long in secrecy that I couldn't believe it'd exploded into this chaotic mess.

"I can't condone whatever's happening here," he said.

"You can't tell Hunter." The words tumbled out of my mouth before I even thought them through. "You can't tell him."

"I don't plan to. Grayson looked ready to kill me when I mentioned it. I'm not quite ready to cross him."

I was thankful that Gareth believed so heavily in the Gods that he had the sense to fear them.

"Scott," he said gently.

I didn't feel comfortable with what was coming.

"Are you going to stop seeing him?" Gareth asked.

I opened my mouth, but nothing came out. I couldn't. I couldn't keep away from Gray because it hurt too much.

"I wish you had handled this better." Gareth sighed.

"Same."

"What's done is done now."

I looked at Gareth and bit my bottom lip, waiting for him to continue. Something in me was hardwired to seek approval from those higher up in the pecking order. But Gareth wouldn't approve of this. I'd broken one of the cardinal rules.

"But I have to put you through the disciplinary, Scott. Holden will let all hell break loose if I don't go through protocol."

My mouth soured with nausea, and the room swayed.

"I'm suspending you from the project for two weeks. James can take over the lab. You can analyse data at home. I need you to clear your head, Scott. I recruited you for a reason. Whatever happens in your personal life shouldn't affect your work, but it does."

There was a faint ringing in my ears as my mouth went numb.

"When you come back, whatever is happening between you

and Grayson — it doesn't affect your work or the rest of my staff. Understood?"

I nodded slowly.

"You can leave."

I got up from my seat and left the office, feeling like the worst person in the world. There was no denying it. The title was mine.

Walking back to the lab, I was completely out of it. I'd been suspended. This would be a mark on my record. They'd question this when I applied for another job and what was I meant to tell them? That I was fucking the subject of the study when it was explicitly forbidden, and my boyfriend at the time walked in on us?

I reached the lab and hesitated before opening the door. The team was there, getting on with work. All of them were completely unaware of how I'd betrayed their trust and put the project at risk.

Gray rose from a bench, but I didn't look at him. Instead, I made a beeline for James. I explained I was taking some extended leave for two weeks and what needed to be done. He was capable, but it was a knife through my heart to hand over my lab to someone, even if it was only temporary.

"I'll be at the end of an email. Send me the data and I'll work through the analysis. It frees you guys up to keep working in the lab."

He asked if I was okay, and all I could do was nod.

"Do a good job. I don't want to be cleaning up a mess when I get back," I told him.

Then I turned and left the lab, blinking back tears. Gray strode after me as I walked through the institute.

"Scott!" he called. "Scott! Quentin!"

He caught up with me and grabbed my arm, forcing me to stop and look at him.

"Don't!" I pulled my arm away from him.

"What did Gareth say?"

I shook my head and kept walking. Gray kept up the pace beside me.

"Don't push me out, Quentin. What happened? What did he

say?"

We made it outside before I turned to him. "I'm suspended for two weeks, Gray. I am suspended from my job!"

"He can't do that."

"He can. He has every right. He could have fired me if he wanted to because I broke the terms of my contract. So really, I'm getting away with it lightly. And I've managed to lose a friend in the process."

I was a cross between angry and upset. The situation had been handled so badly, and it was all my fault. I needed to be on my own to process everything that had happened and figure out how to salvage something from the wreckage.

"Quentin, you'd have left him anyway," Gray said matter-of-factly as I walked away. "At least it's done now."

I stopped in my tracks and turned on him. "Excuse me?"

"You said you were going to leave him today."

"Are you being serious?"

"Were you lying to me?"

The blood pounded in my ears as I looked at Gray, trying to take in what he said.

"No!" I said. "No, I wasn't lying to you."

"So? No harm done."

"Are you kidding me?!" My voice was rising.

Gods were selfish. Stupidly selfish, and it was shining through Gray. He didn't care that Matthew was hurt. Gray got what he wanted, regardless of the consequences, and for him, that was the end of the story. But I felt the guilt, and I'd lost a friend and I'd just been suspended.

"Lots of harm done!" I yelled. "Gods, you can be such a selfish prick sometimes!"

He opened his mouth to respond. But there were wisps of red, and Erik appeared next to Gray. My stomach churned, thinking Hunter might have found out about our secret.

"You need to come to Gareth's. Sorry, Quentin," Erik said. He looked between us. "What are you both doing out here?"

"Why? What's wrong?" Gray asked, ignoring his question.

"Some issues have arisen back home. Hunter expects us to go back there. He wants a meeting before we leave so we're on the same page."

My heart calmed slightly, and Gray turned his focus on me.

"Go," I told him. "I need to go."

Some distance would be good for us. He'd been pig-headed, and I needed to calm down.

"Quentin," Gray said, looking unimpressed.

I looked at him before my eyes flicked to Erik, who looked uncomfortable.

"You need to deal with this," I said.

They needed to keep things as calm as possible or Hunter really would find out, and we'd be in shit. We needed to continue like nothing had happened.

"We need to talk when I get back," he told me viciously.

FORTY SEVEN

GRAYSON

Hunter briefed the Gods before we arrived back in Elysia. The restlessness of the minor Gods had bubbled over, and they wielded their powers loosely at home. Usually, I'd be happy to head back there, but my thoughts were only partially in Elysia with my kin.

Quentin was angry with me. She was upset with how things played out. I only pointed out that our end goal was achieved even if the execution was messier than expected. Holden was a big boy — he'd get over it. It wasn't like they were soulbound.

Quen called me a selfish prick. I was selfish. I was extremely selfish when it came to her. That would remain the case for my entire existence, but I didn't like the way she'd pointed it out. As if it made me the bad guy.

"Gray," Erik said. "I suggest whatever was going on with you and Scott, you leave it back down there. Full attention here."

I looked at my little brother. We needed to talk, but now wasn't the time. Erik had a point; I needed to focus.

We took off across Elysia to cover our respective grounds. Upper Elysia was not off-limits to the minor Gods, but there were many who chose not to walk the highest heavens if they had no business there. They seemed content in the middle heavens, thriving in their own way. But without the elite in position, and with no answer when we'd return permanently, they'd run riot.

Although they outnumbered us, they were less cohesive than the elite, making them easier to overpower.

It took most of the day to talk them down and tidy up the mess they'd caused. By the evening, we'd convened in the council chambers. As I walked down the halls, my crown weighed heavily on my head.

Twelve thrones sat in a semicircle in a stone chamber. Hunter was sitting in the centre, and we all made our way to our seats. Erik sat to the left of Hunter, and I sat on the right. It was clear who was in charge.

Archer strolled into the room, looking bored, and stood before us. Despite his nonchalant facade, I sensed the anger that rolled from him at being summoned.

"You requested my presence," he said shortly.

"Would you like to explain what exactly the minor Gods believe they're playing at?" Hunter asked.

He stood with an expression like butter wouldn't melt. "They have a tendency to get restless. You haven't instilled faith in them the way you're all spending your time with mortals."

I tensed. "You speak as if you aren't there yourself."

Archer's green eyes flicked to me, and he raised an eyebrow.

"Well," he said. "That was the whole reason me and some others chose to go down. Checks and balances and all that. I haven't had time to report to them."

Bullshit. He hadn't reported to them because he wanted to cause unrest and unease.

"Ensure it doesn't happen again, Archer. I would hate to have to put Gods on trial for treason," Hunter said.

He paled but recovered quickly. "Of course not, Hunter. I'll speak to them. Was there anything else you required?"

"You're dismissed."

Archer shot me another look before turning on his heels and leaving us.

"I suggest you all return to your estates. We can head back down in the morning," Hunter said.

He got up from his throne without another word and strode out of the room as everyone began to stir.

I couldn't stay here. I needed to get back down to Quentin. There was nothing else that required my attention. As I went to take steps towards the doors of the chamber, a hand landed on my arm.

"You need to listen to him," Sloan said as Erik joined her side.

"You're going to get caught or found out before you're prepared, if you keep behaving like this," Erik warned me quietly.

"Come and stay at ours tonight, Gray," Sloan coaxed gently. "The children will be thrilled to see you."

"You can tell us what happened," Erik added.

I didn't want to stay. I didn't want to be here, but I sighed and relented. The more I tried to push, the more it was going to look strange to the others, especially Hunter.

The truth was that I wasn't ready to have that conversation just yet. I wanted to enjoy Quen and keep her to myself before contemplating complicating everything further. Although, after the showdown with Holden, we were probably past the stage of keeping a lid on it all.

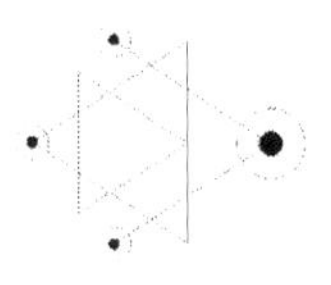

"She didn't mean anything by it," Sloan assured me.

When I finally decided to open up, we'd left the children at home, and we walked through Elysia under a twinkling night sky.

"Knowing Scott, she probably did," Erik muttered, and I slapped him upside the head.

"Even if she did, she's not wrong. We are selfish. And you've been called worse," Sloan pointed out.

"I don't want her to think of me as worse," I grumbled.

Erik lit up. "Why?"

"Curiosity killed the cat, Erik."

He was eager to hear my thoughts. Not only the ones that rattled around my head, but the ones that were buried in my heart and threatened to spill with every single beat.

"Satisfaction bought it back," he quipped, looking pleased with himself.

"Have you thought anymore about what you want to do?" Sloan asked, cutting through the argument before it started.

My head pulsed painfully. Foolishly, I thought I could leave her behind. Part of me still felt like that may be a possibility. What other choice did we have? There couldn't possibly be a future for us. My thoughts had me running in circles until I wanted nothing more than silence. Or Quentin. She calmed the racing thoughts.

"Wait," Erik hissed, flinging his arms out and stopping us from continuing down the street.

"What —"

"Shh," he said quietly, and pulled us to the side.

It took a moment before I realised why my brother had stopped up in our tracks. The walk had taken us close to the reflecting pool and, rather than crystal clear waters that should have mirrored the night sky, the water was a deep forest green.

After a few silent minutes, the surface of the water broke, and Archer's head rose from the depths as he sucked in deep breaths. The look on his face was one of confusion before he waded up to the shore, clothes dripping wet and clinging to him.

"What is he up to?" Sloan mumbled quietly.

Archer glanced around before he wrapped himself in his aura and disappeared from the spot.

"What was he doing in the pool?" I asked, confused.

It was used for gifting. Other than that, there was no need for us to enter it. What was Archer looking for?

"I don't know," Erik mused. "But we should get back in case it's something to piss off Hunter."

As we passed the pool, I glanced at it. The surface was peaceful and reflected the stars in the sky. Was Archer trying to change his responsibility? Was he trying to barter with the pool to have something more useful under his belt?

The smart move would be to tell Hunter what we'd seen. He should know that someone was messing with the pool out of the usual use. But the resentful nature I was built upon won out. I didn't owe Hunter a single thing.

Whatever Archer was doing, we'd find out eventually in a blaze of fiery glory.

Hunter could deal with it when the time came.

FORTY EIGHT

QUENTIN

I felt like a lost lamb when I got home. What was I going to do for two weeks? Banished from the lab, I was left with reams of data, spreadsheets, and databases. I couldn't imagine anything worse than being stuck with non-stop analysis. It was all part of research, but it was tedious and repetitive, and I lacked the focus to get through large portions of it in one sitting.

Concentrating on work would be easier than focusing on what a terrible person I was. There was no way to justify my actions, and I wished I could turn back time and stop myself before causing all the hurt.

When I finally looked at my phone, I saw the messages that Matt had left me that morning to tell me he'd swing by and pick me up. If I hadn't been so swept up in Gray...

A knock on the door made me jump out of my skin. I opened it to see Charlie standing there, looking confused, and I mirrored her expression.

"Do you want to tell me what's going on? Matthew and you are both on two weeks of leave. That doesn't sound right. And when I spoke to him, he said to ask you. He's pissed, Quen," Charlie said. "What's happened?"

Even though Gareth had given us some cover by not labelling our absence as suspension, anyone with half a brain cell could see this wasn't a normal holiday from work.

I moved out of the way to let Charlie into the house.

"He's furious, Quentin. He says he doesn't want to see you and he couldn't care less. What's happened between you both?"

With Charlie sitting on my sofa, everything welled up, and I let out a sob.

"Quen! Oh, my Gods. I'm sorry. Come here." Charlie pulled me into a hug, and I cried harder. "What's happened?"

"He caught me with Gray," I whispered through the tears.

"You live with him, sweetie. They've always had bad blood."

I pulled away and looked at her as she understood the meaning behind my words. I needed someone to talk to, and I'd sat alone with this for too long. Charlie was someone I respected and depended on since we started on the project together.

"Oh Gods, you mean," Charlie started. "You cheated on him?"

I couldn't defend myself. I'd cheated on Matthew.

"I was going to break up with him." But I cringed at how awful and weak the excuse sounded.

"But you didn't!" Charlie looked angry, and I didn't think I'd ever seen her like this before. "You've cheated on him! Gods, he practically worshipped you!"

"You have no idea, Charlotte. He's not perfect."

"He never said he was. Not that it matters. Gods, Quen, why would you do that to him?"

"I didn't do it on purpose!"

I hadn't set out to hurt him. I'd tried my hardest to stay away from Gray while I was with Matthew. I didn't know what made me want Gray so badly.

Charlie got up from the couch.

"Where are you going?" I asked.

"I'm going back to see Matthew."

I stood. "Charlie, you can't tell anyone about this."

"Don't worry, Quentin. I'm not going to spread your dirty, little secret."

The words stung, but she wasn't wrong. We were hiding this the best we could because we both knew it was wrong. It wasn't a long-term relationship. It was sex. But sometimes, it didn't feel that simple. Times where the understanding and the connection went beyond physical and spanned into something more. Not that I could explain that to anyone. I wasn't even brave enough to bring it up with Gray.

Charlie left the house, and the silence was deafening. I felt the tears well up in my eyes again.

What was I doing? Why was I doing this?

I'd hurt a friend and my career had been marked all because of a man. Because of the choices I was making revolving around a man. A man that couldn't even fully commit to me because of what he was. Why was I risking so much?

Making my way upstairs, I flipped open the lid of my laptop. I needed to get away from this. Gareth was right. I needed to clear my head. Reset and refocus. The job had been offered to me on a silver platter and I was meant to be working towards my own research group in my own lab.

My fingers flew across the keyboard as I searched and scanned and found exactly what I was looking for. A flight to New York in two hours.

I needed my brother.

For the entire flight and cab ride to Cass's place, my mind had run so quickly that I wished I possessed a switch to turn it off. My heart and my head waged a war and there was no clear winner. And while they fought it out, I cried more than I had in years.

It was probably the most impulsive thing I'd done in a while, but I needed my big brother. Not just in the sense that I missed him, but I really needed him.

Cass and I were both level-headed children. I had more of a temper, but other than that, we were pretty even. There wasn't an awful lot that he needed to step in for and play up to his role as big brother, but that was what I required from him now.

When I knocked on the door to his home, it took a few moments before Cass answered.

"Quentin? Gods, what are you doing here?" Cass asked, surprised.

"Who is it, sweetheart?" Sophie appeared behind him, and her eyes widened. "Quentin!"

"Come in, duck."

They moved into the house, and I walked in with my rucksack that I'd stuffed with some clothes and my laptop before I left. A few essentials. I had no clue if I was staying for two days or two weeks.

"Why didn't you say you were coming over?" Cass pulled me into a hug, and I clung to him. "Quen?"

"I'll make some coffee," Sophie muttered.

Cass rubbed my back, and I started to cry.

When I joined the Scott family, I was ten years old, and Cass was fifteen. During the entire process, he was a ball of energy that couldn't stop talking. The moment I was adopted, I was overwhelmed, and the first night, I had burst into tears on the bed. It was Cass who found me and took me to the kitchen for a glass of water. Cass, who kept looking out for me from that point onwards. Cass, who became my brother without sharing a single drop of blood.

"Come on, duck. Tell me what's wrong?"

I choked out a laugh at the sound of the old nickname. I used to be obsessed with the ducks at the park when I joined the family.

It was one of the first trips we took as the official Scott family four.

"I don't know what I'm doing with my life," I said, pulling back.

Cass laughed. "Are you kidding me? You've always known what you're doing. Come and sit down."

He guided me over to the couch. It was getting late, but he didn't seem to mind.

"I think I've messed up," I said.

Cass looked concerned. I'd never been into partying. Never touched a drug. Too much of a loner to fall into the bad crowd. Even when I went to uni and our lives were ripped apart by the train accident, Ethan had kept my head straight.

"What's happened, duck?"

I spent the rest of the night telling Cass and Sophie everything. The whole truth of it. I told them who Gray was. How we weren't dating when they came to visit. About Matthew and about how it'd all crashed down around me in the last few hours.

I needed help, and I trusted my brother.

FORTY NINE

GRAYSON

I was itching to head back down and see Quentin. We hadn't parted on the best of terms, but Sloan's question and the events leading up to Holden's tantrum had me thinking.

Quentin chose me. She spent time with me, even if I couldn't guarantee her a relationship. She called me selfish, but there was a reason behind it that I didn't want to admit. But she chose me and that meant I owed her an explanation about what laid between us. I owed her the truth.

"You're going to tell her," Erik said, appearing right next to me.

Everyone had arrived back at the institute and Archer lingered, smirking at us both, before disappearing with the rest. What I'd have given to knock the look off his face. What was the bastard so smug about? Every nerve in my body told me he was planning something, but it slipped low on my priority list.

"Yes," I said curtly, answering Erik. "I want to tell her we're bound."

Erik's smile was so wide I worried he'd hurt himself.

"Gray!" he exclaimed before I hushed him. "Does that mean you've thought about telling her the rest?"

"Let's take it one step at a time."

Just because I couldn't have a relationship with her didn't mean I didn't want one. The more I thought about it, the more I wondered if it could be feasible. She could claim her divinity and join us. It would make things easier. We'd have an eternity with each other. The thought was dizzying.

"Do you love her, Gray?" Erik's question was blunt, and he was grinning at me. He looked like a child, and I felt the blush creep up my neck.

Love and affection were two emotions I'd been starved of. Lust and desire; I was well acquainted with. That was how it started between me and Quen. A simple, undeniable chemistry. But the metamorphosis of our relationship had left me confused. Most of the time, I didn't know what my heart was doing or why. For the first time in my life, I was completely uncertain of what my future held.

I cleared my throat and shrugged. "I don't know."

"I think you do."

"Erik." There was a warning tone in my voice.

I didn't want this conversation with him. It was awkward enough. Erik was blessed with love as his responsibility. It came to him as easy as breathing. The rest of us weren't so lucky.

"It's a simple enough question," he continued. "Do you love her?"

"A reminder, dear brother, that not all of us have your skills, so love is a bit more complicated for the rest of us."

"I think you do."

"Give it a rest."

“I think you do and I'm coming with you."

"No!"

But there was no point. Erik was in his element, and so when I arrived at Quentin's home, Erik was right behind me, still grinning like an idiot.

I sensed it immediately.

"She's not here," I said.

"Grayson." Erik pulled a notepad from the coffee table and handed it to me.

Gone to see Cass. Think we need space - Scott.

It was short, with barely any emotion, and my skin prickled.

Need space? Why the fuck did we need space? I tried to keep my temper in check.

"I'm going there,” I said, feeling my temple throb.

"Right behind you."

If I had it my way, I’d have popped right into Cassidy Scott’s home, but Erik’s aura fought with mine until we landed in a backstreet of a suburb in New York. We made a trek through the streets until we found Cassidy’s home. Erik knocked on the door before I could speak.

"She isn't here," I told him.

"What?" Erik asked over his shoulder.

The door opened and Quen's adopted brother stood there, looking at us both.

"You know," I said.

It wasn't a question. It was a statement, and Cass gave me a nod.

"She isn't here and right now, she doesn't want to see you," Cass said.

I responded, "Well, I would like to see her."

"I'm not sure that's in her best interest."

My aura seeped out and creeped towards Cass. I wasn't in the mood to deal with him. The situation involved me and Quen, and no one else needed to insert themselves into it.

Erik reached a hand out and placed it on my shoulder before saying, "I'm sure she'd appreciate you keeping her brother in one piece."

Cassidy stepped back and Erik made his way into the house with me following behind. The door closed and Cass entered the living room, where we were smothered in a thick, heavy silence.

"You know you can't tell anyone what you know. It'd more than likely cost her life," I told him.

"I'm not an idiot."

Erik sighed and took a seat, neatly folding an ankle over the opposite leg. But Cassidy and I continued to stand, staring at each other.

"How much did she tell you?" I asked.

"Everything."

"Everything?"

"Everything, Grayson."

He was trying to be confident, but Cass, unlike his sister, had a staunch belief in the Gods. He didn't look me directly in the eye, and his voice held a slight tremor. I respected him for attempting to be strong for the sake of his sister.

"Is she okay?" I asked.

Cass softened slightly. "She will be. Quen is nothing if not resilient. I..."

I watched him and even Erik leaned forward, curious about what he wanted to say.

"She's my sister. She's the only family I have. I've watched someone hurt her before and I don't care who you are, but I won't have you hurt her."

"What makes you think I'd hurt her?" I asked, trying to control my rising temper.

"I don't know. I'm not keen to trust you after everything she's told me. I'll be the one picking up the pieces when you leave and head back up there." He gestures his arm up towards the ceiling, signalling to Elysia and beyond.

The front door opened, and I heard Quentin's laugh; the

music only she created, and my heart lifted.

"Maybe," she said. "But if I moved, you'd have double the Scott to put up with. Are you sure you'd —"

The sentence came to an abrupt end when she saw me.

Move? She was thinking about moving?

"Quentin!"

It was Erik that broke the silence as he got up from the couch and moved towards her, hugging her tight. She returned the gesture, but her eyes stayed on me.

"Say the word, duck, and they're out," Cass told her.

"Quentin, I think we should talk," I said to her.

"Sure," she said eventually, overcoming the shock. "We can go to my room."

Cass didn't sound impressed as he said, "You can stay here."

"Cass. I'm a twenty-seven-year-old woman. Can we just not?"

His face flushed pink at the reminder of her age, and Quen turned and left the room. I followed her out. We walked into the guest bedroom, and she sat on the bed, biting her bottom lip.

"You must have left in a hurry," I said to her, unimpressed by her sudden desire to flee.

"Great deal on flights."

"You're a horrible liar."

I joined her on the bed, sitting down opposite her.

"You said you needed space. Why?" I asked.

Quen looked at me and I narrowed my eyes, trying to figure out why she seemed so unsure now when she seemed so positive about us a day or so ago.

"I worked hard my entire life to get where I am," she answered.

"I know you did."

"I can't lose it all because I'm messing around with you."

I hated the way she degraded it to messing around. I was not messing around with her. Not anymore.

"If Gareth wasn't so nice to me, I could have lost my job."

She looked at me. "I think I've lost both my friends."

There was a sinking feeling in me. It was more than sinking. It felt like splintering. Gods, was this what Erik meant about pain if we tried to break the bond? Didn't she feel it? I wanted to tell her, but I was unsure now. She was doubtful, seemed not as invested in this as I was, and I didn't want to force her hand.

"I'm still here," I reminded her, rubbing my chest. She gave me a weak smile, and I pulled her onto my lap. "You still have your job."

"For now."

"What did Gareth say?"

"That whatever is going on between us cannot affect my work anymore. I'm surprised he didn't kick me off your case and reassign me."

"He knows I won't work with anyone else."

It'd been months since my initial demand, but it remained the same. I wouldn't willingly cooperate if I didn't work with her.

Quen relaxed in my arms as she leaned against me, and the pain in my chest eased.

"I'll let you get on with your work," I bartered. "I promise not to be a distraction."

"You can't promise that. You're distracting even when you try not to be."

I chuckled. "Quentin."

"Mmm?"

"If you really believe this isn't what you want, if this will cause an issue with your career, then we can stop."

Even as I said it, I knew I didn't mean it.

Quentin was bound to me in ways she couldn't comprehend. Even I struggled to understand the magnitude of the bond between us. I might have been able to give her days, maybe weeks, of space, but we'd wind up together.

Her hesitation in answering brought on a wave of panic I didn't realise I could possess. And then her hand curled into my shirt, pulling me closer until she hugged me tight. I wrapped my arms around her and buried my face in her hair. It was becoming evident that I needed to figure out a way to solve the issues that would keep us apart.

"I don't want to stop seeing you," she whispered.

"You know, I'm not messing around."

Pulling away, she shot me a questioning look.

I wasn't messing around, but I couldn't commit any more than I had. None of it made sense, and it was driving me to madness.

She didn't push it. Instead, she kissed me and any discomfort in my chest eased away to nothing. I moved us so that she was laying on the bed and caged her in with my arms.

"You can't just disappear when you find things difficult," I told her.

Her cheeks turned pink. "I'm used to doing things on my own."

"Not anymore. You have me."

FIFTY

QUENTIN

The panic had subsided. Spilling all my secrets to Cass and Sophie, and having Gray with me again soothed my soul.

When he suggested stopping, I knew I wouldn't be able to. All those definitive thoughts about work and needing to succeed tampered down in his presence. I didn't want either or. It was a case of finding balance in my life so I could have both. I needed space to calm down, but I couldn't keep away from him, and the damage had been done. We just needed to be less destructive about it — if that was even possible.

Gray leaned over me, crowding my space, and kissing me, nipping at my bottom lip. Insatiable. That was the word that could describe us together.

My mind replayed a single sentence he'd said.

You know, I'm not messing around.

Of course, he was. We both were because it could never be more than this. He'd told me, and I'd accepted it.

A knock on the door interrupted our reconciliation.

"Quentin?" Sophie called.

"Yes, Soph?" I said, turning my head away from Gray, but he just moved the kisses to my cheek and down my neck.

"Just wanted to make sure everything is okay."

I looked back to Gray, and he rested his forehead against mine.

"We're good," I said to her.

"Well, I've already asked Erik, and he's happy to, but would Gray like to stay until you're ready to leave?"

Gray rolled his eyes. "Of course, Erik made this a holiday."

I hit his chest, and he sat up, talking louder so that Sophie could hear through the door.

"I'll be staying until Quentin leaves if that's alright with you, Sophie."

"Perfectly fine!"

It was strange to have Grayson and Erik in the house with us. What was even stranger was the fact that Cass and Sophie knew who they really were.

Over dinner, there were a million questions about the Gods and Elysia, and I could see the jealousy peek through Cass when I mentioned I'd visited the heavens. Gray stayed next to me through dinner, and I traced the numbers — one, four, three — on his hand when it was near mine.

Cass shot disapproving looks at Gray when he first thought we were dating and now, after the truth was out, I caught him giving glances towards us more often, but it was like he couldn't make up his mind if it was safe or not to dislike Gray.

"Quentin," Cass called when we were ready to retire to bed.

Gray stopped. But when I looked to Cass, I knew he was after a private conversation.

"Go on," I said quietly to Gray. "I'll be up in a bit."

Gray hovered for a moment. I'd noticed he didn't like to leave me alone when someone wanted a private word.

"Okay," he said eventually, leaning down to kiss me.

Cass cleared his throat, and I rolled my eyes, pulling Gray

down and kissing him again. He grinned at me and left the room.

"Must you?" Cass asked.

"You and Sophie kiss in front of me."

"That's different."

"How so, Cassidy? Please, enlighten me."

"You're my little sister."

He looked embarrassed because he didn't have a point, and I folded my arms across my chest.

"Did you want to speak to me about something?" I asked.

"About Grayson."

There was a tight ball in my chest. I felt nervous. I imagined this was how it would feel if Dad were sitting there asking questions about my love life. My heart tugged, wondering what my parents would have made of Gray.

"You're staying with him?" Cass asked. I nodded, and he mimicked the movement. "I saw you at dinner, Quen. One, four, three."

I swallowed and felt my cheeks burn. "I —"

"You don't have to explain," he said. "You seem happy with him, duck, but I'm worried about you. I don't want you getting hurt. I want you to make sure you know what you're doing."

My insides twisted. I planned everything in my life. Gray came crashing down into it with all his chaos and had brought nothing but that ever since. I didn't want to think about the end when we were getting started. I knew the numbers I traced on him were a dangerous thing to do, but I could cope. I could get through it when it was time to fall apart.

All my life, I'd been abandoned. When people left you so frequently, you learned to pick up the pieces and carry on. This would be no different. When the time came, Gray would leave, and I'd break, but at least, I'd have the memories of whatever was between us and how it brought me back to life.

"I know what I'm doing," I said.

A lie in its purest form.

"As long as you're sure."

Cass got up from his seat and enveloped me in a hug. I was

glad I'd come to see him. Grateful he didn't judge me.

When I got upstairs, Gray was already in bed — on the left.

"Ah, fuck," I cussed.

"A vital error."

"Let me have the left."

"Not a chance. Get changed and get your ass in bed."

I grumbled, changing into pyjamas, and crawling in beside him. I rested my head on his chest, and Gray played with my hair.

How could you feel so at peace with someone? What was I thinking when I wrote that note? I was so angry, and I took it out on Gray when I shouldn't have.

"I'm sorry for leaving," I said to him.

He kissed the top of my head. "It's fine. We're together now. What did your brother want?"

I laughed. "Just making sure I know what I'm getting myself into. I don't think I could live without him."

Gray tensed under my touch, and I looked at him.

"Everything okay?" I asked.

"There may be a day when you'll have to be without him."

I blinked a few times. "That's a really morbid thought, Gray, and not one I want to touch on."

He looked at me and shook his head. "My apologies. Ignore me."

He kissed my forehead, and I settled down on his chest and let the beat of his heart lull me to sleep.

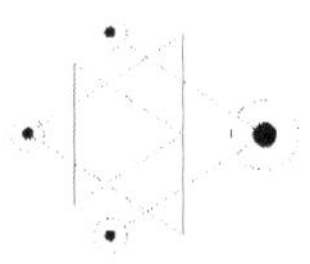

In my dreams, I was back in Elysia, and it was deathly silent. Not even a breeze fluttered through the park, and it made me anxious to move. It'd been some time since my mind had taken me here.

"Archer?" I called cautiously.

"Right here, Scott."

He appeared in front of me, dark hair tousled and green eyes bright. Excitement buzzed from his frame and amplified my nerves.

"Why are you here?" I asked. "Why am I here?"

"I haven't seen you in a while."

"I've been busy," I explained. "I'm visiting my brother."

"Too busy to spend time with me?"

Archer walked towards me and offered an arm. Hesitantly, I took it and we walked.

"Too busy for anyone, really," I commented.

It was a blatant lie. I'd given all my time to Gray.

"You're selfish with your time."

When I glanced up, Archer was watching me carefully.

"I think everyone should be selfish with their time," I replied. "It's a valuable commodity."

"Then I'm honoured you're giving me some of yours."

"Don't flatter yourself, Archer. You're the one invading my dreams. You're stealing my time."

He brought a hand to his chest. "You continue to wound me every time we meet."

I rolled my eyes. "You need thicker skin."

We weren't walking our usual route. We were walking towards the reflecting pool and panic twisted my insides. This was a dream. This was all a dream, and even if the pool wanted me, Archer was a God. I gripped his arm a little harder.

He raised an eyebrow and looked at me. "You seem spooked."

"No," I said, shaking my head. "I just don't understand why we're here."

"It's an important place for Gods. None of us would be who we are without it."

The water sat still and quiet and serene. I knew this was a dream because there weren't any whispers drawing me towards it.

"I wonder…" Archer mused. "What would happen if you were to step into it?"

My heart sank. Why would he say that? Archer wasn't there that night. I hadn't told anyone about what happened. It couldn't be a coincidence that he'd bring up such a random thought.

"I guess we'll never know." He sighed.

What was he doing? The way he spoke was as if he was playing a game.

Archer turned his body to face me, and his bright green eyes bore down on me. It was as if he was searching for something. He moved so that he held my upper arms and I faced him properly.

"Unless you trust me and come back with me," he suggested.

"Come back where?" I asked, unable to tear my eyes off him.

"To Elysia."

My brow furrowed. "Why would I go back to Elysia?"

"They aren't telling you everything, Quentin," he said sadly. "I told you; you can't trust him."

The dream was giving me a headache.

"Archer," I said.

"I'll let you go. I've stayed long enough but think about what I've said. Come and find me if you wish to go back. I only want what's best for you."

When I woke up, I was in Cass's spare room, and I glanced around. The sun was coming through the gap in the curtains, and Gray's face rested an inch or two from my own. His arm was wrapped around my middle, pinning me to his side. He looked at peace when he slept.

Could he really be hiding something from me?

FIFTY ONE

GRAYSON

Quentin decided she wanted to spend the entire two weeks with her brother, and so, she showed me around New York. Cassidy and Sophie attended their shifts at the hospital, and Quen and I worked wherever we felt comfortable. Sometimes from home and at other times in diners and cafes.

Yesterday, I watched with vested interest as she yelled at James over the phone. Barely awake, thanks to the time difference, James had called about an incident in the lab and was met with her wrath. The woman was a force to be reckoned with.

She was finding her feet again after being dealt the blow of the suspension. Quen slowly dusted herself off and buried her embarrassment, rising above it all. Cass was right. Quentin was resilient.

Every day I spent by her side made it more difficult to think about what my life in Elysia would be like without her.

I'd never envied Erik. Or Hunter. I was happy to keep my company sparse if I had a desire, and preferred my own company, anyway. But now…

It was driving me mad how much I thought of a life with her. Waking up to her every morning, draped on my arm for every event, listening to her every idea and thought. The manor would no longer be empty and quiet. Quen's laughter would echo down the hallways. And Sloan mentioned children. Our children?

When we got back to London, I'd find a way for it to happen. I wanted her permanently, and I always got what I wanted.

Waking up the next morning, I found she wasn't beside me. I furrowed my brow and sat up. The clock on the bedside read 9:12 AM. I'd never seen her awake before me. Getting out of bed, I pulled on some sweatpants before heading downstairs. When I entered the kitchen, Sophie was already there making coffee.

"Morning, Gray," she said breezily.

"Sophie, have you seen Quentin?"

She turned around slowly and offered me a smile. I preferred Sophie to Cassidy, but perhaps, that was because I couldn't get him to leave us alone, and Sophie was the one that allowed Quen and I some space.

"She usually needs a wakeup call," I muttered.

Sophie handed me a mug of coffee, and I took it while she made another. I sat at the island, and a few moments later, she joined me.

"She's okay," Sophie said.

That calmed me. "You saw her this morning?"

"She left with Cass earlier."

"Where?"

"A walk."

"You didn't want to join them?"

Quen hadn't asked me to join her, but I wondered if they had extended the invitation to Sophie. I had no definitive role in Quen's life yet, but the trio were family.

"Sweetheart, do you know what today is?"

This was another reason I liked Sophie. I was the God of chaos and she sat opposite me with coffee and called me sweetheart as if I were a lost little boy. She didn't see me as dangerous or cruel. She didn't hold a fear. Sophie operated on kindness, and it was nice to have kindness offered to you when all you were used to was criticism.

"It's Friday," I answered her, matter-of-factly.

She shook her head. "She didn't tell you. Well, that doesn't surprise me."

"Didn't tell me what?"

"It's the anniversary of their parents' deaths."

The news hit me hard, and I nodded. Quen hadn't told me. She was so guarded about her family — more than anything else, more than the work she coveted. She protected her family with every ounce of strength. I wished she'd have said something, but she wasn't an open book at the best of times.

"Cass usually flies out there but since she's here, it made sense to stay."

"I…" I was at a loss for words.

She sipped from her mug and offered me a smile. "Have you ever lost anyone, Grayson?"

It was a personal question, but she didn't hesitate to ask it.

"No. No one I care about. Gods are immortal."

"There's no way of dying?"

I laughed and drank from my mug. "There are ways of dying. Divinity runs in our veins. If you taint the blood, then you taint the divinity and we're vulnerable."

Sophie raised an eyebrow at the information. I wouldn't say any more. There was no reason to reveal every secret.

"I've never lost anyone either," she said. "Cassidy and Quentin have been through a lot. Lost their birth families. Lost their adoptive parents. I can't imagine living what they've been through."

"They're both quite phenomenal." I spoke more for Quen than Cass.

"I would be inclined to agree. Does it bother you, Gray?"

"Hmm?" I took another sip from the mug.

"Does it bother you that one day you'll lose her? I mean, in normal circumstances, one person usually dies before the other, but to live an eternity without them seems such a task."

My face blanched of colour, and I set the mug down. I'd never thought of this. I'd always thought that when I left for Elysia, I'd be able to keep a check on her. I hadn't thought about the fact that one day, she'd no longer exist in the world. That my bound would leave me alone to continue in life.

Sophie realised that what she said had an effect on me.

"I'm sorry, Gray. I didn't mean —"

"No. It's —"

"That's how it would be, right? You'd lose her one day?"

Unless she claimed her divinity. I felt like this was being pushed so much quicker than I'd like. I needed to figure things out. I needed to find a way without putting her in danger. When we returned, I'd see Erik, Sloan, Ig, and Elva. Elva would want to help. She'd want her family back.

Maybe it would be as simple as dunking her in the pool and returning her to earth. Drive by gifting.

"Gray?"

Sophie pulled me out of my thoughts.

"Look after her while you have her. And ignore Cassidy. After Ethan, I think he blames himself for not taking care of her properly and having more of a say in everything. He feels like he should have warned her off him or been more involved to save her from the heartache."

"You have nothing to worry about. I'll always look after her, Sophie. I love her."

The words fell out of my mouth without restraint and a grin stretched across Sophie's face.

I loved her. It was true. I loved Quentin Scott.

Weeks of feeling off balance, of trying to decipher the strange emotion in my heart, boiled down to one simple fact. I loved her more than I'd ever loved anything in my life. No amount of power, no devastating destruction caused by my hands, could compare to how she made me feel.

Erik was going to have a fucking field day when he found out.

"Have you told her?" Sophie asked.

"No."

"You should."

I shrugged and drank the rest of my coffee. I didn't want to discuss it. I'd heard Quentin say the words when she was practically asleep. Admitting it to her without knowing the depth of her feelings was a risk I wasn't sure I wanted to take.

"I'll think about it."

By the time the siblings returned to the house, it was late, and I was helping Sophie in the kitchen as she prepared dinner. She'd coaxed me into an apron that said 'hot stuff cooking' and I did what she asked.

I noticed Quentin standing at the door, watching us with an odd expression on her face. I held an arm out to her, and she walked over, burying herself in my side.

"You could have told me," I whispered.

"I know. I just didn't know how."

"Quen, I'll always be here for you."

"I know you will," she said, reaching up to kiss me. "Hot stuff."

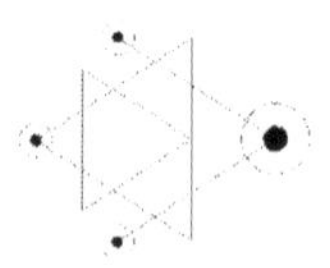

"Would you like to talk about it?"

We laid in bed later in the evening. I'd given her the left side, and she was tucked in against me. My fingers inched their way under her shirt and brushed against the skin of her thigh and hip, making her flush with goosebumps.

"I'm not sure what to say."

"Tell me about them."

She took a deep breath and thought for a while before opening up.

"I was so scared when they first adopted me. I was only ten, and we'd met and spoken, but this was different. I thought maybe they'd made a mistake. The first few nights after the adoption, I couldn't sleep because the fear was so real. Cried my eyes out because I thought maybe they'd return me.

"They did everything they could with us. For us. Dad was easy-going. He was old records and lazy Sunday morning brunches. He thought he could be a gardener, but killed everything he touched when it came to plants. I loved both my parents, but I spent a lot of my spare time with Dad, learning things from him. He was interested in research and introduced me to that side of things."

"And your mother?" I asked.

"She was amazing. I don't think I know anyone who could organise their life the way she did. Mum worked hard, but she was there for me and Cass. Bedtime stories and helping with homework. She was definitely more of the rule enforcer."

Quentin laughed then, kicking my heart from its steady rhythm, and I watched her features brighten.

"Mum wanted to make sure there were rules, but Dad was always teaching us how to bend them."

Her fingers traced numbers again and again across my chest. One. Four. Three.

I pulled her in close. "Do you —" I started and then thought better of it.

"What is it?"

"Do you ever wonder about your birth parents?"

She chewed on her bottom lip and then shrugged. "I looked."

"You looked?"

My voice was a little louder, and she furrowed her brow.

"Yeah."

"What did you find out?"

"Not much. It's like they don't even exist. I was so unwanted they made sure there was no way for me to trace back to them."

I shifted, pulling her so that she was straddling my waist, looking down. The room was dark, but we'd been up for a while.

Quen ran her hands through my hair and kissed me gently. It was a struggle to keep my hands to myself. Physical touch was what I craved whenever she was nearby.

"Listen to me," I said. "You were not unwanted."

She sat up straight and rolled her eyes. "It's fine, Gray. I made my peace with it a long time ago."

"Quentin —"

"What?" she snapped, getting defensive.

"You don't know why they gave you up. They might have had a good reason. Maybe they were trying to protect you."

"Why are you defending them?" Quen crossed her arms across her chest.

"I'm not."

"You are. Gray, honestly, I couldn't care less why they did it or who they are. They gave me up and I'm thankful. I had amazing, loving parents who chose me, and I would have missed out on that. I'm grateful I had as much time as I did with Mum and Dad. I miss them every day."

I rubbed my hands along her bare thighs, and she uncrossed her arms.

"I know," I told her. "I was just curious."

Her hands ran down my arms, moving over muscles. "I just don't like talking about it much." She sighed. "What about your parents?"

"My parents? What about them?"

"Are they still alive?"

"Gods are immortal, Quen. Yes, they're still alive and up in Elysia."

"But they aren't part of the elite?"

"They used to be and then when the prayers for them became less and for us became more, there was a shift in the council.

They're happy though. I think you're much too young to remember them."

She blushed. We rarely discussed age. It was pointless. I had centuries on her.

"What are their responsibilities?"

"Hunting and fertility."

"But I thought Sloan deals with fertility."

I smiled and flipped us so that she was laying under me as I kissed along her jaw.

"She does," I told her. "Sloan became more successful at granting prayers so there was a shift in powers. They get on like a house on fire. No bad blood."

Dotting kisses down her neck, Quen closed her eyes and tilted her head to give me better access.

"She'll love you just as much when you meet her," I said without thinking.

Her eyes snapped open, and she pushed my shoulders until I looked at her properly.

"What's wrong?" I asked.

"When I meet her?" she repeated.

I grinned. "If I've had to sit at dinner with your brother, more than once may I add, I think it's only fair that you sit with my parents."

"I've had dinner with Erik multiple times!"

"It's not the same."

"How so?"

I quirked an eyebrow. "I've yet to meet a person who Erik doesn't love and they don't love him back. It's his thing after all. Quentin, are you nervous?"

"No!"

"Liar."

Any protest she had was hushed when I pressed my lips to hers again and she melted into the embrace. This was something for her to worry about later. An issue we would cross when I'd straighten out everything surrounding it.

We didn't touch on those topics again for the rest of the night, and instead, got lost in shallow breaths and quiet moans. Lost in an uncomplicated tangle of being together in the privacy of darkness.

FIFTY TWO

QUENTIN

The trip home was quicker and cheaper, thanks to Gray and his aura.

"I'm working at Murphy's tonight. Will I see you there?" Gray asked me.

"Maybe. Would you like to see me there?"

I wrapped my arms around his waist, and he looked down at me.

"Are you fishing for compliments, Scott?"

Feigning shock, I said, "Me? Never."

He laughed and shook his head, tucking some hair behind my ear. "Then I won't tell you I would like it very much if I saw you at Murphy's tonight. That I might even go as far as to say it would be the highlight of my shift."

My cheeks coloured. "Yeah, yeah. Alright."

Gray brought his face closer to mine and pulled me in so our bodies were flush together.

"You have become the highlight of my days," he told me quietly.

My stomach flipped at his words, and blood rushed to my face, spreading down my neck. It was an open admission to how he felt and caught me off guard.

There was a knock on the door, and I gratefully broke away from Gray, who smirked.

"I'm going to get that," I told him, still flustered.

"Sure thing."

I couldn't deal with this man. Every time I thought I could do this not serious-serious, not a relationship but still exclusive thing we were doing, he said or did something that made the words dance on the tip of my tongue.

The thoughts wrapped around my head, and when I opened the door, I jumped to see Charlie there.

"Charlie?"

"Hi, Quentin," she said sheepishly. "I was thinking we could talk?"

The last time I'd seen Charlie, she'd been quick to jump to Matt's defence and called what Gray and I had a dirty little secret.

Gray came down the hall and stood behind me.

"Evening, Gray," Charlie said, not looking him in the eye.

"Hello, Charlotte." His words were tight and clipped.

Gray placed his hands on my waist, keeping my body close to his. I'd told him what happened, and he wasn't pleased about it. That was evident by the tension that filled the doorway of my home.

"Gray was just leaving for work so we can talk," I told her.

Behind me, Gray tensed, and I placed my hands over his reassuringly until he spoke.

"I'll see you later."

He kissed me before releasing me from his grip, and I

blushed again at the act of PDA. If you were to assign Gray a love language, it would be physical touch. The moment we were near each other, he'd find a way to get a hand on me.

He moved past us both and walked down the street towards Murphy's.

"Come in," I said, letting Charlie into the house and moving through to the living room.

"So, you two are still...?" Charlie asked, leaving the end of the sentence hanging.

"Yeah."

She nodded. This felt like a conversation on repeat, and every time it made me anxious. I didn't want to hear people say it was a bad idea.

Of course, this was a bad idea. Not only did I break the terms of my contract, but I was willingly entering a relationship — was that the right word? — that held no longevity and would leave me as the injured party.

Charlie took in a deep breath and released it slowly.

"I don't agree with what you did, Quen," she said. "But I've missed you."

I looked over at her and felt a small sense of relief. "I've missed you too. How's Matt?"

"You know Matthew. Bruised ego, but he'll live. He's calmed down a lot from when I first spoke to him."

"I really am sorry. I never meant to hurt him."

"It explains why Gray seemed so damn happy and willing during our sessions. Keep him happy, Quen. It makes my job a lot easier."

"Oh, yeah, because that's why I'm with him. To make your life easier."

"Nothing to do with that body."

"Charlie!"

We laughed together, and I felt some of the sadness that shrouded me, when I left, lifted from my shoulders.

"What?" she asked innocently. "I'm not blind, Quen. That man has the body of a God."

"He is one."

Another fit of giggles.

"You really like him, don't you? I've never seen you like this," she said.

"Like what?"

"You risked work for him. You're happy."

I didn't know why, but that comment hit me hard. Charlie was right. Despite all the difficulties and chaos that Gray had brought into my life, happiness engulfed every aspect of it. I'd lived in a dull sepia until he'd touch it, and everything burst into colour brighter than ever before.

"How about we head to Murphy's and I can catch you up on the wedding planning?" Charlie suggested.

"Sounds great. You go ahead. I just need to do something."

"Okay, but don't be long. I have a lot that we need to catch up on."

We both got up from our seats, and Charlie hugged me. I squeezed her, glad that things were okay between us again. Even after knowing each other for a year or so, Charlie had become a close friend and I should have confided in her in the first place.

"See you there."

Charlie left the house, and I went upstairs.

I walked straight into my room and opened my bedside drawer where the box sat. Scooping it up carefully, I snapped it open to see the engagement ring Ethan gave me. It glittered in the room's light. I gave it a moment before snapping it shut again.

Carrying it back downstairs, I checked my phone for the time. It was seven-thirty. The nearest pawn shop closed at eight.

My feet pounded the pavement as I ran to the shop and as I opened the door, the bell rang to announce my entrance.

"Hello?" I called, taking in some deep breaths.

There was no one around and I assumed the owner must be out the back, so I made my way through the shop, fingers trailing across some things stocked on the shelves.

"Where have you been, angel?"

I jumped out of my skin and whirled around to find Archer

leaning against a set of shelves and watching my movements.

"How did you know I was here?" I asked, clutching my chest.

He arched an eyebrow and laughed. "Are you forgetting I'm a God? If I want to find you, I will."

My cheeks flushed with embarrassment and fear prepared me to bolt from the shop. There was something menacing about the way he'd delivered that last sentence.

Archer made his way towards me, and I backed away slowly. He reached into his pocket and pulled out a cuff, placing it around his wrist.

"I'm playing by the rules," he said. He stepped towards me again and I stood firm. "I didn't want to bother you while you were with family. How are they?"

"They're fine."

The owner appeared and I left Archer to hand in the ring. Once I was done, I turned to find him waiting patiently.

"Perhaps we can get a bite to eat together."

"Actually, I was planning to go to Murphy's," I told him.

"Perfect. I can buy you a drink."

It didn't look like I was going to shake him tonight. "Sure."

We walked to the pub and when we got inside, I saw how busy it was. Most of the tables were taken up with people, so it looked like we'd be at the bar.

Charlie was behind it helping Tyler, and she caught my eye and mouthed an apology. He really needed to sort out his staffing situation. The bar had steadily been doing better over the past few months, and he'd only have Gray until the project was over.

Archer placed a hand on the small of my back, and I jerked away from his touch. A curious expression clouded his face before he made his way over to the bar, where there were free stools.

It was like a magnet. My eyes found Gray's in an instant and he narrowed his eyes before he made a beeline for us.

"What can I get you?" Gray's words were tight, and I started to feel nervous.

"I'll have a beer. Quentin?" Archer said.

"Vodka and coke."

Gray worked on the drinks but kept glancing at us.

"It's nice to finally get you on your own and not in your dreams."

Archer raised a hand and brushed his fingers against my temple. I pulled away and swallowed, knowing Gray wasn't best known for controlling his temper.

A pint of beer slammed down on the bar top, sloshing over the lip of the glass and spilling onto the surface.

"Problem, Grayson?" Archer asked, turning his head to look at Gray.

"Why would there be?"

"You seem to be interrupting my evening with this beautiful woman."

"I didn't realise you kept such questionable company, Scott," Gray said through gritted teeth.

I narrowed my eyes, not appreciating the accusation in his voice. "I bumped into him on the way here."

"We have a habit of bumping into each other, don't we?" Archer said.

My mouth ran dry. Every time Gray had asked me if I'd seen Archer, I'd lied. I was still trying to work out all the cryptic messages that Archer relayed to me through my dreams, and I worried if I told Gray, he'd brush it all under the carpet.

Archer continued, "I'm just trying to convince her to actually let me take her out on a date."

"I'm not allowed to date a God. It's part of my contract," I said automatically.

Archer turned his attention back to me. "I told you before, Gods tend to get what they want and if they want something badly enough, they'll find a way."

"You keep going and Hunter is going to kill you," Gray hissed.

Archer leaned over the bar towards Gray. "It wouldn't be Hunter, though, would it? We both know he won't get his hands dirty."

"What do you mean?" I asked, catching the comment.

"It's nothing," Gray snapped, eyes still on Archer. "If you want to date her, go ahead. It's your funeral," he said nonchalantly.

My eyes went wide.

"Is that you giving me your blessing, Grayson?" Archer implored.

Gray opened his mouth again. But I beat him to it.

"I can't date a God," I repeated. "But if I could, I'd happily take you up on the offer."

"Ah, ah, Grayson. Why so angry?" Archer asked, picking up on the change in the mood.

I looked at Gray, challenging him to say something. Anything. He'd just given up. Thrown me away without a second thought.

"You're both utterly stupid," Gray said coldly before he left us.

FIFTY THREE

GRAYSON

For the entire night, I couldn't tear my eyes away from them. Archer's fingers brushed against her skin, and I wanted to rip his hand clean off his body, regardless of the fact that Quen kept pulling away from his advances.

Archer had been trying to find a way to ruin me for years. To get me back for what I'd done to him. It would be so easy if he found out the truth about us. He had no genuine interest in Quentin, other than to provoke a reaction from me. And if he did that, then we would be neck-deep in trouble. So, I'd told him to do what he wanted. Acted like I didn't give a fuck.

When Archer decided to leave, he caught my eye. Quen's back was to me, but Archer saw me perfectly and leaned down, cupping her cheek and pressing his lips to the other one.

The lights above them popped and shattered, glass splintering everywhere. Quentin immediately turned on her stool to look at me and Archer left the pub while Tyler calmed the commotion.

I walked myself down the bar to where she was sitting and locked eyes with her.

"If he touches you one more time, I swear I'll rip his throat out," I told her, deathly serious.

"No. You don't get to be like that when you practically offered me to him on a plate."

"What did you want me to do? Tell him you're mine and then see what happens? You know what would happen! Why did you tell him you'd date him if you could?"

"If you're going to offer me up as a sacrifice, then you need to deal with the consequences."

"You'll deal with the consequences as well. Do you understand what you're doing?"

"Obviously not. I am stupid after all."

She pushed herself off the stool and made for the exit.

"Quentin! Quen!" I called after her, but she didn't turn around. She disappeared through the door. When I turned, I found Charlotte looking at me. "What?"

"Don't take it out on me. Let her calm down. By the time you go home, she'll probably be more willing to talk."

Charlie made a decent point. Right now, we were both angry, and that wasn't going to help the situation. Every cell in my body wanted to find Archer and rip him to shreds. He had no right to touch what belonged to me. No right to toy with the woman who was mine. I wanted to show him what the God of chaos was truly capable of, because he had no idea.

When I finished my shift, I took the walk home to help myself calm down and to give Quentin time to stop her ass from bouncing off the walls.

Walking up to the door, the lights were on in the house, so

Quen hadn't gone to bed yet. I took in a deep breath and opened the door. I found her sitting on the couch in the living room, reading a book titled *Life explained.*

"Shall we talk?" I asked.

She didn't even look up from the book. "What is there to talk about?"

"Are you being infuriating on purpose?"

"It's a default setting. Kind of like how you being a giant dickhead is your default setting."

"So we're just going to trade petty insults then?"

She snapped the book shut and tossed it into the space next to her before looking up at me.

"I'd rather not talk to you at all," she shot.

She got up from her seat and attempted to move past me, but I grabbed her.

"Get off me!" she yelled.

"No! Tell me what I've done. Tell me what I was meant to do!"

She turned on me, fire blazing in her eyes.

"If you want to date her, go ahead." Quentin had lowered her voice in an attempt to imitate me and although it was childish, I could see how badly it came across.

"He's trying to figure out if anything was going on between us!"

"He probably worked that out from the lights you shattered!"

"He kissed you!"

"He kissed my cheek!"

"No other man is to ever touch you! Have I made myself clear?" I roared.

I'd lost it. The black of my aura pulsed around us ferociously in my rage, but Quen was just as fired up and wasn't backing down.

"You do not get to tell me what I'm allowed to do or who I'm allowed to be around!"

She didn't want to be controlled. She wanted to be free to make her own decisions, but she didn't get the freedom here. The way Archer behaved around her; I could kill him. I could tear him apart so easily. Quentin was mine. She was made for me.

"I can't stand it, Quentin. I can't stand anyone else touching you. I don't want any other being to even entertain the thought that they could have a chance with you."

I always thought that my temper was something to be reckoned with, but Quen was just as bad. For someone who had yet to have their powers gifted to them, she was a nightmare.

"Why not?" she screamed. "What do you care?"

A fucking nightmare.

This woman was stubborn and difficult and there were times I wondered if I could throw her off a cliff and get away with it because the peace it would bring to my life would be bliss. And then somehow, I was always reminded that I knew I wouldn't be able to live without her.

It wasn't the way I planned it. In the back of my mind, I'd planned something more romantic for my first declaration. Quentin deserved a fairy-tale moment that she could look back on in years to come, but nothing ever went to plan when I was with her.

The words bellowed through the room, shattering the lights and the vases until debris littered the floor.

"BECAUSE I LOVE YOU, YOU INSUFFERABLE WOMAN!"

FIFTY FOUR

QUENTIN

I imagined most people thought about the moment that the first declaration of love was made would be done in some cute way. That it'd be a tender moment.

As per usual, for Gray and myself, it was a moment of pure chaos.

I felt the words reverberate around us and ice water was tipped through my veins, dousing the fire that coursed through them, moments before.

Gray just confessed he loved me.

My heart was hammering in my chest as I looked at him. Every ounce of anger I had was flushed out of me by a range of emotions. Confusion, panic, disbelief. You name them, and I was feeling them.

There was a knock on the door that broke me out of my thoughts, and Gray reined himself in enough that his aura disappeared.

"Who the fuck is here at gone midnight?" he hissed, unhappy with the interruption.

A flash of panic ran through me. I'd only had one previous time where there had been a knock on the door at such an unsociable hour. That was the police on the night that my parents died.

"No. No."

My mind ran through the people around me and who it could be. The knock came louder again.

Gray must have sensed my panic because he strode past me to get to the door, and I chased after him.

He wrenched the door open. "Can I help you?"

I got myself to his side, and my heart stopped.

This had to be a joke.

My mind had finally succumbed to years of pressure, and I was hallucinating because what other logical reason could there be.

"Ethan?"

"Hello, Q," he said, running a hand through his blonde hair.

I couldn't believe my eyes that Ethan Blake was standing on the doorstep. The last time I'd seen him was years ago when he walked out of my life, but nothing had changed. He still sported stubble around his jaw. Still styled his hair in a messy way with it sticking up from all angles. Still called me Q like he didn't rip out my heart and step all over it.

"I didn't mean to interrupt," he said, eyes shifting to Gray.

When I glanced up, Gray's jaw was set, and his hands were balled into fists.

"It's fine," I breathed, sure I was a step away from passing out. The three of us stood in awkward silence before I spoke again. "Ethan, what are you doing here?"

"I wanted to talk to you, but I couldn't get a hold of you," he explained.

"So you turn up at the house?"

"It's past midnight." Gray's voice cut across the conversation, cold and sharp.

"Yeah. I realise it's not the most sociable hour. I'm Ethan."

Ethan held his hand out and I had another wave of panic because Gray wasn't wearing a cuff. But Gray just looked at his hand in disgust.

"It's past midnight, Ethan," Gray repeated.

"Sorry," Ethan replied. "I should go."

He turned around, and I stepped over the threshold.

"No!" I called.

"No?" I heard Gray echo behind me.

"You wanted to talk?" I asked Ethan.

"I don't think your friend would be very happy."

"We'll go to the diner."

Ed's was open 24/7 and served the greasiest food. Ethan and I used to finish our assignments there when we were home for the holidays. Tucked in a booth, huddled close together, sharing fries and kisses.

"Go ahead. I'll meet you there," I said to him.

"Sure," he said, looking nervous, turning away.

When I turned around, I don't think I'd ever seen Gray look so livid in all the time I'd known him. His eyes were completely black, and his aura pulsated in violent waves. I moved back towards the house, and he stepped aside to let me in before slamming the door so hard it caused the building to shake.

"You aren't going," Gray told me, voice low and dangerous.

"Excuse me?"

"You're not seeing him, Scott."

I blinked at Gray and the anger I felt before rushed through again. "I told you, you don't get to tell me what I can and can't do."

"You gave your heart to me! You promised it to me! If you so much as look at him, I'll destroy him!"

Gave my heart to Gray? Promised my heart to Gray?

I knew what Gray had said. I knew he said he loved me and every part of me wanted to tell him I loved him, too. But even if I did, even if he did, what was the point?

Gray would leave me. *I love you* were pretty words and maybe I wanted more than that. Maybe I wanted what my parents had. If you loved someone, how could you be okay with leaving them?

I owed it to myself to heal, and that meant hearing what Ethan had to say.

"I have never promised you anything, Gray. And you'll do nothing of the sort. I'll make my own decisions and you cannot force my hand."

Turning away from him, I grabbed my keys from the table in the hallway, but his aura wrapped around my waist, drawing me into his body.

"He's nothing but a mortal!" Gray said to me.

Gray slammed my body against the wall, and I hissed in pain. My heart thumped wildly in my chest as he crowded my space. More than ever, I saw the God who surrounded himself with complete devastation. His hand wrapped around my throat, ensuring I kept my focus on him.

"I could kill him in a heartbeat," Gray said, pressing his nose to mine.

I attempted to push him away but he brought his body closer, pinning me with no hope of escape. His face was in the crook of my neck, stubble grazing roughly against my skin.

"What would you do, Quentin?" Gray asked, words at my ear. "Would you cry over his corpse? Would you mourn?"

I looked at him. To him, mortals were disposable. We meant nothing to Gods. They kept us around for their powers and their egos.

"Maybe the others are right," I said, shaking my head. "Maybe you are a monster."

His aura disappeared from around him. It was as if his temper just dropped away. Grayson straightened up, stepping away from me. I didn't wait for him to say anything. I couldn't even look at him. Instead, I slipped past him and left the house before getting in the car and driving off.

A sharp pain shot through my chest, and breathing deeply, I tried to calm it down. It continued the entire way to Ed's and I rubbed at the spot as I walked into the diner.

Ethan was sitting in our old booth, and I was hit with a pang of nostalgia. I slid in opposite him, our knees brushing together.

"It's nice to see you again, Q."

The words "you too" almost came from my mouth, but it wasn't nice to see Ethan.

He reached out and his hand covered mine. Once, it lit up something inside me, but tonight I didn't feel it. There was a weird pull to see Ethan again, which was why I came. I wanted to see what he had to say for himself.

"Is everything okay?" I asked, pulling my hand away from his.

"I guess so."

"You said you wanted to talk."

"Always wanted to cut to the chase."

Ethan was a gentleman; old-fashioned and knew how to hold a conversation, whereas I rushed to the point. I preferred efficiency over manners.

"You turned up at my door, Ethan."

"Who was that with you?" he asked about Gray.

I was still so mad at Gray for his comments. He had no right to threaten Ethan. The argument banged around my skull. I hated fighting with him. Gray knew how to push my buttons. I never thought Ethan would make him so unnecessarily angry.

"Grayson," I answered, sighing.

"Grayson?"

I shouldn't have called him a monster. I knew he had a temper. I knew he was possessive and jealous. I didn't blame him because I was the same. He told me he loved me, and I was too chicken to tell him the same thing. The truth was, I knew I'd been falling for him for a little while. Despite the temper and the harsh words, I couldn't stop loving him.

"We're seeing each other," I explained.

"Oh."

"What?"

He rubbed the back of his neck "Well, I feel stupid now."

"Why?"

"Austin's getting married."

Austin was Ethan's younger brother, and just as charming as Ethan. I smiled at the thought of him making it up the aisle.

"Congratulations to him."

"Yeah, it's great news. But it got me thinking."

"About?"

"Come on, Q. We'd have been married for a few years by now. I fucked up. I shouldn't have left you like that. We could've been happy together. We were for a long time before I messed it up. I know I did, and I'm sorry. Lately, I've been thinking maybe we could talk and try to fix things between us. I miss you."

My insides twisted as I looked at him. Ethan was once my entire world. I was ready to marry him. 'Til death do us part, I'd have been his partner in everything. When he left, my world shattered. Even though the last few months showed me we were incompatible, losing him had broken me. I didn't think I'd love anyone like that again.

Until Gray. I thought of every night we'd spent together. I thought of every fight we had. I thought of how I caught him looking at me sometimes. He was impulsive and chaotic and would always put his foot in his mouth, but he was supportive and dealt with everything I threw at him. I never thought I'd want someone in my life so badly. I didn't even want Ethan as badly as I did Gray.

Fuck.

Why was I sitting here with Ethan? Why did I agree to talk to him?

I didn't want Ethan. I wanted Gray. I wanted something with Grayson, which meant we needed to sit and talk about this properly and decide what to do. I'd lay it on the line for him so that one way or another, we could figure it out.

"Q? What do you think? I've been thinking about it a lot."

I focused on Ethan again. He rubbed his hand over the

stubble on his jaw. When he first left me, for a short while, I used to dream of him turning up and saying he'd made a mistake, asking for me to take him back. But the reality was that I didn't want him. Not anymore.

"No," I said.

"No?"

"No, Ethan. I don't want to try again," I told him, getting up from the booth. "You said you didn't love me anymore when you left."

"I didn't mean it."

"I don't care. You can't flip a switch like that. I don't know if it's because you're lonely or what, but I don't want this conversation with you. I have no interest in trying to reconcile with someone who couldn't even talk to me about how he felt."

He stood up. "I —"

"I loved you once. But I'm not what you need and you're not what I need."

"But you came here."

"I know, and I think I just realised that this was a mistake."

"Q!"

But I was already walking through the diner and out into the car park. The rain was falling heavily in massive drops, and I heard the thunder before there was a flash of lightning.

Gray rarely said the right things, but what was I meant to expect? He was the God of chaos. Things would never be straight with him. Maybe it was foolish to hope that things could work out between us, but I knew that if I didn't ask him, then I'd regret it for the rest of my life.

I was soaked through by the time I got into the car. I put the key in the ignition and went straight home, but he wasn't there.

Erik's.

Gray always went to Erik when things weren't right.

The rain was getting worse, and I drove carefully through the streets. We were in November, so I wasn't surprised at the rain, but just how heavy it was.

As I drove, the ground shook. It started as a tremor, but it got worse.

Earthquake?

I pulled up at the side of the road, killing the engine.

Then it hit me. This wasn't a natural cause. This was Gray.

I got out of the car, trusting my feet rather than the vehicle to take me safely towards the house.

Whatever Gray was doing, he needed to stop. I pulled my phone from my pocket and tried to call him, but there was no answer. I tried Erik and Sloan, but nothing happened.

I started to run.

FIFTY FIVE

GRAYSON

Whenever I'd been around Quentin, I felt acceptance. I'd been working hard to show her I cared for her. I was used to other people calling me a monster, but to hear her say it gutted me worse than I could have imagined. I didn't even have the will to stop her when she left. Instead, I took myself to Erik's. The pain in my chest was so severe, and I needed it to stop.

When I arrived in their bedroom, I nudged Erik awake. There was a flash of red until he realised it was me.

"Gray?"

Erik's aura illuminated the room, and Sloan woke up.

"What's going on?" Erik asked.

I clutched at my chest as the pain hit me again. Erik jumped out of bed, wide awake.

"Gray! What happened?"

We were wrapped in red, and then we were outside in the garden. The cool night air helped slightly with the feelings, making it easier to breathe.

"You must have got it wrong," I told him.

"What's wrong?"

"She can't be my soulbound."

Erik looked at me in confusion. "Gray, why are you saying that?"

"He turns up, and she leaves with him. I told her. I told her I love her, but she didn't choose me, Erik." I felt the anger swell in me again. "I'd give her anything she wants, but she won't give me the same. She'd pick a mortal over me!"

Erik raised his hand. "You need to calm down."

"HOW?"

There it was. My aura spanned out across the garden. Erik sparked his own up as a protective measure, but I had no reason to hurt my brother. He couldn't help what his responsibility was. He wasn't responsible for her actions.

"She loves you, Grayson. I know she does!" Erik yelled.

I let out a harsh laugh as the heavens opened and great droplets of rain fell from the sky. If she thought I was a monster, then so be it. Why bother to have control?

Sloan came out of the house, her aura around her as she joined her husband.

I'd never envied Erik so much in my life as I did in this moment. To have someone who would choose you every single time without fail. Someone to stand by you and love you no matter how many faults you had.

The pain in my chest worsened as the thunder rumbled overhead.

"Gray, you need to stop this," Sloan pleaded. "You will not

solve anything by behaving this way. Listen to Erik."

But what would be the point in listening to Erik? Why should I care anymore about trying to keep things in check? If I was as bad as they all thought, then why should I not prove them right?

I needed to take my anger out. I didn't want to be calm. I had no desire to listen to Erik. He was lucky to have a soulbound and settled in with no problems. I wasn't interested in hearing him preach to me about giving it time.

A burst of my aura hit him, and he picked himself off the ground while Sloan blocked an attack.

"She'll come around!" Erik bellowed. "I swear it to you, Gray!"

"I couldn't care less what she does. I want rid of this bond!"

This bond was a blight in my life. It had messed with my head and my heart until I couldn't think straight. The pain was already immense, so how much worse could it be if I severed the ties that bound us?

"Please, don't do this, Gray," Sloan said.

The ground shook as my fury seeped into the earth. I'd tear this world apart until I felt better. Everyone could suffer with me until I found it fit to show them mercy.

"You can't break it!" Erik screamed. "I refuse to let you!"

"IT'S NOT YOUR DECISION!"

The tremor I'd set in the earth became more pronounced and shook the world around us violently. I'd bring down buildings and uproot plants. Pure chaos and destruction of a magnitude that only I could manage.

"STOP!"

I did stop, but not because Sloan had yelled at me.

There was a crippling pain in my chest, stronger and sharper than it had been before, and it pulled me down to my knees, knocking the breath out of my lungs.

Erik ran over to me as I clenched my teeth together, trying to ride through the blinding pain. It weakened me, until I felt I might pass out.

"Gray?" Erik asked.

Both auras gone, Erik dropped to his knees and put a hand on my shoulder.

I couldn't describe the pain. It was shattering, splintering, soul tearing. It was white-hot and demanded to be felt. There was no running from it. No reprieve.

"Gray, what is it?"

I heaved as if I was going to be sick. The pain was so undeniably intense.

She was meant to feel everything I felt. Did she feel this now? Did she feel how bad it was?

I searched for Quen, wanting to know if this affected her just as bad as it was affecting me. If my pain was mirrored in my bound.

"No," I whispered.

What I found made me get up to my feet. I pushed through the pain because if I didn't…

My aura took me and Erik, who was still holding me, outside to the front of the house.

"NO!" I cried, the word strangled as I crumpled at the sight.

In the middle of the road, body awkward and small, laid Quentin.

No. No. No.

This couldn't be happening.

I ran towards her and dropped to my knees. There was blood around her head, and I hesitated to touch her.

"ERIK!"

My brother was next to me in a flash, looking forlorn.

"No! No! Stop looking like that!" I yelled.

I heaved again. The pain was unbearable. The ripping feeling in my chest so intense that I was certain it would cleave me open.

Quen was laying before me, and for once, I didn't know what to do.

"We need to fix her. I need to fix her. Erik! Help me!"

"Gray —"

"NO!"

I didn't want to hear him say it. I didn't want him to say that he couldn't save her. Her breathing was so shallow and ragged. Hot tears mingled with the rain that fell down my face.

Sloan joined us, looking like she'd lost all her colour. She placed a hand gently on my shoulder.

"Gray…"

"Please. Please, Sloan. You can help. You can help, can't you? You gift life," I said desperately to my sister-in-law.

Her gift had never been one I worked closely with or took much interest in until now.

Life.

Sloan worked with life, and I needed her to grant me this.

"Gray, it doesn't work like that. I don't gift life in this form."

I screamed out my frustration before it hit me.

"Elva!" I said. "Get Elva! Sloan. Erik. One of you get her!"

Sloan disappeared, and a few moments later, reappeared with Elva and Ignacio in tow. Elva gasped when she saw Quentin on the ground.

"She'll pass soon," Elva whispered mournfully, sensing the ebbing of life.

Goddess of death had given her verdict. She knew when people were ready to go. She sensed when life could no longer continue.

The bile rose up my throat.

Why had I wasted so much time? The arguments had been pointless. Completely trivial. Even if they were unavoidable, I should have followed her to the diner. Waited for her to finish and then taken her home. I should have demanded to know her response to my confession of love.

"Elva, please. Please help."

"I —"

I turned towards her on my knees and dropped my forehead to her feet. Through the rain, I heard the gasps from the others.

"I'm begging you, Elva," I said, speaking to the ground.

"I'm on my knees, and I'm begging you to save her from this."

As Gods, we didn't beg. As Gods, we were prideful to a fault, but I had no pride here. I would give anything because if I lost her, I wasn't sure I could continue to exist.

Elva looked down at me with tears in her eyes.

"She's your family, Elva," I said, lifting my head.

"I'm thinking, Gray."

"Think quicker!"

"The pool," Ignacio said calmly. "She's a demigod. Get her to the pool. If it claims and gifts her before she dies, she'll have her immortality."

"Grayson, we need to go," Erik said.

I turned back to Quen and my heart stopped. I was breaking all the rules for her. Gently, I lifted her from the ground. Usually so animated, she was limp and heavy in my arms, like a rag doll, and a sob escaped my lips.

"Quickly, Gray," Erik urged.

"Hold on, Quentin. I promise you it'll be okay."

I thought I'd seen her vulnerable in the early mornings when she was still in the grip of sleep, but this was something else. The way she laid in my arms with no power in her. This wasn't Quentin. This woman talked in her sleep. She was warm and always had something to say, but now, she was on the edge of mortality, and I was terrified that I was too late.

Once we got into Elysia, we arrived at the edges of the pool. Instantly, the water pulsed steadily, like it'd grown a heartbeat.

"You'll need to take her in, Gray. Just like we've done with the kids." Erik guided me through what I should do.

He stood next to Sloan, and I could see her tear-streaked face staring back at me.

"Bring her home, Gray," Elva said, grasping Ig's hand.

I stepped into the pool without a word. It turned black around me until it resembled a vacuum, but I didn't stop. The water lapped at my waist the further I waded in, but it remained black.

"Why is nothing happening?!" I panicked.

It wanted her the first time she was here, but now it did

nothing. Were we too late? Had we missed our chance?

"Submerge her," Sloan's voice carried out quietly and I nodded.

Taking in a deep breath, I took a few more steps until we both disappeared under the water.

It took moments, but the water changed again. It bubbled and pulsed around us violently. The black cleared away from around us, and instead, the water became golden. We were swimming in a pool of champagne, bright and bubbling and blinding after the darkness.

And then Quentin's gift hit me.

The overwhelming urge of achievement and hard work. Years upon years of certificates and trophies. Praise from everyone around her.

Along with her divinity, Quentin had been gifted the responsibility of success.

FIFTY SIX

QUENTIN

The pain thrummed through my head so badly that I thought my head might split in two. When I tried to take in a breath, my mouth filled with water.

I was drowning.

My eyes snapped open, and I felt the water surrounding me as I kicked and thrashed, hitting something solid a few times.

Where the fuck was I?

I finally broke through the surface and took in deep breaths. My lungs burned from the lack of oxygen, and I coughed and spluttered, heaving in as much air as I could.

A few seconds later, Gray broke the surface opposite me.

"Quentin?" he asked, water dripping down his face.

"Were you trying to drown me? You're a fucking psychopath!"

I went to turn my head to see where I was, but Gray didn't let me. He caught hold of my face and kissed me deeply and fiercely. The moment our lips met, liquid sunshine shot through my veins, heating me up from inside out. His tongue found its way into my mouth, and I let him.

Gods, I was stupid to have walked away from him earlier.

The sound of applause and whooping made me break away from Gray. When I turned my head, I saw the Gods I regarded as friends standing at the edge of the reflecting pool.

"Elysia? Why are we in Elysia? Am I dreaming?" I asked, looking back at Gray.

"You don't remember what happened?"

"I was coming to find you. I had the car, but there was an earthquake. I left it and stepped onto the road. A car…"

Then something happened. It was like a thousand whispers hit me all at once, and I gripped my head in my hands. "Ow!"

Gray didn't let go of me. "Don't focus on them, Quentin."

"What's happening?"

It was like an itch that I couldn't scratch. So many voices, some stronger than others, were coming to me, and I wasn't sure how to get rid of them or if I was going mad. The force of them made me want to crack my skull open.

"What's going on?" I grimaced.

"That's exactly what I want to know."

The voice cut through clear, and I turned to see that Hunter had joined the edge of the pool, and just like that, the colour drained from everyone.

"Grayson," Hunter said. "I suggest you get out of the pool with that mortal, right now."

Hunter's tone turned my blood to ice.

Gray whispered to me, "Stay close to me, okay?"

I nodded, and we made our way out of the pool. There were still a million voices in my head, and everything looked cleaner and sharper than it did before. My focus wavered, making my feet clumsy on solid ground, but Gray kept me upright and the rest of the party crowded around us.

"This is an unauthorised visit with a mortal," Hunter stated.

"We know," Gray replied.

"Care to explain why exactly you are here with her and why you were both in the pool with these lot looking on?"

"I don't particularly care to explain anything to you, if I'm blatantly honest."

Hunter's aura flared into life, and a rush of blue came at Gray. Months ago, I watched both of them come to blows in my lab, and then Gray came home after another run-in with Hunter and was bleeding.

I couldn't let him get hurt again. It broke me inside every time. Immortal or not, seeing him in pain made me ache and long to take it away.

"No!" I cried.

"Quentin, no!"

There was an unfamiliar surge of warmth throughout my body. It began in the centre of my chest and radiated through each limb until my fingers and toes tingled. A blinding golden flash made me throw up my hands and squeeze my eyes shut.

Opening my eyes slowly, the flash had subsided, and I could see Hunter had been knocked on his ass a few yards away from us. I looked to the others, whose eyes were wide, and I had a sinking feeling when I saw tendrils of gold coming from my hands.

"Gray?!" I looked up at him in complete disbelief.

What was happening?

Gray looked panicked. "Listen to me. It'll be okay, but you need to keep a hold on your emotions, alright?"

"I'm smoking from my hands, and you want me to stay calm?!"

The tendrils pulsed out around me.

Hunter got to his feet, and there was another flash of blue that snaked towards me. I threw up my hand where a wall of gold appeared, hidden behind a solid wall of black that Gray projected.

"SOMEONE BETTER TELL ME WHAT THE FUCK IS GOING ON!" Hunter's voice shook me to the core, and I dropped my arms, but Gray kept his aura in place.

"Grayson," Hunter hissed, advancing on him. "What is she?"

I would have liked to know the answer too, although I'd be lying if I said I wasn't terrified to find out. Curiosity did not outweigh my fear. Ignorance was a land that I wished to live in.

"Hunter," Erik said.

Hunter knocked Erik off his feet, and I turned to him, but Gray grabbed my arm and kept me beside him.

"Answer. The. Question," Hunter seethed, looking feral.

Gray looked at me before going back to his brother. "Quentin is a demigoddess."

My head snapped up to him. "What?"

Gray looked at me and I could see it in his eyes that this wasn't a joke, and it wasn't a lie. What he was saying was the truth. And my knees buckled. Gray was there, arms around me, keeping me upright.

"I suggest you all come back to the council chambers, and I'll alert the rest to join us. This needs to be dealt with," Hunter said.

"You'll let us explain."

"The entire council will decide. Get there, now. Don't make me ask again."

"Come on, Grayson," Sloan said, gripping Erik's hand tightly.

Gray's aura wrapped around us, and the next thing I knew, we were in a large stone chamber, where twelve thrones stood at the back of the room. Gray still held onto me, and the others joined us.

"Are you okay?" he asked.

"What's going on? What did you mean back there?"

Gray's hands were on my upper arms. "Listen to me. You have to listen to me now."

"What am I?"

The gold-coloured tendrils pulsed out from me, making everyone but Gray step back.

"Quentin, you need to calm down. We can help you, but you just need to let us in."

I felt out of my depth here. Thin gold wisps fluttered around my hands. They might have been considered beautiful if they didn't cause my amygdala to work overtime. All I could see was a threat, as panic seized my muscles and pushed through my body with every beat of my heart.

"You're a demigoddess, Quentin," Gray told me again gently.

"How? I… How?"

"Your mother was one of us, Quentin. Mallory, your mother, she was my cousin," Elva said.

My head swam with this information, mixed with the various voices that kept pinging around my skull.

My mother.

They thought I was one of them. The pool and the way it called to me. A demigoddess? There was no way it could be true.

Gray was in front of me and took my face in his hands. "You need to get a hold on your emotions, and quickly. He's going to ask the council to vote on this matter and they'll vote against you if they think you're a danger to us. And you're a danger to us if you're not under control. Do you understand?"

I looked at him blankly. Did Gray know about this? Did he know I was supposedly part Goddess?

"Quentin, do you understand me?" His sharp tone jolted me out of my thoughts, and I nodded.

The door to the chamber slammed open, forcing Gray away from me quickly. Without him nearby, without the support, my knees trembled.

"I suggest everyone takes their seats!" Hunter barked.

Twelve Gods and Goddesses took to their thrones, looking regal and divine, and for the first time in my life, I wished I'd prayed. I saw familiar faces and others who I knew the names of but hadn't interacted with. My eyes kept flicking to Gray, but he barely glanced at me as everyone settled down.

Hunter stood up, his eyes boring down on me, reducing me to a few inches tall.

"You've been called here tonight for an emergency meeting," he said, addressing the council but keeping his steady gaze on me. "It seems that we have an abomination in our midst."

The words stung and made me narrow my eyes at him. Abomination? How bad was this? If I was a… With every part of my soul, I wanted this to be a joke or a hallucination, but the golden projections that surrounded me, pushing out into the room, told me otherwise.

The entire room filled with whispers, and I brought my hands to my temples. All the noise was too much to cope with. Sensory overload.

"It seems that there were some of us who knew she existed but failed to report to the council. So, Grayson, would you care to explain to the rest of us exactly who she is and what you know."

The room settled down again, making it a little easier to think. Grayson lifted himself out of the chair with grace but didn't look me in the eye. The weight of a dozen stares fell on me, and I suddenly felt very self-conscious.

"Quentin Scott is a demigoddess," Gray announced.

The words rang around the room, and the space swayed. But I took in a deep breath, trying to stay calm the way Gray had advised me to.

"How is that even possible?" Aria asked.

"It can't be," Malachi muttered.

"They were all destroyed!" she said.

"Obviously not all of them, Aria," Grayson said, rolling his eyes.

"Continue," Waverly called out.

"I found out a few months ago," Gray explained.

"Who?" Aria demanded.

"Mallory. She's Mallory's daughter."

Once again, I felt the eyes on my body and I wrapped my arms around myself, trying to give myself any form of protection against the Gods.

"Mallory had her on earth and left her there. Then —"

"Then she requested death," Elva finished.

There was a thick, heavy silence in the chamber, and my blood chilled. Mallory, whoever this Goddess was, had killed herself after giving birth to me.

"Who else knew about this?" Hunter asked.

Erik twitched in his seat.

"No one. Only I knew," Gray said quickly. "I asked the others to come up here to witness her gifting."

"She was gifted?" Aria asked.

Hunter looked interested. "What is her gift?"

"Success," Gray said.

There were murmurs in the chamber again. I watched Gray, so formal and poised, as he addressed his kin. I was taking in everything he said, but I couldn't believe what was going on. My brain struggled to process all the information, and I wanted to grab Gray and go somewhere private, where he could explain this slowly. I needed to absorb in and ask questions so I could be in control.

"I think the question should be asked now, as there seems to be no need to waste time," Hunter said.

"Hunter," Gray gritted out his name.

"Do you have an objection, Grayson? A reason why we should not?"

Gray was silent.

"No? Then I suggest you sit down."

It took a moment, but then Gray took his seat, hands gripping the arms of the chair until his knuckles were white.

"I ask this council to help decide the fate of this demigoddess." He spat the words with utter distaste. "All of those who believe she should be disposed of."

Disposed of? They were going to kill me?

The panic clawed up through my body and the faint wisps that swirled languidly around my body became solid gold tendrils that stretched outwards, causing gasps from some of the Gods. I couldn't stay calm, not when I might lose my life.

Multiple hands flew into the air. Hunter, Larkin, Aria, Waverly, and Flynn.

"Those who believe she should live. For now."

Another set of hands shot into the air. Gray, Erik, Sloan, Elva, Ig, and to my surprise, Malachi and Bexley. Hunter looked at them all viciously.

"SHE STAYS HERE WITH ME FOR THE TIME BEING," Hunter roared furiously.

"Sloan and I will take her," Erik offered.

"I SAID SHE STAYS WITH ME!"

No one else tried to defy Hunter. Even Grayson sat there, expression schooled into something blank. Hunter came towards me, and I took two steps away from him.

"I can make your life very difficult, so I suggest you listen. For now, you will stay in Elysia while we try to sort out the mess your very existence has made. They'll soon come to their senses and then we'll be rid of you. Until then, you'll stay with me." Hunter gripped my arm and pulled me along with him. "You're all dismissed!" he called to the chamber.

My aura — because that was what it must be, right? — my aura was nothing to his. I didn't know how to control it.

Looking over my shoulder, past Larkin, who was running towards us, I caught Gray's eye.

They were completely black, and Erik stood next to him, keeping a hand on his shoulder.

And then Hunter pulled me out of the chamber, and I lost sight of them.

EPILOGUE

QUENTIN

In hindsight, I could have done so much more. I could have dug in my heels and called out to Gray. But neither of those things happened. Despite my brain struggling through the fog of confusion, I knew calling for Gray would implicate him even further. They were already talking about putting my life on the line. How much more would it take to add Gray to the list? So my mouth remained glued shut as Hunter did as he pleased.

Hunter's home was an icy mix of blue and silver. Bright open space with a minimalist interior. A celebration of him and Larkin, lacking any warmth or personality.

The goosebumps that prickled my skin the moment he had come towards me in the chamber had yet to resolve. I hadn't uttered a single word the entire way here, out of fear. There was too much going on. Too much that I didn't understand.

"I don't want her staying here."

Larkin and Hunter stood by the door of the room, arguing.

I'd been taken upstairs and into a room without explanation. My aura continued to pulse, flickering in and out of life wildly, and forcing me to squeeze my eyes shut.

"What do you expect me to do with her?" Hunter replied.

"Take her to the cells."

"Where they'll all gawk at her? Try to form a relationship with her?"

"Then let Erik and Sloan have her."

"No," he barked. "I want her exactly where I can see her."

The pounding in my head continued steadily and powerfully. Whispers made it difficult to focus on the words, and the growing pressure pulled me down to my knees. They hit the hard flooring, and I hissed in pain. Neither of them moved to help me up.

"What are you planning to do?" Larkin asked. "She's already a liability. She's not coping."

I planted my palms on the ground and tried to force myself back to my feet. The muscles in my arms shook until I quit trying and stayed on the floor. Bashing my head against the wall seemed to be a better option with every passing moment.

"If I had it my way, she wouldn't be here," Hunter muttered sulkily.

Fear ricocheted in my heart. Even with the council voting against it, Hunter remained staunch in his belief that I shouldn't exist.

An image of Cass and Sophie pushed its way to the front of my mind. I wanted my brother. I didn't want to die. There were people who would ask questions. Or did the Gods have a plan to silence them? Could they make people forget I'd ever walked the earth?

The heat surged through me as my aura spanned out across the room. Hunter and Larkin hid behind their own, filtered in a weird mixture of blue, silver, and gold.

"Sorry," I managed to eke the word out weakly.

It felt too late to pray. Even sat on my knees before Hunter and Larkin, sorry was the only word that could spill from my lips. Requesting mercy, begging for them to spare my life — these were the pleas that should be formulating to make sure I walked out of this house alive. But they disappeared before they had the chance to flourish.

Pride was a sin, and I'd meet my end, thanks to it.

"We need to get her to control it," Larkin hissed at her husband. "And I'm not teaching her."

"You'd have to possess some maternal instinct to even take an abomination under your wing."

Larkin looked like she'd been slapped before storming out of the room. Hunter watched her leave before turning on me and I scuttled backwards, terrified of being left alone with a God who seemed intent on murdering me.

"Mallory did a good job in hiding you," he said, stepping towards me. "Right under our noses."

He looked pissed that I'd managed to escape him for years. It must have been a blow to his ego that someone had tricked him. Tricked all of them.

"What to do with you now?" he mused.

I didn't have an answer for him. There was too much missing information to allow me to come up with a plan to save myself. And I didn't trust myself not to make it worse. All it would take was for me to say the wrong thing to seal my fate.

Hunter walked out of the room, locking the door behind him, and I sat back, pulling my knees to my chest and resting my head against them.

We need to get her to control it.

Control.

There were distinct moments in my life where I felt like I'd lost control. When Cass left for the States, the moment the police knocked on the door, Ethan's figure growing smaller as he drove off in his car. And every time, I'd regained the control that I craved and carried on with life. There was no situation that I couldn't dig myself out with logic and reasoning.

But this was beyond my scope. Completely out of my depth, the only way I could describe it was a descent into madness.

There was no chance to catch my breath, no escaping the uncertainty that my future held. The people I relied on, Cass and Gray, couldn't be reached for help. I was stuck until Hunter and the council decided how they would deal with me.

Time became a strange concept. Seconds felt like hours being stuck alone with my barrage of thoughts and the ceaseless whispers. My fingers tangled into my hair, and I tugged hard, wishing for everything to just stop.

The lock clicked, and I heard footsteps coming towards me, heavy and slow. I jammed the heels of my palms into my eyes and wiped them down my cheeks, trying to erase the evidence of tears. My vision was spotty but cleared soon enough.

When I looked up, Archer towered over me with a pair of copper cuffs in his hand. He crouched down, clucking his tongue softly.

"Hunter asked me to bring these when I came to take you," he said. "They'll help."

"Take me?" I croaked.

"You're my responsibility until they decide what to do with you," Archer explained. "We'll make sure you feel at home in lower Elysia. I do warn you, we're a little less refined down there."

Cautiously, I reached my hands out to him, and he clipped them around my wrists. The voices stopped instantly and the gold wisps that had materialised by the shores of the pool disappeared. A fresh wave of tears spilled over onto my cheeks at the relief.

Archer wrapped a hand around my wrist and hauled me to my feet. Gently, he wiped a tear from my face.

"Oh, Quentin. I told you they couldn't be trusted."

Coming Soon

In Desire & Secrets (Tales from Erik and Archer)

Interested in seeing what happened in Of Gods & Monsters from Archer and Erik's point of view? The God of secrets and the God of love had plenty going on during this timeline. Conversations with Grayson and Quentin and trying to unravel the mystery of what binds the pair together. For a fresh perspective, pick up In Desire and Secrets (available 2022).

Elysian Gods #2 – Title to be announced

Quentin Scott has just discovered she is a demigoddess, and half of the elite Gods want to see her dead. But that's only the first of many secrets that have been unleashed. Stuck with Archer in lower Elysia, Quen struggles to control her divinity and more truths come to light that have her questioning if there is anyone that she can trust in the heavens… (available 2022).

Acknowledgments

Alhumdulillah

To Mam, Dad and little sis, thank you for watching my slow descent into madness as I finished this book. The overwhelming support and the eagerness to learn about the process is something I appreciate more than I'll ever be able to put into words.

I am lucky to work with real life magicians. A heartfelt thank you to Books and Moods for the cover design and teaser and to AJ Wolf graphics for the interior design and formatting. I'm grateful to have you all making my book as stunning as it does. Your work is pure magic, and no one can convince me otherwise.

This book wasn't possible without my editor, Zainab. You are the most aggressively loving person I know. Thanks for keeping my ass in line and educating me on grammar and punctuation. You are so enthusiastic about my work and characters that you made me cry and honestly, I hate you for that. But I'll continue to be a hot mess just for you, boo.

For every lab that I've had the pleasure of working in, every scientist that took the time to

Laura Sunday, thank you for betaing the script. Your detailed insight is always deeply appreciated. But more than that, thank you for being such a wonderful friend. The sprints, the laughs, the pure chaos that we're planning to unleash on the world – they're not ready for it. Love you!

Sometimes I had to admit that I had no idea what was going on. I'm a biologist and wanted to step outside my comfort zone. George, you are the Tony Stark to my Bruce Banner. Science bros for life. I'm grateful that you deal with all my 3AM breakdowns over physics with so much grace and kindness. I owe you so many donuts for putting up with me for so long.

No book I have written or will ever write is completed without Ellie. You read so many versions of this story and helped carve it into the final piece. Thank you for helping me keep my head and reading snippets at all hours. You are wonderful and I hope you know I appreciate the very bones of you.

KEEP IN TOUCH

If you want to keep up to date with all the news on my writing and releases you can follow me on:

Instagram:
@zavi_james

Facebook Group:
Zavi James Sanctum

Website:
https://www.zavijames.com/

Printed in Great Britain
by Amazon